A hiss warned him of approaching danger.

xx

Wellen came to an abrupt halt and flattened himself against the nearest wall. He tried not to think of the things he had seen crawling around on other walls in the castle, reminding himself that they could be nothing compared to what moved ahead of him.

The explorer was hard-pressed to make out what shambled slowly toward his location. He was reminded of a beehive with tentacles, but that was all the detail he could make out. He thought that something, some sort of slime, dripped from it, but that was based purely on the sounds the horror made as it moved slowly along.

Wellen was certain that it was coming for him . . . until it suddenly turned and went through one of the walls without so much as a second's hesitation. An illusion? With great care, he stepped over to where the monstrosity had disappeared.

Tentacles burst from the wall, seizing him by the arms and throat . . .

xx   xx   xx

DRAGON TOME

ALSO BY RICHARD A. KNAAK

Firedrake
Ice Dragon
Wolfhelm
Shadow Steed
The Shrouded Realm
Children of the Drake

RICHARD A. KNAAK

DRAGON TOME

ORIGIN OF DRAGONREALM

WARNER BOOKS

A Time Warner Company

WARNER BOOKS EDITION

Copyright © 1992 by Richard A. Knaak

Questar is a registered trademark of Warner Books, Inc.

Cover illustration by Larry Elmore
Cover design by Don Puckey

Warner Books, Inc.
1271 Avenue of the Americas
New York, NY 10020

 A Time Warner Company

Printed in the United States of America

First Printing: July, 1992

10 9 8 7 6 5 4 3 2 1

I

He always knew when it was the most opportune time for an excursion outside. It was all in the book, so to speak. He knew his adversaries' habits better than they themselves did, just as he had known the habits of their predecessors. He had been at this game far longer than either of the two groups now seeking his legacy and he would be at it when they were only whispers in the winds of time.

They ever underestimated him because of his form, he knew. To them, he was a misshapen little gnome, one of the solitary folk who lived for knowledge and gathered what they could of that rare resource. He was incredibly small and wrinkled with age. His arms had the length that his legs had been cheated of and so he seemed to almost shamble rather than walk or run. There was not one single follicle of hair on his head, which often resulted in him looking like a polished egg when the sun shone down. His nose was long and crooked and his eyes were wide and filled with the wisdom of ages. His clothing was simple, consisting of a cloth robe and hood that made him look more like a pile of rumpled laundry than a living creature. He wore simple shoes and a belt from which hung several pouches, but nothing more. There was no need for anything more.

If he looked like a gnome, there was good reason for that; it was he who had given birth to that race when he had taken elfin maidens for mates far in the past. Though those days were past, his offspring continued to spread his mark. It was a sign of his once-great power, one still to be reckoned with even now.

He was no more than a few minutes from his sanctum, but the storm had at last cleared. With the clouds dissipating so fast, it was possible that the dawn would yet reveal a bright, golden sun and a deep blue sky. Dawn was the only thing he really cared about anymore; that and his daily game with those who would seek to steal what was his and his alone.

At the bottom of the hill he paused. From this point on, the land would shield him no longer. Before him stood only wild grass, not nearly high enough to hide even his tiny form. That there was any grass at all was a sign of his own might, for one of his opponents had burned the entire region clean in an attempt to drive the gnome from his sanctum. Left to the weakness of nature, the region would have remained barren. He had no desire to make his home in the middle of a scorched desert, however, and so had sought out the proper spell. That his success only proved to his adversaries the vast extent of his legacy was a moot point. They had seen enough wonders to know that stealing the contents of his citadel would make the victor master over the entire continent.

As for the gnome, he did not care. At this stage in his vast life span, the pursuit of ever more knowledge was all that was important.

To the naked eye, the field looked empty, save for a peculiar structure some distance from where the gnome stood. The structure, a sort of wide, featureless pentagon three stories high, sat in the midst of the wild grass like a benign tyrant surveying its kingdom. If it seemed that there were no windows nor even a door through which to pass, that was because such was the case. If anyone other than he attempted to seek entrance, then that unfortunate visitor would find himself fruitlessly wandering the perimeter of the citadel. Only *he* knew how to enter, which was why *he* held the trump card in the game of wits. His would-be successors dared not kill him out of hand lest they lose the one key.

That did not mean that they did not try other methods, most of which included pain . . . but not death.

It appeared that the field was peaceful, that his adversaries had abandoned their efforts for the night. This might be true of one, for the time being, but not of the other. Always there was at least one.

Shouldering the brace of rabbits that had been his night's work, he began to trudge through, what was to him, the knee-high sea of dancing greenery. From within, tendrils of invisible power, already highly sensitized to the possible plots of the usurpers, stretched ever farther out. If any spell or physical threat came within a hundred yards of him, he would know. Anything beyond that range would not even "dent" the magical shield that surrounded his person and it was likely that anything nearer would do little more. Still, one could grow too complacent. There were always new and more deadly attacks.

Knowing that always added a little spice to his life. It gave his desire for research that extra little flavor, since his very existence might hang in the balance.

When he had nearly cut the distance between himself and his home in half, the squat sorcerer paused. Nothing had as yet disturbed his network of defensive spells, but a sense of foreboding...call it *intuition*...told him that someone or something lay waiting in the near vicinity.

Which one? he wondered. *Who's been silent of late?*

The first spearheads of sunlight rose over the horizon. The aged spellcaster admired the sight for a moment, then resumed his trek. He was still slightly curious about the sensation he felt, but since it did not hint of danger, the gnome was not overly concerned.

Perhaps an enterprising elf? Once or twice, that race had made overtures to him, seeking his friendship, but no longer interested in dallying with the female of the species, he had ignored them. Compared to the other watchers, the elves were inconsequential.

Now his sanctum, his home and place of research, was little more than a hundred feet away and still he had not been attacked. The wizened sorcerer grew bemused, wondering if his handiwork would go wasted this time. He had not even really needed the rabbits, able as he was to summon them to *him*, but the walk and the challenge always stirred his blood. It was almost disappointing.

There *was* that sensation still...

Standing at last before the gray structure, he raised his hand to open the way—and felt every protective spell activate as something hurtled straight down from high in the sky above him.

It was strong, *far* stronger than he had expected. It shrugged off his initial defenses as he might shrug off a leaf that had fallen on his shoulder. Whatever it was must have been high up indeed to have avoided detection sooner and it evidently moved with a speed that would have left even a dragon dumbfounded. The sorcerer dropped his brace of rabbits and focused his attention upward at the startling new threat. Whichever of his present adversaries was responsible for this assault had outdone themselves.

A huge, bat-winged shape formed in the dim light of pre-morning. It shrieked, much the way the night flyer it so resembled did, and reached out with long, taloned fingers for him. Like a bat, those fingers were part of the webbed wings themselves. It had long ears and a body that was essentially humanoid, but that was all the detail he could make out under the circumstances.

Ugly as sin, no doubt, the sorcerer thought even as he moved to defend himself from it.

With a speed remarkable for one of his build, the gnome reached into one of his pouches and removed a small stick. Holding it up above his head, he gave the tip a flick of his thumb. The tip of the stick burst into a brilliant white light, brighter a hundred times more than the sun at its zenith. He was prepared for searing illumination and so his eyes had closed just before his thumb had struck.

The night flyer was not so fortunate.

It squealed, wavered, and finally whirled out of control. Though he suspected it could guide itself by sound as well as by sight, he knew that the light had disoriented it too much for the moment. Its masters might have created it so that it would be used to the light of day, but few things could stare into the gleaming white flare in his hand and not lose their sight permanently. What made the trick more enjoyable to the sorcerer was that the source of the light was a product of nature and not a costly bit of spellcasting. Making the stick had cost him only a few minutes' work.

By no means had he stood still while all this happened. Even as the creature, seven feet in height at *least* if he were any judge, clawed at its eyes, the gnome was already opening up a path for himself in the side of the pentagon. A swift series of gestures with his left hand resulted in a circular hole that formed directly before him. He stepped through, dragging the retrieved rabbits along with him, but paused before sealing the entrance up again.

The beast was already fluttering off into the retreating night, its mission a quick and embarrassing failure. From experience, the gnome knew the mental and physical agony the monstrosity was going through. He felt no sympathy, save for the wasted effort on the part of the beast's creators. Seeing now its sickly white coloring, odd for a creature of the night, he had a good suspicion which of his opponents had been responsible.

"Hmmph! The Lords of the Dead. Of course it would be one of theirs!" Necromancers who had appointed themselves gods. Fools in one way, but still quite challenging and able. They had, with their own vast storehouse of power, created quite a formidable weapon, but one that evidently lacked the cunning needed for its task. Yet, he could hardly believe it had been so short and simple. It was almost anticlimactic after all his expectations.

"Almost farcical, if you ask me," he muttered, though those involved would have hardly questioned *him* on the subject. "Waste of good material! Never use a good weapon with a bad plan!"

Watching the massive shape disappear into the clouds, the gnome's brow suddenly wrinkled. It might *not* be an ill-conceived attempt after all. They should have known by now that such a weak attack would be destined for failure. This might have been an exploratory assault, a preamble to the true attack.

He smiled in anticipation of what their next move might be and when it might take place. Whatever they plotted, he would be ready for it, of course, but the thought that they might have come up with some novel approach stirred his hunger for research. He would *have* to research the possibilities this incident presented, even if it turned out that any such possibilities were nothing more than the products of his inventive imagination.

The hole had just begun to seal itself when he again felt the presence of that patient watcher. Freezing the doorway spell, the bent sorcerer peered outside again. He saw nothing, not that he had *expected* it to be that simple, but in his mind's eye, where the power flowed, there came an image of a tall figure, human perhaps, wrapped in a shroudlike cloak.

That was all. As if his sensing this had broken a fragile

bubble, both the image and the feeling of being watched vanished.

Frowning, the gnome allowed the wall to finish sealing itself up. He had protected his precious legacy from foes human and otherwise for endless millennia and he saw no reason that he could not protect it from one more. Be his rivals birdmen or cloaked sorcerers, they were nothing next to him.

Another image flashed through his mind, but this one was merely a memory of his most persistent and patient adversary yet. He chuckled at some of the clever but futile tricks *that* one had pulled. "Yesss, and that goes for you, too, *lord dragon*!" the aged spellcaster muttered. "The book's mine and that's all there is to it!"

The squat figure resettled the rabbits on his shoulder and trundled down the hall, thoughts of dragons, bats, and such now giving way to memories of the sensual aroma of roast hare. He so enjoyed the peaceful life. This was not at all like his former home, the place that he had abandoned so very, very, *very* long ago.

No, this domain was nothing like Nimth.

II

"There!"

It was Captain Yalso himself who planted the flag. With the aid of his great bulk, he shoved almost two feet of the wooden pole into the soft earth at the inward edge of the beach. As two sailors unfurled the banner—which was actually a ship's identification banner borrowed for just this occasion—a cheer went up from both those who made up the shore party and those watching from the three-masted vessel anchored in the natural harbor. After months of treacherous sailing, the *Heron's Wing* had reached its destination.

The myth was now a fact. There *was* a fabled Dragonrealm! *Or at least a continent in the same general location,* Wellen

Bedlam thought, staring in sour humor at the tiny flag, one that had not even been his idea.

The guiding force as well as the master of this expedition, he should have been the one most excited by this turn of events. His dream had been fulfilled. From the first time his parents had told the children the tales of Lord Drazeree and the Dragon Men to the final days of his own researches in the ruins of the ancient city, he had believed that the Dragonrealm had existed as more than just a storyland. Somewhere there had to have been a basis for such tales.

His entire reputation as a master scholar had been at risk these past few years, but that had hardly been a concern to him. Even when the Master Guardians, who ruled the nebulous region called the Dreamlands from mysterious Sirvak Dragoth, had warned him of the dangers of delving too deeply into the past . . . a shaded threat? . . . he had pressed on. After his researchers had finally, *conclusively*, pointed to the west, beyond the terrible seas, Wellen had somehow gathered the support to finance this expedition. When it had appeared that the effort was about to flounder just as the *Heron's Wing* was about to set sail, he had even taken his own meager finances and spent every last coin to make certain that the ship would leave.

Brushing sand from his brown, cloth shirt, he pulled his long, green cape about him and turned from the merrymakers. Yes, he had made his dream come true, but now Wellen wondered at what cost that might be. In the safe seclusion of his chambers back home, he had only imagined the dangers. The reality of those dangers, however, was more than he truly wanted to face. It bothered him that he of all people might most jeopardize the expedition.

I'm afraid! The thought had burned its way into his soul. *I'm afraid. I've spent my entire life with the deadliest threat to my existence the possibility that I might fail to graduate!*

Sand flew up as he walked aimlessly across the beach. Even with knee-high boots, some of the granules still managed to get inside, making his feet itch. Wellen wished all of his sufferings could be so tiny. How would it look back home if the expedition leader was the first man to crack? How would it look if Prentiss Asaalk had to take over?

Thinking of the northerner, whom other interests had chosen as Bedlam's undesired second, Wellen now recalled his own *physical* deficiencies. It was bad enough that he was afraid, but he had to compete against a man who looked like some demigod hero out of an ancient myth. Where Wellen was short, barely topping the midway point between five feet and six, Asaalk was nearly a foot taller. The shorter man was by no means unathletic, but his broad frame more resembled a flat gate when compared to Prentiss Asaalk's herculean dimensions.

Facially, there was no comparison. Wellen's own features could be called unremarkable at best. Slightly rounded face, simple nose, unassuming mouth . . . only his hazel eyes, which somehow always snared the attention of those he spoke to, rose above the ordinary. Penetrating eyes, however, added up to little compared to the aristocratic features of his second. Not only did Asaalk have the bearing of a leader, but he had the arrogant beauty that all those story heroes had seemed to have, save for the legendary Drazeree.

Despite his constant listing of his faults, however, the short man still found himself very much in charge. For some reason, people were more willing to listen and follow him. It confused Wellen and it almost certainly annoyed the ambitious Asaalk. That added yet another fear to those of the scholar. When would come the point when he led his people into disaster and, should they survive, Prentiss Asaalk finally and irrevocably took his place as leader?

The day was young. The wind fruitlessly tried to tousle his brown hair, which had been cut short in order to save him the trouble of having to take care of it any more than he had to. He pushed a few loose hairs aside, trying not to think of the damnable silver streak that his fingers touched, and paused to stare at the woodlands beyond the beach. They seemed quiet and unassuming, but was anything so in this strange land? A part of him argued that he worried needlessly, but the rest of his mind knew that such worry was the only thing that kept him from growing too dreamy, a dangerous tendency of his youth. Though not quite three decades old, Wellen liked to think that his reckless days had ended with the broken leg and arm he had received because he had been daydreaming instead of making certain that the library ladder was stable.

"So just what're you doing here?"

He nearly jumped, so startled was he to hear the question that he had just been asking himself spoken out loud. Then, realizing it was not he himself who had spoken, Wellen knew that the question had a different, far more mundane basis behind it. He exhaled in relief and turned to face Captain Yalso.

The mariner was ancient, but no one could say just *how* ancient he was. *As old as the seas,* one crewman had said, but if Yalso was that old, he was holding up well for one of his age. Though the hair on his head was shockingly white and his beard stretched down to his chest, the captain was by no means a frail old man. His girth alone proved that, if not also the way he was able to manhandle his crew during the roughest storms and get them working in order to save the *Heron's Wing* and all those on board. He had done that more than once on the long journey. Like most men, it seemed, Yalso also stood several inches taller than Wellen. Again, it always surprised him when men such as the sea captain deferred to him in matters.

"You're driftin' off, you are," Yalso told him in tones designed not to carry beyond the two of them. If there was a man on the ship that could be called Wellen's friend, it was Yalso. Until the scholar had come along, he had been looking at nothing but a long overdue retirement. Wellen had given him one last great adventure . . . the *greatest* one, in fact. No one had ever sailed this far west. No one that had come back to tell of it, that is. The young scholar had had an insistent, knowing way about him, however, and that had been enough for the seaman. He had never lost faith in Wellen.

"I'm sorry," Bedlam muttered. "I keep wondering what we'll find out there." He gestured inland.

"Oh, trees, grass, animals, birds . . ." Yalso winked. "I think maybe a few lost cities, damsels in distress, and gold aplenty . . ."

They both smiled at that image. While there were always those aboard who expected the expedition to find such things, the two were more practical. As far as the captain was concerned, sailing here had been a reward all its own. He had proved once more that he was the best captain there was and that the *Heron's Wing* was the finest lady ever to set sail. Wellen, on the other hand, cared mostly for the history.

His spirits had risen a little, but Wellen could not shake off certain fears. Not after the first attempt to land.

Here be dragons was a warning essential to the tale of this distant land. Dragons they had not seen . . . at least not enough so that they could be identified as such . . . but there were strange dangers aplenty here, of that Wellen was certain.

"You're thinkin' of that blasted city again, aren't you, Master Bedlam? Don't. This here's safe harbor, not like that haunted, monster-laden cove."

Haunted, Wellen could not recall, but the ruined city to the northeast, the wind-swept region that was their first sighting of the legendary Dragonrealm and *was* to have been their initial landing point, was indeed 'monster-laden' as the ancient mariner had just commented.

Their first sight of land had brought a cheer and when the city had first been spotted it was thought that here might be people open to trade. Only when they had sailed closer had the crew and passengers of the three-master noted that the port city was in ruins and had been so for centuries. Part of it had apparently even sunk into the sea. Still, it had been a marvel to see, what with its almost inhuman architecture and beauty, and so they had talked of exploring it, possibly even finding riches long abandoned.

Then, the lookout had seen the sleek, scaled backside in the water.

Sea-blue, that was why no one had noticed them at first. Possibly they had been swimming too deep, also. All that the daring explorers still knew was that suddenly there were several murky shapes in the waters around them that promised leviathans. Captain Yalso was of the opinion that they had come across a breeding ground or something. Prentiss Asaalk had wanted to hunt one. He was, fortunately, in the minority.

The shapes had remained no more than that, ever diving out of sight when the explorers moved closer, but that did not mean that the ship was left alone. When the first tremor rocked the *Heron's Wing,* they knew that several had swum underneath. Oddly, very little damage occurred to the ship, but possibly because Captain Yalso instinctively understood what it was they wanted. Each strike was focused at the bow of the ship, halting the three-master's progress and soon forcing the vessel back.

"They want us out of here!" he had informed Wellen. "They're givin' us a chance to leave in one piece!"

Sure enough, when the *Heron's Wing* had finally turned about and headed away, the fearsome shapes had receded. The explorers had kept sailing and had not looked back until the city and its denizens of the deep were no more than a spot on the horizon.

"Drifting again." The comment scattered the shorter man's

memories. The scholar stared down at the sand beneath his feet, reorienting himself to the present.

Wellen started walking up a small rise, wanting to stand among the foot-high blades of wild grass. "Sorry, captain. I don't mean to do it. It just happens."

"Nothing wrong to dream; that's what got you, got all of us, here. You just have to know where the dreaming ends and the reality begins . . . otherwise ya put your foot in something terrrrible!"

He was never certain whether Captain Yalso affected a salty accent at times or whether the man just switched back and forth without realizing it. Yalso was far more cultured than the short man had expected, but that might have just been the personal prejudice borne of having been highly educated. "I'll try to remember that."

"Good!" The heavy-set sailor joined him, his boots sinking a bit in the soft earth. "If anything happens to you and I have to listen to the blue man's royal orders for very long, then there's gonna be a mutiny!"

The "blue man" was Prentiss Asaalk. For reasons only the Dreamlands might know, Asaalk's folk were blue-skinned. It was not a dye of any sort; they were born a dusky blue from head to toe, including their hair. The only people so colored, they felt it marked them as special, which explained to a great extent Asaalk's arrogant manner. He was a product of his culture.

Still, even for a blue man he could be demanding.

"Come on back to camp, Master Bedlam! If you want a search party ready for tomorrow, we've got plenty to get done before then! I've sent out a few men to scout the nearby area, but I'm goin' to need your presence of mind to keep them enthused and the blue man from takin' over!"

Knowing what an opportunist Asaalk was, Wellen readily agreed. He also knew that keeping himself busy was the best way to maintain a steady rein on his fears and self-doubts. It was one reason he enjoyed his research so much; for a time he could depart from the world and his deficiencies.

Sure enough, when they arrived back among the others the blue man was already attempting to seize control. His expression was bland, much like a king's might be when commanding his subjects.

"There and there," he was saying in a clipped, slightly

accented voice. Though most folk spoke the common tongue in the same manner, the northerners put a certain twist in their inflections, making them sound to Wellen as if the ceremonial daggers they wore on their kilt belts were digging into their abdomens. No one, of course, ever joked about Asaalk's voice, in keeping with his heroic image, he was a deadly swordsman and wrestler. "Create a perimeter here, yes?"

Despite their mild dislike for the blue man, the sailors' minds were so ingrained with the concept of obeying the voice of authority that they were grudgingly following the northerner's commands.

"Thank you kindly, Master Asaalk!" Yalso roared, his beard fluttering as he spoke. "I can take such a meager task off your worthy shoulders!" The captain gave Wellen a conspiratorial glance. "Master Bedlam! Certainly you have something more pressing that would not be so beneath the able control of your second!"

It was likely that Prentiss Asaalk knew very well what the seaman was doing, but the northerner was nothing if not capable of masking his true feelings whenever need be. Instead, he smiled and broke from his self-appointed duties in order to join the two. Yalso, having no intention of submitting himself to the one-man oratories Asaalk thought conversations were supposed to be when he was a part, bowed to the young scholar and made his excuses. He made certain to avoid glancing at the blue man as he departed to organize the camp . . . providing Prentiss Asaalk had left him anything to do.

"Master Bedlam!" Asaalk greeted him with such fervor and pleasure that the expedition leader expected the larger man to envelop him in a bearhug. Asaalk did not, however, choosing instead to cross his arms and stand in cobalt splendor before Wellen like a storybook champion who has just bested his archrival. "Glorious day, yes?"

"The weather seems to be holding—"

"Weather? Not weather!" The blue man smiled broadly, as if appreciating Wellen's comment as a joke between good friends. "The weather is good, yes, but I speak, of course, of our being *here*!" With a finger, he indicated the ground beneath his feet. Asaalk's tendency to emphasize points always reminded Wellen of an actor onstage. He wondered if professional acting was yet another talent of the northerner's. Probably. There were few things that Asaalk did not seem to have some ability in. In fact, Wellen could think of *nothing* so far that was beyond the skills of his second.

Maybe I should let him take over! Then, I might find his limitations! What would happen, however, if Prentiss Asaalk proved to have none, though?

A hand twice as large as his own fell upon his shoulder. He was jostled again and again as the blue man patted him. "This is your day, Master Bedlam! Those who scoffed will hide their faces in shame when we return with our vessel laden with riches, yes?"

Riches? This was to be a voyage of discovery, not plundering! He wanted to shout that in the northerner's perfect countenance, but did not. It would have only made Wellen look ridiculous and Asaalk would not have paid any real attention to his words, anyway. Asaalk was not the only one who sought riches. Most of those aboard, even Captain Yalso, dreamed of returning home with a king's ransom. It was not that they had no interest in the knowledge that might be gained; they were merely of the opinion that one could have knowledge *and* wealth. Asaalk's people had only invested in the expedition because they were certain that the *Heron's Wing* would return with *something* of value . . . providing, of course, that it returned at all. Neither the ship nor Wellen dared return otherwise.

"The city in the north," his mighty second was saying, entirely ignoring the frustration that was evident in the shorter man's eyes. "We could reach it by land, yes? The creatures in the sea would then be no threat! Think what might be there!"

Wellen did and shuddered. "There might be things other than those monsters, things that move about on land. Besides, as ancient as the city looked—what was still above water, I mean—it's probably been picked clean already. Probably hundreds or thousands of years even."

"There is always something . . . and did you not want to find your knowledge? Surely, this must be a good place to seek it, yes? A city as mighty as this might have once known the great Lord Drazeree!"

It was doubtful that things could work out so neatly for him, but the scholar could not deny that a place as massive as the ruined city *might* contain countless answers and endless surprises. There was one other problem, however, that Prentiss Asaalk was evidently oblivious to, but that Wellen could hardly forget.

"It may take too long a journey to reach that land, Prentiss, and we'd spend more than half the time wandering through a mist so thick we wouldn't be able to see a thing around us! Have you forgotten *that*?"

"Pfah!" The tall northerner waved off his concern. "A little fog, yes! I have not forgotten it! I would worry about dragons and demons, but *fog*? Hah! Of what danger can the gray mists of that land be?"

What danger? He had no answer for the massive figure, only a sense of dread that had remained with him all the time they had been within sight of the mist-enshrouded land far south of the ruined city. Certainly, the fog had done nothing to warrant his distrust, but he found it unsettling the way the weather of this realm was so distinctive from one region to the next. The region occupied by the partially sunken city had been sunny and warm. Only two days later, they had entered a storm that had not let up until they came across the mists. Neither the storm nor the fog had shown any sign of relenting. With his scholar's eye for detail, Wellen had noted that the rain had only broken off when the gray cloak became dominant over the distant landscape.

Almost as if someone had *divided* the land between two or more elemental lords.

It was a preposterous notion even to Wellen and so he had not spoken of it to anyone, the captain included.

He held back a sigh and finally said, "We'll see. I'll let everyone know tonight after evening meal. Right now, my only concern is making certain our encampment here is safe and secure."

"You have no need of fear, then! I have placed pickets at the edge of this portion of the beach and I have also men scouting beyond . . . all the way to the first hills. I have our supplies safely ensconced near that sandbar." He pointed at the aforementioned landmark, which was located to Wellen's right. "And I have placed four men by the longboats as a safety precaution. Satisfactory, yes?"

"Are you expecting a war?" It was a rhetorical question, one Wellen had not even meant to ask out loud, but Asaalk's preparations—how he had managed to get everything so organized in so little time astounded the scholar—seemed more apt for someone fully expecting an armed assault.

The blue man flashed him a smile. "I, too, do not take this

land as harmless. I, like you, Master Bedlam, know that caution is a very good thing, yes?"

"*Yes . . .*" He wished his second would stop abusing that last word. It always sounded as if Asaalk were answering his own questions.

"So! There are many things to discuss, but also many things still to do! Tomorrow will begin the glorious trek! I leave you to make your decision, Master Bedlam; I know there is much to consider, yes? You have but to send for me if my assistance in the matter is needed!" Prentiss Asaalk executed an abrupt, ninety-degree bow. "I am your servant."

As the majestic northerner departed, Wellen tried to decide which side of Asaalk he disliked more, the arrogant lord or the patronizing comrade. He finally gave up, knowing in his heart that he would have preferred dealing with neither of them. Whatever side the blue man showed, one could be certain that there was more hidden beneath the facade. Someday, the true Prentiss Asaalk would reveal himself. Wellen hoped he would not have to suffer the misfortune of being around when that occurred.

Yalso would not doubt be upset at the northerner's return to duty, but there was truly nothing Wellen could do about that. For all his faults, no one could deny Asaalk's efficiency. There had been too many instances where his abilities had enabled Wellen to pull the expedition through some crisis. That was what made the man most infuriating. He was as invaluable as he was insufferable.

The blue man's associates had chosen well.

Between the captain and Asaalk, there was actually little for Wellen to do but think. Most of the men had captured a glance of him upon his return with Yalso, and that was all they needed; his mere presence reassured them and renewed their enthusiasm.

Sighing, he stalked his way back to the edge of the beach. The woodlands and the fields beckoned to him. Daring Yalso's wrath, he stepped out into the high grass and wandered slowly toward the nearest tree. His mind was far beyond his physical location, however. Far beyond even the hills in the distance. Somewhere out there, the scholar knew, were mysteries and legends to unravel. Asaalk had a point about the ruined seaport; even stripped by scavengers it would contain many secrets. Who had built it? What were they like? Was the city the last legacy of civilization in the Dragonrealm? None of the stories Wellen recalled had made mention of such a place, but that was not to say it had not existed then. If what he had seen so far held true, then the Dragonrealm was a mighty continent. It might take several expeditions just to map its coastlines. That was something that could wait until later, perhaps after he had achieved his other, more private dream . . . starting a colony. A colony would give him a permanent base for his studies.

His left foot sank a bit in the soft earth, causing him to stumble slightly. Cursing both his daydreaming and his constant worries, he regained his balance. It was while he was wiping the bottom of his boot off on the root of a small tree that he caught a glimpse of something.

He blinked, but it was still there, a black shape moving about within a copse of trees far off in the distance. Wellen had no idea what it was, but his imagination introduced him to several tantalizing possibilities. He took a tentative step toward it, then another.

"*Master* Bedlam!" Yalso's voice seemed to echo through out the land, not to mention the young scholar's head. "If I might have a word with you?"

The captain's voice must have carried, indeed, for Wellen, about to turn to the man, saw the figure bound out of the copse.

It was a stag.

Nothing more.

His disappointment was overshadowed only by the dread of facing the captain of the *Heron's Wing*. He had been warned once by the sailor about wandering off on his own. Despite his being in command of the expedition as a whole, Wellen also had to follow orders, especially where his own safety was concerned. Yalso was a man who had sailed to many exotic places and dealt with countless excursions into the unknown. Until this voyage, Bedlam's closest brush with the unknown had been his examinations.

Steeling himself for another respectful lecture, the scholar made his way back across the soft, grassy earth. Yalso was shaking his head and smiling, but Wellen still felt like a schoolboy caught missing classes. Not wanting the captain to gain the same impression, if he had not already, Wellen met the man's gaze and held it as he walked.

The elder mariner crossed his arms and tried to look like a scolding father. His success was somewhat debatable, since both he and Wellen could not keep from smiling at the scene they presented. "I know there's a siren song that pulls a man at times, Master Bedlam, but I'll not have you wanderin' off on your own, even if ya *are* in charge. *No* man is safe here alone; not until we have a better idea what's out there."

"I was feeling a bit useless."

"The blue devil's got a tendency for making folk feel so. If he wasn't so damned anxious to be top man, he'd make a fine officer on my vessel."

Wellen paused at the edge of the beach and finished wiping off his boot. "I doubt that he'd be satisfied with that."

"You're right on that!" Uncrossing his arms, Yalso heaved his bulk nearer to the scholar. In a quiet voice, he asked, "What was it you saw out there? Someone watchin' us from the woods?"

"No, just a deer."

Yalso chuckled. "Maybe it was some mystical white stag watchin' over the forest!"

"It was a male deer, it was brown, and it scampered off the moment it heard your bellowing."

"They just don't make woodland spirits too strong these days, do they?"

Rising, Wellen shook his head. "Careful, captain. I might find I prefer Asaalk's company to yours if you keep that up."

"That would be *your* nightmare, not mine."

Bedlam took one last lingering glance at the woods and hills beyond the beach. Tomorrow, he would lead the expedition out into that unknown land. The thought drove away much of the good humor that Yalso had brought with him.

"You'll see plenty of that come the morn."

He nodded, then joined the captain on the beach. "I still haven't figured out where exactly we're going."

"Not the city?"

"You, too?"

"Is that where the northerner wants to go?" The sailor scratched his furry chin. "Much as I hate to be agreein' with him, I'd say it's our best bet. We can't stay too long and that would likely be the quickest way to prove our claim here."

"Not to mention possibly making us rich, too."

"I've never been ashamed about the thought." Yalso's eyes gleamed. "You wouldn't deny us that, would ya?"

Wellen raised his arms, dropping them almost immediately after. "I surrender! The city it is, then."

"Now you're talkin'!"

What choice did I have? Wellen wondered. Hopefully, he could keep the men from tearing things apart before he had an opportunity to look the area over. They owed *him* that much, at least.

"Let's get back to camp now," Yalso suggested. He straightened as much as it was possible for him to do and added, "And *this* time you're gonna stay there or I'll clap half a dozen men to your backside who'll see to it that you do!"

The young scholar knew better than to argue. Turning his back on the land of his childhood dreams, at least for this day, he headed back to camp.

This time, Captain Yalso stayed at his backside.

Had he not been interrupted during both brief visits, it is very possible that Wellen would have noticed the print in the soft soil. He had, in fact, stepped in the very same region, but the other print was so large that the mark left by the scholar's boot covered not even a tenth of the area. It is possible that even if he *had* looked down, Wellen might not have noticed it, for the wild grass that had been stamped down into the earth upon the other's arrival had long ago, as plants will do, risen to once more follow the sun. Thus, more than half of the other print was obscured.

Whether or not he would have noticed it was not so important as the fact that Wellen Bedlam would have recognized what creature had made the print even though he had never actually seen one. He would have also likely realized how close the camp might be to one of the monsters.

The print was that of a reptilian beast far larger than any man. A dragon.

A *huge* dragon.

III

Though she sat alone in the midst of the dark wood, she had no fear of the night. The fire was slow and barely illuminated even the surrounding area. Xabene did not care; the fire only existed because she liked to watch the flames dance their brief lives away. She liked the dance because it played at both life and death, as she did.

A flutter of wings warned her of the Necri's coming.

Xabene looked up as the monstrosity descended. In the dim light, she was a study of contrasts, a thing of beauty wrapped in the darkness of death. Her visage could best be described as perfect. Cat eyes that glowed when something drew her interest. Long lashes nearly hid those eyes when they narrowed before the kill. Her skin was unblemished, but as white as ivory. The spellcaster's nose was small and perfectly aligned, while her mouth was full and bloodred. A slight crease in her chin was the only feature that might have marred her countenance, but no man had every truly noticed it, not when confronted with all else she had to offer.

Ebony hair cascaded down to her brow in front and past her shoulders elsewhere, framing her pale features. A single streak of silver coursed down the left side of her head. It was difficult to see where her hair ended and her gown began, for it too was as black as pitch. Xabene had a form that matched her features and the gown emphasized that fact. Thin and cut low both in the front and back, it hardly seemed appropriate for one who spent much of her time in the wilds. Yet, no stain had ever marred it and the sorceress never appeared uncomfortable, no matter what the weather.

Many a man had fallen victim to Xabene's beauty, but that beauty served only herself and those she called master.

As for the Necri, it probably found her as repulsive as she found it. Its clawed feet touching earth, the Necri trotted toward her, looking much like a runner bent forward during a grueling race. The winged abomination did not stop until it was within a few feet of the fire. It then folded its wings about it and stood waiting, white, soulless eyes staring at the tiny human before it.

Xabene knew the danger of the Necri, knew the speed with which it moved and the sharpness of its claws. As if to remind her it had yet more weapons, the massive creature gave her a smile, revealing row upon row of dagger teeth. Though its general form was manlike, everything else was a twisted parody of the animal from which its kind had been spawned, the bat. Had it been able to stand completely straight, the Necri would have been more than seven feet tall; even bent it was almost six. Like Xabene, its flesh was pale, but the pale of something long dead.

A shift in the wind reminded her of something else. The Necri smelled. The odor of carrion and decay clung to it like a shroud. The dark enchantress was fairly used to the smell, having been forced to confront it whenever her masters had summoned her, but coming from this horror it took on an added strength. Given an opportunity, the Necri would be more than happy to add her to its dinner table. It was one of the functions for which it had been created. Human agents might command them for a time, but a Necri's ultimate loyalty was to the Lords of the Dead.

After all, they had *created* the monstrous race.

The snub nose and long ears of the creature twitched as it impatiently waited for her to speak.

Xabene did not rise, although that would have brought her almost eye level with her companion. Instead, she held out one hand so that the Necri could see the small, copper figurine resting on her palm. It represented two figures in struggle. Birdmen. The sorceress had never asked where it had come from . . . one *never* asked the masters such silly questions . . . but she assumed it was an artifact left behind by the Seekers, the avians who had ruled this land before the coming of the Dragon Kings. They had always been fond of using medallions and talismans for their spells. The race still existed, but their power was a mere shadow of their former greatness. Still, Xabene had to admire them if they had been capable of such work as this.

"Do you know what this is?"

The Necri leaned forward, avoiding the light of the fire as much as it could, and studied the copper piece for a moment. It squeaked what the sorceress knew was a positive response. She hid her smile. It always amused her that a monstrosity as deadly as the Necri spoke in a high-pitched squeak.

"Observe." With her free hand, she stroked the side of the figurine.

A blue, spherical light formed above the copper talisman. It turned and pulsated, growing in intensity with the passing of time. The Necri lowered another lid over its eyes to dim the illumination.

The ball of light was now as large as the beast's head. At that point, it ceased growing and a form within began to take shape. Both figures watched with interest as a familiar adversary solidified in the midst of the ball.

The Necri hissed.

"The master of the citadel," Xabene whispered.

Before their eyes, they saw the gnome at work. He was busy scratching away with a feather pen, jotting his notes down. In the background, there were vague images of other things, but only the gnome and his desk were sufficiently in focus to be of any interest.

"Your predecessor achieved this success."

It's eyes focused on her again. The Necri knew what had happened to its predecessor. Damaged permanently in mind as well as body, it had no longer been of use to its creators. They had disposed of it as they saw fit. The winged servant understood that action, but what it did not care for, Xabene knew, was the blindness and madness it had suffered due to the sorceress. It was she who had devised the suicidal plan and had commanded the other Necri to obey, in the name of their mutual lords.

"We have his image trapped. We have the ability to observe him now. The first step to victory and achieving possession of his precious book."

The talons of the creature's hands played against its chest. The squeak it emitted was full of disbelief and contempt.

Xabene was prepared for defiance. No Necri believed that human agents were worthy of their support, but they obeyed because the masters commanded them to do so. A plot hatched by a human, therefore, was sheer madness.

"My work has been approved by the lords themselves. If you care to request an audience with them . . ." She smiled at the Necri's sudden discomfort, revealing her own perfect but somehow predatory teeth. "This image is proof that all is proceeding well."

Disbelief was still evident, but the pale abomination remained quiet. If her plan failed, not that she could foresee *that* happening, the punishment would fall upon *her* head alone, providing that the Necri could prove it had performed its part to the letter. She knew that the winged servant understood that as well.

The image of the gnome vanished as Xabene cupped her free hand over the artifact and withdrew the object from the sight of her ghoulish partner. "We have been given another task, too."

It cocked its head and waited.

"There are strangers in the realm, men from beyond the sea."

For the first time, the Necri's expression caught her by surprise. Puzzlement. Complete puzzlement. The creature could not comprehend the idea of men from beyond the vast body of water. Xabene herself found the thought unsettling. The Dragonrealm was the only world that she had ever known, but the lords had said that these men were from a land beyond and so she knew that it was true.

What was also true was that they were travelling in a direction that would take them much too close to the citadel of the damnable gnome. The Lords of the Dead wanted no other competitors. The Dragon King of this region was trouble enough, thought he would, of course, fail in the end.

The Necri squeaked harshly and flexed his talons in expectation.

She shook her head. "No, we are to watch and wait for a time. The Dragon King will surely note their passage, as will the keeper of the citadel."

Baring its teeth, the batlike monstrosity protested this decision. In the dark of night, it would be easy to pick off several men. Despite its sickly white coloring, it was somehow able to conceal itself from the eyes of all but the most wary.

"The decision was not mine."

Squeaking once more, the Necri grew subdued. It would not go against the wishes of its masters.

"We watch for now," Xabene continued, toying with the copper artifact. "Perhaps later, there will be time for your games."

That mollified the winged horror, at least for the moment. The enchantress wondered just how long it would be able to resist the temptation to slay at least one of the intruders. Long enough, she supposed, for it knew the fate that would await it if the lords discovered its disobedience in this matter.

She pointed to the southeast. "They camp on or near a beach directly south of the hills. Pass within sight of the gnome's citadel and you will have no trouble finding their vessel."

The Necri nodded its understanding. It would find them. Nothing escaped its kind for very long.

Xabene remained silent as the creature spread its expansive wings and turned from her. As it rose into the night sky, a ghostly death on wings, the sorceress pocketed the Seeker artifact and studied the dying flames. She had not informed the Necri of their masters' desire to speak with the leader of the outsiders. They had not required her to and so she had made the decision to leave the horrific beast in the dark.

The Lords of the Dead were very curious about the newcomers. Had the dark enchantress been more daring in her thoughts, she might have almost suspected them of being just a bit frightened as well. Such a thought had never occurred to Xabene, however, for to imagine fright among her masters would have seemed very much like heresy.

In truth, the reason she had not informed the Necri of their lords' desire was because *she* wanted to be the one who brought them the expedition's leader. It would give her an opportunity to ask a few harmless questions of her own.

She smiled. If the newcomers' leader was a man, and she supposed that was the most likely case, then before long he would tell her *everything* she and her lords desired to know.

The dawn had come earlier than they had expected. Under the guidance of Captain Yalso and Prentiss Asaalk, the expedition readied itself. Most of the necessities had been brought ashore the previous evening, including the dozen horses and wagons. Yalso had had the latter reassembled as soon as all the pieces were accounted for. Once more, Wellen felt as useless as the sand on the beach. He knew that was not the case, for it had been his efforts that had brought about the expedition and it was to be his decision when it came to the direction the expedition's future was to take. Certainly, they would investigate the ruined port city first, but there were other priorities. If there was thriving civilization somewhere on this side of the continent, it was up to the party to discover it.

Wellen knew they might find the locals warlike, but the men he had hired, including those of Yalso's crew who were to accompany them, were, for the most part, capable in such situations. He was grateful that the captain had chosen to leave things in the hands of his first mate and had joined the explorers. If there was anyone who knew how to handle a desperate situation, *besides* Prentiss Asaalk, it was the sturdy Yalso.

Around mid-morning, they got underway. Only the scouts and those commanding the expedition had steeds; there simply had not been enough money or room for all those that they would have required. Even enterprising merchants were willing to risk only so much on such a daring venture, and to have carried all that Wellen had needed would have required one, possibly *two* more ships as massive as the *Heron's Wing*. As it was, Wellen, the blue man, and the captain had three of the animals. The scouts had three more. The remaining horses, all draft animals, pulled the wagons along. For the time, their loads would be light, but the expedition hoped to fill those empty wagons with valuables before time considerations made them return to those waiting at the beach encampment.

The first few hours passed as uneventfully as the night. After several miles of walking, most of the men had lost interest in the surrounding landscape which was, even Wellen had to admit, not very different from some of the regions back home.

Wellen called a halt about midway through the afternoon. Asaalk was all for continuing on for a few more hours, but the scholar reminded him that not only was *he* riding and the men were not, but also that most of them had not yet fully gotten their land legs back.

"They've only had a day to recover," he reminded the blue man. "Whatever ground we cover after they've had a short time to rest will be a bonus as far as I'm concerned."

"You plan to travel on until nightfall?" Captain Yalso asked, dismounting.

"I do." Wellen followed suit. After a moment, a reluctant Asaalk joined them on foot. "That should mean about another four, maybe four and a half hours. I'd hoped to reach the hills—"

"Hmmph! Not today!"

The hills were an annoyance to Bedlam. He had estimated them closer and thought they might reach the base of the nearest by the time the sun set, but that was no longer likely.

"Whatever we can add to what we've already traveled,

then." He had no intention of putting the column through a grueling death march.

"There is rain in our future."

The northerner's words made both men look skyward. In the distant northwest, Wellen observed a line of clouds. He shook his head. "Cloud cover, maybe, but those don't look like rain clouds . . . not yet. It'll cool things down a little, at least."

It seemed likely that the white mass would not reach them until some time during the night. If it appeared threatening by then, they could always make arrangements, but Wellen doubted that would be necessary.

The scouts returned just as the column began moving again. Riding beside the scholar, the lead scout, a young, narrow man with a crooked nose and no hair whatsoever, reported their finds.

"All clear up to the hills, Master Bedlam. Not a soul around."

Wellen caught a note of uncertainty in the man's voice and asked, "Does that bother you for some particular reason?"

The scouts looked at one another before the leader finally answered. "Just seems too pretty and too damned organized. My ma had a big garden and I keep feelin' like I'm ridin' in the middle of it now."

"Garden? What does that mean?" Prentiss Asaalk urged his mount closer and stared down the lead scout.

"I mean the hills, what we could see of them, are awfully nice and organized!" His face screwed up as he thought about it. "They're all pretty much identical, too!"

Glancing forward at the distant hills, Wellen had to admit there was something to what the man was saying. The hills *were* nearly identical. They varied in size, true, but not in shape. There was also a definite trend; the hills grew taller the more to the north one looked.

"Preposterous, yes?" Asaalk asked, looking at the scholar.

"I suppose . . ."

"Is that *all* you men have to report?" Captain Yalso asked, sounding both relieved and disgusted. No one wanted to be told that there was danger, but at the same time everyone wanted to know if there was something of interest ahead. The thought of finding nothing but endless woods and fields appealed to no one. While that meant plenty of good land for colonizing, it also meant no riches.

"You told us not to go too far ahead, sir."

That was true. Since the column would be turning north in another day or two, no one had seen much sense in sending the scouts too far west. Wellen was already regretting that decision. Who knew what lay farther inland? Had he not had the others to consider, he would have ridden deeper into the Dragonrealm. Unfortunately, the scholar knew that he would be lucky if they managed to map most of the eastern coastline before they were forced to return home. It might be years before he had another chance, though.

He came to a decision. "Would you men be willing to scout farther west?"

There were nods from all three. The leader asked, "How far should we ride?"

"As far as you can and still be back by the time we've turned north. That'll give you . . . three days."

"*Three* days?" Yalso's half-buried mouth curved upward on the ends. "Change your mind?"

"No, I just want to make certain that we bypass that mist-enshrouded region completely." That, at least, was true. More so, now that he was thinking about it. The sense of foreboding was so great that he almost thought he felt it . . . but that was *ridiculous*. Wellen wore the mark of a spellcaster, the streak of silver in his hair, but he had never so much as manifested the least of skills.

The lying shock of hair was a sore point with him, but he knew better than to brood about it, especially now. Thrusting it from his mind, he told the scouts, "That's all I can give you. Ride at your own pace and be careful. We can't afford to turn around once we get started north."

More enthusiastic than they had been upon returning, the scouts saluted Wellen and rode back the way they had come.

"On horse they should make some distance, yes?" Asaalk looked as if he wanted to join them. In that, he was one with the young Bedlam. "Perhaps they will find something for us, something we may turn to if the city is a loss."

An encouraging thought, but Wellen did not want to get his hopes up. At least they knew the ancient city existed. There might not be another such place on the entire continent. There might be nothing.

Wellen hoped that was not the case, if only because it would mean his dream would become only that, a fool's imaginary wonder.

The rest of the day's excursion passed quietly. Several of Yalso's men had been constantly at work jotting down landmarks that would later be compared for a final map of the region. Now and then, the captain retreated to speak to these men, leaving an uneasy Wellen to ride in silence beside the massive blue man. Fortunately, Asaalk seemed lost in his own thoughts, for he made only one comment when they were alone and that was to point out a rather large bird in the distance. From what little they could make out, the two estimated it to be almost as large as a man. That made the northerner check his bow and Wellen reconsider the tales of the Dragonrealm.

When the sun finally began to sink over the hills and Yalso suggested they stop for the night, he was more than willing to acquiesce. They chose a lightly wooded location that would give them some protection. Any locale would have actually suited Wellen, even a rocky hillside. Exhaustion mingled with anticipation had taken a worse toll on him than he had thought possible.

"You look all done in," the sea captain commented after they had handed their mounts over to one of Yalso's men. Around them, weary souls were preparing meals and bedding. Wellen nodded to a few and tried to look encouraging. He had no idea whether he was succeeding or not.

"The trouble of being a scholar, I suppose. My life has been too sedentary and my body just can't take all of this."

Yalso's expression indicated he did not really believe the shorter man's excuse, but the captain liked Wellen too much to pry, at least for now. "Get some food and then go to sleep as soon as ya can. I'll handle sentries and the like, providin', that is, that the blue devil's not already done *that* again."

The blue man had not joined the two of them, but rather had darted off in the opposite direction as soon as he had dismounted. Wellen did not really care what Asaalk was doing now; the blue man's ambitions had no outlet here in the wilds. Perhaps when they reached the ancient city, he might be able to turn the lure of riches to his advantage, but not at the moment. Wellen had the column moving as quickly and efficiently as possible and he knew that his caution concerning the land to the north was one that most of his men shared.

Food was welcome at this late point in the day, as was the

tent that he found waiting for him when he went to retrieve his things. Both Yalso and Asaalk insisted that the expedition's leader warranted a private tent. To everyone else, it seemed a plain and simple thing, but Wellen always felt embarrassed when he was treated so. He had led a quiet, unrigorous life and so he always carried the fear that no one would respect him if he did not work as they worked and lived as they lived.

Still, the tent *did* give him somewhere private that he could use for his research. His food half-forgotten beside him, the scholar began rummaging through his notes and theories concerning the Dragonrealm. It was always best to check and double-check what he had written earlier. So engrossed did Bedlam become in his work that he did not look up until he realized that someone had called his name.

It was Captain Yalso. "Knew I'd be findin' you porin' over those things! What do you find new in them each night? You were readin' them each night on the ship and here you are again!"

Wellen gathered up his papers. "There's always something new. A different perspective, a clearer thought; it could be anything."

"So you say. Well you may be in charge, but I'm orderin' you to bed . . . les' of course you want to fall off your horse tomorrow!"

Sleep suddenly sounded *so* good. Wellen eyed his dinner, part of which was still untouched. "I'll just finish eating."

"Do it without readin'," suggested the aged mariner. "Just so you know, too, the blue devil's out huntin' with a couple of men. Said there's plenty of game out there."

"Long as he doesn't mistake anyone for a deer."

Yalso grew somber. "He'd better not."

Reading the captain's expression, Wellen shook his head. He doubted that Prentiss Asaalk would bend to anything as crude as murder. A man of pride, the northerner would be more interested in letting his skills prove him the rightful leader of the expedition. Yalso, however, was a man who had lived a far more violent life. Between pirates and such, he had developed a very harsh opinion of life.

The captain, seeing that Wellen would not hear his warnings, switched to a more mundane subject. "The clouds've moved in a lot faster. They may not be rain makers, but I doubt we'll be seein' much sun tomorrow."

After the heat today, that seemed more of a godsend to Wellen. "Means we might get a few extra miles. We'll have to keep an eye out. No telling if the weather here changes abruptly. Wouldn't do to be unprepared for a downpour."

"I'll be keepin' that in mind. That's all I had to tell ya. Get yourself some rest. You'll need it." The bulky seaman started to depart, then paused and added, "If you're *not* asleep in an hour, I'll be havin' the sentries tie ya down!"

Wellen laughed as the captain retired, because he knew very well that Yalso meant what he had said. Organizing his research into a neat pile, he thrust it back into a weathered pouch and then set about finishing his evening meal. There would be days enough to go over it a hundred times and Captain Yalso was correct when he said that Wellen needed rest. Now free of the hypnotic pull of his work, the short scholar felt the renewed weight of exhaustion attempting to overwhelm him.

He wondered whether he would be able to finish his food before sleep finally triumphed.

Wellen gasped and sat up. He had no way of knowing just how much time had passed since he had retired, but he was certain the night was well underway. Outside, he could hear nothing but the sounds of night: insects, birds, and other small, nocturnal creatures. The scholar frowned. None of those sounds had disturbed him; rather, he had the sensation that there was something *else* out there, something beyond his experience.

He gathered his clothes and dressed quietly but quickly. It was still quite possible that Wellen had heard one of the sentries wandering by, but he doubted that. He could not say why he felt doubtful any more than he could explain why these sensations were occurring.

The clouds covered most of the sky, which made the night that much darker. Wellen stepped out of his tent and surveyed the area, trying to identify the few things he could make out from where he stood. He heard a man cough in his sleep and saw the vague shapes of several sleepers. Nothing unusual.

A few tentative steps left him standing in the dark, perplexed and annoyed at what was happening within his head. It if was real, then what was it? If it was all imaginary, then was he suffering from paranoia? Asaalk, if no one else, would welcome that. The young scholar knew that he could not remain leader of the expedition if he started dreaming up imaginary dangers left and right . . . and *above*.

It was *above*. As if he had actually heard or seen it, Wellen knew that whatever it was lurked directly above him.

In the overhanging branches of the nearest tree.

He looked up and perhaps it was the vehemence with which he moved that settled the matter, for a large, dark form suddenly stirred to life. Wellen instinctively let out a yell, bringing the entire camp into frenzied life. The creature in the tree, despite having the advantage, did not fling itself down upon him nor did it flutter off into the night. Instead, it moved about the branches, as if lost or confused.

A hissing noise made the short man stumble away. He saw a long, skinny shape bury itself in the upper portion of the tree's trunk and realized that someone had let loose an arrow. He had no time to wonder who could have moved with such speed and accuracy, however, because the watcher in the branches had finally had enough and was pushing its way out of the tangle.

"What is it? What's happenin'?" Yalso roared from an unknown location to Wellen's right.

Another hiss. The winged figure, just launching itself into the sky, squawked in agony as the shaft bit into it. Wellen watched it tumble toward the ground, wings desperately trying to control its crazed descent. A moment later, it struck the ground with an all-too-solid *thump*.

"Master Bedlam!" Captain Yalso, shirtless, rushed to his side. In his hand he held a torch. "Are you well?"

He could not answer the other man, his eyes snared by the sight before him. In the flickering light, the injured creature became a tale come to life. The humanoid torso, the avian visage, despite its small size—standing, it probably came up to Wellen's chest—it was as a few of the fragmented stories had described.

A Seeker. One of the bird folk in the legends of Lord Drazeree.

Other men were gathering, but Yalso waved them back. The Seeker, whether male or female was hard to say, tugged at the shaft, which had caught it in the thigh. It completely ignored the humans.

An adolescent, Wellen decided. *Small wonder it grew confused instead of departing immediately*.

"I struck it, yes?"

Prentiss Asaalk broke through the gathering men, his long-bow ready. Suddenly, Bedlam wanted to take the man and shake him. The northerner would never understand why, though.

He would have to act quickly. "Everyone remain where you are! Leave this to me!"

Slowly, Wellen walked toward the bleeding avian, his hands out and open for the creature to see. It failed to notice his nearing presence at first, still caught up in its futile attempt to remove the arrow. When it finally did notice him, its reaction was to reach out and try to claw at his legs. Fortunately for Wellen, its desire was greater than its reach. Its swift defense, however, proved too much for it and it slumped to the ground. The scholar continued to move cautiously, noting that the eyes still watched him.

"Don't go any closer," Yalso warned him.

"It's all right."

"We should finish it off, yes? Much easier to study when it cannot snap a finger off." Asaalk's comment made Wellen's gaze shift for a brief time to the Seeker's beak. There was no doubt in his mind that the avian could not only bite off his fingers, but possibly his entire hand. Still, he did not stop.

When he was well within claw range and still the young Seeker had not attacked him again, Wellen dared to kneel down by the injured leg. The eyes of the avian stayed on him at all times, but it now seemed to understand that he, at least, meant it no harm. He touched the shaft carefully, noting how deep it had sunk into the leg. The pain had to be almost unbearable.

"This will hurt. I'm sorry, but I can't help that. There's no other way." Wellen doubted that it could understand him, but he hoped that his soothing tones would relay his intentions.

Though he had lived most of his life in the throes of research, Wellen Bedlam was not unfamiliar with such wounds. Part of his training had included aiding the injured. With raiders such as the Sons of the Wolf forever harassing settlements, it behooved a traveling scholar to have such knowledge.

His hands steady, something that surprised him quite a bit, Wellen carefully worked the shaft outward. The Seeker's breathing grew ragged as the adolescent flyer struggled with the sharp increase in pain. Smiling encouragement and hoping that the bird understood his expression, Wellen continued. The head of the arrow was giving him great difficulty, causing him to wonder just what it looked like. Trust the blue man to utilize a tip with jagged barbs or something equally nasty.

He nearly fell backward when the arrow came loose. The Seeker gasped and shivered, but still did not pass out. He had to admire its stamina. Had it been himself, Wellen was certain he would have blacked out long before. He glanced at the arrowhead. Sure enough, it was lined with hooked ridges. Any animal suffering the misfortune of being struck by one of Asaalk's toys would tear open its wound further when it tried to pull the arrow out with its teeth or claws. In all probability, the head itself would end up remaining lodged in the wound until the victim perished from blood loss or disease.

Thinking of the wound, he turned his gaze back to the leg. Blood continued to streak down the sides. The wound was a good two inches across and probably extended down to the bone. He would have to bind it lest it grow worse, but first he had to inspect it a little closer. There might be other damage.

As his fingers touched the edge of the gaping wound, a wondrous thing happened. Wellen removed his hand as if a snake had been about to bite it, but only because he had hardly been expecting this latest shock.

The wound was closing. It was *healing* itself.

Sorcery! I should have recalled! The Seekers, so the stories went, had ruled the Dragonrealm before the coming of Lord Drazeree. They had a magic of their own.

"What's happenin' there?" Yalso finally dared ask, having grown frustrated with being unable to contribute anything to the situation. "What's it doin' now?"

"Healing itself." *Odd*, Wellen thought. *I thought it would have entailed more than this.*

The Seeker stirred, and rose so quickly to a sitting position that several of the onlookers thought it was about to attack their leader. Asaalk's bow was at the ready, but Wellen held up a shielding hand.

"No!" He made a calming gesture to the Seeker, too. Fear might make it do exactly what everyone had thought it was about to do.

What the avian did do was gingerly touch the closed wound. A taloned finger gently ran the course of the injury, almost as if the Seeker could not quite believe what had happened. Wellen was perplexed; perhaps the young creature had never had to make use of its powers in such a way, but surely it had seen others of its kind heal themselves?

His confusion swelled when the Seeker removed its hand from its leg, reached out slowly, and touched the scholar's arm.

A sensation of gratitude . . . that was the only way Wellen could describe it . . . washed over him. He swayed under its intensity.

Mutterings from the men warned him of their misconceptions. He shook his head and quickly assured them of his safety. "I'm fine! It was only trying to thank me!"

"What do we do with it?" someone asked. "Put it over a fire and cook it?"

Normally, Wellen might have joined in the laughter, but not in this case. He slowly rose and turned to face the others. "We let it go."

"Let it *go*?" It came as no surprise to the scholar that the loudest dissenting voice belonged to Prentiss Asaalk. "So it may bring its flock back to murder us in the night, yes? We should kill it and preserve its hide!"

There were more than a few agreeing nods. Wellen quelled his rising anger. "This is a *child*, gentlemen. You can see that for yourselves. Is there anyone who would like to kill this child? Is there anyone brave enough?"

A cold silence draped itself over the expedition. As he had hoped, putting the killing in such terms had made it an unthinkable act in the eyes of the others. There might have been one or two men who would have performed the horrific deed had they been alone, but no one now dared even speak of it, lest they be marked by their compatriots. Though Wellen had tried to choose men with few familial ties for the expedition, he knew that some *did* have children.

"You heard Master Bedlam!" growled Yalso. He somehow towered over the men. "And a right good decision it is! I'll want no child's death . . . whatever that child *be* . . . on my hands!"

The blue man looked a bit frustrated, but he had lowered his bow and was already replacing the unused arrow into the quiver that had ben slung rather haphazardly across his back.

The Seeker rose, careful to remain behind Bedlam at all times. Wellen encouraged it with a smile, indicating that it could fly off into the sky as soon as it desired. The Seeker spread its wings, but instead, walked up to the short man and placed one clawed hand on his arm again. Once more, there was a sensation of immense gratitude such as only a youngster could convey. Wellen shook his head, trying to indicate that he had done nothing for the adolescent.

Cocking its head to one side, the Seeker released his arm. Expansive wings stretched, flapped, and lifted the avian into the air. There was a collected exhalation from the party. While their homelands were not without wonders, especially for those who lived near the wilds claimed by hidden Sirvak Dragoth, the Seeker was a new creature and one that few besides Wellen recognized from childhood stories.

It hovered over the scholar a moment longer, then turned and soared with remarkable speed into the concealing night.

A youngling, he thought, watching the sky even though he knew he would see nothing more. *The entire camp turned about because of a curious youngster!*

Yalso, as ever, was the rational force among them. He waved the men away, saying, "That's all! It's over! I want everyone back to sleep . . . 'cept you sentries! You I want to keep awake! Lettin' sprats go right past you! If I find another one in here, you can be certain . . ."

The captain's voice trailed off as he followed the men. Asaalk remained just long enough to retrieve his arrows. He picked up the one that had been removed from the avian's thigh by Wellen, ignoring the blood, but the other arrow snapped in two when he tried to free it from the trunk.

"A pity! They are costly."

Bedlam said nothing. He stared at the blue man until Asaalk, seemingly oblivious to Wellen's disgust, bid the scholar good night and retired.

Alone at last, the tired scholar gave the heavens one final scan, then retreated into his tent.

Inside, his other emotions gave way to the wonder of it all. *A Seeker! I saw one!* He could not get the thought out of his mind. The fables and legends bore more truth than he had thought likely. If the Seekers existed, what *else* might? Wellen seriously doubted that he would get any more sleep tonight, so awed was he by the experience. He settled down and stared at the ceiling of his tent, recalling every marvelous detail of the avian. Time would have to be devoted to a piece on the creature before the memories grew indistinct. That meant now. Wellen decided to allow himself a few minutes to regroup his thoughts before he began to write down his notes on this discovery.

Three minutes later, he was sound asleep.

In a tree beyond the camp, its eyes focused on the habitat of he was leader of these new folk, the winged figure watched. No one would notice it here. Learning from experience, however, it had also cloaked itself in warding spells, just to make certain.

The leader of the humans was the one to watch. Already, he had marked himself different from the rest. Soft as he appeared, the others respected his decisions. That meant there was more to him than appearances suggested.

Reluctant as it was to share the information, the watcher knew what would happen if it did not. Closing its eyes, the Necri linked with its unwanted partner. The human called Xabene would be very interested in this particular man, of that the Necri was certain.

It almost pitied him.

IV

Reddish eyes the length of a man opened, taking in the darkness of the cavern. Reptilian eyes, monstrous eyes, filled with vast knowledge.

There was something amiss in his kingdom, something more than just the annoying intrusions by the insignificant creatures calling themselves the Lords of the Dead.

In the darkness of the cavern, the shadowy form of the Dragon King rose, nearly filling the entire chamber.

There was something amiss.

His claws scratched at the rocky floor as he contemplated this affront to his reign. Who *now* dared threaten what was his and what should rightfully be his? Did someone else seek the tome? What was the source of the strange presence? Who was the fool?

His talons gouged great crevices in the rock as he thought of the punishment he would mete out. In the darkness, no one could see his dragon's smile, toothy and full of hunger.

There was something amiss in his kingdom, *oh, yes* . . . but not for very long.

Despite the events of the night, the column was underway soon after dawn. A different mood prevailed. Most now recalled the tales from their youth and were beginning to wonder just what other shocks the Dragonrealm had for them.

Wellen, especially, wondered. As he rode beside Captain Yalso, he could not shake the uneasy feeling that had been with him since the discovery of the Seeker. The young scholar had assumed that the sensation would dwindle away once the avian was gone, but such had not been the case. Waking that morning, he had felt the same, possibly even worse.

Why?

The clouds that had moved in during the night had failed to vanish with the morning. Rain was still not likely; the clouds were not the right type. There were even several patches of clear sky, windows in a wall of mist. Wellen found himself constantly leading the expedition from shadow to light and back to shadow again. Under other circumstances, Wellen might have found it amusing. Not today, not with the sense of foreboding.

"Somethin' wrong?" Yalso asked. "You look all out."

He decided to be honest with the mariner. "I can't help shaking the feeling that something's going to happen. I had the same notion when I woke up and discovered the Seeker!"

Yalso glanced at the telltale mark of silver decorating his companion's head. "But I thought you didn't have any sort of magic, despite that—"

"I *don't!*" Wellen snapped.

Both men stared at one another. Embarrassed, Wellen looked around. The men in the front of the column stared straight ahead. Twisting, he faced Prentiss Asaalk. The blue man met his gaze with an indifferent one, but Wellen was certain it was a mask. Asaalk was likely smiling inside at the shameful display. Bedlam had always prided himself on his ability to hold his temper. For most men, such an act would have been nothing, but for him . . .

A shadow broke across one of the patches of sunlight and vanished.

His anger at himself temporarily put aside, Wellen studied the clouds. The bit of open sky was there, but nothing that could have created the shadow was evident.

"Somethin'?"

The young leader shook his head. "Nothing. Just my imagination running off."

"Umm."

Neither one brought up the subject of sorcery and Wellen's lack thereof. The column moved in relative silence for the next couple hours. Comments were restricted to the notation of landmarks and where the best point to turn north would be. Bedlam finally chose the edge of the hills. The scouts had not yet returned, and he could no longer wait. Somewhere there had to be a break that would allow him a view of the lands beyond.

The column was just entering another patch of sunlit countryside, but Wellen's mind was hardly on something so insignificant. The nearer to the hills they came, the more the lead scouts comment concerning the gardenlike quality of the land came back to haunt him. Was there a break? Did the hills just continue unbroken, as they appeared to do so far?

Had someone arranged them so? Again, it seemed a silly notion, but . . .

For the second time, a huge shadow blotted out the sunlight.

He was not the only one to notice it. Yalso muttered an epithet and even Prentiss Asaalk seemed disturbed. The shadow, however, disappeared from sight before any of the three could look up. Wellen looked at the two for suggestions. The northerner shrugged, weather not being of much import to him unless it was about to storm. The captain thought about it, then suggested, "Clouds."

That was the obvious answer, but it did not settle well with the scholar. He was the first to admit that weather was *not* his forte, but *swift* clouds?

The massive sailor could see that neither man understood him. He tried to explain, "I know most landleggers don't pay *that* much attention to weather, 'cept maybe farmers, but a man on the sea has got to, 'cause if he don't he might find his ship torn apart on the rocks and him takin' the biggest drink of his life . . . and the last, of course."

"And how does that concern us?" the blue man asked.

"There're currents in the air just as there're currents in the ocean. Sometimes, ya got one current going one way and another, lower, goin' a different way."

"And you're saying that it's the same abovè?" Wellen wondered for the first time what knowledge he had ignored by paying so little attention to the sky.

"*Might* be, is what I'm sayin'. I've seen clouds high up go different directions than the ones below them, faster or slower, too."

"Clouds . . ." It was apparent that the blue man was ready to forget this subject. "We have no reason to fear clouds, yes? Not these."

"Maybe."

None of this talk had satisfied Wellen, however. He looked again to the heavens, trying make out something in the patches of clear sky. "I don't think it was a cloud, not a normal one, captain. It moved too fast."

"Then what?"

The scholar had no answer, none, at least, that he could verify. Whatever it was seemed to be gone now.

Or *was* it? The sense of foreboding was so strong that it threatened to drown out all thought. He put a hand to his forehead and closed his eyes for a moment, trying to ease the pounding. Neither Yalso nor Asaalk said anything.

I have no powers! I have no skill! This is all in my mind! Wellen tried deep breaths.

For a brief instant, he felt an inhuman presence in his head.

"Gods!" His head snapped up and though he stared forward, what he saw was beyond mortal vision.

An overwhelming sense of mastery. A hunger that can never be sated. A contempt for lesser things . . . for the tiny warm-bloods below.

"Master Bedlam!" Yalso was shouting. "Listen to me!"

He grabbed the captain's thick forearm. "It's up there! It's up there watching us!"

"What does he speak of?" Asaalk yelled.

"I don't—*Mother of the Sea!*"

Shouting erupted from the ranks even as Wellen joined Yalso and the blue man in gazing up at the source of the growing panic. It had wings that spanned the length of the column with ease. Talons that, even at this distance, must be capable of easily picking up a man and a horse. It had a tail at least as long as its body. When it roared, they could see the vast array of long, sharp teeth in its maw. It was green for the most part, but another color mingled with that green in a manner so subtle that one almost accepted it being there without realizing what it was. Purple or something near it.

Here be dragons, so the stories said.

No one, not even Wellen Bedlam himself, had actually believed that the horrific leviathans of their childhood tales existed. But what flew above them, looking very much like a vulture circling its meal, was no massive, stupid beast like the dragons of home.

As they stared, still unbelieving, it began to dive.

Wellen's shout surprised even him. "Scatter!"

What *else* was there to do? They were not armed to fight such a monstrosity, even if a spellcaster or two had deigned to join the foolhardy quest. The sorcerers of their homelands were too busy fighting each other or simply did not care. Now, that lack might mean the death of every man.

"There's nowhere to run to!" Yalso screamed. "That thing'll tear trees from the earth if we run to the woods! It'll probably scorch the entire field!"

"What else is there to do?"

There was no time for talk after that. The dragon was much too close.

With Yalso and Asaalk behind him, Wellen urged his mount to the hills. The hills offered the best protection and he wished that there was some way to transport his men there. The entire column was facing destruction and *he* was to blame!

A massive shadow raced across the land. The roar of the dragon deafened everyone. The frantic scholar thought that the beast almost *laughed*, but that was impossible, wasn't it? The question became moot as a strong wind caused by the dragon's passing buffeted the riders.

"We must stand and do something!" the blue man shouted. He had a peculiar look in his eyes, but Wellen had no time to decipher it. He was only concerned with saving himself and those who had followed him into this chaos.

"You're welcome to try!" Yalso replied, his eyes glued to the receding backside of the dragon. Its first pass had resulted in little damage and no bloodshed whatsoever. No one thought that the party would be that fortunate on its next pass.

Prentiss Asaalk seemed to be considering his weapons. Wellen shook his head. "You've nothing that could slay that beast! Hiding is the best hope we have!"

The dragon turned in a great arc and began its second dive.

Despite the oncoming danger, the scholar hesitated. His eyes scanned the scene beyond, where men either ran in full panic or buried themselves in whatever bit of cover the landscape provided. Both attempts were futile, save that *some* men might survive with such numbers as they had. From above, the dragon could see them all.

"We can't *do* anything for them!" Captain Yalso cried, taking his arm. The anguish in the sailor's voice surprised Wellen. For all his gruffness, Yalso cared for his crew as if they were his sons. He cared for the rest of the expedition almost as much, since they were under *his* care as well as Bedlam's.

The dragon, persistent as all large drakes were, came toward the earth again, but this time it did not simply pass over and return to the clouds. From its maw, a fine smoke flowed forth, settling on the earth as the drake raced over. Men caught in the midst of it rose and began to run.

The strongest of them ran perhaps five, maybe six steps before clutching their throats and falling face down into the grass, which was itself turning brown and withering.

"No!" Wellen almost whispered the protest, so taken aback was he by the deaths. What sort of weapon was that the dragon had, a poison smoke? "No!"

He urged his anxious steed back toward the dying, his thoughts entirely on their lives and not his own.

"Come back!" Yalso raced after him. "You can't be of any help, Bedlam! You'll only get yourself killed, too!"

The shadow enveloped them then and grew at an alarming rate. The dragon had already turned back.

It did not strike this time, but the wind its streaking form caused was enough to send men falling to the ground. Wellen barely held his place in the saddle and even his steed stumbled in the midst of the blast. He still did not know what he intended to do, only that *something* had to be done.

"It comes again!" Prentiss Asaalk materialized next to him, the blue man's horse already panting from the combination of fear and its rider's great mass.

Even though he knew the leviathan was deadly, the scholar could still not help but admire its grace and beauty. The dragons of home were indeed dull-witted cattle compared to this monster. The vast, batlike wings spread so far that a dozen horsemen on each would have been able to stand their mounts ready and still have no fear that they and their animals would be cramped for space. The scales of the beast shone whenever the sunlight hit it. Truly a wonder to behold . . . but not when it was trying to kill them all.

It was no longer possible to keep track of the men. They were scattered everywhere. Wellen wished he had the dragon's point of view. At least then, he could see where everyone—

A sudden image of landscape seen as though from a mountain peak, yet it kept changing. Tiny, silly figures scurrying about in blind panic, knowing that he was above them, their death. All merely prey to be toyed with except for one who rode, whose mind seemed to reach out . . .

Gasping, Bedlam found himself atop his mount once more. Had he *dreamed* that? Had his wish come true, albeit only for a moment, and granted him the ability to see as the drake did? How could such a thing happen?

You are the one . . .

The voice was in his mind and though no more was said after that, the cloying, inhuman sensation of it remained with him despite the scholar's best efforts to clear his head. He reined his horse to a frantic halt, surprising both Asaalk and Yalso, who rode several lengths past him before they could bring their own frightened animals around. As they rode back to him, the danger to both grew frighteningly clear to Wellen.

He rose in the saddle. "Go back! Ride away! Keep away from me!"

The northerner hesitated, slowing his steed a bit, but Captain Yalso continued on, his weathered visage deep-set in determination not to abandon his friend.

Wellen turned his horse and desperately urged it into motion. The sweating horse needed no encouragement; it broke into a gallop that left the other two riders quickly behind.

"Master Bedlam! Wellen!" Yalso would not be so easily deterred. Wellen, looking back, saw the seaman racing after him, a reluctant Asaalk close behind. He knew that the two men were unwittingly rushing to join him in death.

What the massive beast's limits were, Wellen had no way of knowing. His only hope was to ride and try to block its thoughts. Somehow he and the monster had briefly formed a bond, one that had worked in both directions. He did not think the dragon could read his mind that easily, however; its thought message had seemed forced, as if it had struggled to break in. The frenzied scholar knew that he might be badly mistaken, that the dragon might even now be laughing silently at his suppositions, but there was little he could do about that.

Once more, it was the sudden plunge into deep shadow that warned him of the leviathan's nearness. The black shroud crept up rapidly from behind him. Oddly, his fears were not for himself, but for those who followed.

Someone screamed, "*Jump!*"

Wellen reacted instinctively and dove off his horse.

The animal cried out in horror and pain, but the rolling Bedlam saw only the dust and earth that rose and beat him mercilessly. He heard the thundering of hooves and a voice that sounded like that of the blue man, but little more. As he turned face down again, his nose was pushed against the ground. Wellen grunted as it bent to one side and blood splattered his countenance. The world took on an ethereal quality, fading into and out of existence. As he finally slowed to a stop, it was all he could do to keep from passing out. The stunned explorer refused to give in to his injuries; there was no promise that unconsciousness would save him from the dragon's claws. Wellen, despite his upbringing, was one who preferred to die, if he had to, fighting the loathsome process to the bitter end.

He tasted blood on his lips as he turned over and tried to right himself. A broken nose and torn lips were miniscule wounds. He was thankful that nothing else seemed broken. Had the ground been rocky, it might have been worse.

The dragon was high in the sky, something large squirming in its claws. Wellen's mount. Beast and prey vanished into the clouds.

Captain Yalso rode to him, reining to a stop just in front of the bleeding scholar. "How bad are you?"

"Bruises, nothing more." That was a lie. There was dizziness, too, but he did not want to tell the mariner that. "Leave me; I'll go on foot."

"Don't be bigger fool than you've been! Climb aboard!" Yalso stretched out a hand.

Wellen eyed the captain's mount. It suffered from the combination of the weight of the sailor and the frantic pace it had already been put through. Adding a second body would only kill the animal in short order at this rate. At the very least, it would quickly grow useless for both of them.

The dragon was still above the cloud cover, no doubt finishing off his snack. There could only be seconds before the leviathan returned. "Captain Yalso, if we ride together, we're both lost! If we keep separate, one or both of us could survive!"

"Listen—"

Bedlam would not be silenced. "Go now! You can make it to safety! He wants *me*! Our minds, our thoughts, touched! He will not rest until he has taken me!"

It was obvious that the captain did not understand anything that Wellen was saying, but the grim determination in the scholar's eyes could not be denied. Yalso sighed and gave his companion a weary smile. "At least take the horse!"

"You need it more than me!" Strong the mariner might be, but running was not something his monumental girth allowed him to excel at. *"Go!"*

Yalso blinked, then nodded and rode back in the direction the column had originally travelled from.

Dirty, disheveled, and wracked with pain, Wellen chose a path going opposite that of the captain. By leading the dragon away, he hoped to give the survivors, including Yalso, a chance to make it to safety. Perhaps the drake would even lose interest in them once it had dealt with the one who had invaded its mind.

He was still not certain how he had done that. The silver streak in his hair had always lied; never had Wellen revealed so much as the most modest of sorcerous skills. Why now?

Any theory he might have formed was lost, for the dragon broke through the clouds and dove like an avenging demon toward the spot in which the scholar stood. Wellen broke into a desperate run, knowing he could not outpace a soaring beast such as this. He only hoped his sacrifice would not be in vain. If even a few of the men survived, it would be worth it.

The shadow blanketed the field around him. Wellen stumbled and fell. There was no time left. He had hoped to get farther, to draw the dragon's notice for a bit longer, but such was not to be. He rolled onto his back and watched the descending form grow. What madness made him desire to face his scourge he could not say. Some insane hope, perhaps, that a miracle would yet save him.

Only a short moment from his victim, the dragon suddenly veered off.

The confused and unbelieving human rolled over to watch the monstrosity fly around. The dragon's pattern was erratic, as if he did not know where he was going. Wellen touched the silver in his hair without realizing it. A tentative smile played at his lips as he marvelled at his astonishing escape.

Rising once more to a great height, the green and purple leviathan scoured the earth. Reptilian eyes scanned the very region where Wellen Bedlam lay, but still the beast did not return for him.

"Wellen!"

The horrified voice made him whirl about. He stared in knowing fear as the captain, thinking that the dragon must have injured but not taken the scholar, rode back.

"No!" His shout went unheeded. He was as invisible and silent to Yalso as he was to the drake.

The rider, unfortunately, was not invisible to the menacing form above. Frustrated at losing his prey, the leviathan turned in the air and dove. Captain Yalso realized his mistake at the last moment and tried to leap from his mount as the dragon neared. The winged monstrosity was not to be fooled this time, however. It watched the man and not the beast and when the seaman jumped, unleashed another deadly cloud.

Already knowing it was too late for his companion, Wellen blindly ran west in order to escape the onrushing cloud. Behind him he heard the startled cry of the horse and a mortal cough that could only have issued from a human throat. Wellen did not look back.

The dragon remained low after the attack, evidently searching for its escaped victim. The shadow fell over Wellen and the wind nearly wrenched him from the ground, but still he ran free. Better to just keep running and hope that somehow he might live through this nightmare.

How long he ran, Bedlam could not say. Always it seemed as if the dragon was just behind him. The hills loomed closer and closer. Wellen briefly wondered what had happened to the scouts. Had the dragon caught them sooner? Had something *else* taken them? Such questions only made him run harder, despite the growing pain in his body and the shortness of his breath. It might very well be, he thought, that he would escape the scaly predator only to die of exhaustion.

Something came charging toward him.

A horse. Saddled. One of their own. Wellen had lost his own mount and Yalso's had perished with its rider. That meant that this was Prentiss Asaalk's animal, but then where was the northerner?

He realized he had no time to worry about the blue man. The horse was a gift of circumstances; Wellen could hardly not make use of it. Calling to the animal in as quiet and smooth a voice as he could manage, the battered scholar tried to encourage it over to him. At first the horse was skittish . . . and with good reason, of course . . . but then it slowly trotted his way. When the animal was within arm's length, Bedlam reached out, stroked its muzzle, and carefully sought out the reins. There was no blood to be seen. Other than being frightened and exhausted, the steed was healthy. Again, he wondered what had become of the blue man. While Wellen had hardly cared for Prentiss Asaalk, he did not hate him enough to see him dead or injured.

A quick glance skyward revealed the dragon still searching fruitlessly for the tiny figure who had vanished before his very eyes. Wellen thanked whatever gods had chosen to protect him and mounted. He did not dare ride east, not with the poisonous mists still enshrouding most of the region, and his inability to return to the ships left him with few other options. Riding north or south would leave him too open for his own tastes. Wellen had no idea how long he would remain invisible to the drake and whether or not this protection extended to other dangers. The horse had not been blinded; other creatures might also be able to see him.

That left the west and the hills, the destination he had been fleeing toward already.

Turning the nervous steed about, Wellen rode. Now able to relax a bit physically, if not mentally, the scholar found himself fighting the exhaustion that his earlier panic had kept at bay. He shook his head and tried to clear his thoughts, never assuming for a moment that he was free of danger. The drake might come in his direction and bury this part of the field under a cloud of death. It might finally pierce the mysterious barrier—one which Wellen could not believe *he* was responsible for—and once more be able to see the human morsel who had escaped it.

Sweat dripped down from his forehead, stinging his eyes. Wellen wiped his arm across. As he lowered his arm, he noticed a stain of red across his sleeve. The bleeding scholar knew it was a good thing that he could not see his countenance; between his broken nose and the wounds he had garnered during his fall, he probably looked more dead than alive. That he felt no pain from his wounds worried him, and for the first time he tried to take stock of his injuries. It was impossible to do so now, however, for between the horse's bouncing gait and his own exhaustion, the injured man could not keep track of what he was doing.

The first of the hills was nearly within reach when a second, louder roar shook the rider.

Wellen fought for control of the horse, then twisted, with effort, to an angle where he could study the cloudy sky over the plains.

Something moved about the clouds that *dwarfed* the leviathan that had destroyed the expedition.

Something *purple*?

He wiped his eyes clean again and stared. Whatever it was chose not to reveal itself again, but it was still there. He knew that, if only because the drake was rising swiftly to meet the newcomer. Yet, the monster's movements were not those of a beast about to attack, but rather those of a lesser creature answering the summons of a greater.

There and then, Bedlam knew he did *not* desire to remain where he was any longer.

With a last effort, he guided the stumbling horse into the hill region. The way was rough going at first. It almost seemed as if the same being who had shaped the hills with such uniformity had placed them so no path ever went straight, or remained level, for that matter. The path twisted and wound with such frequency that when Wellen and his horse finally reached a smooth, clear point, he paused and studied it. The thought of a subtle trap wormed its way through his clouding mind, but he soon rejected it. For what reason he did so remained unclear to him; the scholar could only recall that it seemed to make sense.

Wellen looked back on occasion, but after the first few minutes, the hills permanently blocked his view of the plains and the eastern sky. He could not hear either the dragon or the newcomer, which he assumed, with much trepidation, had to be yet *another* of the species. But that did not mean that they had departed.

The longer he rode, the more difficult it became for Wellen

Bedlam to remain conscious. The leap and its aftermath had taken much more out of him than he had first supposed. Once in a while, Wellen found himself stirring from periods that he could only describe as blankness. He had been neither conscious or asleep, merely *not there*. When he tentatively checked both his broken nose and the forehead wound, he found both still bleeding profusely.

"I hope you can go on without my help," he muttered to the horse. The sound of his own voice, as dry and cracked as it was, kept him somewhat coherent. He began talking to himself more and more, not caring how mad he might sound. Besides, who was out here to listen to him besides the scholar himself?

"I had this dream once." Wellen forced himself to turn his head so that he could study the landscape around him. More and more trees were dotting the path. He vaguely wondered if that meant he was coming to the western edge of the hills. "I had a dream that I would become a great warlock, a sorcerer without com—compare."

He coughed. The noise echoed throughout the area.

"Kept waiting for those magnificent powers to manifest them—themselves. They never did." Wellen glanced at his mount, as if waiting for it to respond. He started to think about what sort of life the animal had enjoyed before being picked for this expedition. "Bet you wished you were back in the stable. Nice and boring, but safe." A ragged laugh. "I had a life like that . . . and to think I wanted out of it."

The hills kept rising before him, shattering any idea that an end might be in sight. Wellen scratched his nose despite both the blood his hand came away with and the fact that since the nose was numb it had not itched in the first place. "Should I . . . should I stay here or go . . . go beyond the edge?"

Something fluttered about the trees, something fairly large. Wellen doubted that a dragon could hide itself so well, then thought of the young Seeker. Could one of the legendary avians be watching him? He leaned in the direction of the noise, and an owl darted out of the trees and off into the sky.

Wellen wanted to laugh, but there was not enough strength left for that. He satisfied himself with a brief smile, then once more concentrated on the myriad path running through the hills.

There had been no sign of the dragon or dragons for some time now, but not once did the scholar think to turn around. He was committed. This far into the hills, he was determined to at least complete the crossing. Beyond the sloping, turning land there was something so valuable that it needed dragons to guard it. Bedlam was certain that such had been the drake's purpose in being here, to guard what lay beyond the hills.

The horse shied.

Wellen twisted in the saddle, gazing up in full expectation of sighting a diving form.

He saw nothing. The sky that was visible here was clear, save for a few high clouds. Now, there was nowhere the dragon could have hidden. Frustrated and worn, he turned to shout at the skittish animal . . . and saw the grisly remains poking out from behind some high bushes.

They were recognizable as a horse and a man, but little more. From the shreds of clothing that still lingered on the bloody torso of the unfortunate rider, Wellen knew it was one of the expedition scouts. Some force had torn the man quite literally apart, much the way one might tear apart an orange.

Weakened as he was already, the scholar did not have the stamina to resist the sickening sight. Half falling from the saddle, he went to his knees and vomited. Little more than spittle and blood issued forth, but the act itself was nearly enough to make him completely collapse. Wellen succeeded in maintaining consciousness, but that was all. For more than ten minutes, the hapless rider kneeled where he was, trying to pull himself together.

No dragon had killed the man. If such had been the case, not a shred of clothing would have been found. This deed had been performed by a smaller but savage creature, something perhaps the size of a . . . of a *Seeker*? Wellen could not see the avians killing so, however. The legends and his encounter with the adolescent Seeker were enough to convince him that the bird folk, however dangerous they might be, were capable of more *civilized* methods of death. More likely, an animal of some sort had gotten the unsuspecting scout while he had been engaged in studying the landscape.

So where were the *other* scouts, and why had they left his body unburied?

He was afraid he knew the answer already. Dragging himself to his feet, Wellen took hold of his mount's reins and, forcing himself to endure the sight of the ravaged remains, continued down the path. Each step tore at his already fragile system, wracking him further. Nevertheless, Wellen continued until he found what he was looking for.

All in all, the other two had not gotten very far from their comrade before whatever horror had murdered the first had caught up to them. One of the figures, the man Bedlam recalled as the spokesman of the trio, was actually in recognizable shape. Perhaps the beast had tired by that point. What did matter was that Wellen was now absolutely alone in the Dragonrealm. The scouts were dead, Yalso had perished, and the scholar had found no trace of Prentiss Asaalk, save the blue man's mount. Any survivors from the column were undoubtedly on their way to the waiting ships. There had to be a few, despite the thoroughness of the dragon. He had no doubt that the acting commander would order both vessels underway once he heard what had happened to the grand expedition. With such tales to tell, it was doubtful that anyone would risk returning to this continent for years to come.

He would be *alone* in the Dragonrealm.

His dream had become a nightmare.

Wellen desperately wanted to do something about the remains of the three men, but he barely had the strength to stand, much less dig a grave or build a pyre. In fact, as shameful as it might seem, Wellen did not even want to remain in the same area any longer. In his present state, he could barely stomach the rising stench.

Disgusted with himself, the expedition leader tried to remount his horse. The animal was understandably nervous and Wellen's first two attempts failed miscrably. Wincing at the pain coursing through his body, Wellen took a tighter hold on the reins and whispered to the beast. The voice calmed the horse to a point where the young Bedlam finally felt it was safe to try again. Carefully, he started to swing himself upward.

In the undergrowth near one of the bodies, a heavy form moved toward them. The horse shied. Wellen, caught midway, could only hold on. He did not even have the breath to talk to the shifting steed.

The creature in the undergrowth hissed and crawled out from cover. The scholar, turned to face it by the movements of his panicking mount, marked it immediately as a carrion creature, one of the lesser drakes that always seemed to have a nose for finding the dead. Unless there were more than a dozen, such beasts rarely attacked the living. They were possibly the biggest cowards amongst their kind.

The horse, already at its wits' end from everything else, saw only teeth and claws. It rose onto its hind legs and kicked wildly. Try as best as he could, Wellen could not maintain his grip. He fell to the earth, striking his head on the flattened path.

The drake hissed again, but held its ground, unwilling to give up the morsels it had found. Wellen had a blurred glimpse of hooves and then was bowled to one side as the horse, unwilling to contest with the newcomer, caught him a glancing blow. It galloped off even as its former rider rolled to a stop.

Wellen tried to rise, but much like the steed, he too was at his limit. Even when he heard a louder hiss and saw the second drake appear, the strength would not come to him. The drakes were cowards, yes, but not when it came to the helpless. Wellen had as much chance of fending them off as he did of casting a spell. The bitter irony that here his lack of true power would finally prove his undoing, made him curse the heavens for ever having created the silver mark as the symbol of sorcery.

"Such, such language," came a voice.

The drakes froze, then scattered as if one of their more violent cousins had come for them. Wellen tried to turn over and see his rescuer, but that was now beyond him.

"Where . . . who . . . ?"

Darkness coalesced in front of him, taking on the vague shape of a cloak and hood. In the deep shadows cast by the hood, he barely made out the general visage of a man. That was all he could tell about his rescuer. The massive robe all but buried its wearer within.

"You should be more careful, Dru," the cloak said.

Wellen tried to speak, but then even breathing became difficult and he passed out.

V

Xabene stood by the long-dead campfire, her silence condemning the Necri in front of her as no words could. The Necri refused to be cowed by this mortal creature. It had performed its part as commanded.

At last, the enchantress turned on the monster. "You were caught up in your *entertainment*, weren't you? You were too busy with your *playthings* to keep an eye on the leader of the newcomers!"

The pale, batlike servant hissed. Through its own peculiar method of communication, it had let known all that had happened, but Xabene still did not believe it.

She shook her head. Time and time again she had warned her masters that the Necri had only limited uses. They were too savage, too single-minded. While it had vented its eagerness upon the outsiders' scouts, the dragons had struck at the column itself, slaying most and scattering the few survivors. The winged monstrosity claimed it had followed the short one who was leader, but somehow the two had become separated in the hills. The dark sorceress was certain that *she* would not have lost track of a man, but then men were her forte.

What bothered her most was the sensation she had felt at roughly the time the Necri indicated it had lost sight, both normal and magical, of the human. It was a feeling she had only associated with two other forces, the gnome and the Lords of the Dead . . . yet she was certain it was neither.

"We have to find him again! *You*"—she stared into the white, dead eyes of her inhuman partner—"have to find him, or the failure will be on *your* head!"

The Necri bared its long, glistening teeth, but it did not argue. Their masters were not ones to debate the reasons for failure, they would merely execute punishment. Still, both knew that it was just as likely that they could find fault with

Xabene. After all, it had been her duty to back up the Necri in its mission.

Yet, she too, only came up blank when she sought to tear away the darkness that had enveloped the outsider leader.

At least we have your face, she thought. The Necri had been able to relay that much to her. A short man, true, but not unsightly. A learned man from what the Necri's sensitive ears had picked up during its visitation to the men's camp.

Also a man who wore the mark of the warlock, the sorcerer, yet did not display any power whatsoever.

You will be so much more entertaining then most, she thought to the mind image of the one called Wellen Bedlam. She hoped that her masters would leave something of him when they were done; it was rare that she encountered a man who wanted more than conquest, riches, or even women. Here was one that wanted knowledge, too.

Certainly he would make a better companion than that! Xabene decided sourly, giving her monstrous counterpart a glare that would have chilled most mortal creatures. The Necri only twitched its long ears and waited for her to return her attention to it. She buried all personal thoughts of the missing outsider in that secret part of her mind that no one, not even the Lords of the Dead, could touch.

"He has to be somewhere," she told the Necri.

Its nose wrinkled as if it had smelled something unpleasant, though what a carrion beast such as this could find unpleasant was a good question. Xabene knew what the response truly meant; the Necri was not one for the nuances of human speech and thought. Its kind had no use nor could even comprehend the use of obvious statements such as the last.

"We have no choice but to search until we find him."

This time, it shook its head. Searching the hills would take it days, perhaps weeks, even with the use of its sorcerous powers.

"Would you rather we go to the masters and tell them of our—"

The Necri had begun to vehemently shake its head, but then something beyond Xabene made its soulless orbs widen in outright fear.

The sorceress whirled about, thinking that perhaps the Dragon Kings had seen past her spells of concealment.

An odd, greenish hole had opened up behind her, one that stood in open air. It was nearly a third again her height and twice as wide as the Necri. Though nothing was visible within, she could already detect the sweet scent of decay emanating from the hole.

Now beside her, the Necri hissed. It was not a challenging call, but rather a meek, fearful response to something they both recognized.

The Lords of the Dead *already* knew of their failure, and they had come to their own decision concerning the twosome.

From within the hole, a second Necri emerged.

"Awake, are you?"

Wellen opened a pair of protesting eyes and tried to focus on his surroundings. For a time, there was little more than a vague light. Then, things slowly began to take form.

To say he was in a cavern was to understate matters. This simple cavern was tall enough to house a castle in its midst. Much of it did not seem natural, as if some ancient had carved out most of it, then left a good deal abandoned. He wondered whether it was the same being that had possibly shaped the landscape.

"No, the cavern is not the work of any Dragon King."

The scholar rose quickly to a sitting position, then waited for the wracking pain to punish him for his transgression. When nothing happened, he looked down at himself. Not only were the blood, scars, and dirt gone from his hands, but his garments looked new. Wellen put a hand to his nose and delighted in the sensation of skin touching skin. There was no blood when he pulled the fingers away. A quick inspection of his forehead wound revealed that it, too, neither bled nor pained him.

He finally recalled the voice and also remembered the murky figure that had rescued him from the minor drakes.

It . . . *he* . . . was seated on a stone throne overlooking much of the cavern. Only the voice lent any clue to the identity of the figure and that only of the gender. The hood and robe obscured so perfectly that Wellen Bedlam would have almost assumed he was staring at a pile of clothing rather than a man.

"I took you for another," the cloak said. "I sometimes forget that so much time has passed. He's likely dead by now, don't you think?"

"Who?" the confused Bedlam asked. He thought of Yalso, but the figure surely did not mean the sea captain.

"Dru . . . but then, you didn't know him. Still, I see him in you."

"Who are you? I mean . . . I thank you for what you've done, but I don't know where I am or why you—"

The robe waved him to silence, revealing by the act the fact that the figure did indeed have a hand. A gloved one. Like the robe, it was dark gray. Everything about the figure seemed to be gray.

"I've watched you for the past day. You're here because I thought you someone else . . . then it was too late. I decided to continue rescuing you, after all."

Wellen began to wonder whether his host was completely rational.

"No, sometimes I lapse and forget where and when I am." The hood leaned forward, revealing just a bit of proud chin and stern mouth. "The forgetting of *when* is by far the worst, I warn you."

"Are you reading my thoughts?"

"Something like that. It is so much easier when you are conscious, though. Besides, you've hardly kept them hidden, now have you?"

Though he had never manifested power, Wellen did know of mental shields from his studies. He raised one instantly.

"Now is that any way to build *trust*?" The hooded warlock rose, but made no threatening gestures. "Well, I've always believed in the sanctity of one's privacy, so I have no qualms if you desire to protect yourself." The hood tilted to one side. "Besides, I'm certain we'll come to an understanding before long."

"Who *are* you?"

The warlock turned from him, seemingly caught up in other matters now. He moved to a table where a collection of artifacts and drawings were scattered and began to collect the latter. The table, as far as Wellen was concerned, had not been there a moment ago.

The cloaked figure finally managed to respond to the scholar's question. "I am the shadow of the past, a ghost of your past . . . and even mine. Whatever name I had, it hardly matters now. Those who knew it are dead. Dust. My people live on in you and those above, but the memory of greatness has been forgotten." The warlock shrugged, his back still to Wellen. "You may call me Shade; it's appropriate as anything and I have become attached to it over the past few centuries."

"Past few—" Bedlam cut off the remainder of his stunned

reply. He knew that spellcasters could extend their lives, but that was generally limited to three or four hundred years. Though the one called Shade had not indicated otherwise, Wellen suspected that he was speaking of much more than four hundred years. There was a presence about the warlock so alien, so ancient, that the expedition leader would have been willing to judge the sorcerer in terms of *millennia* rather than centuries.

He realized that his fantastic host had turned to him once more. In the left hand was a plate upon which fruit had been piled. Wellen was aware that the plate had been nowhere in sight, just as the table had been earlier.

"It would be best if you ate. I have tended to your wounds and replaced your clothing. You will need to be at your best when the time comes."

The temptation to ask the warlock exactly what it was the scholar had to be ready for was great, but Wellen decided to wait until after he had eaten. The food would give him strength he might need in case his host proved to be too unstable. The shorter man did not know how he might defeat a master warlock, but he was prepared to try, if necessary.

"I thank you. I could use food."

The plate floated from Shade's hand and landed in Wellen's lap. "When your constitution is a bit stronger, then perhaps you can try something other than the fruit. For now, it will serve to revive your strength."

Wellen tore into the food, finding his hunger suddenly growing into a monster as huge as the dragon that had slaughtered his men. Thinking of the drake made him pause. The warlock also paused, as if he, too, knew what his guest was thinking. Bedlam wondered just how strong the mental shields he had put up really were. Was Shade reading his mind again?

"Something disturbs you?"

"I was thinking about the dragon and the attack."

"Oh." The cloth-enshrouded spellcaster shrugged again, apparently deciding that the deaths of so many good men were of little consequence to him. "You find that such things happen here."

"Is that *all* you can say?" At last roused to anger, Wellen Bedlam rose, spilling the plate of partially eaten fruit all over the smooth cavern floor. "They died needlessly!"

Quietly, patiently, the warlock said, "I have seen more deaths in my life than there are fish in the seas. Only my own now concerns me . . . even after so many failures."

The scholar stood where he was, shaking in frustration. He could think of nothing to say to his host that would likely break through the apathy that had built up over a lifetime at least tenfold, possibly a hundredfold or a thousandfold longer than his own.

Bitterness growing, Wellen reached down and retrieved the fruit. There would come a time, he reflected, when the warlock would regret those words. When death finally came for the man, the angry scholar hoped Shade would recall what he had said now and how he had reacted. Wellen's men at least had their leader to mourn them; no one would ever wish to mourn for someone such as Shade.

For a time, he ate in silence. The dark spellcaster seemed satisfied to simply stare his way. He tried not to stare back, but more and more the shadows that hid the warlock's visage bothered him. What did Shade truly look like? What effects would living so long have on mortal flesh?

Wellen knew he would get no answers if he chose to question Shade about his past. It might be that the warlock barely remembered his own history.

As he completed his meal, something else began to nag at the scholar, something concerning the cavern. Wellen looked up and scanned the area, ignoring Shade's suddenly stiffening posture. What was it about this place...?

For the first time, he realized that he could see *nothing* of the cavern, save the walls, the throne, and the table... and the last only because the warlock had walked over to it. Every time Bedlam sought to focus on an object, he found his eyes turning away and seeking some view of less significance. With concentration, he was able to make out a series of tables, but what lay upon them, the curious explorer could not say.

"So you pierce the mists," his gray, nebulous host commented. "So there is a bit of Dru within you after all."

At the mention of the last, Wellen lost concentration. The cavern once more became a place of the almost-seen, the shadowlands. He hardly cared. Twice, perhaps more, Shade had made mention of the name "Dru." "Do you speak of Lord Drazeree?"

"Drazeree? Lord?" Shade chuckled. It was a dry sound, as if the warlock had only just rediscovered it now. "I speak of things long dead, my friend. I speak of myself and others."

A typical Shade answer, Wellen was realizing. There was no point in pursuing the matter. His speculations would have to remain just that. Still, if this warlock *was* what he claimed, a contemporary of the legendary lord, would that not make him over . . .

The confused scholar shook his head. *No one* could live so long.

Shade surprised him then by reaching up and pulling back his hood.

Perhaps, he amended, *one* could *live so long!*

From a distance, the warlock would have resembled an elder scholar, a man nearing the end of his term, but not yet ready to give up the fight. There was strength there, incredible strength. In any other being, that would have been all Wellen noticed . . . if not for the fact that Shade's skin looked so dry, he wondered whether it would turn to powder at his touch.

It was the skin of a man who *should* have been dead, but *was not*.

Tearing his gaze from the stretched, parchment skin, he met the eyes of the sorcerer. Too late, Wellen Bedlam wished he had not abandoned his previous view. The eyes of Shade were *crystalline*. Not eyes created from crystal, but actual ones like Wellen's own that merely exhibited perfectly the attributes of gems.

If the eyes were the mirror of the soul, then the warlock no longer suffered the existence of the latter. Outside, he might still live; inside, he had died long, long ago.

Why the words that came then should choose this moment to be blurted out was a question the explorer would wonder later, but Wellen suddenly found himself asking, "What do you plan to do with me?"

Questions like that had been the death knell of many a character in the plays the scholar had enjoyed back home. Under present circumstances, it would have hardly been surprising to find real life similar.

Again, the dry chuckle. Shade smiled, but it was forced, as if it, too, had only now been rediscovered and its true use still uncertain to the hermitic spellcaster. "I plan to help you . . . if you choose to help *me*."

He was acting much more lucid, but Wellen was hardly encouraged by that. What would a warlock of his host's obvious abilities need with a mortal who could only dream of casting spells? "I can think of no way that I would be of use to you," Wellen admitted, knowing he might very well be throwing away his life but unable to lie under present circumstances. "I ask again; what do you plan to do with me?"

Shade walked slowly about the cavern, and as he walked, the chamber grew more distinct. Tables and alchemical equipment filled the chamber. Crystalline artifacts flowed with power. Diagrams and patterns that Bedlam had never come across before were hewed into the very stone. The scholar within Wellen desperately wanted to inspect each and every artifact and experiment. He wondered why the warlock would be willing to reveal so much. Either he was extending his trust to his guest or he had no fear that anything Wellen did would be a danger to him. "When I saw you . . . and I came to realize how lost my mind was then . . . I thought you another, a man of great courage and strength." The hooded warlock paused and stared at one of the blank cavern walls. He whispered something, a name, Wellen believed, then seemed to recall himself. "A man of ingenuity and determination. A man who could help me with a situation that prevents me from achieving my goal."

"And that is?" Daring the nebulous figure's wrath, the scholar purposely phrased his question so that it might be referring to either the problem or the goal.

The crystalline eyes narrowed and focused on Wellen as the warlock turned to him. Wellen had never thought to stare Death in the face before, but surely here was the closest earthly equivalent.

"You know as well as I. Your reason for journeying here was too transparent. I know the true reason was carefully *buried* within the folds of your mind." The crystalline eyes seemed to burn. "I know that you've come for the *book*."

"What book?"

Shade frowned, causing Wellen to fear that the warlock thought he was being patronized. "You know its appearance. A massive tome with a stylized dragon on the cover. It is possibly green, though it may be another color. It is kept there by a gnome who is the only one who knows the way in and out."

The scholar hesitated, but finally asked the next logical question. "In and out of *what*?"

A sigh. "Beyond the western edge of the hills lies another field like the one in which you were . . ." Shade shrugged and let the last part hang. "In this field is a single structure, a five-walled place with neither doors nor windows."

The curious explorer wanted to ask what purpose was served

by such a place, but he suspected that the gray warlock would not care for yet another interruption at this juncture.

"The tome lies within. The gnome has guarded it jealously for..." Glittering eyes blinked and Shade seemed to lose track of his present surroundings for a time. At last he shook himself and finished, "...for as long as I can recall."

"I know nothing about any book, gnome, or bizarre structure sitting out in the middle of nowhere," Wellen responded in flat tones. He took a step toward his host. "I came here only because I had grown up on legends of such a land. I—"

"Ridiculous." For the warlock, there seemed to be no answer but his own that would satisfy. He cut off yet another attempt by Wellen to explain, then slowly returned to the throne that he had been seated in when the scholar had first awakened. Shade pulled the hood back over his head, all but obscuring the upper half of his visage, and sat down again. His breathing was quick and short.

"We have... things to discuss... you and I. The book, your... being here, and *what* you are."

"What I *am*?"

The shadowy spellcaster settled back, seeming to sink into the very rock. "What the lands have made you... what sort of power... and, more important, what sort of monstrosity... hides within you... that I do not see."

The tone was cool, almost indifferent, but Wellen read a well-nurtured fear behind it, one the spectral sorcerer had carried for very, very long. It concerned not just his mortality, though that was a part of it, but something more, something at least equally important. He hoped he would not remain with the warlock long enough to find out. Shade was as dangerous to Wellen as the dragon, and the fear within the ancient figure might one day prove too much.

A mad man with great power was a man to be feared.

He dared to respond, not wanting Shade to think that his silence was an acknowledgment of the accuracy of the warlock's dark statement. "I'm no monster. I'm as human as anybody."

At that, the master warlock *did* laugh, but laugh so that Wellen feared for his existence. Only madness, never humor, tinged the laughter of his host. Bedlam had thought the chuckle dry and unnerving; the laugh made him wish to find a place to bury himself.

From the dark within his hood, the eyes of Shade *gleamed*. Though the cloaked figure had not moved in the slightest, it was as if he loomed directly over Wellen, so forceful was his presence. "*Nobody* is human, anymore!" he informed his anxious guest, the authority in his voice almost making his words believable. "Nobody on this forsaken world is human anymore, save for *me*! The lands have changed you *all*, no matter how you might appear!"

As if punctuating his insane words, a roar echoed throughout the cavern. The scholar looked about, trying to find the source and cursing himself for being impotent against the chaos around him.

The roar was followed by another and then another. Wellen readily identified their source, the knowledge turning him as pale as ivory. He had heard dragons roar before.

"Pay them no mind," Shade commented in disdain, acting as if he had completely forgotten his outburst. "They often grow lively this time of day. Merely the clan males reaffirming their status with one another."

"Dragons?" Wellen stared wide-eyed at his host. "There *are* dragons here?" What sort of fool lived among dragons, especially ones like the horror that had killed his men.

"They never come this deep into the caverns. They fear the older magics." This satisfied the warlock, but not the scholar.

"You *live* beneath dragons?" Visions of the monstrosity in the air made the explorer shake. What if they chose now to start descending into this chamber?

"I live beneath the foremost of the dragon clans," Shade corrected him. Straightening just a bit, the warlock used his hands to indicate the entire cavern. "Welcome to the interior of Kivan Grath, emperor of the vast and treacherous Tyber Mountains!" The eyes glittered again, then faded into the darkness that was so much a part of Shade. "A most appropriate place, I think, for the dwellings of the Dragon Emperor...don't you *agree*?"

Wellen neither agreed nor disagreed with the warlock. He could only stand, stare, and once more curse the silver streak in his hair that should have promised so much but instead only *mocked* his continual helplessness.

VI

Amidst the clutter, the gnome worked feverishly. Tables and shelves filled the tiny room that he had set aside for his research and upon each table and shelf were notes, discarded experiments, and miscellaneous artifacts that he had either created or located over the years. Once every hundred years or so, he cleared everything away in order to make room for more.

At the moment, the gnarled spellcaster was completing his notes. The feather pen, animated by his abilities, danced about the sheet of paper, scribbling down its master's every notion as he thought it. When that sheet was filled, the pen would lift and the paper would fly off to join those which had preceded it. The pile was already several dozen sheets high. A new piece landed below the quill, which dropped down and hurriedly resumed its momentous task. Even as swift as it was, the pen had to work hard to keep pace with the gnome's thoughts.

Time, be it measured in hours or days, meant nothing to him when he worked. He had long diverged from his original course, that being the possible explanation for the weak assault by the potentially deadly night creature controlled by the Lords of the Dead. When he had thought about that particular situation at all . . . and that had been rare . . . the gnome had decided that the attack was a ploy and that his adversaries had hooked a more subtle spell to his person. Locating it had been child's play. In the end, the short mage had chosen to leave it attached; while they watched him, he watched them. Besides, they now only saw what he permitted them to see.

The gnome had been at this game much too long to be taken in by a trick such as this. Once again, he marvelled at his own brilliance.

"End," he abruptly informed the pen. It straightened, shifted to one side of the sheet it had been writing on, and laid down.

He stretched out a hand toward the pile of papers, which

leaped to him. With his free hand, he indicated an uncluttered spot on the table.

A book materialized on that spot. It was green, or perhaps red, or perhaps any of a number of colors, depending on how one looked at it. On the front was a stylized dragon.

Placing the sheets to the right of the tome, the wizened figure took hold of the book and carefully turned the cover over.

The front page was blank. Taking the first sheet of notes in one hand and the quill in the other, the gnome began to write. This part he always did by hand, for this would be the final version of his research, and because of that he liked to savor each and every word.

So used to this task, he finished the first page in only a little more than a minute. He pulled the pen back and allowed the page to turn itself.

A tug in his mind warned him that someone had activated the watcher spell planted during the attack. The gnome carelessly released a spell of his own, one which would give the faraway observers something to interest them. This time it would be him in the midst of some suitably brilliant experiment. Of course, if they tried to follow his work, their own experiment would *somehow* go awry. He doubted they would watch for that long, however. They were only concerned with books.

Finished with the second page, he began work on the third. The thrill of his own brilliant discoveries urged him on and on with his writing. That suited him just fine.

After all, he had an entire book to fill.

They stood atop the peak of one of the Tyber Mountains, Shade observing the land below and beyond and Wellen observing that he was going to freeze to death if he did not stumble to it first. The two of them were here, apparently, because the master warlock simply liked the view.

A day had passed since Wellen had first woken in the cavern. The spellcaster had taken him to this place once before, shortly after his talk of how all those around him were monsters in disguise. He had still not yet explained that insane statement, nor had he "decided" about Wellen himself, who was supposed to be just as monstrous as the rest of humanity. The scholar chose not to bring up the subject, fearing it would only be detrimental to his own chances. There was so much he already dared not bring up. Shade was nothing if not mercurial; he brought up and dropped subjects as rapidly as he breathed.

"Here is your kingdom, Father," the shadowy figure whispered.

Wellen had already learned to pretend to ignore these various comments that his host muttered. Shade lived half in another world and time. He talked of and to a vast panorama of folk, many of them apparently related to him. The scholar had already counted five certain brothers and two more likely candidates. None of the names were familiar to him save *Dru*, which he believed *must* be the basis for Lord Drazeree, and another that sounded like *Sharissa*, the legendary lord's daughter.

If it were not all simply a case of madness, then the cloth-enshrouded figure beside him was many, many millennia old.

Shade turned from his musings and observed his hapless companion. "You should clothe yourself better."

"I *told* you that I have *no* power of my own!" Wellen had long gone beyond the point of civility where this question was concerned. Try as he might, he could not convince the other that the silver streak was only a mistake, not a sign of greatness.

"Very well, if you insist." Without so much as a negligible wave of a hand, Shade clothed Wellen in a furred cloak with hood.

"Thank you," Bedlam replied, his voice on edge.

The warlock missed his sarcasm. "Not at all."

"Are we through here?"

"A moment more."

Knowing protest was futile, Wellen tried to occupy his thoughts. He had been awash with relief when he had been told they would be leaving the caverns, not to mention the drakes who lived above, but that relief had died quickly when the scholar had learned where the two of them were headed. Worse yet, Wellen, who had never experienced teleportation, nearly lost his meal upon arrival. It was not the trip itself, which had been so swift that he had missed it by blinking, but rather the abruptness. To find himself going from the depths of a cavern to the precarious heights of a mountain peak had nearly been too much. He was disgusted with his weaknesses.

Despite having dropped the subject, it was obvious Shade still believed that he was here to obtain the mysterious dragon tome. All of Wellen's protests had gone unheeded. He knew that he could have opened his mind to the warlock, but to Bedlam his mind was the only private place he had left, and the sanctity of that was not something he was ready to give up.

Besides, the warlock would have likely claimed his thoughts all false, the product of a clever spellcaster like himself.

So far, he did not know why his companion wanted the tome, but Wellen was beginning to suspect it had to do with the pale warlock's incredible age, since that seemed the one topic Shade continued to recall. What part the book played was still a question whose answer or, quite possibly, *answers*, evaded the scholar.

"Do you hear them?"

Wellen could hear nothing but the wind howling.

"They'll not see us, of course, not unless I will it. My power is forever beyond them now that they've changed. I reestablished the link to Nimth, only this time no one noticed it because I was so much more careful." Shade had mentioned the place called Nimth before, but always talked of it as if it existed *elsewhere*. Several scholars and spellcasters had begun to debate about worlds beyond this one and the emptiness termed the Void. The latter was a realm of nothingness which those who used certain types of teleportation passed through before arriving at their destinations.

While much of what Shade said had little bearing on what Wellen knew or understood, there were always a few tidbits that made the younger man pay fairly close attention. One was the status of the legendary Dragonrealm. Wellen had been horrified to discover that the old saying was more than true. Not only were there dragons here, but many of them were intelligent, such as the one that had devastated the column and the many who lived in the upper caverns of Kivan Grath. Worse yet . . . they ruled the *entire* continent!

"We have spent enough time here," the gray warlock suddenly announced.

Wellen let out a gasp. The two of them were now standing on a small hill overlooking a town of some sort. The shaking scholar was surprised to see people in the distance, apparently unconcerned about the fact that they lived in a land ruled by monsters.

"Mito Pica."

He glanced at the warlock. "What?"

"Mito Pica." Shade indicated the village. "It will be a grand and glorious city in another century or two. Much traffic flows through it."

"How can they hope to build anything with the dragons

loose?'' Despite his question, Wellen Bedlam could already see that the village *was* thriving. There was new construction going on in the western portion of the village.

"The Baron of Mito Pica obeys the edicts of the ruling Dragon King. His people perform the tasks that come down from the ruling drakes. In return, they are left in peace."

"They . . . they *deal* with those beasts?'' Throwing off the warm cloak given to him by Shade, Wellen took a few steps forward in order to better view the village. *Sycophants!* An entire community of them! Dealing with murderous monsters that—

A restraining hand caught his shoulder. Wellen discovered two things. The first was that, in his anger, he had started down toward Mito Pica. The second was that the warlock was not only a being of great magical power, but also great *physical* strength.

"It would not do to go wandering down there. Not for our needs. As to your question, they deal with the dragons because doing so allows them to live and flourish. The Dragon King's folk have become dependent on many services performed by the . . . the *humans*.'' Shade seemed reluctant to actually use the word *human* to describe his fellows, but apparently had come upon no other word that satisfied him.

"What could they want that humans have?'' *Besides the flesh on their bones*, Wellen added bitterly.

Shade shook his hooded head and looked down at the scholar as a disappointed schoolmaster might at student who has not lived up to his potential. "The drakes are not mere beasts. They are thinking creatures. Despite their savage nature . . .'' Here the warlock paused, seeming to drift off. "Yessss . . . their nature has always been rather savage."

Wellen was already thinking of his brief contact with the mind of the attacking dragon, an act he still had no satisfactory explanation for. In retrospect, he could recall the complex workings of that mind.

"The humans tend their food herds,'' Shade continued, not, evidently, noticing his own lapse. "They act as trade emissaries between the various clans because two drakes of opposing groups tend to become combative after a time. Humans are beneath them, but the Dragon Kings know their skills at trade. There are many other ways that the human race has proven itself worthy of survival. The population has grown continuously because of that." The warlock shook his voluminous cloak, as if trying to rid himself of something not to his taste. "Not bad, considering how few survived the original chaos."

Forcing himself not to ask about the last statement, which he knew that Shade would not explain anyway, Wellen decided to deal with his own immediate future. "And we have some reason for coming here now?"

"We do, but our route will be quicker and more subtle."

Wellen barely had time to prepare himself before they teleported again.

This time, he found himself in, of all places, a smithy. The smithy, actually a barn, was filled with all sorts of metal creations, including a few that he could not identify. To Wellen's right, an open doorway taunted him with false promises of escape. Ahead, a heavy, muscular man, nearly bald, was hard at work on something that his back hid from the sight of the scholar.

"Master Bearn."

The smith seemed not at all startled by the voice. With great deliberation, he put aside what he was working on and turned to face the twosome.

"Master Gerrod. Good to see you, sir."

Wellen made note of the educated tones of the smith, but his interest focused more on the name Shade had given himself. He debated whether or not Gerrod might be the warlock's true title, then decided that the cloth-enshrouded spellcaster would hardly have utilized it. Shade had probably chosen the name at random, not because it had any meaning.

Bearn seemed not to notice the scholar, which was fine with Wellen.

The warlock's visage was shadowed by his hood, but his voice hinted at his anxiousness when he asked, "And have you completed my task?"

In response to the question, Master Bearn seemed to shrink. He now appeared only slightly overwhelming. His tone was bitter. "I have not. In the year since last, I have made many breakthroughs, but none worthy of your project." Bearn spread his hands, "If you should choose to go to another, I would understand."

"You are the most suited for the task, Master Bearn, as your father and grandfather were before you. Each of you has presented me with discoveries which, while not of use for that

which I have described, have proved worthy in other ways."
The almost soothing voice of the warlock surprised Wellen,
who had not expected to find so much humanity still remaining
in the shrouded figure.

"Here." A pouch materialized in one of the smith's empty
hands. The smith gripped it, causing the pouch's contents to
jingle. "Until next year, Master Bearn."

"I have *not* earned it—"

For a brief breath, the crystalline eyes burst through the
darkness caused by the overshadowing hood and glowed with
an inner fire that, even after millennia, had evidently not been
extinguished. "When you or your descendents *have* completed
my commission, smith, it will be worth *all* the money your
family has been paid . . . and more!"

Bearn went down on one knee and thanked the warlock.

Shade gripped Wellen's shoulder. "Come."

As simple as that, they stood on a rocky hillside. Wellen
started to look around, then gasped and covered his eyes when
the glittering brilliance almost blinded him.

"The peninsula . . . can be quite bright when the sun is
sinking," Shade informed him. The warlock pressed something
into the scholar's hand. "Put this on. It goes . . . over your
eyes."

Wellen cautiously looked down at the object. It was a pair of
transparent lenses attached to some sort of frame. A notch in
the center seemed to indicate it should rest on his nose. After a
few tries, he got the artifact to fit, if not comfortably.

He looked up . . . and was dazzled.

Even with the protective lenses on, the landscape still sparkled. He had seen crystalline deposits before and so he knew
what was causing the magnificent glitter, but the sheer immen-
sity of *this* place. . . .

"It's . . . it's . . ."

Beside him, Shade nodded. "It is. That is why he and they
have chosen this place."

Wellen was suddenly wary again. "'He'? 'They'?"

The cloth-enshrouded figure pulled his voluminous cloak
tighter. "The first you have no need to be concerned about. He
never interferes. He has no interest. As for the latter . . . they
are here now."

And the earth at Bedlam's feet erupted.

They burrowed free of the rocky soil, two monstrosities that overwhelmed both men in size. Their clawed hands were good for both digging and grasping. They had dusky brown shells that covered most of their bodies, and their heads were long and ended in a peculiar, tapering mouth. Even with the lenses on, he could see that they, like their land, glittered.

One of the creatures hooted. It was a long, baleful sound that made Wellen's heart flutter. At the same time, however, the scholar in him was fascinated by these incredible creatures. Interest and reason, the latter reminding him that he had no chance of escape anyway, kept him riveted where he was.

"He is with me," the warlock informed the beast who had sounded.

The second horror also hooted, albeit at a higher pitch. Though the sounds meant nothing to Wellen, other than that both creatures appeared disturbed, the ancient spellcaster evidently understood them perfectly.

"Not yet. You have not completed your end of the bargain. Have you found it? Is there one?"

The two armored figures eyed one another, seeming to confer . . . and then one dared to reach out and try to snare Wellen.

Its speed was so unbelievable for so bulky a beast that the scholar, on his own, would have moved much too slowly. Even as the huge, taloned hand closed on his shirt, however, he found himself standing several feet behind Shade, who now was positioned directly between his mortal companion and the earth dwellers.

Shade reached out and touched the would-be attacker with only the tip of his gloved index finger.

It squealed and began folding into itself. The other one, sensing that they had overstepped their bounds, backed away and sounded a similar squeal. The warlock paid the second no mind, but watched the first. Wellen, daring to step closer, could not help but watch also.

Like the armadillo it so closely resembled, the monster folded itself into its shell. Yet, the change did not stop there. Rolled tight into a ball, the hapless monstrosity squealed what was obviously a frantic plea to forgive its transgression. Shade simply folded his arms. As the other watched, the rolled-up form stiffened, grew more indistinct. Wellen noted that the monster looked more and more almost like a . . . like a *rock*.

That was what it was. The image was no longer indistinct.

Where once the mighty beast had been was now a large, quite real, boulder.

A short, dry chuckle escaped the warlock. "Not much of a change in personality when you think of it."

The survivor fell to its knees.

"Get up," the spectral figure commanded. Wellen saw a different Shade now. The warlock had multiple personalities, likely developed from his eternity of near isolation.

The armored monster obeyed.

"You have to watch the Quel," Shade informed his companion offhandedly. "They have vile tempers." To the sole remaining Quel, he said, "Your companion will return to normal in two days, long enough for him to contemplate the foolishness of his actions. *We* have a bargain. Just because you have been unable to fulfill it so far is no reason to demand things from me! If you no longer wish to deal with me, you can always deal with *him*!"

The plaintive hoot the kneeling Quel emitted left no question as to the beast's opinion on the last suggestion. Whoever it was that Shade spoke of, the Quel feared almost as much and hated more.

"I thought not. I shall return next year then, as agreed. Perhaps your successors will be more fortunate."

The finality in Shade's tone was signal enough to the lone Quel that its presence was no longer required. It cast one disturbed glance at its ensorcelled companion, then dug its claw into the hard earth below.

With a speed and skill that would have been the envy of many animals, the creature burrowed into the ground. In only a few breaths it had vanished below the surface. In only a few more, there was barely even a sign that it had ever been there. Only a small mound of unsettled dirt. The Quel evidently filled in its tunnel behind it as it burrowed. Wellen wondered about its lung capacity.

"Nothing," Shade whispered to himself, "but the pieces will slowly gather." He did not bother to clarify for his companion. "Perhaps in another century the preparations for this spell will be ready..."

Wellen, carefully silent, shivered then, but not because of anything the warlock had said or done. The shivering came on its own and, while it existed for only a brief time, its reappearance made him stiffen, for the sensation was akin to those he had felt just prior to his experiences with both the Seeker and the dragon. He shifted his position as he tried to calm down.

The warlock, sensing something was amiss, whirled around. "I had almost forgotten." He began to revert to the dark, dreaming persona that Wellen had met first. "It is time to talk again . . .

"Time to speak of lives and how they change . . . or perhaps how they are *changed* literally," Shade added, now sitting once more upon the throne in the cavern.

Spitting out a very unscholarly epithet, Wellen tried to orient himself *again*. He only barely heard the shadowy figure's words. The constant shifting from one location to another was wreaking mental havoc on him. He did not know if he simply hated the teleporting or the fact that he always found himself so helpless. Dragons and spellcasters; what chance did he have? Despite the drake clans above, Wellen hoped that the he and Shade would remain in *this* location for awhile; at least until he ceased feeling like a leaf caught in a whirlwind.

As if purposely choosing a moment when Wellen was most open to attack, the sensation of impending danger struck him again. This time, it lasted longer than a few seconds. Like the last occurrence, however, it eventually did pass, again leaving no reason for its existence. Was it merely because he was a captive of the warlock? Was it possible that he was just *imagining* the sensation?

That will make two *madmen*, the bitter warrior silently cursed.

Shade, half lost in his thoughts, barely even noticed his "guest." He looked skyward, staring through the cavern ceiling to some place beyond, both in time and space. "Do you know, monster, what it is like . . . to live so long . . . but to live in constant fear for . . . your very self?"

The scholar thought he had a fair idea of the latter portion of the question, but it would hardly have been to his benefit to mention who was presently the cause of that fear.

"Dru Zeree. . . ." The dreaming warlock gestured. A vague apparition began to take form before him. "He always seemed to see so much, yet he could not see what was happening."

The apparition swelled and coalesced, gradually taking on a more distinct appearance. It was a man, one who swayed back and forth like a leaf in the wind. Wellen squinted, noting the height, the beard, and the streak of silver. Was this Dru Zeree?

Was this truly what the legendary Lord Drazeree had looked like, or was it a stylized phantasm, an image borne of ancient but colored memories?

"Master Zeree. . . ." Shade whispered. He met the gaze of the misty figure. "What did you finally become?"

Wellen could have told him, but he knew that Shade would never believe the legends. The warlock would refuse to believe that his companion of old had lived a long, fruitful life and that there were those, like the scholar himself, who had some claim that they might be his descendents. Shade would hardly care anyway; to him Dru Zeree had become a monster like all the rest.

Bedlam wondered if Shade had ever looked in the mirror to see what *he* had become.

Another form began to materialize on the warlock's other side. Shade barely paid any attention to it at first, caught up as he was in some one-sided conversation with the ghostly Dru Zeree, but when he did, he fairly buried himself in the depths of his cavernous cloak. His voice was barely a whisper, but Wellen, watching the new specter take shape, already knew who now haunted the spellcaster.

"Sharissa . . ." The warlock whispered.

The depths of his insanity were ever surprising the explorer. It was clear from Shade's reaction that even though he was responsible for conjuring up these apparitions of the far past, he did not entirely control them, at least, not on a conscious level. He had, in fact, succeeded only too well in haunting himself.

What price immortality?

She was tall, albeit not so much as the other conjured ghost, and slim. A magnificent robe of white covered her very female form and silver-blue hair cascaded down her back. She was beautiful, so *very* beautiful, this possible distant relation of Wellen's, that the scholar knew she must not be real. He was seeing her, and Dru Zeree, as the hooded spellcaster *wanted* to recall them, not as they had been. Still, there had to be some truth to their appearances. They were too distinct to be entirely fashioned from Shade's madness.

Rising, the warlock joined the shades of his past. As he moved and talked, they floated about him, taking in his words and responding in silent mouthings that the ancient spellcaster evidently heard.

"I did care for you, Sharissa," he told the female image, "though I knew you would never be mine."

Her smile brought sunshine. She said something that made Shade laugh, much to Wellen's astonishment. The laugh was young in direct contradiction to his deathly countenance and his previous, darker moods. "Yes, I think I knew that. I just did not want to admit it."

Fascinated, Wellen stepped closer. Now might have been the perfect time to seek escape, but he found he could not pull himself away from the fantastic tableau before him. That this scene confirmed the madness of his captor was not so important as what it revealed about the history of Wellen's kind.

Though it was not likely pretending to him, Shade took the insubstantial hand of the Sharissa image and pretended to pull her nearer. "I hated most of all to think of you changed. I thought you would be a physical horror, like my brethren... like my father. Now I see, though, that you of all of them could not suffer such a fate." The image put a hand to his cheek. He moved as if truly being caressed. "I see that you could only have become a *goddess*!"

Is this what near-immortality does to one? Wellen found himself saddened despite his own predicament. *Is there a point where your existence becomes only a never-ending look back at your failures, your losses?*

The Sharissa image wavered around the edges. The explorer glanced at the unmoving figure of Dru Zeree. It, like the other, was just beginning to grow indistinct. Shade was slowly returning to the present, Wellen assumed. Soon, he would recall his 'guest' and the questioning would begin again.

Then he looked closely at the warlock and discovered that he also had grown vague around the edges.

Wellen blinked and tried once more. If anything, Shade had become even more murky. *What becomes of him?*

Somewhat belatedly, the sensation of possible danger returned.

On the dais, Shade was still caught up in his conversation with the two phantasms. Wellen found he could no longer hear the warlock. In fact, he could not hear *anything*. The scholar turned uncertainly and scanned the cavern chamber, his fears almost immediately justified.

It was not just the warlock who was fading, but rather the *entire* cavern.

Or was it Wellen himself?

"Shade!" he called frantically, hoping to stir the dreaming spellcaster. To his growing horror, the shout emerged as no more than a whisper, one that even he found barely audible. Wellen started forward, but despite movement, he drew no closer to the dais.

The domain of Shade dwindled without pause. Bedlam finally stopped running. The effort was futile and he was only expending his own energy. Yet, he could not just give up. There was no telling what had become of him. It was even possible that the dream-struck sorcerer himself has been responsible for the scholar's predicament, though Wellen was of the opinion that the source was from somewhere beyond.

A tiny gleam before him caught his attention. With nothing but emptiness now surrounding him, he focused on the gleam with the fervor of a starving man eyeing a crumb of bread. The gleam seemed to slowly grow in intensity, but Wellen doubted his senses at first. It seemed too much to hope that he would so quickly leave this oblivion. Not with the way his luck had turned so far.

I am destined to be some sort of human ball, forever being tossed or carried from one place to another! Despite that thought, however, he did not regret coming to the Dragonrealm. He had already seen and learned so much. His despair lay in the fact that no one else would ever hear of his discoveries. All he had come across would again sink into the mire of legend, especially if no one else in the expedition returned. Had the others turned around and sailed home? Did the dragon continue east and destroy the rest of his expedition? How many *had* died?

Wellen tensed as the gleam defined itself. Suddenly, he found himself staring at a medallion of gold. It drew his eyes as Shade's crystalline orbs had. He tried to turn away, not trusting, but this time his will was not strong enough. The medallion pulsated . . . at least, he thought it did . . . and pulled him closer and closer. Resistance was useless.

Shapes representing many things formed around the artifact. A scene grew around him. Wellen felt like a character in a painting who watches as the artist draws in the world around him. He saw trees and hills, but what he saw most of were a number of figures who surrounded him. Almost immediately, it was evident that they were not human. One of them was holding the medallion at chest level.

He made out wings on the still-vague images and knew then who had taken him from the very sanctum of Shade.

The Seekers.

Beneath his boots, he felt the solidity of earth. The wind caressed his countenance. The sounds of birds and other forest life assailed his ears. A rich forest landscape surrounded him.

As, he reminded himself, so did the avians.

The one with the medallion lowered it and stalked toward him. Like the bird it so resembled, it cocked its head to one side as it observed him. Wellen could not help but fix his own gaze on the sharp, predatory beak. It was quite clear that here was a creature who made meat part of its diet.

The Seeker leader, if that was what it was, came within arm's length of him and stopped. Wellen swallowed but tried to give no other sign of his uncertainty. He had no idea why he was here, but the feeling of impending danger was still with him, not that he needed to be told how precarious his position had become.

Gazing behind the human, the avian nodded.

Strong, taloned hands took hold of his arm. The talons dug into his flesh, but not enough to hurt.

Raising a hand to Wellen's face, the apparent leader displayed its own long, sharp talons. The captured scholar needed no one to tell him what those claws could do to his unprotected body.

It came as a surprise, then, when the leader stepped back, the threat of the talons receding with it. Bedlam doubted he was safe yet, at least not if his peculiar new sense was correct.

The tall avian turned back to the circle of winged figures. As if reacting to a silent command, the circle broke open. Through the opening stepped another Seeker, this one smaller than the others. A female?

It joined the first and turned to study Wellen. One clawed hand went to its leg as if it were trying to indicate something. The human's eyes widened as realization struck.

Before Wellen stood the young Seeker he had protected from the expedition. He breathed a sigh of relief, deciding that it had convinced the others to save the one who had aided it earlier. The Seekers were a strange, alien race, but gratitude, it appeared, was a concept they shared with humanity.

The smile was just spreading across his visage when the talons of the young avian shot toward him.

VII

They were displeased with her. Her masters were displeased with her. Xabene shuddered. The Lords of the Dead had *never* found fault with her skills before. She had seen others fall victim to their displeasure, but the thought that she now balanced on a precipice. . . .

For the first time, she began to regret her pact with them. They had always given her what she had felt the world owed her and in return she had given them absolute loyalty. The enchantress had never had cause to wonder what would happen to her if she could not fulfill her end of the bargain. Now that thought was ever in her mind, reminding her that those dismissed by the demonic lords did not merely ride off into the distance.

It was a combination of things that had brought about the fall from favor. One had been the suspicion that her watchdog spell, the one she had sacrificed a Necri for, had failed. Her masters were of the opinion that the gnome had tricked them again, that he knew he was being watched. The other thing that had endangered her was the loss of the man called Wellen Bedlam, the one who evidently had led the ill-fated expedition. He had survived the dragon, but somewhere in the hills, both she and her monstrous companion had lost him . . . and to that mysterious personage whom the lords refused to discuss . . . but clearly worried about.

To her right, the Necri she had been paired with hissed in consternation. A sick joke, the beautiful sorceress decided. A sick joke that she and the beast were allies in spirit, too. They were bound by their mutual failure and now they had only one chance.

A dozen other Necri stood scattered around them. Here to aid the two, supposedly. Yet these monsters did not treat either her or their counterpart as superiors. Rather, they seemed more like executioners awaiting the signal to swing the ax and put an end to their predecessors.

"Be silent!" she warned them. Let them think that they were the cause of her lack of concentration.

She would have preferred to work her spells at night, when she was more comfortable, but the masters had deemed time of the essence. Her only bit of satisfaction lay in the knowledge that the band of Necri found the sunlight far more distressing than she did. Had her own existence not been at risk, Xabene would have stretched the working of the spells for as long as possible, just to watch the pale horrors squirm.

In her smooth, deceiving hands, she held a tattered notebook. It was her special prize, the one thing that had redeemed her so far in the eyes of the lords. She had suspected that some object of the expedition's leader might remain in the field. The dragon that had attacked the column had not been particular about clearing away the carnage. A search by the Necri and herself had brought this item, evidently something that had fallen out of one of the saddlebags on Bedlam's unfortunate mount.

The notebook was well used. His trace was strong. Given a little time, she would be able to locate him.

Given a little room, too! The Necri were starting to cluster together, trying to draw comfort from one another in the revealing light of day. Unfortunately, that meant that they were crowding her.

"Away from me, you decaying misfits!"

They gave her a little breathing room. She sighed. Now there were no more excuses. This time, Xabene knew that she had to succeed.

Sliding the notebook so that it rested on the palm of one hand, she stroked the top of the foreigner's journal as a child might stroke a beloved puppy. Love had nothing to do with this, however. Rather, the constant, active contact stirred the trace, made her connection with it stronger. The stronger the contact, the better her chances of reaching out and finding the notebook's owner.

What is your own world like, Wellen Bedlam? she wondered as she concentrated on the spell. *What wonders exist over there?* From what she had glanced at in his journal, he was an intelligent if somewhat isolated man. A knowledgeable scholar, but one lacking in practical experience. Still, someone closer to her own ways than most of those she had encountered during her service to the lords. For them, Xabene had generally had one of two purposes, both designed to put them into the debt of her masters.

A pity that we may not have time to talk, Master Bedlam.

There came a tugging in her mind. She forgot all else as she opened herself to the link. An image slowly formed before the raven-haired enchantress, an image of a forest and . . . and . . . the view was being blocked by whatever or whoever was with the man. There were several figures, however. Xabene tried to delve into the mind of her target, but found a very impressive wall blocking her probe. The spellcaster pondered her dilemma for a moment, then used her link to pick up peripheral information about the region.

She recognized the place, which in turn answered the other question. Xabene smiled, an entrancing yet chilling sight that, this time, did not involve humor in any way. She knew who was with the man, even though she did not know how he had come to be in their talons rather than the grip of the cloaked warlock. *You are very popular, my scholar. I look forward to meeting you face-to-face . . . should the Seekers leave anything left of yours by the time they're through with you.*

There was no time to lose. It might already be too late to save him from the avians, but she had to try, if only for her own sake. Xabene broke the link and leaped to her feet, the notebook crushed in one slim hand.

"I've found him!" The Necri stirred, at last able to do something. Her own demonic companion hissed a sigh of relief and almost looked thankful, although the savage visage of the batlike creature was hardly designed for such expressions. "We must hurry! Even now the bird folk might be finishing with him!"

Xabene revealed to them the image she had conjured and where it was located. The Necri, to their damnable credit, wasted no time. In rapid progression, the horrific bat creatures took to the sky, a line of unreal terrors that scattered the few birds nearby and brought silence to the forest with their sudden activity. The sunlight did not deter them, for they knew that the responsibility was now as much on their bone-white shoulders as it was on Xabene's.

The enchantress watched them vanish into the distance. Alone, for even her Necri companion had joined in the flight, she contemplated her own plans.

The Seekers would meet her masters' servants with all the

power they had. Chaos would reign. If the outsider was not already dead, there was a good chance that he might die in the madness of combat. For some reason, a dead man was of no use to the Lords of the Dead. They had made it clear that they wanted him alive if at all possible. That in itself interested Xabene, who began to wonder at this sudden limit to their power. Why had she not noticed it sooner?

For now, that did not matter. Wellen Bedlam, explorer and scholar, did. Which meant that Xabene herself would have to join the battle . . . and enter the very thick of it. She hoped that the man was worth the trouble.

If not, she would make certain he knew that before she was through with him.

Wellen gasped as the talons came at him. He prayed that at least the attack would finish him quickly, else he would suffer horribly. It seemed that fate had stopped toying with him at last. He almost looked forward to death, if only because it might mean an end to his being tossed and chased about the Dragonrealm like a cat's prey.

The talons, when they touched his flesh, were astonishingly gentle. He barely even felt them.

Was this a test?

A vision assailed his mind. Wellen was so stunned, he tried to back away. The avians holding his arms tightened their grips, preventing any escape. Unable to resist, the scholar gave in and allowed the vision to take root.

He saw a world in which everything was slightly distorted. Odd men came forth and, with a start, he realized that he was the foremost of them. The others were various men from the column, including a menacing, much more avian-appearing version of Prentiss Asaalk. The group was surrounding something and the blue man looked ready to pounce on whatever it was.

It was the young Seeker, the explorer realized. He was seeing the event as the feathered creature had. It . . . were there different sexes among the race? . . . was trying to explain something.

He felt a touch in his mind, a feeling of acknowledgement. The concepts being revealed to him almost made Wellen gasp. Communication through images in the mind was not unknown, but not with such efficiency, such skill. Yet here was a race that did it on a daily basis!

Gradually, the entire scenario unfolded. Most important was the last part, where Wellen Bedlam had refused to allow the hatchling to die and then had healed the deadly wound.

Healed it? He tried to think in the negative, to deny that he could have ever performed such a feat. Magic was not for him. He pictured himself casting a spell and failing, hoping the meaning got across. It did, but the bird creature sent back another image, one of him casting a series of spells, each progressively more successful. The Seeker was of the opinion that the ability was there. In its mind, Wellen had already proved that.

It was useless to argue. Moreover, the tantalizing thought that he *might* yet become a sorcerer of some skill appealed to him. There were so many things he could have done if magic had been there to aid him. So many things . . .

An urgent touch by the young avian informed him that there was more. Wellen opened up his mind to the link. This time, he saw the hatchling returning to the flock. It was well received, for there were few young in this aerie, a magnificent old castle that the Seekers had taken over and made their own after the unknown builders had abandoned it. The birth rate among their kind had been at a low since some ancient disaster. It had happened long ago, but the Seekers were *still* trying to recover. What it was Wellen was not told. He sensed fear in the mind of the adolescent being before him and knew from contact that this fear touched the adults as well.

The Seekers had noted his deed, but little more. It was not until the devastation of the column that they tried to aid the one who had proven his worth to an otherwise proud race. Wellen had the suspicion that the Seekers looked down on the other races, but his act had raised him almost to their level. He did not feel insulted by that; humans could do worse.

Shade had reached him first, much to the consternation of the Seekers. The warlock and the birds were old acquaintances. It said something about Wellen that they had attempted a rescue. Shade was both respected and feared; to the Seekers he was almost a demon. His madness was his only weakness, at least so far as they knew, and they had dared exploit it this once. *They* had instigated the visions from the past, drawing them from the warlock's drifting mind in a rare moment of strength. Still, the spell summoning Bedlam had barely succeeded. There had even been a point where the Seekers had almost lost their target to the Void.

The scholar shivered, happy that he had not known that then. He had wondered why the bird folk had foregone their advantage and not attacked their adversary. But now Wellen knew that they barely had had enough strength to free him. Entrancing Shade for a brief time and actually doing him harm were two different things. Many avians in the past had learned the folly of assaulting the warlock. If left alone, he generally left them alone. If disturbed . . . the images that flashed across Wellen's mind stunned him. Never had he heard of a spellcaster with power of such magnitude. Even the mysterious Dragon Kings feared him, if what the images indicated were true.

And all that power in the hands of a madman! What would Shade do when he discovered his "guest" missing? The young Seeker reassured him that they could protect him from the threat, but he was doubtful.

At last, contact was broken. Wellen looked at his inhuman companions with new respect and hope. He still had no idea where they hoped to hide him, but he was willing to go along with their plan. What choice did he actually have? Whether they lied or not, he was definitely helpless before them. Yet, where once he had revealed magical skill, could he not again? If given time . . .

"What happens now?"

Though contact had been broken, he was certain they understood him. The young one pointed skyward. Wellen looked up, but saw only clouds and blue. He turned his gaze earthward again, focusing on the hatchling. "I don't—"

The two Seekers who held his arms rose into the air, taking their prize with them.

It took a moment, but Wellen regained his composure. He was certain he was safe in the claws of the avians, not only because the sensation of danger had vanished but also because the Seekers had had too much opportunity to prove themselves his enemies. He was helpless, something that seemed to be the pattern of his life since coming to the Dragonrealm. Admittedly, Wellen was not so certain that Shade had meant him harm, but with as unpredictable a force as the shadowy warlock, he preferred not to find out.

Fears and doubts fell behind him as he and his two guardians rose above the trees. Flight was something new to the explorer and he marvelled at the experience. The sights below could certainly not compare to his excursions with Shade, but Wellen much preferred this method to standing and shivering on the top of a chilling, inhospitable mountain peak.

Other Seekers joined the trio. He saw no sign of the young one. Likely they had not wanted to take any risks with it. It? Though contact with the adolescent had not lasted that long, he had come away with the vague notion that the young one had been female. It was hard to say and he had noticed that, to his eyes, the adults all looked more or less alike. Wellen scanned the small flock fluttering around him. They were probably males, if only because what little he had learned about their history made that seem more likely. With births so few, a race would be mad to waste its females on a task such as this. Wellen had no misconceptions concerning his own worth; he was probably fortunate that the young Seeker had been female. It explained even more why the avians had finally chosen to rescue him.

They flew for what was probably two or three hours, with periodic stops to allow different pairs to take control of the wingless human. The avians were strong, but carrying so much dead weight—not a term Wellen liked to use for himself but true nevertheless—would tire anyone after a short while. As time progressed, the sun slowly moved on a downward arc on the scholar's right side, which meant that the party was heading more or less straight south. He hoped they would reach their destination before nightfall. While not a child afraid of the dark, Wellen did not care for the thought of flying blind or coming to a rest in some mysterious wood. It was a foolish fear, since the avians obviously knew what they were doing, but Wellen had already gone through enough for anyone. He only wanted a safe and secure place in which to rest and hide from the world for a time.

His head began to pound. Wellen grimaced, thinking that a headache was mild in comparison to what he had already suffered.

As if taking umbrage with that thought, the pounding grew incessant. Had it not been for its intensity, which was becoming staggering, Bedlam almost would have thought that it was—*a warning*.

He quickly glanced around, almost dislodging himself from

the grips of his guardians. One of the Seekers squawked at him, no doubt reminding him that humans did not fly and so he should stop squirming. Wellen shook his head and tried to indicate that something might be wrong. The avian blinked and turned its attention back to the flight.

Around him, the other Seekers flew with an equal lack of concern. By rights, that should have been enough to satisfy him, for they certainly had to know their homeland better than he, but the warning would not cease. He looked below, thinking that there might be a threat from that direction. The incredible height from which he peered down gave him an excellent view of the region for miles around, but the most dangerous thing he noted was a small pack of minor drakes at work on a kill. They were of the wingless variety and fairly slow-witted from the looks of them, hardly a threat.

So what was there, other than being dropped, that would endanger him? Wellen tried to look up, but the angle at which he was being held allowed him to scan only those areas ahead of the flock. Twisting around only threatened to loosen his companions' grips, something he did not want to cause. Yet, where else was there to look?

At last, unable to resist the constant nagging in his mind, he carefully tried to turn enough to see. The Seekers holding him squawked, but he merely shook his head. His attempt was not entirely successful, as it would have required the ability to twist his neck in a complete circle, but he was able to shift enough so that he could see some of the clouds just behind and above them.

The explorer stared narrow-eyed at the clouds. It had been clouds which had hidden the dragon that had murdered his companions.

He could not take the risk. Twisting back, he regained the attention of one of the avians and shouted, "The clouds! I think there's something in the clouds!"

The Seeker merely looked at him, one eye cocked as usual. He repeated the warning, wondering if it understood his words at all. Wellen had no right to assume that all Seekers understood human common language. In fact, it surprised him that people on this continent still spoke the same tongue. Why was that?

Time for questions later! he reprimanded the scholar within. His two guardians matched gazes, possibly speaking in that silent manner of the race, but nothing more happened. If they had mulled over his warning at all, either they had not believed it or they thought it not important enough. Perhaps they had even known in advance but were merely allowing possible watchers to fall into some secret trap. He hoped but did not believe the last was the case.

Minutes later, the flock began to descend. As the earth rushed toward him, the human searched for a possible destination. He saw nothing but more hills and woods. Only another pause, then. Wellen quickly scanned the rest of the landscape and noted some hills far to the southeast. Their regularity made him wonder if they were the same hills where Shade had first rescued him from the scavengers.

Thinking of the warlock made him wonder what the murky figure had thought when he had woken from his musings. Had he even gotten that far? Was Shade still conversing with the images of long-dead companions? For all the danger that the ancient warlock represented, Wellen could not help feeling sorry for him, for all the years of fear and uncertainty he knew the spellcaster had gone through.

His feet touched the ground, erasing such notions. The avians released him once they were certain momentum would not send him tumbling forward. Around him, the other creatures landed. None of his companions were at all concerned, but the broad human was not so certain. While very nebulous, his sudden ability to detect danger had not failed. Each time there had been a threat, however remote it might have been.

Able to stretch his legs, Wellen went through a methodical listing of possibilities. Why would he not see a danger, yet feel its presence? First, because it was not there. Second, because it was far away...which did not seem that likely to him. Third...he paced, both to think and work his muscles more...third...

Because it doesn't *want* to be seen? Shade's cavern had been masked by a spell, but Wellen *had* seen through it, much to the warlock's surprise. That meant that he had more than average potential. Would it be possible to do the same here?

Not exactly certain what he should be doing but willing to experiment, Wellen Bedlam tried to open up his mind completely. He had not been concentrating when he had broken Shade's spell, so he suspected that such a route would not work here. As with many things, trying too hard often led to failure.

Perhaps if he allowed his premonition to guide him, he might find something.

To his surprise, he found himself turning his gaze to the east and high up in the sky. There was no conscious effort; Wellen simply moved. Still, he saw nothing, despite scanning the sky carefully, and doubt began to resurface.

Then vague outlines began to take shape in the sky above them. He could not tell what they were, but he could see that they were closing the distance between themselves and the flock in swift fashion.

Grabbing hold of the nearest avian, he pointed at the oncoming shapes. "We're about to be attacked!"

A number of the Seekers looked in the direction the explorer pointed, but none of them reacted as if they had seen what he did. The one that Wellen had grabbed hold of gave him a glance whose meaning was the same in either human or avian terms. Wellen refused to give up, however. He took the Seeker's claw and pressed it against his own forehead. With as much will as he could muster, the human envisioned what he had discovered.

Almost instantly, the avian pulled back his hand, eyes wide. At first, Wellen was not certain he had succeeded, but then the Seekers as a whole turned toward the sky. A change came over the flock. Their feathers bristled and they readied their talons for combat.

Wellen saw that the shapes were nearly upon them.

The bird folk began to take to the air, save for one that remained by him. As they rose, a transformation took place among the winged figures descending. Their cloaking spell uncovered, they evidently saw no more use for it. Just before the two groups met, the last shreds of sorcery burned away, revealing in its place . . . horror.

"Gods!" Bedlam had expected birdlike creatures, thinking that the wings meant the attackers *must* be like his avian allies. These were not, however. The monstrosities that the Seekers now faced resembled another flier, the bat. Yet, no bat ever resembled these. The attackers were as tall, if not taller, than Wellen and almost as manlike as the bird folk. Where the avians wore the mantle of civilization, however, the bat creatures were without a doubt savage killers.

He did not doubt that it was he they were after. Coincidence could only be stretched so far.

Why? Why does everyone want me? Whatever the reason, Wellen knew it was a mistake. He knew nothing and had nothing anyone would desire. For some insane reason, though, fate had chosen Wellen Bedlam to be its jester.

The two sides were evenly matched in terms of numbers, but the Seekers were badly lacking otherwise. They had power, true, but so did the bats. Spells were unleashed and spells were cancelled out. A few did some damage, but most caused a flash or a crackling sound and nothing more. The bats were also not mere animals; they moved with too much skill and daring and reacted too efficiently when attacked to be thought of as such. It was physical strength that would decide victory and that, unfortunately, belonged to the deathly pale horrors.

Even as he realized that, Wellen saw a Seeker plummet to the earth, its chest a gaping, blood-covered hole. Another was torn apart by two monsters who then threw the remains about. Intelligent, yes, but bloodlust clouded their senses a bit. One of the two died suddenly when a Seeker came from nowhere and slashed the back of its throat completely open. The other reacted, however, and raced to meet its companion's killer.

The Seeker beside Wellen put a claw on his shoulder. The human nodded, knowing without looking what the avian wanted. Assured, his feathered guardian leaped into the air to do its part in a battle it must have known was lost already. Wellen could not have blamed it; he would have done the same had he some way of assisting. His sorcerous abilities were limited to say the very least. The explorer had a knife, but his sword had been taken from him. Wellen pulled the blade free nonetheless, knowing he would need it whether his next decision proved to be running or fighting.

Either way, he expected to be dead or a prisoner before the sun had set.

"Run! This way!" a voice, female, called.

The voice came from his right. Wellen searched that region, but saw no one.

"Run, I said!" A figure, as female as the voice, materialized next to one of the trees. The woman wore a long cloak that blended in with the colors of the forest, which was the reason he had not noticed her at first. She waved for him to come to her. "Hurry! It's your only chance!"

It twisted Wellen's stomach to abandon the Seekers, who were giving their lives for him because he had saved one of their most precious ones, but they fought in great part to keep him from the bats and this looked like the only way their desire might still be fulfilled.

Still holding the blade ready, the harried scholar ran toward her. All the while he wondered. *What now? Who else wants me?*

"A little farther!"

He tore through the foliage and came up next to her. For one brief breath, Wellen froze and stared at the exotic, pale countenance. Then, she broke the spell by tossing a cloak like her own at him.

"Put this on over your other clothing!"

With all their power, he doubted that the cloaks, however much they resembled the forest, would fool the bats for very long. While he was donning the bulky garment, though, Wellen noticed that its pattern *shifted*.

"It adjusts to whatever your surroundings resemble. Precisely adjusts."

True camouflage. It was still doubtful that the trick would work for more than a few minutes, but any time it bought might give Wellen time to think of something else . . . that was what he *hoped*.

When he was finished, she gave him a very brief inspection. "That'll do! Follow me!"

The two moved swiftly through the woods. Wellen marvelled at how the branches and the grass never seemed to touch his guide. She moved like the wind, something he wished was possible for him, for every bit of foliage grabbed at his garments or sought out his face.

The sounds of battle had died down. Wellen heard a heart-stopping shriek of anger that no Seeker would have been capable of unleashing and suspected that the bat creatures had discovered him missing. It would not be long now. The only positive note, and it was indeed a slim one, was that of the dozen or so monsters, at least a few had likely died or been badly wounded by the unfortunate bird folk. With their numbers diminished, they would not be able to cover the region as thoroughly as they might have before.

It gave him slim hope.

His guide, who moved like an elf but did not resemble one, slowed and reached out a hand. Wellen grasped it, feeling a tingle run through him that had nothing to do with warnings of danger. He had time to think of how smooth and cool that hand was before she commanded, "Close your eyes and hold tight!"

Close my eyes? "Why?"

Her smile was a bit crooked, but the perfection of her lips made him ignore that. "To live."

He could hardly argue with that. Wellen shut his eyes and prayed it would not be his last mistake.

There was a ripple, as if he had struck and passed through the surface of a lake. Wellen heard the distant shriek of a bat creature, but it broke off abruptly. He collided with his rescuer, who had stopped running almost at the same moment as the shriek had ceased.

"You can open your eyes again."

Once more, he was stunned by her beauty. The hair was at least as black as night, if not more so, and it worked to perfectly accent her ivory skin. His gaze met her own. Wellen thought of the cat people in the mountains east of his homeland. With eyes such as hers he would have almost suspected her of being a crossbreed.

"You may relax now. We'll be safe here for a time." Seeing that he was sweating from all the clothing, she added, "You can take that off, too. It was just a precaution. I didn't know how fast they might be after us."

"Who are you? What were those things? How did you know where I was?"

"Such an inquisitive man." Her change in demeanor was disconcerting. She talked as if they had not been pursued by ungodly fiends but rather had been out for a stroll after a picnic. "I like that. You don't demand like so many I've known. Polite even under the circumstances."

"Then perhaps you would be so kind as to answer some of my questions," he returned, undoing the cloak. Wellen hated to part with it, especially without examining it, but the heat was getting to him.

Slender fingers worked as she began to remove her own cloak. "My name is Xabene."

"Xabene." Her name was all he could think of to say, for the woman dropped her cloak at that point.

"And yours?"

"Wellen. Bedlam."

"An interesting name." She reached toward him with two

smooth, pale arms. "May I?" When he blinked, the raven-haired woman added, "May I take the cloak?"

The scholar pulled himself together. Handing her the fascinating garment, he asked again, "What were those things that attacked the Seekers?"

She began folding his cloak. "Those were the Necri. You wouldn't like them."

"I didn't." Bedlam noticed that the garment in her hands kept decreasing in size as she continued to fold it. The bundle was now only half as big as when Xabene had started. "What did they want of me?"

"Probably the same thing that the birds wanted." The bundle now fit into the palm of her hand, yet she still folded. "Do you know what *they* wanted from you?"

He watched as the cloak became a tiny square of cloth. When Xabene seemed satisfied, and the bundle was hardly bigger than a large coin, she deposited it into a pouch at her waist.

"*Do* you know?" she asked again.

"They were rescuing me. I saved the life of one of their young."

Her visible impression of him rose. He felt unreasonably pleased at that. "It's not many a human that the birds respect at all."

"It seems to be the only good piece of luck that I've had since coming here." *Other than now,* he added in silence. Xabene's mere presence disconcerted him.

"And where did you come from?"

"Overseas." An unanswered question of his own nagged at him again. "Why did you rescue me? How could you even know I'd be there?"

She did not seem inclined to take it any further at that point. Bending over, Xabene retrieved her own cloak. She bundled it up rather than folded it. "There's a time for questions later. I've been remiss." Her smile bewitched. "I know of a place where we can be alone . . . and talk in peace."

The idea of actually being able to relax and exchange information appealed so much to the brown-haired man that he was almost able to forget the bloodshed he was responsible for. Perhaps Xabene would be able to shed light on the situation, including the secret of the mysterious dragon tome that Shade had wanted and thought that Wellen had come to steal.

Admittedly, he did not mind the thought of remaining with Xabene for a time.

The lithe, commanding woman was crumpling the second cloak together. Like the first, it seemed to shrink as she packed the cloth tighter. Since she had not bothered to fold it, the garment ended up resembling a small pile of loose material shoved together. When it was no larger than the other, she put it away.

"You are a sorceress."

"Sorceress, witch, enchantress...the titles all mean the same thing now, but, yes, I am." Her eyes half-closed and she gave him a look that reminded him of a child who thinks it has disappointed a parent. "Does that bother you so much?"

"Not at all. You might be able to help me." Perhaps she would be able to instruct him in the development of his own abilities. For the first time in quite some while, he felt truly encouraged.

Xabene almost came to him. "I'm so glad. So many people do not understand. Now come. We have just a short distance to cover, but the sun is about to set." The enchantress reached out and took his hand again. "You don't want to be out here at night. There's no telling what sort of dark things might be roaming about."

He allowed her to lead him along, but they only had gone a few paces when he pulled her to a halt.

"What is it?"

Wellen pointed to the east. The trees had kept much of the landscape in that direction hidden, and now was the first time he had been able to get some bearing on his location. To his surprise, the sight before him was very, very familiar. "Those hills. Are there others like them?"

"None." There was something in her tone that hinted he should not waste any more time, but Wellen wanted to be certain. "I think...they look like the ones where I was rescued by...where I was rescued." He decided not to mention Shade, not wanting to worry Xabene further.

"If you think that those hills look familiar, they probably do. The first Dragon King of this region is supposed to have raised them up that way. That was when their power seemed limitless. The present ones can't do that as far as I know, although you shouldn't underestimate them."

"I won't." More questions to ask. Who *were* the Dragon

Kings? He was just about to return his attention to the trek at hand when he noticed a tiny structure vaguely east of the two of them but not quite as far as the hills. It seemed to be sitting in the middle of nowhere. Nothing else existed around it, save empty field and a few wooded regions. Why would someone build such a place here? "What is that building?"

For the first time, she looked at him with suspicion. "That's the citadel of the gnome. It's where he works and where he keeps his secrets. No one get in or out of that gray place but him."

Wellen was not deterred. "I think . . . I think I have to go see him."

"No." Her voice was flat. "You don't want to see the gnome."

"Why, is he dangerous?"

She shrugged. "There's a vast, ruined city on the eastern edge of the Dragonrealm. Part of it extends into the sea now."

The city guarded by the sea serpents. "I remember it. We passed it on our way to the southern shores."

"A good thing. The Dragon King who took it over is very possessive." Her smile held no warmth. "It'd been in ruins for over a thousand years before that."

"What had that got to do with the gnome?"

Xabene laughed. "Who do you think made it that way?"

He gave her a doubtful look. "Not *him*?"

"Of course. Now tell me; is *that* dangerous enough for you?"

VIII

"I have waited so very long for the book," the Dragon King Purple rumbled. He lay just outside of the caverns where the clans made their home. The setting sun reflected off his scales, causing him to glitter. Purple might have seemed a strange color for a dragon, but he felt it quite regal . . . and no one laughed at a purple dragon, anyway. No one who lived for very long after, that is.

"My sire waited. So too did his predecessor. They waited, but they never succeeded." The great drake's foreclaws gouged ravines in the rocky, unrelenting soil. The region just around the clan caves had been baked hard by generations of fire-breathing beasts, yet it was no match for the Dragon King's might.

The tiny human figure before the leviathan did not look up. That was one of the first rules the Dragon King taught those within his presence; you knelt and looked down, showed the proper respect until given permission to stand. Ashy remains attested to those who did not obey with sufficient swiftness.

"I will *not* allow this task to fall to *my* successor! I *will* have the gnome's secrets!"

Those few drakes in attendance tried to make themselves as small as the human. When the dragon lord grew angry, it did not matter whether the one who suffered the consequences was human, drake, or otherwise.

Purple eyed his human. "I spared your life because I desired information. You were fortunate, for the one who decimated your kind was too eager for his own good. He disobeyed. He will not do so again."

The other dragons hissed and the human shivered. A reptilian smile, so very toothy, spread across the Dragon King's horrendous visage. There was no question as to his authority in his kingdom.

He brought his massive head lower to the earth, the better to further terrify his man-toy. The tiny creatures were so predictable, it was pathetic.

"You claim that you did not come here for the book, which I do not believe. I suspect now, though, that you are not the one who led. There is another and he is the one I seek. You are hardly clever enough to hope to gain entrance to the gnome's infernal lair!"

"No, my great and imperial lord!" came the muffled response.

"So." Purple pulled back, his countenance masked in an expression of nonchalance . . . or as close as was capable for one of his kind. "Who, then? All of your companions are dead. Your vessels are scattered. Can you give me a reason why I should prolong your existence?"

"The one who commands still lives!"

"Indeed?"

"I saw him escape into the hills! He rode a horse he had stolen!"

"The hills . . ." The leviathan was having difficulty hiding his interest. These outsiders, as weak as they were, would not have dared come from so great a distance if they had not had a plan they felt sufficient to outwit the cursed gnome. The Dragon King Purple was certain of that, for it was the way he would have thought, and of course his cunning was paramount. "He is one of your learned ones?"

"He is very learned! It was by his decision that we have come to this damn—this land!"

There was hatred in those tones. The Dragon King found that amusing. It was something that might be played upon later. "And what is this human's name?"

His puppet dared to look up, knowing that his life relied on this next moment. As he stared at the insignificant creature, the drake lord marvelled at its coloring. *Perhaps I shall give him to Irillian. He is, after all, more to their liking, being blue*.

Prentiss Asaalk, looking much more worn and beaten, responded, "His name is Wellen Bedlam!"

Xabene's choice for a hiding place was not what Wellen had expected. When she had first revealed it to him in the first minutes of night, he had stared at the giant, misshapen form, not certain that what he saw was what she wanted him to see.

"The tree?"

"It's more than just a tree," she had assured him. In the darkness, the enchantress had been almost invisible despite her pale skin.

In truth, it *had* proved to be more than just a tree. Much, much more.

It was almost another *world*.

She had led him to a crack in the side of the trunk. It had been a tall, narrow thing, hardly big enough for him to even slip his fingers into. On the other hand, Xabene's slender fingers had fit perfectly. While Wellen had watched, mystified, she had run her fingers up and down the crack. The enchantress had performed the strange deed twice, then had stood back.

With a groan, the crack had *widened*. It had continued to widen until it was somehow spread far enough apart to admit the two humans.

"Come with me," she had whispered, her hand seizing his to assure that he would not be left behind . . . or possibly choose to turn and run from her.

If the outside of the tree had stunned him, the inside had *overwhelmed* him. From without, the trunk had looked massive enough, if it had been hollowed out, to contain five or six people . . . provided, of course, that they had stood still and barely breathed. From within, however, the tree had revealed a chamber almost as great as the vast, ageless cavern Shade called his domain.

Even now, hours later, Wellen could still not believe it.

He sat cross-legged on a fur, one of many covering this part of the floor. Xabene lounged nearby, uncomfortably close. She smiled as she noticed him once more surveying the unbelievable room. It had been, other than his tales of his life back home, one of the most prevalent subjects they had spoken about.

There were shelves along nearly all the walls and tables upon which books and various artifacts had been neatly organized. A rack of jars attested to the enchantress's interest in alchemy. Specimens of many small but exotic creatures floated in other jars nearby. A desk with writing supplies resting atop it stood in one corner. There were even two subchambers, one filled with various items the raven-haired spellcaster had collected over the years and the other sealed off. Wellen, unable to find a good reason to pry about the closed chamber, tried to ignore it from then on.

"Is it that disconcerting here?" she asked from where she lay.

Wellen tried not to pay too much attention to the way her gown, which somehow had never so much as snagged against a branch or bush *once* during the trip outside, molded itself to what little of her body it covered. He had no doubt that she was aware of her physical attributes, but he was not trusting enough to think that she merely found him attractive. Nothing could be accepted at face value, even so perfect a face, in the Dragonrealm.

Her question was safe enough. "It is disconcerting, yes, but at the same time I feel so at home. The books, the experiments, the collections . . . I might almost be back in my own study."

It might have been wishful thinking on his part, but he thought she was pleased. Certainly her next words sounded sincere. "I'd hoped you would find my secret place to your liking. There is much similarity between us, I think."

"I still don't understand how this chamber came to be, though. The skill with which the spell was cast is astounding."

She nodded, shifting closer as she replied, "It is, as I said, very ancient. Before the Dragon Kings, the birds, the Quel, or even those that came before them. We are not exactly in the same world once we enter the tree. You might call it a pocket world, one created long ago by someone and then abandoned. I found it purely by chance."

Wellen mulled that over. This place reminded him of Sirvak Dragoth. He wondered if there might be a connection, but since Xabene had never been across the sea, he could hardly have asked her to make a comparison.

She reached forward and handed him a mug that must have been conjured by sorcery, for he could not recall her holding it the moment prior. Wellen readily took the proffered mug, as he had had food and drink previous to this, and sipped it approvingly. After so many meals aboard the ship, he still found fresh food a grand novelty. The brief life of the expeditionary force had not been a long enough time for him to reaccustom himself to normal meals.

Throughout most of their time here, Xabene had offered little information about herself. She admitted to having seen Wellen earlier during the Seeker's flight. It had been her intention to rescue him from the bird folk, whom most humans did not trust. That circumstances had caused that rescue to come off a little differently was just the workings of fate.

He did not, of course, completely believe the story, just as he did not believe some of the other things she told him about. Most of her explanations twisted or turned whenever they grew too close to what he suspected was the truth. The puzzling thing was that he had felt no premonition of danger since entering this place. It pleased him that he could feel safe in the presence of the enchantress, as safe as any man would *be* from her, that it, but it perplexed him that all her deceit did not present some sort of threat. Almost everything else in the Dragonrealm had.

Since she had not mentioned Shade, Wellen chose to continue to keep his time with the warlock secret. There was no single particular reason; at some point he had just decided it would be better if he kept silent.

His mind was just beginning to drift when the mug nearly slipped from his hand. After the day's events, Wellen was worn almost to nothing. Even the rest Shade had allowed him had not been sufficient, for the scholar had found himself shifting and waking constantly, each time feeling the eyes of the hooded warlock upon him.

"Let me take that," Xabene offered, retrieving the mug from a drowsy Bedlam. "You look exhausted."

"I feel exhausted." Had it been just a little too sudden? The thought that his food or drink might have been drugged had occurred early on, but the lack of warning had made him complacent. Now, the novice warlock was wondering if his own small skills had betrayed him. Not possible . . . or could it be that he could be drugged as long as no harm was meant to him?

Wellen grimaced. His thoughts were all muddled.

With gentle pressure, the pale enchantress pushed him down onto the furs. Her action had just the opposite effect from what it should have; the weary explorer stirred at her closeness. For a moment, their eyes locked. Xabene stared as if seeing something new, then, with lips parted, whispered, "You have demanding eyes, Wellen Bedlam. What is it they demand now?"

"Sleep," he blurted, half-mumbling the word. Her catlike eyes widened, almost tempting him to a knowing smile. If she had expected his defenses to be down, she did not yet know him well enough.

He drifted off after that, his last memory that of the frustrated sorceress folding her arms across her exquisite form and glaring at him.

She never looked more beautiful.

He had a dream, the only one he could remember, that is, and it included Xabene, the monstrous batlike creatures, and a figure who reminded Wellen of nothing less than Death itself. There were words and tones filled with anger and supplication. That was all there was to the dream, save that a vague sense of danger touched him. As the dream, or rather nightmare, faded, however, so too did the warning.

Puzzled but relieved, Wellen Bedlam sank deeper into slumber.

* * *

When he finally woke, it was as if the last few moments of the night before, especially his rejection of Xabene's advances, had never happened. As fresh, somehow, as the morning itself, she gently prodded him to consciousness. Wellen, on the other hand, felt as if he had slept among the very animals from which the furs on the floor had been skinned.

"I have some clothes for you." The smile was back and possibly even warmer than the day before. Having witnessed many a play during his years of study, Wellen came to the conclusion that the enchantress was as good an actress as any he had seen. "There is also a place where you may renew yourself."

The latter proved to be the mysterious subchamber the brown-haired scholar had wondered about during his initial hours in the tree. His first glimpse of it was as stupifying as his first glimpse of the tree itself.

The Dragonrealm is truly a place of wonders, a magical paradise . . . when it is not trying to kill you!

It was, as Xabene explained it, a pocket world within a pocket world. What it truly was, was a tiny woodland scene with, of all things, a stream running in a complete circle around the rest of the view. There was no end or beginning to the stream; it just went around and around.

"The water is always fresh," she assured him.

It was cold, but marvelously so. Wellen spent half his time enjoying the luxury and the other half trying to investigate the astonishing creation. The trees and grass were very real. A light source he could not locate played at being the sun.

With some reluctance he finally abandoned the place, knowing that it was time to move on. For the first time, the scholar was relatively able to decide his own fate. He had come up with the only choice that seemed reasonable to him. Wellen hoped that Xabene would join him, but if she did not, he would move on without her . . . even if it meant confrontation. The enchantress might not like the thought of losing him before she succeeded in gaining whatever it was she wanted. The explorer was under no delusion that her interest in him was strictly personal.

The clothing he now wore was an exact replica of that he had arrived with, save that it was both clean and untorn. The boots were still his own, however, being a very servicable pair that Xabene must have decided did not need to be replaced. As for the sorceress, she was clad much the way he had seen her the day before. There were subtle differences in the style of her gown, but it still served the same purpose he now knew all her clothing seemed to have been designed for; addling the senses of men. It was certainly not practical for the outdoors, although the enchantress had not seemed at all put out by the weather.

It came to him then that despite her words of warning concerning the gnome, she also had an interest in the enigmatic book. She had been too quick to warn him about staying away and her attitude had revealed her belief that he was there for the same purpose she was. That was the connection that Wellen had somehow not been able to make yesterday—the reason for which she had *actually* rescued him.

One question remained; did she herself have masters or was she, like Shade, a single force?

He blinked. Vague memories of voices and the smell of sulfur. A flapping of wings. Had that happened during the night? The memories slipped free and escaped as Wellen was forced to focus his attention on Xabene. She was seated on the furs, a small table filled with meats and other items before her. He noticed that none of the food had been touched and that the majority of it was placed near the side where he would have to sit.

"Are you hungry?"

He was, but was too restless to sit down. Wellen took a piece of fruit, confident that it was safe, and bit into it. After he had swallowed the first bite, the explorer said, "I need your help."

Xabene's eyes narrowed in interest. "In what way?"

"I want to speak to this gnome."

She looked at him as if he had asked her to marry a Seeker. "The gnome? After what I told you?"

"You told me only that he destroyed a city long, long ago. I think there must be more to it than that. I also think that if the gnome were so powerful and so evil, he would have conquered the Dragonrealm long ago. For that matter, how do you know it's the same gnome? Could he have really lived so long?"

"Throughout time as far back as legends go there's always been a gnome there. From what I've seen and heard, he has looked the same for generations. Could he really be that old?" Xabene shook her head. "I've heard of stranger things!"

"He appears to be my only hope of ever extricating myself from this chaotic farce."

"There is the matter of the Dragon King of this land. It was one of his that tore apart your expedition and slaughtered your friends!''

He winced at her casual way of speaking about the massacre. ''He cannot be too great a threat or else you would not keep returning to this place.'' Wellen indicated the tree chamber. ''Although it could also be that other things draw you to this region. You've a great interest in books, I've seen.''

Xabene crossed her arms and met his gaze. Her words were not accusatory, only confirming. ''You already know that I've an interest in the gnome's book. You've known for quite awhile. If you'd asked, I wouldn't have denied it.''

''But you would not have mentioned it otherwise.'' He smiled. ''Am I your prisoner? It seems to be a habit with me.''

''I could have conjured up some chains at any time. Have I?''

''No.'' The scholar did not add that her not having done so did not preclude his captivity. He hesitated, pretending as if the thought was only just occurring to him, and then suggested, ''It might be the case that my needs coincide with your needs.''

Her interest was instantly piqued. She moved closer, using every step to her advantage. Wellen worked hard to prevent the facade he wore from cracking. Xabene played her role well. From many another woman, Xabene's manner would have seemed overdone, too obvious. Not so from the enchantress. It *was* her. She was so natural that Wellen almost shivered. What could she do to a man who *did* succumb to her charms?

Not all the answers that flashed through his mind were pleasant.

''Are you speaking of the book?'' she asked. ''Or other things?''

''*The book.*'' His reply was a bit too quick and, unlike the night before, not at all to his advantage. Both of them knew it.

''Then you are saying that if I help you gain an opportunity to confront the gnome . . . and there's no guarantee that he'll even bother to acknowledge you standing outside his citadel . . . you'll help me obtain the book?''

''If that is possible; I cannot promise that the chance will arise.''

From her tone, the sorceress seemed to think otherwise, likely because she still assumed that Wellen secretly *did* want the dragon tome. He did not attempt to dissuade her. If it helped him escape this madness, all the better.

I was willing to risk death to reach this land, but I'm not willing to risk it for something I care nothing about! Given the opportunity, he would have been more than willing to take the gnome's damnable opus, throw it as far as he could, and then sit back and watch the others fight over it.

Xabene looked him over and visibly contemplated his offer. He had no doubt about the outcome, however.

"All right. I agree." She turned away with a whirl, as ever, perfectly orchestrated, and added, "But we'll have to move in swift fashion. This place does not allow spells to extend beyond it; we'll have to transfer from outside."

"No."

"No what?"

He waited until she was looking at him again. "No more teleportation. Not after what I have been through."

"Traveling any other way will take too long. The more time we linger in the vicinity of the pentagon, the more chance that one of the Dragon King's sentinels will see us! If not his minions, then those of someone else interested in the gnome's secrets!"

Deep down, he knew that Xabene had the right of it, that taking their time would only increase their risk. Wellen was adamant, however. He had been pulled along like a toy once too often. Magic was not yet his element and it might never be. His premonitions of danger aside, he felt lost in its presence. Wellen wanted some semblance of control over the situation and sorcery, especially teleportation, left him feeling defenseless and befuddled.

The enchantress saw that it was useless to argue. If she wanted to maintain his trust, she could only give in.

"As you like it, then." Even when she merely shrugged, the ivory-skinned witch exuded her charms. "I could summon up a pair of mounts, but it could mean waiting for quite some time. They might be very near, but they also might be very far."

"Would it take longer than walking?"

She sniffed, not caring for that suggestion at all. Wellen knew his hostess thought him mad and it might be that she was correct. He was not so certain about his sanity, either.

"I will not walk to the gnome's citadel. That is asking *too* much, Wellen Bedlam."

The night before, she had been calling him strictly by his

first name; now, she had become more formal. It was the one inconsistency. If she sought to draw him in, why distance him so? Calling him by his full name reminded both of them that they were relative strangers.

Wellen knew not to press. "Very well, we'll ride."

Her smile returned. All was well, indeed. On the surface. "It will not take so long, I think. This will not be the first time I've summoned these particular mounts. They *should* be fairly near."

She had yet to call them horses. *Were* they?

"I'll have to summon them from outside, of course." It was one of the things Xabene had explained to him after their arrival here. Spells worked within or without the tree's tiny world, but only if the sorcerer was in the same region. A spell cast in the tree would not make it to the Dragonrealm. At the same time, someone utilizing magic in the Dragonrealm could not send their spell into the tree. It made for a wonderful sense of security as far as Wellen was concerned.

"I'll join you," he replied. While keeping the enchantress in sight was a pleasant task in one way, Wellen was aware that his future might depend on being wary when it came to Xabene. She might decide at some point that he had overextended his usefulness . . . and *then* what would happen?

"Of course."

Where gaining entrance to the tree had required physical effort from the enchantress, leaving proved to be not so cumbersome. As the two walked to the hidden doorway, it slowly split open. Bedlam noted that it opened only enough to allow one person through at a time. He wondered whether this was the way it worked or if Xabene had caused it to part only so far.

It was early morning, just after sunrise. Even before he stepped back out into the Dragonrealm, Wellen knew that. It surprised him, for he had come to assume that his slumber had lasted far longer. So much the better. While night might have its uses, he preferred movement during the day. Too many things stalked this land after dark. At least in the daylight he would have a chance to see what was coming for him. Wellen had never been good at stealth.

"This will only take a moment." She turned from him and faced north. He took a step away from the shielding tree and breathed in the sweet morning air.

The inside of Wellen's head fairly screamed.

"Xabene!"

Too late did he realize what the world within the vast tree had done to him. His own powers had become muted in there because the danger was outside and he was inside. Now the warnings ripped through his mind, as if stored up and waiting for the first chance to tell him the truth.

There came a rustling noise in the woods beyond. Something large moved with great speed toward the duo. It trampled through the underbush. Wellen glanced at the enchantress and saw that she was still caught up in the summoning. He turned his gaze from her to his hands, as if staring at them would somehow unleash the power he supposedly contained. Bedlam felt no different, however, and almost immediately gave up the attempt as hopeless. As the unseen threat neared, the desperate scholar quickly searched the surrounding ground and located a broken tree limb. His head ached with the urgency of the situation. Wellen wanted to laugh at how sad his defenses would be. Anything that caused such dire warnings to ring in his head had to be monstrous. The stick would probably annoy rather than harm it or them.

"Xabene!" he hissed, trying one last time to awaken her.

"What?"

Her sudden, calm voice threw his guard completely off. He was about to turn to her when two massive shapes crushed through the foliage and raced toward the enchantress and him.

Wellen raised the branch then dropped it when he saw what had joined them. He knew his face was red.

Two horses. A black and a spotted one. The mounts that the sorceress had been summoning. They were the danger? It hardly seemed possible.

The animals trotted to within a few yards of the duo but refused to come nearer when Xabene called to them. She noticed the branch in Wellen's hand. "You won't need that. Throw it far away so that they see you don't mean them any harm."

"I—" The sensation would not leave, yet how could these horses be a threat? Wellen reluctantly threw the stick far to his right, then revealed his open palms to the animals. He felt foolish, but the enchantress nodded her approval.

"Do not underestimate them, Wellen Bedlam. These are very intelligent creatures."

He knew of legends revolving around a demon horse whom Lord Drazeree, or rather *Dru Zeree*, had befriended, but neither of these could be the demon.

So why was his head still pounding? "Xabene . . . there's something wrong here."

"Nonsense." Her tone might have been a bit sharp; Wellen could not be certain. He had not explained his peculiar ability to sense possible danger, mostly because he still did not understand it himself. It had also been his one reliable weapon . . . until now, perhaps. "The Dragon King is nowhere near and I sense nothing else."

Were her abilities superior to his? The novice warlock was willing to believe that. Xabene was a sorceress of no little ability. To think that his skills could in any way be more finely tuned than hers was presumptuous to say the least.

The spotted horse trotted up and tried to smell him. Wellen backed away before the nose touched him, not knowing why he did but glad regardless. Both animals disturbed him despite their innocent appearances.

"I think your horse has been chosen for you," Xabene commented wryly. "If you have no objections, then mount up so that we may be gone from here."

He looked the horse over. "There are no reins. No saddle, either."

"And there will be none. These animals will not accept them. You may trust that they will not lose us, though. I have ridden both of them countless times."

Still not assured but unable to argue, since it had been *his* choice to enact this plan, Wellen reached over the spotted one's backside in order to get a good enough grip to help himself up.

His fingers barely grazed the animal's skin. Wellen withdrew them as if the horse had tried to bite him.

Xabene, already atop her mount, looked down at the confused figure. "What is it now?"

"There's . . . I . . ." How could he describe what had happened when he hardly knew what had happened himself? When his fingers had touched the flesh of the spotted horse, they had not felt the warmth of life, but a coldness that he could only associate with the *long dead*.

Brief images of the dream flashed through his mind. Xabene. The figure she had been speaking to. A figure that brought up thoughts of ancient tombs and corpses long putrifying.

"Are you having second thoughts?" the enchantress asked coyly, her interruption banishing the dream images to his subconscious again.

"No." Gritting his teeth, Wellen searched his clothes, then recalled that these were not his originals. Knowing that he looked more like a plaintive child than a grown, educated researcher, the scholar asked, "Do you have a pair of gloves?"

"Look in the belt pouch just under your left arm."

"I looked there already."

"I know."

Removing the gloves from the pouch a moment later, he reflected upon how spellcasters seemed to have an annoying habit of playing games with those unable to reciprocate in like fashion. While having had little personal experience with sorcerers, a *planned* maneuver on his part, Wellen had heard more than one tale. Whether a master mage or a permanent novice, sorcerers were all the same. They enjoyed toying with their *lessers*.

It in no way helped to constantly recall that he was, by the loosest of definitions, a spellcaster himself.

The gloves on, he tentatively mounted the horse. It was an extremely calm creature, but that failed to sooth his distrust. The sensation of danger, or perhaps it was just possible threat, continued to plague him.

"Are you ready?"

He was not, but it was too late to back down. With a mask of bravado in place, he simply responded, "Lead on."

Xabene gently touched one side of her mount's neck and whispered in an ear. The animal started off on a slow trot, which, despite her interesting, almost lounging manner of sitting, did not dislodge the alluring black-clad woman. She and her horse were almost one, an effect amplified by the way her clothing melded with the color of the steed.

Wellen's own beast followed. He was certain that its first movements would send him sliding off, but the horse's body countered his every shift. After a few moments, Wellen grew a little more comfortable about his chances of staying on. He still did not trust the horse, however. Even with the gloves and pants, the sickly feel of the horse's cold flesh belied its outward appearance. If not for Xabene's words and his own inability to put his finger on exactly what was amiss, he would have leaped to the ground and followed the sorceress on foot instead.

It would be no more mad than this journey I've chosen to take.

He settled in and tried not to think about the animal beneath. It was not as it he had nothing else to consider. There was still the matter of his upcoming confrontation with the gnome, providing the latter even deigned to meet him. What would he do if the end result of his quest turned out to be either sunstroke or finding himself a tidbit for one of the Dragon King's minions?

For that matter, what would he do if the gnome *did* appear?

Now there, the explorer thought, was a *truly* disturbing aspect!

From where they huddled in the treetops, trying their best to avoid the unforgivable light, the seven remaining Necri, including the one who had originally accompanied Xabene, watched as the enchantress and the other mortal rode off. The one Necri in particular noted the man's discomfort with the beasts the Lords of the Dead had secretly provided. The batlike horror could not blame the human for his distaste; the two mounts had been dead far too long. Their meat was tasteless and dry. Only the glamour cast upon them made the horses seem so lifelike.

The Necri who had served alongside Xabene pondered the sorceress's plot. On the surface, it seemed reasonable, but her other plans had failed in the end. On her head and its would lay the most blame. The others . . . the masters might choose to include them in the punishment . . . but more likely was the possibility that they would be made to watch the slow, painful elimination of the two who had failed greatest, despite more than one chance to redeem themselves.

It would be the female's fault, then, if *it* perished so ignobly. No battle. No blood. Not the way a Necri desired to ends it existence.

It had already noted the hesitation with which the enchantress had acted now and then where the man was concerned. The winged horror still recalled the betrayal, when she had taken him while the Necri had been fighting the feathered ones. *That* had not been part of the plan. Xabene had not spoken of that, even with it.

The Necri glanced back at its anxiously awaiting fellows, then turned its blank eyes back to the receding figures. It hissed in frustration, ever mindful that its existence now depended upon a human female.

The toothy maw opened and closed. The claws that had torn stronger foes to bloody gobbets flexed. If she failed, then before it perished it would do its best to see that the sorceress died first. Slowly, too.

After all, a good death was one that could be savored for a time. Even if that time would be short-lived.

While the Necri watched Wellen and the enchantress, another watched them both from a short distance behind. Even though no tree or hill provided adequate cover, the batlike horror neither noticed him or the telltale stench of his odd sorcery.

This will do just *fine,* Shade decided. *They head to the citadel. I could not have planned it better myself!*

IX

The Lords of the Dead gathered in a world where light was but a dim memory. They were eleven and always had been ever since they had discovered the path to godhood. There were vague outlines to each, hints of what they once had been, but anyone who sought to ferret out details of their features would find that little remained but the memories. They were not much more than emaciated figures, some worse than others but all of them reminiscent of the long dead.

Such was the price of their rule. They only knew that they had carved for themselves an empire of sorts, one that stretched beyond the boundaries of this plane into the world of the Dragonrealm. They were the final judges. When those in the Dragonrealm died, it was only to become vassals for them. Someday, their subjects would also include the living and then their empire would be complete.

So they had always liked to believe.

Their kingdom was decay. Things long dead slowly rotted or

were eaten by scavengers, yet never entirely disappeared. Lakes and rivers of dark, moldering green were the only color in the landscape, save for clouds of sulfur that rose above volcanic vents. Ungodly creatures scuttled about, seeking food and trying to escape being food.

The sky was a black cloud that rolled and turned, ever threatening a storm. No moon or stars existed here. The only light came from the vents and it was just barely enough to let the scavengers sight their next meals.

In the citadel, the Lords of the Dead took their places. A huge pentagram marked the floor of the room. Ten of the shrouded forms moved toward points and corners of the pattern, while the eleventh waited for them to take their places. As nominal leader, his place would be at the center, where the array of power would be the strongest.

To his eyes, they had not changed at all over the millennia. None of the Lords of the Dead saw themselves or their compatriots as other than the armored, dragonhelmed sorcerers of long ago. It was a measure of their power, not to mention their madness, that they had never seen their kingdom as it truly was. To them, they had rebuilt the magnificent world of their kind. In truth, there *was* a close resemblance between this place and that ancient world, for their birthplace, forever barred to them, had also become a twisted reflection of its inhabitants. It was why they had come here in the first place, to escape the destruction their people had caused.

When the others had moved into position, the leader joined them. He stepped into the very center of the pentagram, then turned around in one complete circle so as to acknowledge the presence of each and every one.

"The pattern is complete," he intoned. His voice was nearly emotionless, though he did not realize it. "The power flows. Who will be first to speak?"

A shorter specter shifted just enough to warrant the attention of the others. His voice was almost identical in timbre to the leader. "The servant Xabene rides with the outsider."

"Where did they find horses?"

"The animals were ours, ensorcelled to seem living."

The spokesman nodded slowly. "Then, they are on their way to the gnome's accursed sanctum."

"Yes." The shorter figure lowered his shadowed head, a sign that he was finished speaking.

Another, this one akin in size and shape to the master speaker, moved forward one step. "The Necri are upset. Many were lost in battling the Sheeka. They slaughtered the bird folk, but they felt that the servant Xabene had wasted them, not informing them of her own plan until afterward."

The leader turned, setting in motion a wave of sulfur that wafted throughout the featureless, dank room. Moss on the walls withered, but the other lords did not notice. They had long passed beyond the normal senses of men. "Her actions have been questionable of late."

"The outsider's doing?"

"Perhaps." The ruling lord waited for his counterpart to withdraw, but the other was not yet finished.

"There is . . . one more thing."

Hesitation. The coven leader arched a brow he no longer had at the sudden show of uncertainty. "That is?"

"*He* has taken an interest in the outsider and the gnome. It may be that he too desires the book."

No one had to ask who it was the one spoke of. He had been the bane in their existence for longer than they cared to recall, ever since they had sought to steal the power that he had brought with him from the birthworld. Unfortunately, his link made him stronger than they and he had refused to see the inevitable and die. Century after century he had kept himself alive by one means or another.

Now he was after the gnome's secrets. That meant that he was growing desperate, but it also meant that their own plans were in jeopardy, for it anyone understood them, it was he who now called himself *Shade*.

Shade. The name was a mockery. The Lords of the Dead preferred the use of his true name, when they could recall it, for it served to remind them that he was, after all, no more than their errant relation.

"There is no choice," the ruling speaker intoned. "We cannot allow the dragon tome to belong to anyone but ourselves. Even if it means confronting . . . our cousin." He found that this time he could not recall the name. There were many things he especially had forgotten over time. With effort, the name would come, but like so many other such moments, it made more sense to utilize that effort for their plots than for recalling little-needed things like the past.

One whose memory in regard to Shade was a bit stronger

than the others, supplied the name that the others could not recall. "Gerrod. His name is Gerrod, Ephraim."

Ephraim, who realized with a start that he had forgotten his *own* name as well, moved from the center, breaking the pattern. The others saw determination etched into his features, but only because they shared the same delusion when it came to one another. "Then we will know what to call him when we summon him later . . . from the lists of the dead."

The gnome's citadel did not loom over them, but regardless, its presence unnerved them both. It was not as big as Wellen had thought, but the fact that it stood here was impressive enough. From what he had learned, the citadel was as solid a landmark as the mountains Shade had dragged him to . . . was it only a day or two earlier?

"Do what you must and hurry," Xabene demanded, her eyes darting this way and that. He knew she expected to see a dragon or some other threat come swooping down from the sky or springing up from the earth. In truth, the scholar was somewhat surprised at his change of luck. The determination to reach this place had dwindled the nearer they had come. It was almost as if geas had been put on him, one that had now served its purpose.

His head throbbed with undefined warnings of danger, but Wellen was beginning to understand a little about how the ability worked. There were things with the potential to threaten him and things which *were* a danger to his existence. The horses, a mystery yet unsolved, were one of the former. Shade he considered one of the latter.

Xabene was an enigma. Bedlam knew she should have been one or the other, yet she was still one of the few things that apparently did *not* mean him harm. That was contradictory to everything he knew or thought he knew about her.

He dismounted and walked toward the blank, ominous structure. After a moment's hesitation, the enchantress followed suit. Wellen had expected that. Xabene wanted to get in more then he did. In fact, had it been up to him, he would have turned around now and ridden back as if a thousand hungry dragons were nipping at his heels.

Too late now. He glanced at the wall that rose before him. Not a leviathan, but still more than three times, probably more than four times, his height. Careful to avoid touching it, the curious explorer leaned close enough to inspect the substance from which the edifice had been built. It looked like stone, possibly marble, but there were differences. He started to walk along the side, trying to find a place where blocks had been joined together, but more and more it seemed that the gnome's citadel had either been carved from some single massive rock or that it had been formed and baked into shape, like a clay pot. Neither theory was very plausible. There had to be another explanation. Lost in curiosity, he continued along the wall.

"Where are you going?"

Wellen glanced back. "I have to look it over. How do you think he breathes in there? There's no opening that I can see. Are there vents or windows on the top?"

"No." She folded her arms in aggravation. "Is this necessary? I though you had some plan to make the gnome listen to you."

"Plan?" Wellen turned the corner. After a moment, he heard the soft steps of Xabene behind him. "Until this morning, I hadn't even thought about coming here. I was going to ask you to help me get back to the coast so I could see if the *Heron's Wing* was still anchored there." He began to walk faster. "It was not until this morning that I felt I had to come here. I don't even know what I expected from him."

"Do you mean I—" Xabene snapped, her words cut off so abruptly that the scholar turned to see if something was the matter.

"What was that you were saying?"

"Nothing."

Nothing? Wellen pondered the possibility that Xabene had been responsible for his overnight change of mind. Could the vague recollections he had assumed were dreams actually be some true scene? If so, why did he not sense any danger from Xabene?

Wellen continued around the ancient structure until he had come back to his starting point. The enchantress followed him all the way, her expression sour and possibly a bit fearful. Of what?

"Did you find anything?"

He shook his head. "Only that I have wasted my time. Have you ever touched it?"

Hesitation, then, "Yes."

"Nothing happened?"

"See for yourself."

Taking a deep breath, Wellen reached forward. His fingers grazed the surface. When no bolt of lightening smote him, he planted his palm flat against the wall.

"Extraordinary, wasn't it?" Xabene asked, the sarcasm in her tone sharp and biting.

The disappointed explorer removed his hand. The wall felt like any wall, save a little smoother. He had no idea what he had been hoping for, just that he had been . . . hoping.

"And so it ends," the enchantress chided. Wellen met her gaze. Xabene looked away and began to walk to the horses. For some reason, Wellen saw that she was more upset with herself rather than with him. Another puzzle.

The logical thing would have been to follow his companion, remount, and ride off. In a few years, he might be able to forget his debacle, providing he lived that long. Yet, now that Wellen found himself here, he knew he could not just walk away. There had to be something else he could do.

Facing the wall, the scholar quietly spoke. It might be that he talked only for his own benefit, but at least he could say he had tried. Perhaps the proper words could do what force had not.

"I do not know if you can hear me in there, but my name is Wellen Bedlam. I've come from across the seas to explore this continent." He shrugged. "I have no designs on your secrets. My only reason for coming here was to see if you could help me return to my land. Right now I want nothing more than to begin my studies anew."

A breeze tossed his hair about. The gray, flat face of the edifice remained as indifferent as it had before. No magical portal opened in the side. No voice boomed in the heavens. For all he knew, the gnome might not even be inside.

Xabene, mounted and ready to retreat from this disaster, leaned forward and called, "What was that you were saying?"

He was about to turn and tell her when a tingle ran through him. It was not a premonition of danger, but rather some effect from outside his body. Wellen stared at the blank wall for a few seconds, then reached out and touched it.

With a yelp, he pulled his hand back. His fingertips felt as they had been *burned*. A belated throbbing warned him that he should not touch the wall.

"What did you do?" the stunned sorceress cried.

Explanations had to wait. The tingle increased. Though he sensed no danger to himself, Wellen stepped back just in case.

The entire pentagon shimmered.

"No! Don't!" Xabene tried to urge her mount forward, but it was strangely still, almost like a frozen corpse. She cursed the animal, then called to Wellen. "Get away! You might be killed!"

He could not. The shimmering structure nearly had him hypnotized. A panoramic display of colors surrounded the gnome's citadel, a display that grew brighter with each passing breath.

"Wellen!"

Bedlam put a hand over his eyes to shield them from the brilliance.

With what sounded like a hiss, the entire building *vanished*.

"Lords of the Dead!" Xabene swore.

Slowly, Wellen took a step toward where the edifice had stood. His hope that it had merely been an illusion and that the gray structure still stood there, invisible, was quickly shattered. For all practical purposes, the gnome's sanctum might never have been built. Grass as high as his waist fluttered in the light breeze. There were no indentations, no fragments. The citadel was simply gone.

The enchantress leaped from her mount and ran over to him. She took him by the arms and spun him around to face her, displaying at the same time incredible strength for one of her size. "What did you *do*? What spell did you cast?"

Spell? He realized that she had taken his words, unintelligible to her, as some sort of complex spell. He knew that sorcerers sometimes found need for vocal guides, what the ignorant called "magic words," but surely she did not think that *he* was capable of such sorcery?

Or was he? The novice warlock gazed thoughtfully at his hands. *Had* he somehow unleashed a spell of such potency that it had taken the entire building, gnome, book, and all?

"This was not his fault."

The two turned at the sound of the voice, Wellen's heart sinking, for he knew all too well to whom it belonged. Xabene, on the other hand, ignorant of who faced them now, took a step toward the newcomer and held up a fist that crackled with power. The disappearance had wracked her far more than it had

Bedlam. He, after all, had only wanted escape; *she* wanted the tome . . . and not, Wellen suspected now, for herself.

"Who are you?" the enchantress demanded. "This is your doing, then?"

"You may call me Shade," the hooded warlock advised her quietly. As usual, his deathly visage was half-obscured by shadow. "And I am no more responsible for this than Master Bedlam here."

Wellen could not meet her gaze. "You know him? You lied all the time? The book *was* what you wanted?"

"No! Shade assumed I did, just as you have! He's the one who wants it."

Xabene looked from her companion to the elderly but potent figure before her. "The dragon tome is mine!"

To their surprise, Shade simply walked toward them. Wellen quickly stepped aside. The enraged enchantress, confused by the peculiar action, finally stepped away just before Shade would have walked into her. The shadowy warlock continued on a few more feet until he was at the edge of where the citadel had been. He went down on one knee and studied the grass with avid interest.

"A masterful piece of work. Worthy of him."

Despite circumstances, Wellen was interested. "Worthy of who?"

"The gnome, of course."

A movement by Xabene drew the explorer's attention. In horror, he watched as she stretched out her hand and pointed at the shrouded backside of Shade.

"Xa—" was as far as he managed before her spell was unleashed.

With perfect timing, Shade raising a single gloved finger. Xabene's attack faded with only a spark to mark its brief existence.

"There will be no more of that," the kneeling figure commented in an absent manner, still studying the ground. "For Master Bedlam's sake, I will forgive it this once."

The disheveled sorceress began to shake. She looked at Wellen with sudden pleading in her eyes. He frowned, not understanding her growing fear, and joined her. To his further consternation, Xabene fell against him and started crying.

"What is it? What's wrong?" he whispered. There was no reason to include Shade in this, whatever it might be.

"She has failed her masters," the hooded warlock interjected. He rose, his back still to them as he surveyed the field. "They will, of course, see that she pays appropriately for that failure. This is, after all, a very important task and they do not generally take failure well. Still, do not take all of her anguish to heart. She's hardly given up."

Xabene's shivering had grown worse as Shade had talked. Her tears had lessened, though. She looked up at Wellen, gave him a shadow of her seductress's smile, and then focused on the cold figure of the ancient warlock.

"Who are you that you know so much? Who are you that thinks you can best the gods?"

Grimacing, Wellen quickly whispered, "Take care! He's mad!"

"They are no more gods than I am." Shade faced them.

"Their power—" began the scholar.

"Has its limits. You may trust me on that." He cocked his head to one side, almost resembling a Seeker. "They and I are related, as a matter of fact, though neither side is willing to admit it at times. We also have a tendency to forget, it being so long."

His explanation was hardly what she had expected. "How could you—"

"Cousins, actually. Perhaps half brothers in some cases. Father... he had a tendency to... share."

Wellen, mind busy in what was so far a futile attempt to find a way to extricate the two of them from Shade's hands, recognized the telltale signs of the aged warlock's insanity seizing control again. Shade was beginning to drift back in time.

"Xabene." He tried to keep his voice as low as possible, hoping that she would be able to understand him and that Shade, in his present state, would not pay attention regardless of his exceptional hearing. "Forget what I said earlier. Teleport us away from here now!"

He was gratified to see her nod slightly. She, too, realized that this situation was beyond her abilities, especially if all the master warlock had said were true.

Xabene tensed in his arms and then—

Nothing. Nothing, save that Shade was walking up to them and Wellen discovered that he... and Xabene... could not move so much as a finger.

"I think we should go elsewhere to discuss this further," the warlock suggested offhandedly. This close, even the shadows could not hide the fact of his parchment skin. He looked ready to crackle. "There will be others along shortly and they will raise a fuss."

The Dragon King! The reptilian monarch of this land would surely know of the catastrophe before very long, unless, of course, he knew already. The choice was not one that he would have preferred to face, but Wellen decided that departing with Shade certainly had to be better than awaiting the scaly presence of the angry drake lord.

"I'm not going anywhere with you!" Xabene swore.

"Then you may remain here, if that is your desire." He stretched out a hand toward Wellen. "Come, Master Bedlam."

"I won't"—Wellen discovered himself now standing *next* to Shade—"leave her!" he sputtered, mentally cursing teleportation and its misuses.

"Wellen!" The enchantress, also released from the movement spell, rushed to his side. Whatever her goals, she evidently did not want to separate herself from him. He wondered how much of it had to do with fear for herself because of her failure and how much had to do with the chance that she still might be able to redeem herself in the eyes of her masters if she remained with Wellen and Shade. Possibly she was evenly split; the short scholar *still* had no delusions about her attraction to him. What did he have to offer?

"We all go together then." The corners of the warlock's mouth crooked upward at the sight of the twosome holding one another for reassurance. Shade seemed most coherent when he had an audience or something that particularly piqued his interest. If not for his indifferent attitude toward the lives and deaths of others, Wellen might almost have been able to like him. As it was, the best he could do was again pity the aged spellcaster.

The shrouded figure began to curl within himself. It was something he had always done prior to teleporting himself, but this was the first time that Wellen had actually paid attention to it. He wondered if that was the way he had looked when the hooded warlock had teleported him.

A force tugged at the duo, Shade's spell pulling them in. Bedlam and the enchantress held one another tight, if only because neither of them cared for the idea of entrusting themselves to their spectral companion. Wellen thought the spell was drawn out much more than it had been in the past and wondered what Shade might be doing differently. He glanced back up at the warlock.

Shade, twisted sideways in a manner that turned the anxious scholar's stomach, froze . . . and *untwisted* with a scream.

The cloth-enshrouded figure crumpled to the ground, his spell dissipating even before his face struck the grassy earth. At the same time, Wellen felt a heavy weight he had not noticed earlier lift from his mind. A cold shiver passed through him as he realized what it might be. He looked down at the motionless form.

"What happened to him?" Xabene separated herself from Wellen and took a tentative step toward Shade. She leaned forward and studied the warlock.

"I think . . ." It was insane, but he could see no other explanation. "I think *I* might have fought him off."

"You?" The enchantress rose and inspected him, trying to see something that neither she nor Wellen had noticed before. "You think you stopped him?"

Her disbelief was reasonable. He shrugged. "When he started to collapse, I felt different, as if something had been accomplished or . . ." The confused man spread his hands in surrender. "I cannot explain exactly how I felt. It just makes sense somehow. I knew that I wanted his spell to fail. The thought of teleporting again . . ."

"Perhaps you have something there. Now that I think of it, I thought I sensed a difference in you, but my first notion was that it was just an effect of his sorcery." She dared to prod the still form with her foot. "His power . . . so different, yet still like theirs . . ."

Her masters. Shade had spoken about them, called them *kin* of all things. The idea that Xabene followed such masters repulsed him. What had she spouted after the disappearance of the citadel? *Lords of the Dead?* His eyes flashed to the two horses, still standing quietly exactly where the duo had left them. Wellen's hands curled as he thought of the flesh he had touched. Now he understood.

A horrible thought sprouted from that memory. Could Xabene be like the horses?

He stared at her pale skin, such a contrast to her raven-black hair and the dark gown she wore. Impossible. There was too much vibrance in her, even if most of it worked to trick men into doing her bidding. She could never be one of the walking dead.

She caught him staring at her and, despite the situation, smiled. It was not a smile that beguiled, but rather one that he thought was tinged with open pleasure at his interest in her. Again, though, Wellen could not forget that the enchantress had already proven herself competent at playacting.

"There's nothing more to be gained here." Xabene glared at the innocent-looking field. "I can't sense it anywhere. Are you certain that it wasn't you?"

"No, but he was." He wondered what they would do with the warlock. Leave him? Abandoning an unconscious Shade to the whims of the Dragonrealm did not appeal to the explorer. There was also the thought that the ancient warlock, should he escape harm, would immediately set off after them.

"Him. Should we find some peace for a time, I would like to hear about the circumstances of your acquaintance. You seemed to have forgotten to tell me earlier."

He met her reprimand with one of his own. "As you seem to have forgotten your masters."

Xabene bit her lip. "No, I could never forget them. They, on the other hand, might be more than willing to forget about me."

"For failing?"

"I never have before. I never thought I *could*. It was so perfect!"

His head was throbbing harder. Turning his gaze to the sky, he scanned the region. At last, Wellen discovered a tiny dot on the northern horizon, one that was rapidly growing larger.

"Xabene, whatever our differences, they can wait. I think we have to leave—*fast*."

"You sense something?" From her tone, she had not. Wellen was vaguely interested to note how his sorcerous abilities, however limited, occasionally proved themselves superior to those of much more powerful spellcasters. He tucked the fact away for later contemplation. Their lives were what mattered now.

"I sense *and* see something. Look north."

She obeyed. "I don't . . . no . . . I do see it."

"Dragon?"

"I wish it were only that simple. Try *dragons*!"

Squinting proved Xabene was correct. There were three of them. They flew in a formation, much the way birds did, with the flock leader in the front.

"Wellen." Since Shade's intrusion, she had gone back to speaking to him in more familiar terms. Whether that was good or bad was something only time would reveal. "Whatever has come between us, I agree that we are together in this at least. You were the one able to overcome our friend here; can you also summon up a portal or teleport us away from here before it is too late?"

"What about you?" The thought of trying to perform a conscious spell, something he had really yet to do, unsettled him. "Shade is no barrier now. Your powers—"

"Are not sufficient. I tried at the moment he collapsed, hoping to take us away before he recovered. Instead, I found my abilities reduced to almost nothing." She glared at the prone figure in bitterness. "Much the way they were *before* I made my pact."

It was up to him, then. "All right. Any suggestions?"

"It differs with everyone, but this might help. Think of us elsewhere. Pick a place you know and trust. A stable place."

Pick a place he knew? He was a stranger in this land. When had he had time to become familiar with *any* part of this realm? Wellen looked around in frustration, trying to stir an idea to the surface.

He caught sight of the hills to the east. Their unreal uniformity was something he could never forget.

"I have it. The hills."

"Then think of us there. Wish that we were there. That is all I can tell you. The rest happens within your mind."

The would-be warlock tried. He pictured the symmetrical hills and tried to recall various parts of the range. Choosing one, Wellen formed an image of himself and Xabene standing there, safe and sound.

Nothing happened. After several precious seconds, he shook his head. "What now?"

Her eyes on the rapidly approaching leviathans, Xabene suggested, "The horses . . ."

Both their mounts were gone. Neither Wellen nor the sorceress could recall when the beasts had vanished. Xabene was particularly upset. "They've abandoned me! I failed them and this is my reward!"

Running would have been futile. Wellen doubted that even the horses would have been fast enough to escape the soaring drakes. Were they just to stand there, then? What else was there?

It came to him. "Can you cast illusion?"

She understood. "I might be able to do that. We have to huddle together, though. The less space I have to cover, the better."

Wellen nodded and walked over to Shade.

"What do you think you're doing?" Xabene demanded.

"He doesn't deserve to lie here helpless. He could have killed you rather than muted your spells. Besides, we might need Shade to help us later. If you cannot accept that, think how much more carefully they'll search this area if they find him."

His pointed was not arguable. With some distaste, she joined the explorer and took hold of the unconscious warlock. "It will be better if we kneel or sit."

"We do not have much time remaining."

"I know." She closed her eyes. A breath or two later, she opened them again. A triumphant smile played on her full lips. "I've done it!"

Wellen, who still saw the three of them sitting . . . in *Shade's* case, lying . . . in the middle of the field, frowned, not having noticed anything. "I don't see any change!"

"*We* are not the ones who should, but you can feel it, can't you?"

"Feel?" Concentrating, he did finally notice it. A tingling, much like what he had felt just before the citadel had vanished, but almost unnoticeable. In fact, Bedlam had to concentrate hard just to continue sensing it.

"Now," Xabene said, moving closer to him, "we have to hope it fools *them*!"

Even as she whispered, the dragons, reptilian visages twisted in fury, swooped down toward the field.

X

One fear that Wellen had tried to stop thinking about was that even if the dragons did not notice them, one of them might decide to *land* upon the very bit of ground that the hapless humans had chosen for their spell. That, fortunately, proved not to be the case. The nearest drake was more than twice its length from the still figures.

If there *was* a problem, it lay in that the trio were within the triangle formed by the three behemoths. None of the drakes wanted to be too close to where the building had stood, just in case it came back, Wellen supposed.

They were giants. Wellen's scholarly curiosity came into play even while part of him prayed for a quick and painless end if he and the others were caught. The drakes had jaws capable of easily swallowing a horse and rider and sharp, daggerlike teeth stained by the bloody meat diet their kind preferred. Their claws looked strong and deadly enough to tear apart mountainsides, which made it more amazing that the citadel had looked unmarred by battle. At least two of them were larger than the leviathan that had slaughtered the column. The third could not have been much smaller. All three were of the same coloring, a dark green mixed with hints of purple. On the dragons, it was actually a beautiful color, especially when the sunlight caused their scales to glitter a bit.

He forgot all about colors and scales when the smallest of the three *spoke*. "It issss asss feared! There issss no trace!"

Wellen almost smiled, so fascinated by the sights and sounds. This was the first time he had actually heard one of the monsters talk like a man. The dragon that had killed Yalso had laughed, if the scholar recalled correctly, but had never really talked much, if at all.

Thought of the friendly sea captain and all those others that had perished turned the would-be smile to a scowl.

"But it wassss here!" roared another. An old scar ran across its torso, one that indicated a wound almost mortal, for it looked as if it had run long and deep. That the dragon had lived to see it heal spoke of the fate of the one who had caused the wound.

A sudden, low groan by Wellen's side made him tense.

"Wassss there ssssomething I heard?" asked the short one, raising its head to listen.

"I heard nothing," muttered the third.

Shade was beginning to stir. Wellen matched frantic glances with Xabene.

"It wassss ssssomething!" insisted the smaller one. His stature in no way detracted from his leadership. The other dragons clearly respected his power.

The three menacing beasts twisted their heads around and began to scan the field. The eyes of the scarred one glanced over to where the trio hid, but did not stop.

The waking sorcerer shifted.

"Ssssomething?" roared the smaller one, its burning eyes focusing on a point just a few paces to Wellen's right.

"Nothing." The one with the scar clearly wanted to be gone from this place. "There issss *nothing* here."

Xabene's hand came down and covered Shade's mouth just as the warlock was about to mutter something. His eyes flashed open, gleaming crystalline orbs that almost made the enchantress, who had never seen them unshadowed, cry out. She was able to smother it at the last moment.

This time, they were fortunate. The drakes had not noted anything.

"He will not be pleassssed!"

"What elsssse can we do? There issss nothing! Perhaps the gnome hasss destroyed hissss infernal sssself!"

"Would that sssssuch were true," agreed the leader.

The dragon with the great scar abruptly raised its head. "I ssssmell manlingssss!"

A shift in the wind. Neither Wellen nor Xabene had counted on that. The scholar silently cursed his stupidity. A boy on his first hunt would have known to prepare for such a situation.

The other behemoths sniffed.

"I smell nothing!" argued the third.

"It issss the gnome'ssss doing!" hissed the leader. "A ploy to confuse ussss while he furtherssss hissss plotssss!"

They were taking much too long. Although Shade was

awake enough to be aware of the danger, Wellen doubted that
the warlock would remain complacent for more than a few
minutes, shorter, if his madness flared.

If they would only finish their search and depart! he thought,
eyeing the smaller dragon, whose decision was the one upon
which their lives hinged. If only that creature would satisfy
itself and give up! There was nothing for them to see. Wellen
knew that all too well.

He felt a tug.

Wellen blinked, and found himself facing two dragons.

"What ailssss you?" one of them, the *scarred* one, hissed
anxiously.

The explorer, stunned, eyed first the one who had spoken,
then the other, who looked as frantic as Wellen felt. As for the
third, the leader, he was . . . he was . . .

He was *Wellen*.

I've leaped into its mind! Unlike the first time, when he had
touched the thoughts of the dragon in the sky, Bedlam had
complete control. There were no thoughts of puny humans and
how well they might taste. He was himself. How long that
would last and what happened afterward were two very good
questions, but Wellen had been given an opportunity that he
dared not miss.

"There is no more to be seen here!" Belatedly, he recalled
how the dragons had a tendency to hiss. "If the gnome issss
gone, it issss our lord who issss besssst suited to find him!"

It proved easy to convince them. In what might have been a
flash of insight from his host's mind, Wellen realized that all
three leviathans feared the might of the gnarled gnome. That
said much for the tiny sorcerer's power, that *three* such as these
would fear to face his sorcery together.

With a swiftness that almost caught him napping, the other
two drakes lifted into the air. The wind created by their vast
wings stormed over the field. Wellen wondered how the others
were taking it, then realized that he was still trapped inside the
dragon's body. Unless he wanted to live his life out as one of
the beasts, Bedlam had to find a way back or—

No sooner was the desire made known than Wellen found
himself clutching onto Xabene and even Shade as the three
behemoths rose higher and higher into the heavens. The wind
threw grass and dust all about, nearly choking the humans.
Even Shade seemed disinclined to do more than cover himself,

easier for the warlock with his expansive cloak, and wait for things to settle.

Gradually, the situation did. The wind became no more than a light breeze again and the dust and grass returned to the earth from which they had been torn. As for the dragons, they were already far to the north of the field by the time Wellen and Xabene looked up.

It was also at this time that they noticed that the third member of their party was no longer huddled beside them.

"You have my gratitude," Shade said, standing over them. He might have been talking about some minor gift they had given him, so disinterested did he sound. The warlock peered around at the open field. "So the drakes are at a loss, too."

Xabene was silent, perhaps measuring her chances against Shade, but Wellen was not going to wait for the ancient sorcerer to make their decisions for them. He had shown the master warlock that he could be entrusted with his life; now he intended to show the hooded titan that he could be respected and listened to, also.

Strengthening his resolve, he stood before Shade. "You just thanked me. I don't think you realize just how much you owe to us."

The near smile returned to the undead countenance, but no words escaped the lips to condemn Wellen for his impertinence. Shade was amused at the very least.

Wellen pushed on. "You lay unconscious, my doing, I admit—"

"Yours?" He had the warlock's interest now. The smile was not so deprecating anymore.

"Mine." The novice spellcaster waved it aside as something that could be discussed later, when he had finally had an opportunity to try to puzzle it all out for himself. "What matters is that we could have easily left you there, helpless, for the drakes to discover! The Dragon King would have found you most interesting considering what had happened here!"

"Indeed." Shade's gaze drifted to Xabene, who had come to stand behind and to one side of the angry scholar. Her left hand rested on Wellen's shoulder. "You have forever forsaken your masters now, female. I am the one being they can never forgive you for saving. Had the dragons seized me, they might have even forgiven you for losing the gnome and the book."

Xabene did not say anything, for which Wellen was appreciative, but the crushing strength with which she grasped his shoulder was a sure indication that the weary enchantress had not considered that.

The warlock returned his attention to the short figure before him. Standing face to half-face, Wellen knew that even if he had been of a more normal stature, he still would have not quite stood at eye level with the cloth-enshrouded titan. Shade was several inches above average and had such a commanding presence that he seemed even taller.

"You are correct in part it seems, Master Bedlam. I owe you, but not for simply saving my existence." Shade reached up and pulled back the hood. His glittering eyes flashed into and out of existence as he blinked in the sunlight. Xabene inhaled sharply, still not used to the sight. Wellen, too, found the eyes arresting. Who *was* Shade that he looked so? There was the name, Gerrod, but that hardly explained anything about the man. He was not even certain the name was a true one. That he had known legends also said something about him, but hardly enough.

Who was the man?

The warlock brushed hair back from his eyes. "I owe you for something just as essential to me. For the past few years it has become increasingly difficult to retain my mind. I've seen *so* much time go by, but so slowly! It has a withering effect, I can tell you."

And through nearly all of it you've been alone. The scholar was amazed that Shade had retained as much of his sanity as he had.

"You are an anchor, Master Bedlam, an anchor that has enabled me to plant my feet firmly on the ground again. Part of it was due to the simple fact that I pursued you, thus giving myself active purpose. That was minor, however. In truth, what drew me back more than anything else was seeing myself . . . in *you*."

"This is all very pretty," Xabene interrupted. Her hand continued to squeeze Wellen's shoulder. She was nervous about remaining here and he could not blame her for being that way. "But there must be a better time and place to discuss this than in this field."

"Indeed there is." Shade pulled the hood forward without thinking. Wellen felt as if some gate had been shut. For only the space of a few breaths, he had captured a glimpse of the man behind the shadows. Now, the master warlock, the mask, stood before him. "And I shall take us *all* there, since no one else seems able."

Shade started to curl within himself, then paused. He glanced at Wellen, an appraising look spread across the portion of his visage that the explorer could see. "You have far greater potential than I imagined, Master Bedlam."

"What do you mean?"

"I find I still cannot teleport no matter which variation of the spell I try. You seem to have anchored me *too* well to the earth."

With neither Wellen nor Xabene able to cast such a spell themselves, Shade was their only hope. "Do I need to remove whatever I did?"

"That would be kind."

He tried to think of the spell being removed. Vaguely, Wellen saw a spectrum of colors that seemed to beckon to him, but when he tried to reach out with his thoughts, the spectrum vanished.

Shade shook his head. "It appears that we are destined to walk."

"We could summon something," the novice warlock suggested, trying to make up for his mistake. As a scholar and researcher with some success over the past few years, he had forgotten what it felt like to be a first-year student. The Dragonrealm had brought all those humiliating memories back a thousandfold.

"Risky, Master Bedlam. At this point, we're liable to summon back our scaly friends. No, walking is our best bet. The only thing that remains now is a destination." Shade frowned in thought. "My own sanctum, I regret to say, is both much too far away and too dangerous to reach from here. We would have to cross the clan caverns of Purple, who would be delighted to see all of us. A shame, Mito Pica is beyond that and west of Mito Pica is the Dagora Forest. We could find aid there."

Xabene was aghast at the idea. "Dagora Forest! The Green Dragon rules there!"

"Yes, I know. His line has always proved a benevolent one where humanity is concerned."

"I will not willingly place myself in the claws of *any* Dragon King!"

The warlock laughed, a raspy sound. "You have a spirit much in common with one I knew in my youthful days! Then *where*, my lady, do you desire to go? We have already spent much too much time jabbering with one another! Purple himself may return here before long, and he and your former masters were hardly the only ones interested in the gnome's treasures!''

"There's the tree." Wellen stared down Xabene, who flashed dagger eyes at him for betraying her secret place to the fearsome warlock. "We really don't have a choice, Xabene."

"Not anymore," she snarled. Despite her anger, the enchantress did not argue. "We could probably make it there just after nightfall."

"A tree?" It was clear that Shade desired to ask questions, but the spellcaster held back, likely because he and Wellen both knew that Xabene would not readily volunteer answers.

Although it was Xabene who led the trio, she being the only one who knew exactly where the tree was, it was Wellen who found himself in command. Neither of his companions trusted one another very far, but both had faith in the outsider. Wellen had proved himself time and again. Trust was evidently a rare and precious commodity in the Dragonrealm.

The walk was not so strenuous at first. Xabene had the worst of it; though she still moved with astonishing grace, she was no longer immune to the landscape. Things scratched her legs now and snagged on her clothing. As the journey progressed, she became more tight-lipped. Wellen began to understand just how much of her power had been granted to her by the mysterious Lords of the Dead. Without their favor, Xabene had little more ability than he did.

For all that the enchantress had lost, Wellen found her even more desirable that ever. He knew why; she had lost none of her beauty, but now she seemed *human*. Little things affected her. Xabene no longer passed through the world. She was now a part of it.

They contemplated running, but a near fall by Wellen quickly squashed that suggestion. The nigh uniform look of the grassy plains hid the fact that there were treacherous gullies and holes. It was amazing that the horses had not thrown them at some point, but then the creatures had been more than they had seemed. The Lords of the Dead had probably calculated for worse dangers than uneven ground.

Shade ever remained behind them, keeping pace but never catching up. *He* might have been out for a stroll. He had no trouble with footing and neither the grass nor the insect life sought his attention. Wellen, who could not make his abilities work for him in regard to the infestation problem, envied the warlock. What made it worse was that the sun, quite triumphant in its efforts to heat up the world, had also failed to touch Shade.

It hardly seemed fair.

There was still no sign of activity. Each moment, Wellen expected hordes of dragons or flocks of batlike creatures to come swooping down. The latter especially bothered him. It was not just that the three of them would be hard pressed to defend themselves in the open field. What bothered the scholar more was a realization that the woman beside him had once been a servant of the same masters who controlled the winged terrors. He had not forgotten the slaughtered scouts or the massacred Seekers. There was no doubt now that Xabene must have known, too, possibly even plotted the second attack.

What other horrors was she responsible for?

"We have trouble," the enchantress warned. Wellen was almost grateful, for now the answer to his question could be safely put off for a time.

Riders were approaching. At least a dozen. They were small figures in the distance, but they obviously were heading toward the trio. A banner fluttered above the newcomers, but it was impossible to make out in the wind caused by their passage.

Wellen's first impulse was to run. He had only the knife and a few untrustworthy magical abilities. Run where though? The closest shelter was a clump of trees a hundred or so yards to the south and it was hardly sufficient to hide or protect them from the determined horsemen. There was nowhere, in fact, where the trio could escape before the riders caught up to them. The newcomers were familiar with the land, that was evident in the easy manner in which they navigated the plains without falling prey to the many hidden gullies.

"We have to make a stand here," he informed his companions. "Unless we split up. It might be that one of us could get away."

"Not likely," Xabene countered. "Not with at least four riders apiece to chase us down." Her hands opened and closed, the frustration of no longer having the power to deal trouble to her enemies tearing at her. "Repeating the illusion would not do any good, either. They've seen us and I do not doubt that at least one of them has some sorcerous ability. They will be ready for most any trick that I can still muster."

"We will do nothing."

They looked at Shade, who calmly walked up to them, then continued past until he had the lead. "We will do nothing at all."

"He's betrayed us!" the pale woman snarled. Xabene looked ready to take the master warlock on no matter how great the imbalance of ability between the two.

"Be silent and observe." The tall, hooded figure took up a stance of authority, his voluminous cloak fluttering loosely in a wind that seemed stronger around him than it did anywhere else.

Wellen knew they had no choice. Shade had volunteered his services and the other two could only hope that he knew what he was doing. The scholar had not seen any lapses in sanity so far since the ancient warlock had woken; that, he hoped, was a good sign.

The riders were close enough now that Wellen could see they were soldiers. Most were clad in a cloth-and-chain combination of armor. The patrol leader, a large, black man with graying hair, wore a more elaborate chain-and-plate outfit. A purple cape danced behind him. Wellen did not have to ask which human solders would be allowed such free access in this region. Only those who served the lord of the land. A glimpse of the full banner verified all too well that assumption, for he saw a winged, masterful drake posed in triumph. The leviathan was clearly purple.

He began to fear that he had overestimated Shade's sanity. The warlock was asking them to wait to be captured by men serving the Purple Dragon.

Xabene had come to a similar conclusion. Pulling Wellen back a step, she whispered, "He's mad! Why else wait to be captured by servants of a deadly enemy? Look! He has no intention of fighting! With his power, I could have killed them all!"

"Which makes it fortunate, does it not, that I am the only one with the ability to do so," the shadowy spellcaster called back. Both of them had forgotten Shade's uncanny hearing. "Rest easy, though. You have my word that I know what I am doing."

The promise had little effect on either Wellen or Xabene. The explorer doubted that Shade was even concerned about their misgivings. He had given his word and that was that. They would have to trust him.

"We've little choice in the matter," Wellen reminded her. "If he wanted to betray us, he could have done so much earlier. Why give us to the patrol when he could have easily turned us over to the Dragon King's own kind?"

"Why indeed?" Shade asked, his back turned to them. He calmly watched as the riders spread out in a manner meant to cut off escape. Bedlam tried his best to look as unconcerned, but the surly visages that began to surround them would have made it nigh impossible for the bravest of men to not reveal at least a little uncertainty.

The patrol leader urged his bay charger toward Shade, not stopping until the mount's flaring nostrils were almost in the warlock's shadowy visage. Shade gave the rider and animal the same expression of indifference that he had given to Wellen and Xabene earlier.

"Master Shade." The black man nodded in respect. He had a short, well-groomed beard and an aristocratic countenance. In comparison to the four other dark-skinned men in his party, he was night itself.

I am surrounded by shadows, Wellen could not help thinking. Compared to Shade, Xabene, and now this man, he looked positively colorful in his simple green and brown clothing. Everyone else was black, white, and *Shades*—the pun could not be resisted—of gray.

The late Prentiss Asaalk would have stood out like a flower in the desert.

"Benton Lore. Commander." Shade added the rank after a disappointed expression began creeping over Lore's face.

"I'd not been expecting to see you again, sirrah. Three years it has been since last we were in this position. I gather it is you who are the cause of our routine being disturbed."

"Not this time."

"No?" Lore gazed at Wellen and the enchantress. Not surprisingly, he spent more of the time studying Xabene. "You will, of course, explain all of this to me . . . and my lord."

The meticulous politeness was becoming too much for the explorer. Why was the warlock on such terms with a servant, a traitorous *human* servant, of the Purple Dragon?

The patrol leader studied his chief captive again. "You seem . . . more fit."

"It is the company I've been keeping."

Lore misunderstood, his eyes briefly flashing to Xabene, who scowled back. "And such splendid company!"

"Careful," Shade teased. "She has killed men for less than making that assumption."

"Well can I believe that." Lore leaned forward in the saddle. "May I ask how you escaped the notice of the three drakes? I must admit I was surprised to discover you here after they departed."

"In time, we all meet again."

It was refreshing to the scholar to see someone other than himself perplexed by the warlock's inscrutability. "If you ... say so." The soldier straightened again. "I will not bother to try to decipher that response. Oh, by the way, you are my prisoners, sirrah."

"Of course. You have my bond."

The commander was satisfied with that. "And your friends? Their bonds?"

Shade shrugged. "Of Master Bedlam, I can promise you a word of honor. Of the female ... I can promise you that she'll remain with him. No more than that, though."

Benton Lore snapped his fingers. One of the men began unlooping rope from the back of his saddle. "Then she will have to be properly bound."

"What?" Xabene's eyes first grew round as the moons, then as narrow as a dagger on its side, not to mention as sharp as the selfsame weapon. She was all set to summon up what little skill was left to her and teach the soldier a lasting lesson.

Wellen seized the rising hand and forced it down. He matched gazes with Commander Lore and, to his hidden pleasure, forced the other man to look away, if only for a second. "I'll be responsible for her. There's no need for the rope."

The massive officer chuckled. "You may change your mind before long, Master ... Bedlam, was it not, sirrah? Very well, I accept your bond for her, also."

At a nod from Lore, the man who had been unwinding rope returned it to the saddle. The patrol leader then pointed at Shade and Wellen. Several riders broke from the ring, two converging on the scholar. Each one grabbed him by an arm and lifted. Wellen found himself deposited on the back end of one of the large mounts. He saw that the same had happened to the warlock.

Benton Lore, in an amazing show of strength, pulled Xabene up and almost threw her over the front of his saddle. At the last second, he allowed her to slip into a sitting position. The enchantress had death written on her face, but Lore only laughed. "You would tempt many a man, Milady Xabene, tempt or terrorize them!"

As her hand came up, the dark man caught her wrist. The smile took on a slightly taunting atmosphere. "Temper, temper, milady! You would ruin your fine nails on my tough hide! Lest you think your spells would do you better, let Master Shade yonder tell you otherwise!"

"You would be wise to listen to him, child," the hooded warlock chastised. "Commander Lore has a bit of talent of his own."

"He has no streak of silver in his hair!" she argued, not wanting to give the soldier any more advantage over the trio than he already had.

"I am, milady, a bit of a confusing situation for my friend Shade here . . . for my master, too. Rather than explain, I ask that both you and Master Bedlam inspect my graying hair.

Both of them stared uncertainly at Lore's head. At first, Wellen saw only the coming of the elder years. Then, he noticed what was almost a twinkle. Trying not to slip from the horse, he leaned forward for a better view.

Lore turned his head to the side. Wellen again saw the twinkle and this time knew what it meant. "There's silver in your hair," he blurted, "but it's scattered about like little *bits!*"

"I prefer to think of it as 'peppered,' but, yes, that is more or less correct, Master Bedlam."

"Showing that even the 'gods' are not perfect." Shade seemed to find much satisfaction in that, the explorer noticed, almost as if he had known those very gods he spoke of . . . known and cared little for.

"So"—Lore made certain that Xabene was secure—"if there is no other reason to delay, it is time to leave this place."

One of the other soldiers, apparently the commander's second, ordered the riders into a more military formation and then faced them northwest. When the patrol was ready, Benton Lore gave the signal to advance.

A short distance into their journey, Wellen began to have suspicions about Commander Benton Lore and his men. It was not just because of his inexplicable relationship with the aged warlock, although that was a good part of it, but also the officer's choice of routes out of the gnome's former domain. Once clear of the field, the party made no attempt to turn due north, the direction that the dragons had indicated was where their infernal monarch awaited. Bedlam was certain that the Dragon King would have desired to question the three humans as soon as possible. Any delay was likely to cost those responsible, yet Lore was heading farther and farther away.

Why?

Although on the surface it was a ridiculous gamble, the scholar leaned close to the guard he was riding with and asked, "Where are we going?"

The man did not respond, but his eyes narrowed as if Wellen's question had hit too close to the truth. *Only I have no idea what that truth is!*

Xabene was more or less hidden by Lore's expansive backside, but Wellen could see Shade, who rode a little ahead on his right. His visage remained hidden by the wide hood of his cloak regardless of the gusty wind caused by the patrol's quick pace. Nonetheless, the warlock's body radiated a sense of satisfaction with the present situation.

What lay northwest of their location? Xabene had given him vague lessons in the geography of the Dragonrealm, but most of those lessons had melted away. The veteran scholar tried to recall the maps he had been shown. Unfortunately, only a few names came to mind, most off in the wrong directions. Lochivar was the mist-enshrouded land to the east; far, far north of it was Irillian By The Sea, the city that the gnome had supposedly ravaged centuries earlier. Mito Pica, the thriving village that Shade had dragged him to was more or less north, although it might be west enough to be their destination. He doubted that, however.

His head, strangely enough, disturbed him very little. If the signs were to be believed, he was in less danger now than he had been when the trio had been walking. Wellen wanted to accept that, but found it impossible to do so. There were so *many* things he found impossible to accept. The list, he thought, must surely stretch longer than his arm.

At least we aren't teleporting, Wellen thought, trying to boost his morale. It was not the greatest of comforts, but it was one of the few he had at the moment.

Then a massive hole in the very air opened wide, right before the racing charger of Benton Lore.

In the comfort of his sanctum, the gnome laughed as he observed the havoc and consternation his spell had caused among those who would have his secrets. Dragons in a panic and humans racing hither and thither. Would-be gods afraid to step upon the very world they desired to rule.

"*Children!* All of them . . . nothing but children! They cannot even see what lies under their noses!"

He leaned back and once more observed. The best, the wizened sorcerer knew, was yet to come.

XI

"It seemssss that you will forever be a thorn in my sssside, warlock!"

The Dragon King was a horribly magnificent being, so large that he was forced to lie nearly flat on the cavern floor in order to speak to the small band of humans brought before him. His eyes were fiery red and, in the glow of the torches his servants had placed about the chamber, his scaly form glittered like the stars on a clear night. Each paw could have enveloped a horse.

He was everything the other dragons were and more. He radiated majesty and power. When he moved, it was with a grace that a creature of his form and bulk should have been denied.

Only . . . the Dragon King before Wellen and his companions was not purple in any way, but rather *emerald green*.

"I have never attempted to disturb you, Your Majesty," Shade returned with politeness. "Our paths have only crossed in times of necessity."

"Necessssity on your part, *not* mine!" Nevertheless, the Dragon King smiled. Xabene unconsciously pressed her side against the scholar's and he, in turn swallowed hard at the toothy sight. "Sssstill, you may be of ssssome usssse to me thissss—this time!"

"I live to serve." The master warlock bowed.

"Or be sssserved."

Wellen chose the moment to observe Benton Lore. The soldier had removed his cloak and donned a new one upon arrival here. Green dominated the garment. The banner standing tall over the patrol also had changed; it now bore the stylized image of a proud, almost *thoughtful* dragon.

They were in the domain of the Green Dragon. That was the Dagora Forest. Northwest of the field, but much farther than a day's swift ride. This was the drake lord that Shade had called sympathetic to humans.

The portal had been the work of Benton Lore. The disguises he and his men had worn would have only served to momentarily fool a true servant of the Dragon King Purple, and so the patrol had planned to be in and out of the region once they found out what they wanted to know. Unfortunately or fortunately, depending on how one looked at it, Lore had sensed Shade and the others. He had judged rightly that the shadowy warlock and his companions would garner his master much more information than the patrol could have obtained in such limited time. More important, it meant getting out with their skins intact, always desirable for any sane spy.

The cavern of the Green Dragon was much like the one Shade lived in, save that it seemed more alive. The warlock's citadel had reflected its master; it resembled more a ghost of the past, a memory. There had been nothing there that sparkled with life. It was a gray place for a gray figure. Not so this cavern. While that might have been in part to the bustling activity and someone's attempt to decorate the carved-out chamber with amenities a human noble would have appreciated—sculptures and the like—it had more to do with the smells. Benton Lore had explained that the dragons here had a slightly different system and so methane, not sulfur, tainted the air.

"I must admit," the warlock was saying, "that I had not expected to sense Commander Lore nearby just when we needed his services."

The dragon acknowledged Lore with what was an almost affectionate nod. "The commander is a very valued servant. He looked at the situation, saw what needed to be done, and performed his duty in exemplary fashion."

They were all quick to note the change in their host's voice. The Dragon King was being very precise in his speech, as if the sibilance that was common among the dragons embarrassed him.

"Quite a coincidence that he should be riding under the banner of your brother at the time."

"Quite." The short, succinct response informed them that the drake lord wanted no more said on that subject. Spying on the domain of a fellow Dragon King probably had worse potential repercussions than if one human monarch had spied upon another. The lords of the Dragonrealm were not afraid to use their might, whatever the consequences.

"I don't like this at all!" the enchantress whispered. "They're all too polite!"

Green chuckled. Had he heard Xabene?" "As I said, it may be that you can serve me, warlock. Lore has told me what he knows already. Now, you tell me what happened to the gnome. Tell me what you did."

As politely as it was requested, no one doubted that the Dragon King was to be obeyed or else. Wellen only hoped Shade's mind continued to function in the present. It would not do for him to start drifting just when it appeared their lives might be in danger.

The warlock was far from mad at the moment, however, Bedlam discovered just how in control the shadowy figure was when Shade stepped aside and, with a vague smile at the scholar, informed the drake, "You will find Master Bedlam a much more reliable fountain of information than myself."

Wellen blinked, refusing to believe what he knew he had just heard.

"The *outsssssider . . .*" The Dragon King Green's interest made Wellen feel like a rabbit held up before a hungry wolf. He steeled himself. Now that Shade had pushed him before the leviathan, there was no choice but to hope that he would impress the dragon enough to earn his continued existence.

"I am Wellen Bedlam, Your Majesty." He bowed, trying to think of the emerald behemoth as just another noble.

"From across the sea! Fascinating!"

"Yes, my lord." Did the Dragon King sound almost child-like in his enthusiasm?

"You must tell me all about it when things are calmer! I have gathered artifacts and legends that connect your lands and ours, but until your coming, it was only my dream, nothing more!"

This is a dragon? Wellen was both befuddled and bemused. He felt more at ease. However great and ferocious a leviathan this drake lord was, he had interests so very much akin to the scholar's that it almost might have been enjoyable to forget all else and just compare findings.

Benton Lore, perhaps used to this type of behavior, cleared his throat. Green blinked, looked the black man's way, then nodded. "Perhaps later." A puff of smoke escaped the flaring nostrils. "Tell me now, Master Wellen Bedlam, of the gnome, his citadel, and your part in this."

Wellen did, omitting nothing. It might have been an elaborate ploy, but he was tempted to trust the Dragon King more than he had most other beings he had met since the massacre. That the great beast shared his interests in the far past had much to do with it, but Wellen tried not to think that such a reason alone had swayed him. It was also that he sensed almost no danger at all from the emerald monarch. Considering the premonitions he had felt prior to this during various other encounters, a dragon who was little or no threat was something quite easily noticed.

As he spoke, Wellen grew more and more relaxed. He felt again in charge of himself. True, his future was still in the talons of the Dragon King, but the interest with which everyone listened to what he had to say was near enough to make him feel it was so. By the time he was through, Wellen was feeling more like his old self than he had since he had made the terrible mistake of boarding the *Heron's Wing* back home.

The Dragonrealm is my home now, such as it is, he reminded himself. *I have to make it a place I can live or else I'm lost!* There was no doubt in his mind that the remainder of the expedition had either lifted anchor and headed east or had been decimated by one threat or another, most likely by the clans of the Dragon King Purple.

When the scholar was finished, Green addressed Shade again. "And you?"

"I find his account as accurate as any I could give. There is nothing I can add, save that I believe this was the gnome's masterful work. Master Bedlam merely fell prey to his somewhat peculiar sense of humor. The gnome has simply come up with a new way to confound us all."

"It would sssseem strange if he did not. My predecessor was of the belief that the gnome finds this all some ssssort of game. I am inclined to believe that. He acts too precisely, introduces us to his tricks at too perfect a moment, to be doing this haphazardly."

"He was the greatest of his kind," Shade remarked somewhat distantly. For a breath or two, Wellen feared that the warlock's mind was slipping away. The ancient warlock visibly pulled himself together and retreated in the security of his enveloping cloak.

"I must consider all you have told me," the Dragon King declared. "I must also consider what to do about your predicament, Master Shade. It issss humorous that you have been laid low by so untrained a warlock, though."

"It is only my ability to teleport anything to anywhere. My talents for all else are still exceptional."

"I will do what I can for you. I think there is something in one of the tomes I have gathered. This will require much more than simple blink-of-an-eye sorcery." The reptilian monarch raised his head and summoned Commander Lore. "Thesssse three will be my guestssss . . . guests! You will guide Master Shade and the dam to appropriate quarters. Master Bedlam, however, issss to remain with me."

"Wellen!" Xabene refused to budge from his side, seeing in him her only ally. Both of them knew that Lore and the others were fully aware of who *her* masters had been.

"I assure you, Mistress Xabene, you are in no danger whatsoever." Benton Lore smiled at her discomfort. "We will treat you as you deserve."

Now it was Wellen who did not trust the commander. He stood ready to fight the soldier, if necessary, even though Lore outweighed him by a good sixty pounds or so, and all of it well-honed muscle.

"Rest easy, Master Wellen Bedlam." The Dragon King tried to look pleasant, not something he had been born to achieve. Instead, the leviathan looked hungry. "Your female will be treated as an honored guest." He eyed the enchantress. "Sssso long assss she recallssss who issss ssssovereign of thissss realm!"

Bowing to the inevitable, the sultry enchantress took a moment to urgently whisper in Wellen's ear. "See me when you can!"

Taking her arm, Benton Lore led Xabene away. Shade followed behind them. Most of the officer's men formed a very secure "honor guard" around the visitors. The hint was not lost. Xabene went meekly.

When they were alone, save for a few solitary human guards who could only be there for show's sake, the massive head tilted down toward Wellen. "Tell me about your life, human."

More relaxed then before, Bedlam gave him a brief discourse, skipping quickly through his young years, save when his interest in the legends had first arisen, and then concentrating on his time spent in research and studying. He told of his dream, of the actual voyage, the storms, and the pleasure of the expedition when it had at last sighted land. With bitterness, he told of the ill-fated column and its fate.

That part of the tale made the Dragon King hiss in anger. Although Wellen had never met the Green Dragon's counterpart, he felt certain that they were as far apart as could be. What were the others like?

He finished with the attack by the ghoulish, batlike terrors. The drake lord's eyes widened as he spoke of the monsters and the ferocity with which they had slaughtered the avians. It was clear even before he was very far into the tale that the leviathan knew of the creatures.

"The infernal onessss who think themselves godssss sent thosssse monstrossssities after you! The creaturessss are not natural beings! The Nccri are like golems of flesh! They only exist because of the foul necromancy of the Lords of the Dead!" The Dragon King hesitated, then, in a calmer voice added, "You know that your female followed their path of decay. I could smell their tainted touch upon her."

"I know she did. She does not any longer."

"That is ssssomething time will tell."

"Meaning?" Was there something Wellen did not know about Xabene that the drake lord did?

"Meaning many things or nothing at all. Hmmmph! I sound like Shade now! I will not detain you much longer, human. You are in need of sustenance and rest. Besides, there are things I must do myself."

"I haven't minded."

The head cocked to one side. "I am not what you expected, am I?"

Wellen had no trouble with the truth. "You are what I hoped

for, Your Majesty. What I expected . . . I perhaps discovered all too much of.''

''Well said! I find, as the dark one has probably told you, that I have an affinity for your short-lived kind. More so than any of my brethren.''

''Are they all so . . . so different from each other, your . . . brothers?''

That brought a laugh. ''They are . . . and we are not actual brothers, if that is what confuses you. We call one another brethren because we are equals, just as the ancient covenant of the first of our forebears declared. Equal, save that the *Emperor* has final say on all things.'' At the sight of the confusion spreading over the scholar's visage, the Dragon King shook his head. ''Never mind our ways for now, human. Just know that most will tolerate your kind, you being so adaptable to our needs, but only a few actually care. I have worked so that my successor . . . the eldest of my own get . . . will likewise care.''

''If I may ask, why?''

The dragon grew serious. ''Because one before me foresaw a time when it might be humans who control the destiny of the realm . . . and I would have our races live together rather than watch my kind fade away as sssso many racesss did before ussss. So I will impress upon my get and so he who follows me will impress upon his.''

Benton Lore rejoined them. Instead of armor, he wore an elegant, forest-green tunic that ended in a kilt much like that once worn by Prentiss Asaalk. A short sword hung at his side and a cape similar to the one he had worn earlier covered his shoulders and back. ''Your Majesty needed me? I thought I felt your summons.''

''I did, my loyal ssssservant. It is time that Master Wellen Bedlam wassss returned to hissss companions.'' The drake lord's sibilance seemed to grow more pronounced every time he became distracted or emotional, Wellen thought. If not for that, it would have actually been possible for the scholar to forget that he talked to a gigantic, winged beast.

''We will talk again, human. The matter of the gnome and Brother Purple is a priority and we can certainly not forget about the most irritating Lords of the Dead! They have surely not played their last hand!''

There was no gesture of dismissal, but Commander Lore suddenly bowed, indicating with his hand that Wellen should follow suit. When the weary explorer had, Lore turned to him and said, "If you will come with me, sirrah, there are fine quarters awaiting." His voice dropping to a whisper and his face breaking into a smile, the dark-skinned warrior added, "You will also find a volatile but glorious visitor waiting there, too. She has refused to leave until she has seen you again."

Certain that Xabene's concern was more for herself than for him, Wellen did not respond to the latter statements. Instead, he turned back to the Dragon King, who watched them with veiled amusement, and said, "Your Majesty, I look forward to our next discussion."

"As do I," the reptilian monarch rumbled.

With Lore leading, the two humans departed the cavern of the Green Dragon.

Xabene fairly flung herself on him when he entered his new quarters. Benton Lore stayed only long enough to give flustered Wellen a look of barely concealed mirth, then departed.

As soon as he was gone, the enchantress released her hold. She looked at the scholar with a calculating expression. "What did you talk about with the monster?"

"We talked of many things," Bedlam replied, a bit disgusted with her behavior. "I told him about myself. We discussed this land a bit."

"All nicely civil, I suppose."

His anger stirred. "As a matter of fact, it *was*. More civil than this conversation, in fact."

She looked chastised, but he knew better by now. "I *was* worried about you, you know."

"Because I might be all that stands between you and the Green Dragon," he retorted. Wellen studied the room. It had been purposely carved out of the wall, as much of the cavern system had. He wondered whether the drakes or an earlier race was responsible. The chamber was actually rather roomy, almost as much so as the one in Xabene's tree. Emerald and blue drapery covering most of the walls nearly gave the place the illusion of being other than a cave. Cavern plant life, mostly mosses or fungi of a sort, added to the decor. Someone with an eye had sculpted them into astonishing shapes and patterns, further enhancing the wonderland appearance of Wellen's quarters.

Almost mundane by comparison were the desk and bed, despite the fact that an artisan had obviously carved the wooden parts. Wine of some sort sat waiting on a table next to the bed. A rich, bright green carpet, which turned out to be *grass* when the intrigued scholar inspected it closer, covered all but the entranceway of the chamber.

Xabene had remained silent and brooding after his comment. When she saw that he had run out of things to inspect, however, she reinstigated the conversation.

"We're no safer here than we were in the field, you know."

"I am; you might not be."

"*Wellen.*" The seductress was back. "I would never harm you."

"I know." He said it with such conviction that she stepped back to stare at him.

"You *do* know!" she blurted. "I can see it in your face! But . . ."

How could he know when she herself did not? Wellen knew too little about his ability to answer that question. He also knew too much about Xabene. She was not the sort of person who liked being predictable to others.

Best, he thought, to turn to another, albeit sensitive, subject than this one. "What do you think the Lords of the Dead will do?"

She was wary. "Do you think I know?"

"No, but you're far more familiar with them than I am. I hoped you might be able to guess."

His response was acceptable to her. "I don't know! If what that walking corpse of yours says is true, they will not tolerate his presence! Lords! He looked more like one of their servants than I ever did! How old do you think he is?"

"As old as they are and don't try to turn from the question I asked, Xabene. Please."

The enchantress was genuinely worried. Whenever the subject of her former masters arose, Wellen caught a glimpse of the hidden Xabene. *How the offer of power must have appealed to her! She must have been so afraid before that!* Someday, he would ask her about her early past.

Someday? That was assuming that they were still together and, more important, had survived this chaos.

"I think . . . I think they will strike after we leave here. They must know where we are; that would require the least of their power. Maybe they'll wait until we've left the safety of the Dagora Forest."

"But they *will* strike?"

The look on her otherwise beautiful face told him all he needed to know, but the sorceress added, "Oh, they will. When they do, we'll be lucky if any of us survive!" Her hands shook. She clasped them together. "I won't talk of them any more. Talking draws their attention." The wine attracted her. "If you can withstand my presence a little longer, Wellen, I think I need some of that."

Xabene sat down on the bed and waited in silence while he poured wine for both of them. He handed a goblet to her, and sat down beside. The sorceress sipped the clear, golden elixir.

When he saw that she had calmed somewhat, Wellen dared ask, "How did you come to be one of their servants?"

She looked at first as if he had taken his knife and cut her throat. Then, the look faded into an expression of resignation. "You want some tragic tale, don't you, Wellen Bedlam? You want to hear how I turned to them in desperation? How they were my last chance? Not at all! I was a minor witch, someone destined to life in a small village where I would do little things for little people but be shunned otherwise! I turned to the Lords of the Dead because I saw that my life would be a wasted nothing, that I'd grow old, live uselessly, and die to be buried and forgotten! Forgotten like so many before me and so many after me."

"Xabene—"

"They gave me power to do what I wanted! I could go anywhere and look down upon those who would have looked down on me! I *was* power!" She turned away from him, swallowed a large portion of wine, and finished, "So much for your idealistic imagination! Not what *you* thought, was it?"

Rising, the bitter enchantress tossed the goblet to the floor. The remainder of her wine slowly sank into the grassy surface.

"If you'll excuse me, Wellen Bedlam, I think it's time I rested. I'd like to leave in the morn if you can persuade our host to let me. There doesn't seem to be much need for me here . . . and I think I'd only attract more trouble, isn't that so?"

He could not respond, still overwhelmed as he was by her initial outburst. Xabene seemed ready to take the slightest thing as a provocation. His question perhaps had pushed too much at something she no longer cared to recall, but he had done it with their safety in mind. It was his own attempt in trying to understand the ivory-skinned enchantress.

Xabene stared at him for several seconds, waiting for *what* he could not say. Then, frustrated, the proud goddess stalked out of the chamber.

The exhausted scholar fell back on the bed, all too aware that he had missed something that he should not have. Under better circumstances, it would likely have been very obvious. Now, though, his mind churned so much that Wellen found it a wonder that he had been able to keep as much straight as he had.

He fell asleep still trying to make sense of it all.

In her own chamber, nearly identical to Wellen's, Xabene fell onto her bed and tried to bury her turmoil in one of the pillows. What she felt was unfamiliar to her and, because of that, frightening. The enchantress also hated losing control, a thing that had not happened since before her pact with the Lords of the Dead.

Some of what she had shown the outsider Wellen Bedlam had been playacting. It was so much a part of her nature now that she found she could not avoid using that ability, even when events might have warranted otherwise. He, especially, encouraged her playacting, although he did not know that. There was something about him that made her afraid to reveal too much of herself, yet desire to.

He would be gone after this was over, one way or another. They might die, but, if they were fortunate enough to escape with their lives, he would find his way back to his home. Why would he desire to remain in a land that had tried to kill him almost before he had even set foot upon its shores?

The thought that he would leave tore at her. The enchantress grimaced, recognizing the unfamiliar feeling. *Not me! It could never happen to me! I'm stronger. It would serve me no purpose to care for him! It would make no sense!*

Part of her mind argued that those she had seen under that selfsame spell never cared about whether it made sense. They just succumbed.

"Not with *him*," she muttered. *Certainly not so swiftly, either!*

Xabene closed her eyes and began to drift away from the true world, never actually falling asleep but sinking into a state where she sensed things around her but only from a great distance. It was a pleasant sensation, for her fears and anxieties became tiny, insignificant creatures of no concern to her. Once more she was the powerful enchantress. Men fell prey to her form while her spells wreaked havoc with their plots.

All except one man.

He can be yours . . . if that is your desire . . .

Her dreams took on a different twist. A horribly familiar darkness slowly crept through her mind.

You are deserving of a second chance . . .

Xabene's nose twitched as she relived the memory of a chamber filled with the smell of sulfur and decay. She saw the multitude of scavengers crawl over and through things that had been rotting since, it seemed, time itself began. A pool lay before her, one covered with a thick layer of fetid slime. The pool bubbled, as if something lurked beneath it.

Let your power be yours again . . . all that is asked is this one . . .

A distorted, monstrous image of Shade loomed over her dream self. He laughed at her insignificance, his crystalline eyes gleaming. She would not be sorry when Wellen and she parted company from the mad warlock.

Your power . . . and the man . . . yours . . . for so small a price . . .

What was the price? Her brow wrinkled as she struggled to understand. What price?

A doorway formed in her thoughts. Not anything that *she* had ever imagined. The rest of the scene around her, the pool and Shade, faded as the doorway strengthened. There was no actual door, but the sorceress knew somehow that something still barred whatever waited on the other side. Some sort of barrier.

The power to be respected . . . more power than ever before . . . to make yourself feared by those who would otherwise make you fear them . . .

It was tempting . . . and the power would also give her back the self-control that she had been losing.

Open the door . . . that is all that must be done . . .

Open it? How? Her image reached out and touched the darkness in the center. There was nothing before her, yet her hand would not go through.

The barrier exists only in you . . . *but you are also the key . . .*

The barrier *and* the key. To power. She wanted that power.

Slowly, her image pushed at the invisible barrier. This time, it began to give where her hand was. Xabene knew that she did not have to destroy the entire barrier. All she had to do was make a hole . . . then the Lords of the Dead could act.

So close to reattaining her desires. The barrier struggled, but it was already straining to her limits. She had no qualms about betraying Shade. In her eyes, he was deadly, a mad creature that would bring only death to her and Wellen and then depart, laughing at their foolishness in believing in him.

The barrier gave. One finger burst through its membrane. She felt a tug on the other side, as if they were trying to help pull her completely through. Only a little more . . .

Then, pain struck her and she realized just *what* barrier it was that she was fighting.

Herself. A part of her that did not want to give in again to her former lords . . . but why?

Once asked, the answer, since it came from her own mind, was instantly known. To betray Shade was also to betray Wellen . . . both his belief in her and in himself . . . for the Lords of the Dead saw much potential in him.

They also knew that he would never become one of their servants.

"No!" Xabene called out in the scene. She tried to withdraw her hand, but whatever tugged at her held the sorceress and, in fact, pulled her farther in.

She screamed, but whether in the real world or the dreamland, she never knew, for the barrier broke then and the enchantress was overwhelmed by what had been waiting for her all this time.

Waiting in hunger.

XII

"Issss thissss the one?"

Prentiss Asaalk, looking much more fit than he had after his capture and feeling a bit more in control of himself, studied the image the crystal revealed to him. He stood in the imperial chamber of the Dragon King Purple, the monarch of the realm stretched out before him in all his horrific splendor. Unlike the "throne room" of the Green Dragon, that of Purple was barely more than the cavern itself. Only those things that the drake lord thought necessary to his pursuit of knowledge, and the power that such knowledge would in turn lead to, were present.

Asaalk was very respectful in both manner and response, despite now being granted the privilege of gazing at the glory of his new master. The blue man had been treated well these past few days, but he knew that his footing was still precarious. Wellen Bedlam was still loose and the drake lord was growing furious, especially after the debacle involving the gnome's cursed citadel.

"That is not him, no." The image was that of a strange old . . . *old?* Asaalk thought he looked a thousand years *dead* . . . clad in a cloak and hood that seemed ready to swallow him.

"Then, I know who it musssst be." The leviathan raised a foreclaw. A human clad in a robe of deepest purple touched the crystal. The sheer size of the dragon made it impossible for him to manipulate such tiny objects without endangering them. The artifact was also so sensitive that to use his vast sorcerous power might have resulted in the drake lord destroying its effectiveness.

Prentiss Asaalk had noticed many humans working for the Dragon King. They did all the things that the drake clans found beneath them and also those things that the tinier, more adept hands of men could do better. The blue man had also come to realize that for all the drakes there were in the clans, they were actually few in number. Humans already outnumbered them and would increase that margin before too long. It would be interesting, he thought, to see what the future held.

His future held nothing but oblivion if Bedlam was not discovered soon . . . and then what? Asaalk would have to find a new way to make himself valuable. *So I will, yes!*

"Concentrate on what floatsss before you, human, or elsssse I shall feed you to my get as a sssspecial treat!"

The blue man looked up . . . and gasped. His eyes narrowed and his mouth curled in bitterness. He could never forget the face now. "It is him, yes! It is Wellen Bedlam!"

He had come to hate that face for putting him in this

situation. Had *he* been in charge of this expedition, this would have never happened.

"Ssssoooo . . ." The leviathan raised his head. As far as the northerner was concerned, there were far too many teeth in the smile of the Purple Dragon. "Brother Green treadssss where he should not!"

The statement made no sense to Asaalk, but he remained silent. If the reptilian monarch deigned to explain his outburst, Asaalk would be more than pleased. If not . . . he would have to live without the knowledge.

The important thing was to *live*.

"Your Bedlam issss in the care of my brother to the northwessssst! The Dagora Foresssst! Green hassss grown too pressssumptuoussss! I shall tear his kingdom asssssunder! There will be carnage everywhere! Hissss damssss will become mine; hissss get will feed my own!"

Another Dragon King had Wellen Bedlam and had stolen him . . . somehow . . . from this one. The blue man understood that much. He also understood that his captor was speaking of a war between the clans of two leviathans, with Asaalk caught in the midst! In desperation, he sought ways to prevent the coming war. Asaalk was a survivor. Better to throw himself into a plot of his own making than sit by idly waiting for death to come for him.

A solution came to him. It was not the best, but time did not warrant long and careful planning. While it had risk to him, he preferred it over doing nothing. "My great and honorable lord!"

He was forced to call twice more before the Dragon King noticed him. The head of the behemoth swung down and Asaalk found himself staring into a dripping tunnel from which there was no returning. Sulfur and the smell of blood combatted with one another to smother him. He stifled the look of disgust that was attempting to surface, knowing that it would only lessen his chances of convincing his new master of the worth of the plan.

"Sssspeak, manling! Or should I ssssimply dissssspense with your annoying pressssence now?"

"My lord, I have a plan which may gain you what you desire without the danger of loss!"

His phrasing, he discovered, did not entirely agree with the leviathan. "Do you think my clanssss *cowardly*?"

"By no means, great lord! That which I meant was . . . was that why risk what you seek? Such a war would likely kill Wellen Bedlam!" A new thought, based upon what he had learned about the society of the drakes, gave him more ammunition. "The Emperor would surely not like seeing your two lands torn apart either! He would grow suspicious and learn of what you have hidden from him!"

Purple's mouth clamped shut. Asaalk had never seen a dragon caught unaware before, but here was such a sight.

"The tome musssst be mine!" the drake lord muttered. "Only I have the right to it!"

"It was found, after all, in your proud domain, yes?"

The handful of human servants in the chamber were all staring at Asaalk. He flashed them an arrogant smile, to show them who had their master's ear now.

"What issss your plan?"

Here it was. Always it seemed that his existence depended upon something. "It is simplicity itself, yes. Master Bedlam and those who control him will leave the other kingdom soon. They must, for they, too, want what is rightfully yours." He spit on the cavern floor to show what he thought of their presumptuousness. "When they leave, they will find one waiting for them. One who will gain their trust and lead Wellen Bedlam into your very claws. That one will be me, yes."

"You? And why should I trusssst you, human? If I let you loosssse, you will ssssimply try to run!"

"How could I run from you? I am merely a manling. Besides, I have come to see that my desires are best served by serving you, yes." There was truth to that. If he was condemned to live out his life in the Dragonrealm, it made sense to choose a path leading to power. The drakes *were* the lords of the realm and Asaalk had learned enough about the others to know that his chances were probably best with this one. There was just enough similarity between himself and the Dragon King to make that so.

Of course, by that same reasoning, there was less reason for the leviathan to trust him.

"A pretty little ssssspeach . . . and a plan which, while ssssimple, might be acceptable! There musssst be a few *minor* alterationsssss, though! I musssst alsssso ensure your obedience!"

Prentiss Asaalk had known that would be the case and steeled himself. Whatever happened, it could not be too severe, else it ruin his chances of tricking Master Bedlam. While the squat little scholar had led a sheltered life, he was by no means a fool, save perhaps in being too naive at critical times.

The Dragon King tilted his head and eyed one of the guards standing just behind the blue man. "Ssssee to it that thissss one issss fitted for a collar! Then . . . return with him to me!

Would it not have risked his new status, the blue man would have exhaled a tremendous sigh of relief. The collar was what he had hoped for. He had seen the sorcerous toy in action. There were other, stricter methods that Purple used to keep his more enterprising servants at bay, but the collar was the simplest. Most humans needed nothing; they were cowed by the drake lord's mere presence. Collars and such were for those too crafty or too important to be left unguarded, people who might actually *defy* their rightful monarch.

The collar, despite the little tricks it contained, was something Prentiss Asaalk knew he could circumvent. The blue man had tricks of his own that no one, not even his late and unlamented companions in the expedition, knew about.

As he was led away, much more respectfully than when he had first been dragged in here days ago, the northerner began to think that life in the Dragonrealm might not be so terrible . . . once he had made a few changes in the way things were done.

The look on Wellen Bedlam's terrified visage would be good enough incentive, too.

"Wake up, lad!"

Wellen was once more on the *Heron's Wing*. He was trying his best to sleep, but Captain Yalso kept shaking him. Part of him knew that was wrong, for Yalso was dead, but the image was insistent. Somewhat distractedly, he noticed that his head was trying to warn him of some danger.

"I said for you to be wakin' up!" A beefy hand slapped him on the right side of his face. His eyes opened wide but, as is often the case with those startled to consciousness, he could focus on nothing. He only knew that the torches that had lit the chamber were still burning, albeit not nearly so brightly.

"That's better!"

The startled scholar blinked, looked up at the source of the voice, and then tried to scramble off the other side of the bed. Unfortunately, a steely grip around his arm kept him from going anywhere.

Captain Yalso's pale visage came within an inch of his own. "Someone might think you're not pleased to be seein' me, Master Bedlam!"

"You . . . you're *dead*!"

The sea captain smiled. "That I am, lad."

The next connection was not difficult to make. "The Lords of the Dead! *They* sent you!"

Still keeping his hold on Wellen, Yalso sat his heavy bulk down on the edge of the bed. "That they did. A queer lot, them lords, but their power can't be argued with. I heard me name and there I was!"

Bedlam noticed that Yalso never breathed, even when he spoke. That should have made it impossible for him to speak at the very least, but the corpse seemed unimpeded by that fact. Yalso also stunk like a fish left rotting on the deck during a hot, sunny day. "It . . . it's good to see you, captain. I mean that, regardless of the circumstances. I wish . . ."

The undead mariner nodded his sad agreement. "I know. We made our choices and that's all there is to it."

"How did you get here?"

"How else? Through your comely lass."

"Xabene? But she—"

"Was made an offer that sounded too good. Can't blame the girl; I was in her shoes not too long ago." Yalso stood up, his hold on Wellen's arm never easing. "Speakin' of which, it's time we got goin'! I've got a bargain to keep and you're part of it, Master Wellen." With one hand, he lifted Wellen up and stood him on his feet. "Good to see you're wearin' your clothes, my boy! Would hate to think I had to drag you naked before their like!"

The befuddled explorer gazed down at his crumpled clothing, which he vaguely recalled having fallen asleep in earlier. Then, realizing the import of the ghoul's words, he asked, "Where are we going? What's to happen to me?"

Yalso tried to look comforting, but his ghastly appearance had the opposite effect. Wellen, having more time to observe him, noticed that the words he heard were not in sync with the movements of the late captain's mouth.

"No need to be worryin' too much, *friend*. They've promised not to harm ya. They just want to be knowin' what *you* know."

The hapless explorer tried to pry the death grip loose, but

touching the sailor's hand was like touching the cold flesh of the horse Xabene had summoned for him. Wellen drew his own hand away and shivered. Yalso's face darkened.

"D'you think *I* like it? They've offered me a new chance at life, Master Bedlam. I just have to bring you to them to answer some questions! Then I bring you back and they give me what the cursed sky serpent stole from me! Is it too much to ask ya, then, to help me out? You're still livin', you are! *You* escaped!"

The bulky corpse began to drag him toward the hall. Wellen forced himself to touch the hand again and struggled to free himself. "Yalso! Listen to me! I've mourned the deaths of all of you and I wish I could bring you back, but you can't trust the Lords of the Dead to keep their promise! They've only resurrected you because they know I feel guilty about what happened!" It was true; he had still not forgiven himself for ever having put together the expedition. "They know I won't fight you as much as I can!"

Small cracks had materialized in the mariner's hands and face while Bedlam had talked. They reminded Wellen of the sort of cracks a badly formed clay pot might develop on hardening. The sight made him nauseous. Yalso did not bleed as living people did. Even as the unnerved scholar watched, a dark, thick substance began to drip from the wounds. What was slowly seeping out of the corpse was blood, he realized, but it had long ago congealed.

The undead captain did not notice what was happening to him. "I can't take that chance, Master Bedlam! I'll not stay dead if I have a choice about it! C'mon, man! You'll be okay! They've promised to give you to your lass! Ya can't call *that* a fate worse than death, now can you?"

"Where *is* Xabene?" Had she really betrayed him? It seemed reasonable to suppose that she had to have been their key to the protected realm of the Green Dragon. Like the tragic figure before him, Xabene had been made an offer that encompassed all she could ever want. Life without power was as horrible to her as being dead was to Captain Yalso.

"She's *fine*," the corpse replied in what was supposed to be soothing tones. The cracks has spread so much that the mariner was now covered with dripping wounds, none of which he had yet noticed. Yalso's visage was taking on a less-than-pleased expression. "Now, come with me, Master Bedlam, so that what needs to be done *will* be done!"

"I cannot, captain!" Wellen lifted his knees into the stomach of his undead companion.

The sailor shook his head. Bedlam's kick had not even slowed him. "You shouldn'a fought me, Master Bedlam. Now, I'm afraid I'll have to take you more forcible like."

Yalso's eyes turned up, becoming pale white orbs. More and more the scent of death permeated from his body. "I'll have to make you more agreeable. I'm sorry, lad, but it's me *life* I'm talkin' about!"

This is not the captain! Wellen told himself. *Yalso was never this way in life and he'd not be this way in death!* This was a shadow of the man, manipulated by the soulless necromancers Shade claimed were his kin.

The scholar fought the rage that welled within him. What the Lords of the Dead had done to Captain Yalso was unforgivable. "Captain, if I could give you what you desire, I would!"

A brief spark of the old mariner resurfaced. Yalso's horrific visage twisted into a look of genuine sadness at what the two had come to. "I know ya would. I...I really can't help meself! They promised me, though!"

"They promised Xabene many things, but I've seen that they like to take back those promises! Think of how they've treated her!" Wellen was gambling that the enchantress had not been so willing to return to the fold as the corpse had said. Perhaps she had been tempted, even almost succumbed to their offerings, but if she had accepted, why send Yalso, then, instead of her? Xabene was not one to leave something she had started to others. *She* would have gone after Wellen, if only to erase her earlier failure.

"I—" Yalso froze, caught between whatever he had been told and what his mind argued might be the truth. Wellen's spirit rallied, although not for his own sake. That Yalso hesitated meant Bedlam had been correct concerning the raven-crested sorceress. Xabene had not betrayed him.

"I have to..." Though the captain's loyalties, enforced or otherwise, tied him to where he stood, it was all too likely that the necromancers' power would prevail in the end. Wellen could not hope that the undead mariner would decay away if stalled long enough. The Lords of the Dead surely had that contingency covered.

Power within, if there was ever a time for you to come forth, it's now! He wished with all his might for some spell to save him from the clutches of his rotting captor, but nothing happened. His mind still screamed uselessly of the danger he was in, yet no other bit of sorcery sought to free him of that danger.

For that matter, he wondered why no one was rushing to his aid. With the arguing, it would have made sense for a guard or two to come bursting in . . . unless the forces behind Yalso had taken care of that beforehand.

Staring at the entranceway, Wellen abruptly spotted his one chance for salvation. It would mean risking all, however, for if he failed, his plan would only serve to turn his late comrade against him.

"I know it's hard, Captain Yalso," he said in his most understanding voice. "You still have time to consider everything. I could be wrong. Perhaps if we start on our way to wherever it was you were trying to lead me to? By that time, you might be able to think clearer."

Yalso's now blank eyes stared his way. "What are you trying to do, Master Bedlam?"

"Help you."

"Help me . . . all right."

Wellen had banked on this shambling parody being less than the living sailor or else his plan would have failed in that instant.

As the captain turned them both toward the entranceway, Wellen stared at the torches that were still burning on each side.

Yalso only held him by one arm, too.

His captor was silent, either still engaged in mental battle with himself or simply deciding that speech was an unnecessary drain on his false life. Wellen walked almost beside him, trying to keep up his show of support until the end. "It's always possible that there's another way, captain. Shade is a masterful warlock, perhaps he—"

"He'll be dead, lad, like I've been."

Wellen almost gave himself away at the announcement. Just how great an attack was this? Did the Lords of the Dead seek to take on *all* of their adversaries while they slumbered under the mantle of false security? Was even the Green Dragon in danger? If so, it only made Wellen's need to free himself that much greater.

The torch on his side was almost in his grasp. Another two

steps. Then, it was only one. Still Yalso did not notice. Would he react as Bedlam assumed?

The final step. The burning torch was within reach.

Wellen lunged for it.

"You shouldn'a had, Master Bedlam!" a sad Yalso announced. He pulled hard on Wellen's arm, nearly yanking his prisoner off the floor. His strength was enough that the explorer could not help but fall toward him.

Which was what Wellen had wanted. Prepared, he added his own strength to the zombie's. The two crashed into one another and, despite Yalso's dead weight, both living and unliving were sent stumbling into the torch on the captain's side.

The horse that Xabene, or rather the Lords of the Dead, had provided had been a cold, lifeless thing like the unfortunate Yalso. It had felt like a dry, long-dead corpse, although at the time the realization had not sunk in. Wellen had wondered just how dry both the mount and the unliving captain were.

The answer was . . . *very.*

Yalso's back and far side burst into flames like kindling.

"Put it out!" roared the sailor. His visage, already crumbling, was half ablaze. He released his charge without thinking, trying desperately to beat out the flames. Bedlam did not pause, backing quickly to the other torch and taking it from its stand. With it, he confronted the macabre figure.

There were tears in his eyes. If he had thought there was actually a way to resurrect his friend. . . . "I'm sorry, Yalso, I am."

"You will *come* to us!" a chorus of voices decreed. What was left of the sailor's face no longer resembled him. Yalso was gone; the Lords of the Dead had taken complete command. One of the corpse's hands was completely burned away. The other, flames wrapped around it like a glove, reached for the waiting human.

Wellen thrust the torch at the horror's midsection. The flames rushed up the length of the torso, turning the entire top half of the ghoul into an inferno. The furnishings and curtains behind it were also ablaze. Bedlam, sweating from the heat and half blinded by the light, backed out of the chamber. The thing that had once been Captain Yalso tried to follow, but the flames had spread to its legs and, being so much dry timber, they easily crumpled under the combination of sapping flame and the creature's still-bulky form.

He watched the corpse burn for a few breaths, his face tear-streaked and his mind recalling Yalso as he had known him in life. Wellen had no doubt that a part of the captain had been there, but at the same time, it had been the necromancers who had guided the strings.

No one should make a mockery of life like they do!

There was no time to mourn Yalso and, he reminded himself, he had done so before. It was the living who were important now. Falling back to the cavern corridor, Wellen started to throw the torch away, then remembered that Shade and Xabene might face attacks similar to the one on him. The torch might prove handy. The enchantress, he suspected, was in less danger. If he understood correctly, the Lords of the Dead needed her to maintain penetration of the Dragon King's lair. He was under no misconceptions about his chances of trying to free her on his own. He had only escaped because the necromancers were probably concentrating their power on their most dangerous adversary. Shade.

It was Shade who represented Wellen's best, possibly only, hope of freeing Xabene, yet, he found he could not bear the thought of rushing to the warlock first. He *had* to see if he could help her.

The tunnel was dead silent. He heard neither drakes nor battle sounds. Either all were killed or they were unaware of what was going on. Likely the latter, for the disarrayed explorer doubted that the death lords could defeat the hooded warlock *and* destroy the combined drake clans.

Benton Lore had placed all three outsiders within only a few minutes from one another, yet Wellen saw nothing. Had Shade been caught unaware or in the throes of his madness? Wellen started down the tunnel, still trying to convince himself to rush to the warlock first. What if they had acted against Shade as they had against him? It was the one area where Bedlam held the advantage. The Seekers had struck at the shadowy spellcaster, successfully releasing his memories and using them as distractions. Could the Lords of the Dead have utilized the same trick, only more effectively?

Turning a corner, he stumbled to a halt.

There were two human guards standing in the tunnel, facing one another. Human guards for human guest, Bedlam decided. They looked neither ensorcelled nor dead. Both of them looked his way and one brandished a short sword.

"Identify yourself!"

"Master Wellen Bedlam! What are—"

"One of the outsiders brought in by the commander," the other sentry, an older man, explained to his compatriot. To Wellen, he said, "You should not be wandering the system, Master Bedlam. Those unfamiliar can get lost very easy. It's sometimes hard to explain to the drake's young that they shouldn't have eaten a guest of His Majesty."

"Haven't you *heard* anything?"

"No, should we have?" The sentries looked skeptical. Wellen knew he looked like a wild man.

"I was just attacked by a man who I last saw dead at the claws of a dragon!"

"Then, he couldna been much trouble, could he?" the younger one asked, chuckling.

"Your master—"

"Save your breath on these blind ones," came a voice that was doom incarnate. Wellen was reminded of the tones a judge used when sentencing someone to death . . . or perhaps it was the voice of the executioner himself.

It was all and neither.

It was Shade.

He stood in the midst of the tunnel, directly behind the two guards, who whirled and readied their weapons. Shade raised a finger and the two soldiers fell against the sides of the corridor. They were conscious, but they could not move. Not even speak.

"Shade! Were you—" He stopped as he caught sight of the warlock's tattered garments. Even the cloak and hood had been torn. The ancient spellcaster still wore the hood over his head, but it failed now to hide the burning rage in those jarring, crystalline eyes. Shade teetered on the brink of an insane rage and it was possible that he had even begun plummeting over that brink.

"They have gone too far this time," the warlock muttered. He did not seem entirely focused on Wellen. "They chose the one they thought I could not deny in the end, the one most likely to bring me down."

Memories of the two phantasms floating around mad Shade's head returned. Sharissa and Dru Zeree. Had it been one of them? The woman? Had they used her?

"They, of course, had never defied him until then. *They*

would never have believed that I could have defied him so."
Shade turned to the elder guard. The man, unable to move
anything but his eyes, could only stare back in fright. "You.
Tell your commander... tell your liege... that the necromancers have invaded his domain. *Now!*"

Suddenly free, the sentry ran. Wellen fell flat against the
wall as the man sped past, obviously under a geas or some
similar magical compulsion.

Shade recalled the other sentry. "There may be risk. You had
better go with him."

Compelled, the wisecracking soldier hurried off to join his
compatriot.

"I will not sacrifice any more lives to them," the hooded
sorcerer commented coldly. To Wellen, he said, "I come to
save you, but I find you coming to save us."

"I was..." Wellen could not get his tongue to work for
him. Listening to the sorcerer speak, he had been reminded of
Captain Yalso.

A bit more rationality, but perhaps even more chilling anger,
returned to the warlock. "Yes, my cousins no doubt sent
someone they thought you might hesitate to resist. Like myself,
however, you found that you could." At the shorter man's
unasked question, Shade added, "What they sent me wore the
shape and form of my dear, unlamented father, but it was not
his spirit. I know. That was their fatal mistake. They could
re-create the form, but they could *not* imitate the spirit of the
Patriarch of the Tezerenee. It would be unmistakable to me."
To Wellen's surprise, Shade actually shivered. "I cannot say
what I would have done if it *had* been him..."

"Shade..."

"They will pay for this debacle..."

"Shade!" Bedlam stepped directly in front of his companion
and forced the warlock to look at him. The expression he
received almost made him regret his action, but it was too late.
Besides... "Shade, Xabene needs us! She's the way they
were able to pierce the Dragon King's defenses! She's their
key!"

A grim smile stretched his dry skin to its utmost. "And ours.
Come."

Without preamble, the two of them materialized in the
enchantress's chamber. Wellen barely noticed this time, his

concern for the pale sorceress far outweighing his dislike for teleportation.

She lay on the bed, almost serene.

"Xabene?" He started to go to her, but the shadowy warlock stayed him with an arm.

"They would hardly leave her like this without another trap."

"Are you certain?"

"We are kin. We were Vraad. Worse, we were all Tezerenee."

The names meant nothing to him, but if Shade understood the necromancers, Wellen would bow to his judgement.

"What could it be?"

Given a task, the master warlock once more gained a stronger foothold in reality. He took a tentative step toward the motionless figure. "Something surrounding her, deadly to the touch, would be the obvious way."

Wellen's head, which had been screaming danger since his awakening, somehow succeeded in becoming even more adamant. The danger seemed much closer than a spell surrounding Xabene, almost as if a great *physical* threat was lurking . . . *above?*

Hanging from the cavern ceiling, motionless until Wellen's glance upward, were the Necri.

"Shade!" was all the harried scholar had time to shout before the winged horrors were upon them. Four dove at Shade, while only two found Wellen of interest. He held up the dying torch, a pitiful thing by now, and wielded it like a sword in the desperate hope that it would have sufficient flame to ward off the oncoming pair that had chosen him for their meal.

His torch became a sunburst, swelling upward in size yet never so much as singeing his fingers. It caught the first batlike monstrosity by surprise, turning the creature into a living fireball that squeaked once and dropped to the chamber floor. Wellen jumped back, but did not lose track of the second horror, which had now grown much more cautious.

An explosion shook the furnishings and forced Wellen to fight for balance. He was pelted by a rainstorm of stench-ridden gobbets of white flesh and a sickly sweet liquid he did not care to identify, although he had his suspicions. The Necri above was also showered by the ungodly rain, but where the human shook in disgust, the demonic creature was aquiver with rising fury. It hissed.

Wellen's protective flame winked out of existence.

The Necri dove, claws bared and maw wide open.

He fell to the floor and rolled aside. Claws raked his backside, causing him to scream. Fortunately for the scholar, the winged terror had either overestimated the width of the chamber or its own ability to maneuver in closed spaces. As it turned to finish its prey, it caught one winged arm against the rock wall. The sudden loss of the one wing forced the Necri into a short-lived spiral that ended with the monster colliding fully with the wall.

Panting and wincing from the jagged cuts, Wellen leaped up and charged the Necri's backside. He raised the dead torch above his head, then brought it down as hard as he could. Not once did he consider the creature's skull, suspecting that it was solid as it looked. Instead, Bedlam utilized his momentum and weight as much as possible and focused the head of the torch onto the less protected neck.

The monster's neck did not crack; Wellen had never thought it would. The blow did, however, send the Necri to the ground, shrieking in agony. Wellen struck again and again. The batlike creature twisted in frustration and confusion, succeeding at last in throwing the scholar from its backside. Still, even free of the human, the Necri could not rise at first.

An inhuman roar filled with agony overwhelmed Bedlam from behind, but he had no time to see what had caused it. The torch was beyond him now. That left only his knife. Wellen wished he had asked the Green Dragon for a new sword, but doubted that the drake lord would have given him one so readily. After all, what reason had there possibly been for Wellen needing a sword while in the safe claws of Dagora's monarch?

What, indeed. Only ghouls and savage horrors from beyond!

Wishing there were another way, for his own sake, Wellen pulled out the knife and attacked the slowly rising Necri.

The demonic servant of the Lords of the Dead turned to face him . . . a moment too late. The blade, intended for the neck, caught the beast in the snout. Wellen was startled but relieved to discover that the Necri did not have impossibly thick skin near that region. The knife sank all the way to the hilt. A thick, brackish fluid covered both the hilt and the scholar's hand. It stung terribly, making Wellen release the blade without thinking.

The Necri was squealing, trying to grasp the slick hilt and remove it. It took a halfhearted swipe at its human target, but the knife insisted on attention. The batlike terror clawed futilely at the moist blade, only doing more damage to its snout. Wellen fell back against the edge of the bed and looked around in desperation for something to finish the beast. Even wounded as it was, the Necri would soon enough come for him . . . and now it partly blocked the only way out.

Benton Lore, wielding a falchion, chose to materialize in that selfsame entranceway, followed closely behind by at least two or three guards bearing similar short swords. He looked in horror at the necromancers' servant, then immediately brought the wide blade down on the neck of the wounded monster. The falchion sank deep into the Necri, splattering more of the foul liquid over the area.

The Necri shivered once . . . and collapsed.

The commander quickly wiped the blade off on one of the cloths decorating the nearby walls. Disgusted, he looked at the battered and worn outsider and demanded, "What is happening here?"

Wellen did not answer him, but turned instead to Shade, who he feared might already be a victim of the other Necri.

He was not. The shadowy warlock glanced his way as he dropped the tattered remnants of a Necri arm to the ground. Shade appeared tired, but the fury had not left him. The course of the battle had knocked his hood back and Wellen heard Benton Lore and the other soldiers mutter at the sight before them. If anything, Shade seemed almost as much a demon as the savage beasts he and the scholar had fought.

"You took your time getting here, Lore." In contrast to his appearance, the ancient sorcerer's voice was almost nonchalant, as if Benton Lore had been a few minutes late to a noble's party.

"Not our fault. We were barely more than two or three minutes . . . and that because a barrier of some sort blocked our way in this hall until moments ago."

Two or three minutes? Wellen blinked. Had it only been that long?

"Two or three minutes in battle with these can seem like an eternity. Fortunately, they prefer tooth and claw to their magic, else they might have utilized the latter to better advantage. Typical of the lack of thought that their creators suffer from."

"Xabene!" Mention of the Lords of the Dead brought the

disheveled explorer to his senses. He rushed to the still enchantress's side and reached for her.

"Stay!" Shade was suddenly there on her other side, his gloved hands gripping Wellen's wrists with such strength that the mortal grunted in pain. The warlock pushed him back. "The link must stay intact. I need it."

"I cannot let her stay like that! Not even for you!"

Shade's smile was mocking. "Would it make a difference, Master Bedlam, if I told you that breaking the link would not return her?"

"What does that mean? Who is responsible for this transgression?" asked Lore, coming up to the foot of the bed. He glanced down at the unmoving Xabene. "What has happened to her?"

"Always this need for infernal explanations," Shade mocked. "She is the link that the Lords of the Dead used to invade your liege's kingdom. Her body and mind are here, but her spirit, her *ka*, now resides in *their* domain."

"She's *dead*?" Wellen paled.

"I did not say that. I said that her spirit resides in their kingdom, though I cannot say how long before she does die. I sincerely doubt her former masters will have any use for her once they realize they have failed."

"I should think they would know by now," Benton Lore commented, pointing at the still sizzling remains of one of the Necri the hooded warlock had destroyed.

The smile creeped onto Shade's face. "I have seen to it that they do not . . . for a time. Time enough, if there are no more interruptions, for me to do what I must."

Wellen looked the warlock in the eye, not an easy thing to do even now. "You have to save her!"

"If that is possible; my hands will be filled . . . with my cousins. Now if someone joined me . . ." He stared pointedly back at the scholar.

Wellen nodded without hesitation.

"We shall come, too." Lore snapped his fingers. The guards quickly lined up in two columns.

Shade winked at the scholar, such a disconcerting sight that Wellen almost thought he had imagined it. "I think not, Commander Lore."

He seized the explorer's hands again.

The world twisted in and out . . . and so did Wellen.

It was so dark that his first thought was that someone had doused all the torches in Xabene's chamber. Then the terrible stench of sulfur and rotting flesh informed him that he was elsewhere.

A blazing light formed in the air only a yard to his right. In its glow, he saw a wretched landscape. The few things that resembled plant life were twisted and black. The scholar was reminded of terrain after a horrible battle in which the only true victors were the carrion crows and their ilk. Things, frightened by the intense light, scurried into holes. A few did not move fast enough and were swallowed up by less frightened, much larger monstrosities that failed to resolve into any distinct shapes when Bedlam tried to see them better.

"I once knew a place like this," came Shade's voice. Somehow, he had not seen the warlock. Wellen finally made out the shrouded form standing an arm's length from the floating light. "In some ways, I have never left it."

The tone was all too familiar to the younger man. It was the same one that the ancient spellcaster generally used as he was slipping into madness. Wellen rushed to prevent that. "Where are we?"

His spectral companion, seeming almost as much a part of this nightmare world as the things that had hidden from the illumination, quietly responded, "We are in the reflection of another place, a world that long ago died yet still is . . . and only they would think to re-create such despair." A cloak-covered arm rose and a gloved finger pointed ahead. Wellen followed with his eyes and saw something, some *structure* in the distance. "And there is where they wait."

The warlock began walking, the ball of light ever floating ahead. Wellen kept pace, knowing that to lose Shade and the light was to lose more than his life, for here were things that fed on souls as well.

Here were the Lords of the Dead.

XIII

In the field abandoned by the gnome, there occurred a strange thing. It happened when no one seemed to be looking that way, curious since, until that point, countless prying eyes had studied the land in a futile attempt to understand what the citadel's master had done.

The pentagon rematerialized...but not quite in the same place. Then it disappeared again.

Wellen and Shade stood at the front gate of the twisted castle that served as the meeting place of the Lords of the Dead. The magical ball of light that the master warlock had summoned was their only illumination, but it served to give the anxious scholar some idea of how the bizarre structure looked.

What it looked like a hodgepodge collection of many places all fixed together by insane craftsmen. Towers jutted at impossible angles and the style of architecture in one region sparred with an entirely different style next to it. The only thing they all had in common was a presence of despair and decay...and madness, too, Wellen corrected himself.

"Shall we go inside?" the hooded figure asked rhetorically.

And just like that, they *were*.

Shade looked up into the darkness. "Come out, my cousins, and let us speak of family!"

Save the scattering of tiny, hideous forms at the silence-shattering call, there was no response.

As willing as Bedlam was to save Xabene, he wondered what his companion thought he could do against the ageless necromancers. His own abilities were too unpredictable, too reluctant. They had saved him from one of the Necri, but seemingly abandoned him to the other. The only skill he trusted was his ability to sense oncoming danger and that was of no use to him now, for the screaming in his head only told him

162

what his normal senses had from the beginning. This was not a place for a living mortal.

"We shall have to go to them," Shade informed him. "I would recommend staying near my side for now."

Where else would I dare go? the explorer wanted to ask. Too many larger things moved about at the edge of the sorcerous illumination, as if biding their time. Wellen tried not to contemplate what would happen if the light spell failed.

Shade began leading him through a moss-covered hall. The stench was, if anything, worse within the walls than without. Now and then, a large mass lying sprawled on the floor required them to step carefully. The entire place seemed orchestrated to emphasize what it was the Lords of the Dead were. The scholar whispered so to his dread ally, not so much out of fear of discovery, but because the silence was so absolute that any noise was an intrusion that struck to the soul.

His words did not surprise the shadowy form beside him. A dry, sardonic chuckle escaped the mass of cloth. "There has ever been in my family a sense of the theatrical. Still, I doubt this world we see is the one that they perceive. It has been said that the one most susceptible to an illusion is often the one who has cast it, for he of all people *must* believe in its worth."

Rolling the last past over in his mind, Wellen dared ask, "Who said that?"

"I did."

Somehow, Wellen found that the answer did not surprise him.

The hall abruptly ended at a flight of stairs leading up . . . and *up*. Even when Shade expanded the ball of light, they could see no end.

"I see they are expecting us." Shade raised a gloved hand. In the extended brilliance, Bedlam noted that his clothing and that of his companion had been repaired. It was a bit consoling, he admitted to himself, that Shade was powerful enough to deign to reclothe them while still concentrating on the danger at hand. Wellen knew he himself would have been hard pressed to conjure even a good glove, if even that much was possible for him.

"Enough of these childlike games." The warlock's hand folded into a fist as he called out, "By the dragon banner, I demand a confrontation!"

"The banner is torn," mocked a whispering voice.

"The staff is broken," said another.

"And the clan is dead," uttered a third.

The staircase was gone. For that matter, their entire surroundings had changed, though Wellen would have sworn it was the room that had come to *them*, not the other way around. They stood in a chamber where an immense pentagram had been etched into the floor. A dark circle marked each point and corner of the pentagram, eleven circles all told when the one in the center, one fairly close to the duo, was counted, too.

"*We* are all that remains of the glory," said yet a new voice from almost behind them.

Bedlam whirled, but Shade seemed not at all put out by the sudden intrusion. He stood his ground and Wellen, trusting his judgement in this case, relaxed, but only a bit. They were, after all, in the sanctum of the Lords of the Dead.

A shape began to coalesce in the region where the last voice had originated. Basically manlike, but in the way a cloud can look like a person. Temporary. Always shifting, as if the memory was hard to recall. Wellen had an impression of a fully armored figured wearing a cape. The more he stared, the more the impression became clearer. The necromancer, for it *surely* had to be one of them, wore a helm with some sort of intricate design. Much of his countenance was covered, which the scholar thought was probably a good thing.

"What do you see?" Shade whispered.

Wellen hastily described it.

"You perceive memories. To me, there is a walking cadaver, a thing less alive than the false father I confronted in my chambers. It wears the armor that you mention, but it is rusting and ill-fitting on so emaciated a torso. *All* of them look so. Yet, even I see only memories."

"All of them?" He looked around and discovered that there were ten other murky figures around them, each one standing near a darkened circle. When they had appeared he could not say. "Are they . . . dead?"

"For all that they should be, they are not."

"We are immortal, cousin," said the one nearest to them.

"No more than I."

"We have become the gods we once were and *more*."

"*Gods?*" Shade laughed. "We were never gods. Just spoiled children with godlike powers, children who did not know how to use those powers." The warlock pretended to look around. "And I see you have learned nothing in that regard."

"Our kingdom is a paradise." As the leader spoke, the

others moved to the center of their respective circles. "We have re-created the Nimth of old."

"True . . . you have re-created the twisted, sick child we left behind."

The air crackled with barely suppressed power. Despite their air of indifference, Wellen could see that the Lords of the Dead were very much disturbed by both the intruders and the words of their cousin. He wondered why Shade did nothing. Surely his companion saw what was happening around him?

"We have mastered life and death."

The hooded warlock purposely turned away from the speaker and addressed Bedlam. "They think that because they can steal a piece of a dying person's ka, that they have captured the entire thing. They think that a scavenger stealing a morsel is the same as a hunter catching his prey. Have you ever seen such naïvety?"

"*You* demanded confrontation and we have given it to you!" The necromancers grew larger. The nauseating stench they raised made Wellen's eyes water.

"The female is your responsibility, Master Bedlam," Shade remarked quietly. "Follow her trail. You cannot miss it from here."

"His words are ensorcelled," one of the other necromancers commented. "He hides something from us."

"To little avail," intoned the leader. He took his place in the center and faced the warlock. "To little avail, cousin."

Shade wrapped himself tightly in his cloak and turned around to stare at the thing that claimed kinship. "Nothing I do is to little avail, Ephraim."

The ball of light circling above the duo's heads became a nova.

It was as if the necromancers' world itself screeched in agony. A howl rose among the Lords of the Dead as the blinding illumination revealed to all what they truly were. Wellen swallowed hard. Neither the image he had seen nor the view Shade had described left him ready for the dark mages' true forms. Wellen found it hard to believe that these things could be alive in any sense.

A hand caught his shoulder and a voice, Shade's voice whispered, "Now is the time, scholar. Find her and take her from here. Go!"

Propelled in part by the warlock's hand, he ran blindly toward the only exit he could see.

The light died. Not faded away. Died. Wellen felt it, just as he felt the summoning of great strength by the Lords of the Dead. The running explorer stumbled, then discovered that despite the absence of illumination, he could still see the arched exit. Wellen increased his pace, regretting for the thousandth time that he had not been able to secure some sort of weapon, such as the falchion that Lore had carried. His knife was gone now, too. Now he only had his sorcerous skills to trust, not a great consolation in this dismal place.

It occurred to him that he was running without thought, that Xabene could be on the opposite side of the necromancers' citadel. For some reason, though, the novice mage was almost certain he was on the right trail, almost as if the two of them were linked to one another.

A hiss warned him of approaching danger. Wellen came to an abrupt halt and flattened himself against the nearest wall. He tried not to think of the things he had seen crawling around on other walls in the castle, reminding himself that they could be nothing compared to what moved ahead of him.

Whatever source, be it Shade's doing or some stirring of his own power, allowed him to see in the darkness, he was hard pressed to make out what shambled slowly toward his location. Wellen was reminded of a beehive with tentacles, but that was all the detail he could make out. He thought that something, some sort of slime, dripped from it, but that was based purely on the sounds the horror made as it moved slowly along.

Wellen was certain that it was coming for him, until it suddenly turned and went *through* one of the walls without so much as a second's hesitation. An illusion? With great care, the curious explorer stepped over to where the monstrosity had disappeared. Just before the wall, he stepped into something moist, certain evidence that what he had seen had not been the product of overtaxed imagination. The scholar within could not help taking a moment to study the phenomenon.

Tentacles burst from the wall, *seizing* him by the arms and throat.

Crying out, Bedlam tried to pull back. The thing proved stronger, however, and he found himself slowly but surely edging toward the wall. Wellen wondered what would happen when he and the stone met, then decided that it was a question better left forever unanswered. Frantically, the would-be war-lock tried to summon up some sort of spell.

Nothing happened. He cursed his premonitions; the ability

was so overwhelmed by the necromancers' kingdom that the warnings had become one constant headache, with no definition between near and not-so-near danger. Such was the trouble of becoming too accustomed to sorcery; one could forget it had limits.

In desperation, Wellen gave up attempting sorcery and tried the only thing he could think of. Bracing himself, he kicked the stone from where the tentacles projected.

If anything, the tentacles pulled with more fervor.

"Let me help you," came a quiet but, somehow, commanding voice. A single, delicate hand, female, reached out and touched one of the tentacles.

The appendage unwound and snapped back into the wall with such haste that it took part of Wellen's sleeve with it. Again the graceful hand, attached to a slim arm clad in white gossamer, reached out and touched a tentacle.

Whatever was happening, the beast had decided it had happened once too often. Wellen fell back as the tentacles were frantically withdrawn. He coughed as air rushed into his lungs. There was no doubt in his mind that he had scars around his throat and wrists. Still trying to draw breath and also watching to make certain that the wall stalker did not attempt to renew its attack, he said, "My . . . my thanks!"

"I would always help one of my children."

He raised his head and twisted around to see who had saved him.

She was taller than him and nearly as tall as Shade. Her well-formed figure was outlined in white, making her appear to be some snow goddess, and her hair, long and flowing, was silver-blue. A streak of very solid silver also ran through her hair.

His next statement died as he studied her more closely. The hall behind her was visible *through* her.

She smiled, almost a bit sadly, and somehow the smile made up for the fact that she was one of the undead. This was not Yalso. This was not one of the necromancers' toys. Here was one who could not, *would* not, hurt him.

"Tell him I always cared about what happened to him," she whispered. Then, in slightly lighter tones she added, "There are still a few facets of crystal in *your* eyes."

"Wait!" He knew without knowing how, that she was leaving. "What—"

The white wraith pointed backward at the hall behind her. "She lies that way. You won't be impeded anymore. I can see to that before I go."

She was growing less distinct, looking more and more like a bit of smoke in the wind than a woman.

He hesitated, then asked, "Did I . . . did I summon you?"

"I will never belong to the children of the drake," was her dwindling response.

Wellen shook then, feeling as if he had both found and lost something. He rose, thinking that the spirit had looked familiar, almost like . . . like the phantasm that had haunted Shade? Lady Sharissa?

Did she call me one of her children? The scholar found that hard to believe. If true, the bloodline had grown diluted over time. Many families, including his own, had laid claim to being descended either from the Lord Drazeree's . . . *Dru Zeree's* . . . daughter or from the children his elven bride had borne him. He had liked to think there was some truth, had even subconsciously used it as a reason for his obsession, but to actually *be*. . . .

As astonished as he was, Wellen recalled what his true task was and rose. If he was a descendent of the legendary lord, it behooved him to prove himself more than he had so far.

Wellen followed the path both his mind and the wraith's words told him was the true one. He was relieved to discover that she had not lied about one thing; nothing larger than a hand-sized, dead-white spider crossed his path and it had retreated quickly. All the time, the castle was silent. What had happened to Shade and the Lords of the Dead was an enigma. Wellen had expected the castle to rock from the intensity of their battle. He had anticipated explosions, thunder, and the screams of massive monsters brought into the fray by both sides. The silence, however, reminded him too much of the invasion of the Green Dragon's domain. The scholar was unfamiliar with sorcerous duels, but he assumed that they involved *some* noise.

Turning a corner, he found a wooden door. There was no question in his mind that this was his destination. This was where Xabene, or a part of her, was kept. He had no idea what he would find behind the door. A wraith, like the one in the hall? Conjectures were useless; it was easy enough to find out.

As Bedlam reached for the handle, the citadel *shook.*

A roar like a thousand storms raging all around nearly deafened him. Wellen put his hands to his ears and fell to one knee as the floor began to ripple beneath his feet. Pieces of stone dropped from the ceiling as shock wave after shock wave rocked the castle. It was as if all the effects of battle had been saved up for this one movement. Perhaps Shade had confined the battle somehow so that Wellen could find Xabene without too much trouble. If so, it boded ill that the hooded warlock's intentions had failed.

The stone floor tilted, nearly sending the hapless rescuer crashing into the opposite wall. He tried to grab the handle again, but it stayed just out of reach. Wellen managed to stand in one place, but then his boots started to *sink* into the stone floor. Not wanting to sink through to whatever lay below, or worse, find himself *trapped* in the very stone itself, the determined explorer struggled his way back to the more solid walls and pulled himself up by what little fingerhold he could find. The floor still had some solidity, too. With effort, he found himself making progress toward Xabene's chamber again.

A flurry of tentacles in his face made him throw himself to one side. A wall stalker sprouted full-grown next to his chest, but it had no interest in him. Wellen watched as the monster frantically wiggled its multitude of appendages in a useless attempt to stay attached to the wall. With what must have been a despairing hiss, the creature lost total control and plummeted to the floor.

It did not fall through as he expected. Instead, the wall stalker struggled as a drowning man might. One or two tentacles of the beehive creature shot in his direction, but not far enough. The thing rolled about in the liquid floor. It seemed to be trying to *swim* its way to the opposing wall. Unfortunately, the wall stalker was not built for that. All it succeeded in doing was miring itself further.

As abruptly as it had liquified, the stone floor reverted to normal . . . much to the distress of the necromancers' pet.

Wellen swore as he turned away from the stomach-wrenching sight. As simple as it had been for the wall stalker to shift through stone, there was evidently some conscious effort needed. Caught unaware as it struggled, the monstrosity was *crushed* in the sudden reversion. A shower of entrails and fluids narrowly missed Bedlam. A wave of sulfur made his nose burn and his eyes water, but fortunately, it was only a momentary thing.

Testing the stone, Wellen dared put his full weight on the floor again. Tremors still shook the castle. Although there were no windows here, he did not doubt that if there had been he would have seen a panoramic display of colored explosions lighting the generally dismal landscape. Light seemed a key element in dealing with the Lords of the Dead. They and most of their abominations had an aversion to it. Only a few servants, mostly humans like Xabene and reluctant creatures like the Necri, the latter of whom probably *preferred* the night, were likely to be of any use during the daytime.

He touched the door. To his surprise, it swung open easily. Almost too easily, he thought, but then it was doubtful that the necromancers had contemplated someone actually invading their citadel. Either that or once they had made use of Xabene, she had become unimportant to them.

"Xabene?" His voice echoed.

He stepped into the chamber, not understanding. Xabene *had* to be here. It felt correct. Shade had said he would be able to follow the trail; the wraith of Lady Sharissa had pointed the way. This *was* the place.

It's not her true body I'm looking for, Wellen reminded himself. *It's her spirit.*

Follow the trail . . . he had followed it to the room, but could it be followed farther?

Slowly, he wound his way into the middle of the room. There did seem to be more to the path. It was as if he was at his destination but not.

As he circled the center, still tracking the trail, the scholar saw a form shimmer into and out of existence.

A woman on a platform.

He continued to circle the center, finding somehow that the trail overlapped itself again and again but did not come to a definite conclusion. *What sort of mad sorcery is at work here?*

Wellen glimpsed the image again. It *was* Xabene. She seemed a little more solid now, although the image itself lasted little longer than it had the first glimpse. The enchantress was stretched out much the way she had been in the Dragonrealm, yet now she was more ephemeral, more like a dream.

This is not her true body. Would he be able to touch her, much less wake her? Wellen tried calling out to her again, hoping that his voice would do what his hands might not. "Xabene! Awaken!"

She remained as she was, but the image of her grew more constant, albeit still ghostly. Bedlam circled like a vulture, both marvelling and despairing at the way the path seemed destined to go on forever. Still, each revolution appeared to bring him closer to his goal. Closer, but never actually there.

"Xabene!" The chamber quivered as another tremor shook the castle. A piece of ceiling stone crashed to the floor just to the right of the scholar. Neither the sudden crash nor the tremor so much as caused the sleeping enchantress to shift.

She must wake! he thought, *before the entire citadel comes crashing down on us!* Or just him, he corrected. It might be that Xabene was beyond the physical danger. "Xabene!"

Her eyes opened wide and stared skyward. He was overjoyed until he realized that nothing else was happening. Xabene merely lay on the platform, arms crossed, and watched the ceiling. She made no move to acknowledge him nor did she appear to notice the destruction going on around her.

"Xabene, I won't leave without you!"

The enchantress turned her eyes toward him. Though her mouth did not move, he had the impression that she spoke his name.

Madness or not, he seized the straw. Wellen held out his hand. "I have come to take you back with me."

She stretched out a hand toward his. It was not insubstantial, as he had assumed it would be, but very light. Slowly, her ghostlike form rose from the eerie platform and joined him. Xabene said nothing else, but the enchantress did smile.

Now what? Shade had not told him what to do after this. Wellen had assumed that he would recognize the way back when the time came, but nothing struck a chord.

Shade! What do I do?

In the chamber of the pentagram, the twelve still stood. The eleven Lords of the Dead and Shade. None of them had moved so much as a foot or even a finger in all the time, yet the signs of their savage battle were everywhere. The ceiling was gone, opening the chamber to the pitch-black sky that was occasionally lit by fire. Portions of the castle lay strewn about both the room and the landscape. Things glowed or melted or died, depending on the spell that had been cast.

Near the center, whirlwinds failing to dislodge his hood,

stood Shade. He stared ahead at the one called Ephraim, but his mind, like theirs, was all over the landscape.

One part of his mind heard Wellen's anxious thoughts.

Slowly smiling, an act which instantly pushed the Lords of the Dead to renewed efforts, the warlock responded.

Xabene's spirit, her *ka* as Shade had called it, turned toward one of the far walls with such abruptness that Wellen expected to see a horde of tentacled stalkers come crawling through. That was not the case. Instead, his unworldly companion began trying to pull him toward the wall. Uncertain but not knowing anything better to try, he allowed her to lead him, careful never to lose his hold. The enchantress's hand was so light it was almost possible to forget one was holding it. That could prove dangerous. If he and the ka were separated, Xabene might never wake.

He might never return.

She continued ahead, even when it was evident that the wall was not going to move for her. Bedlam started to warn her, then closed his mouth as first her fingers and then her arm disappeared through the stone. Within seconds, the enchantress had vanished, save for the hand the scholar still held.

"Xabene!" *She* might be able to walk through walls, but Wellen could hardly be expected to follow—

His own hand sank into the stone without even the slightest tingle.

Gritting his teeth and closing his eyes, the novice warlock allowed himself to be led through. He did not open his eyes until he was certain that enough time had passed.

Wellen almost regretted reopening his eyes. They had left the castle interior and the spirit was now pulling him along with even greater force, almost as if she were nearing an important destination.

It would not have been so bad if the two of them had not been more than twenty feet above the ground.

He knew that Xabene did not have to fear falling, but he wondered what held *him* up. Certainly not his own skills. Could it be that Shade was aiding him again?

They flew swiftly over the landscape. Wellen dared to look back. For the past few moments, the citadel had been deathly quiet, but he doubted that the battle was over. If Shade had won, he would have joined them. If the warlock had fallen victim to the Lords of the Dead, the two mere mortals would hardly have been allowed to escape.

Something began to take form ahead of them. It resembled Shade's ball of light, but much, much larger. Xabene's spirit focused on it.

Behind them, there was a slow, building growl of thunder. It did not end after a few seconds, but continued to grow in intensity. Wellen did not have to be told that the final show-down was coming. When his wraithlike companion picked up her pace, he did not argue.

They were nearly upon the fiery sphere. It was wide enough to admit a score of riders traveling side-by-side and taller than the gnome's citadel. The heat made Wellen sweat, but he would have been willing to face the burning might of the sun, if only to escape this place.

He *assumed* this was escape.

With a final effort, Xabene dragged the two of them into the inferno.

"—back here, warlock!"

Wellen Bedlam looked up at the startled countenance of Benton Lore, who actually dropped his sword as he stared at the battered and torn figure lying in a heap on the rug next to Xabene's bed. The officer retrieved his weapon and, still stunned, stared into Wellen's face.

"Master Bedlam!"

The worn scholar tried to say something, but only a low croak escaped his now parched lips. He felt as if all fluid had been drained from his body.

"Get him water!"

One of Lore's men brought a mug. Wellen accepted the water and gulped it down. A sense of reality finally returned to him. "We're back!"

"You barely left! First the two of you vanish, then a second later, *you* return! What *happened* to you?"

He was not certain he had heard the officer's words correctly. "Only a few seconds?"

"No more."

"I do not—" The stench of the dead Necri attacked his sense of smell. What was left of the monsters had not been removed, something that Lore would have definitely had done at first opportunity. Memories came tumbling back to him. With an effort he would not have thought left in him, Bedlam whirled around and pulled himself up. "Xabene!"

His heart sank. The pale enchantress lay as she had before.

"What did you expect?" Commander Lore asked in open curiosity.

Wellen wanted to tell him about all that had occurred and how *hours*, not seconds, had passed, but he could not take his eyes from the still figure. For all she had to answer for, he did not want to lose her. When he had been younger, the scholar had smiled in mild amusement at stories of people who were drawn together almost from the first they had met, despite their differences. Now, Wellen was not smiling, for with him it was true.

He put a hand on her arm.

Xabene stirred.

The soldiers tensed, as if expecting some new trap, but Lore signalled them to relax. "What have you done, Master Bedlam?"

"Nothing!"

She opened her eyes wide, quickly scanning the chamber as if unable to believe where she was. Then the enchantress focused on Wellen. To his surprise, Xabene turned away.

"I'm sorry . . . it was so tempting at first."

"What was?"

Xabene turned back. Her expression was hard, cynical, but her eyes were moist. "What do you think? They offered me all that power back . . . and more . . ."

"And did you accept their offer?" Benton Lore asked. His manner was easy but his falchion was ready. Wellen glared at him, but the soldier did not lower the blade.

"I almost did . . . but then I realized what that would mean."

"Yet, you still let them through!"

"I had no *choice* by then! They were too strong!" She tried to rise, but it became apparent almost immediately that her strength was far from replenished. "Too strong!"

"Commander Lore, I will vouch for her!" Wellen understood the officer's concern, but Lore seemed too determined to have *someone* to punish for the embarrassing intrusion. "She was hardly an honored guest! You also might recall what Shade said . . . not too long ago . . . about how she would have died before very long if the part of her the Lords of the Dead had stolen had not been returned."

Lore was by no means convinced, but he quieted nonetheless. "And where is Master Shade? Will he be returning shortly, too?"

"He isn't here?" Xabene looked around, as if expecting the shadowy warlock to materialize in some corner. "But he was the one who showed me the way back!"

"He stayed behind." The rolling thunder echoed in Bedlam's mind. "He was still fighting the necromancers. Shade must have wanted us out of the way."

"But I thought that she was the only path open to you," Benton Lore commented, forgetting his distrust of Xabene for a time. "If she is awake and well now, then that path is closed to him."

Taking the enchantress by the arms, Wellen asked, "Can you open the path again? Can you?"

"No!" She looked away, not wanting to see his disappointment. "They've severed the link! I'm cut off from them forever! I'll never be . . ." Xabene's voice faced away as she contemplated her future.

The thunder seemed to roll even louder in his head. He closed his eyes and tried to will it away. "Then, Shade's trapped in their domain."

XIV

The rest of the night passed without any sign of Shade's return. Wellen was surprised at the depth of emotion he felt for the peculiar, often tragic, warlock. Shade had saved him more than once and the last time for no reason at all. His only comfort lay in the fact that the Lords of the Dead had been conspicuously absent, too. They had not attempted a second invasion. Wellen could only hope that if the warlock had perished, he had at least taken the necromancers with him.

Xabene was still asleep on his arm when Benton Lore quietly returned to their chamber. The enchantress, in a complete reversal of the sort of personality she had exhibited upon their first encounter, had pleaded with the weary scholar to remain with her. He could hardly blame her. Had he suffered as she had, it was likely he would have made the same request.

"Good morning," the black man quietly said with just a touch of mirth in his eyes. "Sleep well?"

The scholar shook his head. He had dozed, but nothing more. Each sound had made him think that either Shade or the Lords of the Dead had finally made a reappearance.

Hearing Lore, the enchantress stirred. When she realized where she was lying, she quickly sat up. "What is it?"

"Morning, nothing more."

"Morning . . ." Xabene grew wistful. "I used to love the nights . . ."

"His Majesty would like to see you," Lore announced.

Wellen looked down at his ruined clothing. "Do we have some time or are we required there now?"

"You have time to make yourself presentable, of course. Her presence is not required."

Before Xabene could say anything, the scholar replied, "I think he will want both of us there."

"As you wish." The commander snapped his fingers. Two human servants brought in food and fresh clothing. Benton Lore seemed more than just a loyal soldier serving a Dragon King. He was more of a major-domo, ever making certain that the kingdom, *his* kingdom, ran as smoothly as possible. Lore was probably almost as much the ruler as the Green Dragon. "A guard will be posted outside. When you are ready, you will be brought before His Majesty. Until then."

The officer departed, leaving Wellen and Xabene in the care of the servants, who, it seemed, were there to see that the duo did not dawdle. The two chose to eat first, hunger having quickly stirred once they were awake.

"What do you do now?" Xabene asked between bites of a juicy fruit called a srevo.

"What *we* do depends on the Dragon King." Whether she was distancing herself for his sake or her own, Wellen had no intention of parting just yet.

A passing smile, only a shadow of the once-seductive one. "And what do you think he'll want of *us*?"

Wellen knew the answer to that one without thinking about it. "It will have something to do with the gnome, I'm certain. What else is there?"

She grimaced. "You're probably right."
They ate in silence after that.

At first, it seemed he was wrong.

"I have utilized all options open to me," the dragon informed them almost immediately upon their arrival. "And I find no trace of either the Lords of the Dead or Shade. None of the gateways that they use are open and my power is insufficient to break through the lock spells they have set. Insufficient, that is, for the time being."

The Dragon King's almost clinical manner reminded Wellen of one of his instructors in school. An image of the drake lord teaching a bored class formed in his mind. He quickly stifled it and waited for the reptilian monarch to continue.

It almost seemed as if the Green Dragon was hesitant to add to what he had already said. "Your warlock friend still lacksssss hisss . . . *his* ability to teleport, that is, if your spell still holds true."

Consternation filled the novice sorcerer. He had completely forgotten about the accidental 'curse' he had laid upon the hooded warlock. Shade had brought them to the domain of the Lords of the Dead and then had shown them the way out, but in neither case had he needed to rely on a spell of teleportation, although what spell Shade *had* used to send them to the necromancers' foul kingdom was beyond him. Wellen was almost certain that the warlock *had* materialized in the hall during the initial chaos, but if the Green Dragon had not had an opportunity to free Shade of Bedlam's blunder, then the scholar was mistaken. In the rush of things, it had probably just seemed as if the warlock had teleported.

"Then, he has no chance." In a sense, Wellen realized that *he* had condemned the ancient spellcaster to his fate.

"That is where you might be wrong."

"You know something?"

"I fear you will not like it, human."

He knew then what the Dragon King was suggesting. "You want me to go and seek out the gnome."

"Insanity!" Xabene, who had kept quiet since their arrival, mostly because the reptilian monarch had stared her down almost immediately, dared step toward the massive figure lying before them. Benton Lore and several guards readied their weapons. While Wellen could not fault their loyalty, he did find it hard to think that *they* could possibly protect the Dragon

King better than he himself could. What were swords and spears compared to *one* paw?

"I merely offered the choice, female," snarled Green. The enchantress, staring up at his open jaws, stepped back behind the dubious protection of Wellen's body. "I feel that Master Bedlam would have wanted to know regardless."

"Thank you, yes." The idea of returning to the field and seeking out the hermitic gnome, a creature who had baffled and foiled would-be conquerers for as long as anyone could remember, appeared ludicrous on the surface. It also appeared ludicrous below the surface.

And yet . . .

"Shade might be dead," Xabene reminded him, seeing the calculating look on his visage. "Could he possibly hold on for so long?"

He remembered the rolling thunder again. If the shadowy warlock was dead, however, why were the Lords of the Dead not moving? Surely they still wanted Wellen. There was also Xabene. He doubted that they would leave her be.

It was no use mulling it over and over. The explorer knew what his decision was already. He had to know. He had to *try.* "How can I do what no one else has in all these centuries? How can I gain entrance to the gnome's citadel?"

The burning eyes of his host lowered. "That, I fear, I do not know. I cannot even ssssay how you might find the curssssed place!"

"Then why bring it up?" Xabene asked, her voice and stance mocking.

"Because I *am* in debt to the gray one!" The Dragon King would say no more about that. "And if I knew of a way to send mysssself to hissss . . . his aid, I would."

"Wellen, listen to me!" The raven-tressed woman turned to him so that they faced each other. She moved close, too close for his peace of mind, and said, "It would be madness to put yourself in the claws of Purple. While he is a lover of knowledge, like this one, he lacks any care for humanity. As long as you are useful to him, you stay alive! Become useless and you perish!"

"She is correct in what she says."

He knew that, but it made no difference. Somehow, he had to find a way. Wellen silently pondered his own abilities, physical and otherwise, and tried to find something that would aid him.

There was not much. He was a researcher, a would-be explorer, a man of books who lived for knowledge but did not always use it to his benefit. Wellen admitted to himself that he knew facts, not the world. It was not an entirely shameful thing. Even now, the thought of merely conversing with the gnome, learning a few of the things the master of the citadel had learned, exchanging knowledge...

Exchanging knowledge?

Would it work?

The others, even the Dragon King, had waited in silence, seeing that this was an inner struggle on which everything here hinged. Wellen smiled at Xabene, thanking her for what he was certain was true concern, then turned so that he faced Lore and his monarch, too.

"I think I have a plan."

"Indeed?" The lord of the Dagora Forest lowered his tremendous head. Benton Lore looked skeptical, but that was the way prime ministers and major-domos were supposed to look as far as Wellen was concerned.

"What can you tell me about the gnome?"

Green acceded to his second. "Lore?"

The pepper-haired soldier thought. "There is not much, my lord. No one knows much about him. If he has a name, it has never reached the ears of a talespinner. Legend says that it is the same gnome, that he is immortal, but I find that hard to believe."

"What about Shade?" Xabene could not help asking slyly.

"Shade is Shade. He is an entirely different matter."

"Of *course.*"

The commander went on. "Now and then it's claimed he is seen in human settlements. I have even heard he appears in the aeries of the Seekers or, more doubtful, the underworld dwellings of the imaginary Quel."

"They are not imaginary," Wellen commented, recalling the massive, armored monsters.

"No?" The Dragon King was interested in pursuing the subject, but held back while Lore continued.

"No one knows what he does when he appears. He is seen and then not seen."

Wellen scratched his chin. "What sort of people have seen him?"

"My spies, but I assume they are not who you mean.

Learned folk for the most part. People whose word I can trust in this matter. There have been others, some trustworthy, some not, but the majority are as I said.''

"I think he must love knowledge," the scholar commented. He knew that his idea might be foolhardy, but no more than some of those ideas attempted already. How many more ridiculous plots had been hatched over the millennia as desperation grew among those seeking the dragon tome and its owner?

"What do you propose?" Lore asked, his doubts in whatever Wellen had planned quite evident.

"Something simple and straightforward, but it still required knowing *where* the citadel is."

"I think . . . there may be a way," Xabene interjected. She did not want to speak, but if Wellen intended to seek out the gnome again, everyone knew that she would go with him. Therefore, it behooved her to increase their chances of success as much as possible.

"And what might that be, female?" asked the Dragon King. He was as doubtful of her suggestions as Benton Lore had been of whatever plan Bedlam had come up with.

The enchantress grew thoughtful. "I'd rather not say until I've had a chance to try it. There is a problem, though."

"Of course."

"Not one beyond the skill of the enterprising Commander Lore, however," she added, smiling knowingly at the officer. "I need you to gather grass from the region where the structure rested. Grass and cloth for weaving."

"Grass?" Lore was incredulous.

"You shall have whatever you desire, female," the reptilian patriarch interrupted. His nostrils flared, sending tiny clouds of smoke flying. "But I shall expect some results. Your skills are not what they used to be."

Xabene was more confident now, despite the polite reminder of her present status. "If you can get me what I need today, than two days from now should be sufficient to find out if I'm correct, Your Majesty. What I hope to do doesn't require much sorcery. Just concentration, cunning, and some talent for *weaving*." She looked at her hands in disgust. "Something I thought I'd never have to do again."

"And you, Wellen Bedlam," the Dragon King said. "Is there anything beyond the usual preparations that you will need for this undertaking?"

He could think of only one thing. "Luck."

Green chuckled. The sound echoed. "That, I am afraid, is a treasure likely beyond even the gnome."

Perhaps because of the task Xabene had set before him, Benton Lore had been determined to retrieve the grass himself. He presented her with his catch only two hours after the audience with the Green Dragon. The major-domo's eyes dared the enchantress to tell him that he had failed in any way. Xabene, however, indicated she was quite satisfied with the bundle of wild grass. She took it and other materials she had requested to her chamber, where some of the other human servants had set up a device to aid her in her weaving. With it, the enchantress promised that even with her rusting skills would be able to finish the project by nightfall. Wellen was almost certain that she actually looked forward to the work, if only to keep her mind off of her former masters.

The explorer's own plans were so simple that he had much time on his hands. Part of that time he spent with the Dragon King, who more and more became simply a fellow scholar and not an emerald-scaled leviathan who could have swallowed him whole. The drake lord told him more about the Dragonrealm and how the Dragon Kings ruled it.

There were thirteen kings and twenty-five or so dukes. The truth as to their origins was lost to the drakes; as far as most were concerned, the past really did not matter. It was where the Green Dragon differed from most of his brethren. "The past matters very greatly. We are but the most recent monarchs of this land. I do not think, human, that I am remisssss in believing that our predecessorsssss also thought that they would rule forever."

It was a sobering thought even to the human. He thought of his own race and the ever-growing menace of the Sons of the Wolf back home. Most thought the raiders were a temporary menace, but Wellen sometimes wondered.

As she had promised, Xabene did finish the weaving portion of her plan. The enchantress forbid anyone to touch or even look at her work, but not because she was embarrassed about its quality. With her meager magic, the sorceress-turned-weaver had instigated the next step, which would take all night to complete itself and was so sensitive to outside influence that even Bedlam, with his limited abilities, might disturb it.

The night passed so uneventfully that Wellen, unable to believe it, found he still could not sleep. Again, the sounds around him made him think of either Shade or the Lords of the Dead. Sleep finally did come, but then his dreams were haunted by cloth-enshrouded specters and rotting ghouls that slowly stalked him.

Morning, as horribly quick as it came, was a blessing by comparison.

Xabene remained ensconced in her chambers. What she was doing was still a mystery, since she had forbidden even Wellen to enter, but the smell of melting wax wafted from the entranceway. Feeling rather useless, again, he decided to see if he could convince the Dragon King to teach him how to bring his abilities to the surface and use them with some consistency. The idea had originally come to him because of the constant nagging in his head. His premonitions could not cope with dragons nearby, even if those creatures were either indifferent or, in the case of the monarch himself, fairly friendly. It was especially irritating this morning.

The dragon, however, had been reluctant so far to instruct him. As with many things, he had not said why. Wellen, who had seen few other drakes during his stay here, had an idea why. Making use of humans was one thing. While Bedlam knew that Benton Lore was very important to the leviathan and even respected by the Green Dragon's clans, part of that respect was due to the knowledge that he was fiercely loyal to his lord. He had been born and raised in one of the human settlements and considered it as much his land as his lord's.

The scholar, on the other hand, was an outsider. Not merely someone from a neighboring kingdom, but from a land beyond the control of any Dragon King. He was an enigma and, as Wellen had discovered, the drakes disliked, perhaps even *feared*, enigmas.

A guard met him in the tunnel just a few yards from his destination. "Your presence is requested by His Majesty."

"I was just going to him."

The guard insisted on leading him back the short distance. Protocol was protocol even in the kingdoms of the Dragon Kings.

Raising his head, the emerald behemoth acknowledged the human's arrival. "Master Bedlam. So good of you to come so quickly."

"I was on my way to see you when your guardsman found me."

"Then you heard."

"Heard?" Wellen's hopes rose. "Shade's returned?"

"Alas, no. This concerns an intruder captured in the eastern edge of my forest. A most unique human."

"And how does that concern me?"

The dragon's mouth curled into a toothy smile. "He claims to know you."

"Know me?" Wellen tried to recall who had been left in charge of the *Heron's Wing*. With all that had happened, however, he could not even summon up a distinct face, much less a name. "Who?"

Turning his head, the dragon commanded, "You may bring the creature in."

Two guards stepped from a side corridor into the cavern chamber. Between them was one of the last people that the explorer had ever thought to see again.

"Asaalk!"

"Master Bedlam, would you so kindly please tell these two that I am friend, not foe?" The blue man partially turned so that Wellen could see the ropes that bound his arms back.

"You do know thissss . . . this creature?" The drake lord was visibly amused by the northerner's blue skin.

"I do, Your Majesty. He is likely the only other survivor of the column, unless, of course, some made it back to those waiting for us." The hopeful explorer looked to Asaalk for confirmation.

"Alas, I do not know," Prentiss Asaalk replied with great sadness. "Until yesterday, I was a prisoner of the beast who rules the land to the east, yes!"

"The Purple Dragon?"

"The Lord Purple, yes. I was not laughing, either, despite his peculiar appearance. He is not a forgiving master."

"He is not," agreed the Green Dragon, interjecting at this point. "It issss a wonder you succeeded to escape!"

Prentiss Asaalk bowed. "Master Bedlam will tell you that I can be enterprising when I need to be, yes?"

Wellen nodded. Deep down, he was sorry that it had not been Yalso who had survived, although he knew that could not have ever been the case, having witnessed the captain's death himself. He was ashamed that he was less thrilled by Asaalk's survival than he would have been if the mariner had walked through the door. The blue man had probably gone through at least as much hell as he had.

The huge dragon nodded to the guards. From their faces, they were not that pleased to release the blue man, but when their master commanded they obeyed.

"My great thanks, Your August Majesty!" Asaalk rubbed his arms where rope marked had formed.

"In gratitude, you will tell us all, in detail, of your captivity and your escape."

"Only too gladly!" With gusto, Prentiss Asaalk talked about being thrown from his horse and stumbling his way north. Twice he had thought that the dragon was coming for him, but both times it veered away. The northerner, weaponless, had nevertheless continued on bravely to the north. There were incidents, but his skills of survival had always come through for him in the end.

Until he had been spotted by servants of the Purple Dragon. His strength depleted, the northerner had been easily captured. Asaalk was taken before the drake lord himself and only quick thinking had saved his life. He had immediately discerned that here was a beast who admired knowledge and gathered it to him as if it were gold.

"And what did you have to offer him?" the Green Dragon interrupted.

"I told him of my homeland and of the place I came from. I...embellished a bit for him, yes, in order to keep his interest." The blue man glanced at Bedlam. "You, I think, would have done the same."

Wellen nodded.

Asaalk skimmed through his captivity, something the scholar could not blame him for doing. It could not have been a pleasant time. Escape had come by accident. He had been fitted with a magical collar to keep him under control, but after a couple of days, he had discovered that the control was weakening. His probing fingers came across a crack that had formed when they had sealed the device around his neck.

"By the end of the third day, it threatened me no more. I wasted no time, yes. When my chance came, I *walked* out of their lives like a cat." The rest of his tale the blue man summed up in a few sentences. He had headed west, knowing from information he had gathered that here he might find sanctuary.

"And what do I find, but a face so familiar to me! This is fate, yes?"

The northerner's exaggerated speech pattern made Wellen wince. He was certain by now that Asaalk's shifting from one manner of speech to another was calculated. Now and then, the blue man might slip, but for the most part, he seemed to purposely change. Why he continued to do that was something the scholar doubted he wanted to know about. Perhaps now that he was safe again, the blue man's ambitions were returning. Did Asaalk think he could toy with the Dragon King?

It hardly mattered for now, Bedlam reminded himself. What Prentiss Asaalk chose to do was up to him. Wellen had his own path to follow.

The northerner apparently did not think so. He strode up to the shorter man, clasped him on the shoulders, and bellowed, "It is good to see you again, yes! I thought you dead! Now, the two of us can leave this place together and return home!"

"Home?" Once, he had planned to try and start a colony here, one that would not have to deal with the machinations occurring across the sea. That idea had died a lamented death with the unfortunates in the column. "How can we return? The *Heron's Wing* is . . ."

"Is still anchored off the shore where we left it. It has not been so long since we departed, has it?"

It had not been, but Wellen had assumed that the rest of the expedition had either departed in haste or been taken by the minions of Purple. "It's still there?"

"Before my escape,"—here Asaalk gave him a theatrical impression of craftiness—"I gained access to a device that could study most every region of the cursed purple one's kingdom, including the shore."

"Ssssuch a device is known to me," Green interrupted. "All of us control such artifacts. There are other methods available assss well."

Home! It almost seemed too good to be true! "Could we see the ship from here?"

"That issss doubtful. While we may call one another *brethren*, each of ussss . . . each of us guards our domain very carefully. Not that we do not have our spies, of course. Finding out about this vessel is another concern, however. Purple is particularly jealous at the moment, what with his prize stolen, and so he has stepped up his defenses. Perhaps after a time I will be able to overcome his spells. It would take many days of work.''

"We can't afford to wait," Wellen reminded him. "Shade can't afford to wait. As soon as Xabene completes her work, we have to move." Even now, it was probably too late. Yet, he still could not believe that Shade was dead.

Asaalk listened with great attentiveness. "Please. What is it you speak of? Who is this Xabene?"

"I'm Xabene." The enchantress was standing by the entrance to the Green Dragon's imperial chamber. How long she had stood there, Wellen did not know. Somehow, she had found yet another form-enhancing outfit, again black, but this time it was a little more practical. Still a gown, yet it was sturdier, more able to combat the elements and plant life.

She was no less desirable and she likely knew it.

The lengthy northerner eyed her with open appreciation. He shook his head and said to Wellen, "Here I struggle and you have found this one! All adventures should be so treacherous!"

"Oh, it was . . . for both of us." The enchantress gave him a winning smile, which made Bedlam scowl. She then smiled at Wellen and joined him, giving clear indication to Prentiss Asaalk where her interests lay.

"Human relations are always sssso amusing," the reptilian monarch baldly stated, "but there are other, more pressing, concerns. How goes your task, female?"

The enchantress did not take kindly to the drake lord's general refusal to acknowledge that she had a name. "It goes well, dragon. I have to return in an hour and begin the next stage." She had been up for hours already, but fatigue was not evident. Sorcery gave Xabene life where nothing else could. "After the next stage, we just have to let it sit until it is ready."

"And when will that be?"

"Tomorrow sometime." She held her head high. "As I promised. It should function perfectly for our purposes. I could, of course, do more if I had the time."

"What is it we speak of?" Asaalk wanted to know.

Wellen saw no harm in telling him. "A way of tracking down an elusive building."

"You jest."

"Did the Dragon King Purple never speak of the gnome?" The northerner nodded. "There was talk of such a creature and his sanctum, yes. For a time, I was questioned, but I knew nothing. What does this have to do with a building that . . . *hides*?''

"It vanished. I was standing almost as close to it as I am to you."

"Aaaah! This explains much, yes! Small wonder they did not expend so much effort on me! I know of the value that the Dragon King put on the place. If it is gone, he would be very furious."

The Green Dragon chuckled at that. "He issss, indeed, human! He would rather his get all be slaughtered than lose the gnome."

"It is a book he wants, I think."

Green's more vicious counterpart had evidently told Asaalk more than Wellen had first imagined. "That's right. A book."

"And you also want this book?"

The scholar was saved from trying to explain by Xabene, who cryptically said, "Among other things, if possible."

Prentiss Asaalk seemed to measure Wellen. "And you plan to go to this place then? You plan to risk the evil of the land's monarch?"

"I do."

"I have not found you only to lose you again!" The blue man put a companionable hand on the explorer's shoulder. Wellen tried not to wince at the strength Asaalk used when he squeezed. "Then *I* must go with you!"

"That won't be necessary," Xabene blurted.

"But it will! I must see to it that Master Bedlam here survives to return home and claim his glory!"

The enchantress grew rigid and glanced at Wellen. She did not appear to like it when the blue man spoke of him departing. The thought had been discussed on and off, but no one had truly believed he would be leaving. Until Asaalk's return, it had been assumed that there was no longer a vessel waiting for him. Without a good ship, the explorer was trapped here. Now, however, it appeared he had a definite means of escape. Whether he made use of it was up to Wellen.

Prentiss Asaalk was not going to back down. Bedlam knew the man well enough to realize that. It might be that the northerner *would* come in handy. They could hardly go marching in with Benton Lore and his soldiers and expect the gnome to listen. More important, they could hardly expect the dragon Purple to ignore a small army. A diversion had been planned by the lord of the Dagora Forest, but this would only work if it was more noticeable than the truth. Three or four people riding swiftly and shielded by some spell of the Green Dragon would have a better chance of avoiding detection. If one of those people, Prentiss Asaalk, knew something about the workings of Purple's kingdom, it might increase their chances. While the Green Dragon was the best source of information, they could hardly bring him along.

"All right," Wellen told him, trying not to sigh in resignation. He turned to Xabene, but she was finding ways to avoid his eyes. The time was coming for the two of them to ask and answer some questions for one another.

It may be that the Dragon King saw some of this, though it was more likely he had his own questions and answers to discuss. "Human," he said to Asaalk. "These guards will take you to a place where you may feed and rest. I have things that I must discuss with Master Bedlam. You will be summoned when your presence is required."

The northerner bowed and obediently followed his guards out. Wellen knew that Asaalk did not like being dismissed like that, but protesting to a dragon was utter foolishness.

When it was certain that the northerner was far enough away that he could not possibly hear them converse, the Dragon King asked, "You trust this peculiar-skinned human, Master Bedlam?"

"I do." He was basing his assumption on pure conjecture; with his head throbbing as it was, Asaalk could have been ready to murder him and he would not have known. Still, the two of them shared a bond. They were outsiders in a mad world.

Green tilted his head to one side and called out, "You may enter now, Benton Lore."

The black man stepped in from one of the outer corridors. "Yes, Your Majesty."

"You are certain, Wellen Bedlam, that you might trust this man?"

"I am . . . I *think* so, anyway." What were they driving at? What was wrong with Prentiss Asaalk? From Xabene's perplexed expression, he gathered she did not understand, either. Disliking the man in general was one thing, but sinister mysteries was another.

"Lore, tell him what you ssssensed."

The pepper-haired warlock looked at the curious duo and calmly reported, "Nothing."

Wellen shrugged. "So what then is the problem? If you sensed nothing amiss, then why should—"

"That was not what I said," Lore interrputed. "I said I sensed *nothing*. Your companion is magically blank to me."

"Assss he isss to *me*," added the leviathan.

"I do not understand."

The reptilian monarch smiled grimly, his toothy smile, as ever, making Wellen uneasy. "What Lore seeks to say, is that as far as the blue-skinned one is concerned, we do not feel his presence on a magical level."

"He does not exist," completed Lore. "Bodily, yes, but the man you call Prentiss Asaalk is not altogether *human*."

XV

Wellen spent several hours with Prentiss Asaalk, but unlike the Green Dragon and Benton Lore, not once did he sense anything amiss. Asaalk seemed a bit more flamboyant than he recalled, but not enough that the scholar could interpret the difference as anything significant. Still, Wellen was willing to think about what his host had said. The Dragon King was of the opinion that Asaalk might be a spy of sorts for the Purple Dragon. It might not be the blue man at all, but rather something or someone made to resemble him. Bedlam was therefore careful about what he discussed with the possible double and regretted that the subjects of Xabene's work and the gnome had come up.

In order to keep everything seemingly normal, Asaalk had been given one of the chambers near those of Wellen and the enchantress. The guards, however, were tripled in strength. No one informed Asaalk that there had ever been a change in numbers.

Day had passed into the night, although that was not a simple thing to realize in the perpetually lit caverns. Wellen first knew it from the exhaustion that threatened to overtake him. A short conversation with Lore had verified the lateness of the hour. Asaalk had already retired and his chamber was carefully watched. No one wanted a repeat of the attack by the Lords of the Dead. The Green Dragon was very certain that this was a ploy set up by his counterpart to the southeast and not the necromancers. The style was identifiable, the leviathan had informed him, even if the plot was not one of Purple's most cunning. Its flaws had been spotted almost instantly by the master of the Dagora Forest.

The Green Dragon intended to turn that ploy against its originator.

"He thinks we do not suspect that this creature is possibly not the real human. The frustration of losing the gnome has made him act in too much hassssste!" The reptilian monarch had greatly enjoyed his counterpart's gross error.

Wellen was not so confident. He could not help wondering if there was more to the situation than they knew. Had the other Dragon King grown *that* careless?

The scholar paused when he reached Xabene's chamber. A thick curtain covered the entranceway, but he could tell it was dark within. Wellen had wanted to talk to her, but waking the enchantress would not start the conversation off in the correct mood. This had to be done just right.

He continued on to his own chamber, nodded to a couple human guards . . . did the rest of Green's clan have *nothing* to do with humans? . . . and brushed aside the curtain as he entered.

Xabene lay casually across his bed, waiting for him. She smiled slyly at his dumbfounded expression. "I had to talk to you, Wellen Bedlam."

Her formal use of his name did not bode well. He strode to the bed and stood before her, arms crossed. With languid movements, the well-formed sorceress rose and faced him.

"Still untrusting?"

"I trust you." He stepped back when she came too near. Xabene laughed lightly at his reaction.

"I can see that you do. Don't worry, I won't come any closer than this . . . unless you decide to let me."

"What do you want?"

She folded her own arms and turned away. Wellen could not help but follow every detail of her movement. The ebony-haired enchantress had resumed her role of seductress. Bedlam was not certain whether he welcomed the return or not.

"I've wanted many things in my life. Most of them were beyond me before I sold myself to the Lords of the Dead for power. When I was finally able to gather those things, I discovered that they were not what I had expected. There were always other things, though, so I was not unhappy so long as I had those goals, those treasures, to pursue."

Xabene turned around again. Wellen broke the momentary silence to ask, "What does that have to do with me? Am I supposed to be like those treasures? You no longer have to toy with me for the necromancers; does that mean it's time to turn elsewhere?"

In response, she took hold of Wellen and kissed him hard. Like a candle's flame abruptly doused, the world around the scholar winked out of existence. His world was now the woman in his arms. Shade, the gnome, the Lords of the Dead, the Dragon Kings . . . they seemed such distant things that he was almost tempted to believe he had dreamed them.

When they finally separated, Xabene once more had a calculating look in her eye, but this time Bedlam had a better idea of what it concerned. "I still don't believe in love at first sight," she said. "But I do believe that two people can find that they are meant for one another. I was bothered by that thought when I first noticed how I reacted to you. You struck something within me that should have been as dead as . . ." Xabene forced the unspoken thought away. "Let's just say that I knew I was yours even when I fought not to be."

"I'm not certain I understand some of that."

"It doesn't matter, but something else does. You know what I was like, Wellen; you know what I've done. Can you accept me as I am now?"

He blinked. "I thought I had."

"Kissing me doesn't necessarily answer that. I've done far more with men before and neither side thought of love."

"Are you the same Xabene as then?"

"Only in form."

"You almost sound like Shade," the scholar commented. "My answer still holds. If what I've seen these past few days is the true you . . . and not some playacting like both you and Asaalk seem to enjoy . . . then I have no intention of giving you up."

"What about your vessel?"

Wellen had forgotten about that. "If it exists, which is doubtful, it has room for one more." He grimaced. "It has room for *many* more now. More likely, the Dragonrealm is now *my* home."

She took hold of him again. "Do you still intend your madness with the gnome?"

"I do. I owe Shade that much."

Xabene sighed. "I suppose I do too." The enchantress kissed him briefly, then began to lead him toward the bed. "If we are destined to walk arm-in-arm into the maw of Purple, then, let us do it as one, not two."

"Xabene . . ."

A finger to his lips silenced him. "No argument, please." She smiled and though her smile was seductive, it was not calculating, this time. "After all, tomorrow may be too late."

He could not argue that no matter how much he might have wanted to. Tomorrow was all too likely to end in disaster . . . and one or both of them would probably be dead.

The blame, much like the choice, would be his.

All too soon it was the next day. With much enthusiasm, Xabene revealed her handiwork to Wellen and the others. There was no way of avoiding the inclusion of Prentiss Asaalk, or whatever or whoever the blue figure might actually be, from the gathering. If Asaalk was other than he appeared, to exclude him was to warn the one who had sent him that the plot had been uncovered. The Green Dragon did not care for events to occur that way.

At Lore's order, two servants had brought a large, oak table into the cavern chamber so that the enchantress could better display her handiwork. The results, needless to say, were curious enough to bring even the Dragon King to silence.

"Thissss issss a tapestry of ssssorts," the leviathan finally stated.

"It is," she responded. "Given more time, I could have made it much more elaborate, but that would've probably taken years."

"Time we do not have," Wellen agreed. If this worked, they would likely be leaving soon after. The Dragon King wanted everything perfectly coordinated. It was possible that the citadel would move again, too. The nearer they were when they did their final check of its location, the less chance they had of riding fruitlessly back and forth across the plains.

"How does it work?" Asaalk asked rather eagerly.

The tapestry was fairly simple. Three feet in length and two across, it barely fit what Wellen would have thought the size requirements of a tapestry. He recalled the huge, intricate cloths hanging in the great houses and the university corridors. This . . . this seemed more something to wrap a small baby in.

Its pattern was also simple, although time, again, had played a hand in that. The explorer recognized a crude representation of the region where the gnome's five-sided citadel had stood until recently. The material used to weave that section was different from the rest. He suspected it was the grass Xabene had requested. That she had been able to make use of it in her weaving indicated that some of her sorcery still remained.

The hills and grasslands were easy to identify, but one mark puzzled him. A five-pointed star. He assumed it must represent the citadel, but it stood far away from the field, almost as if it were part of some other illustration not yet complete.

Wellen repeated Asaalk's question.

"The best way to explain it is to show you," Xabene replied. She turned the tapestry toward her, then pulled a small crystal from a pouch on her waist. Nothing their eyes, she held up the piece. "I used this in an attempt to spy on the gnome while he worked. I also used this and . . ." Her eyes lit up and she rummaged through the pouch. Xabene retrieved a tattered notebook and thrust it toward Wellen. ". . . and *this* to search for you."

He looked at the ragged object. It was his notebook. The scholar felt a momentary rush of affection, as if a favored pet had been returned to him. The journal was all he really had left from his once-peaceful life.

"It occurred to me," the enchantress continued, "that I could use the crystal in another way." So saying, Xabene lowered the crystal onto the waxy star. She held it in place for several seconds, closing her eyes during that period and whispering something to herself. When she opened them again, there was an intense eagerness.

"What did you do?" Prentiss Asaalk asked. Everyone, including the Dragon King, had turned their attention to the sorceress during her brief display.

She glanced down at the tapestry, smiled widely, and indicated that they, too, should study her creation.

The star was no longer situated under the crystal. It now marked a spot in the northwestern region outlined on the tapestry.

Xabene leaned back and put her hands on her hips, pride at her accomplishment radiating from her. "*There* is where the gnome is!"

"So simple!" Wellen marvelled. He touched the star lightly, almost afraid he would nudge it away. Examination proved, however, that it was as much a part of the illustration as the plains were.

"Not so simple. I had to chip the crystal to make this work. There are fragments incorporated in the wax. Only because of them does the tapestry work."

One observer, however, was not so impressed with the results and what they indicated. "That cannot be! From all that my ssssourcessss have informed me, there hassss been no ssssign of the citadel! It doessss not ssssit there! Not sssso closssse!"

"It must!" The enchantress looked ready to fight to protect her success. She had proven that her abilities were worth something even without the added power that the Lords of the Dead had given to her. One Dragon King was not going to make that success a failure. "I planned it all out carefully! If the star is there, then that's where the building is!"

"Then where issss it, female? Floating high in the sssssky? I think one of my cousins would have sssseen it there!"

Wellen's eyes narrowed as he considered the suggestion. The sky, obviously, was not a proper choice, but what if the gnome had travelled in the opposite direction? He recalled how the Quel had burst from the ground. They *lived* down there; why not the gnome?

The short scholar leaned over the area where the star was located. "He's taken it below and shielded it."

"What?" Prentiss Asaalk stepped back as if struck. Not the reaction Wellen would have expected from the true northerner, but it was possible that Asaalk, out of his depth now, was truly surprised.

"What do you sssspeak . . . speak of, Master Bedlam? The cursed gnome has taken it *under* the surface?"

"Why not? Is it beyond him?"

"Hardly! Yet . . ." The Green Dragon could come up with no argument against Bedlam's suggestion. Xabene was visibly grateful for his quick thinking.

Pressing on, Wellen added, "We have to move as quickly as possible. You were the one who first said that. He could send it elsewhere at any time. An entire army might waste weeks hunting him, even if he's only limited to the plains . . . which we do *not* know is a certainty."

The Dragon King shifted. His claws scraped at the rocky surface of the cavern floor. "Below . . . and *moving*. Hissss skillssss never cease to amaze me!"

"A question, Master Bedlam," the blue man said. "How will you speak with the gnome even if you do find where he is located? He will be far underground, yes? It will make for difficult hearing."

"I doubt if the gnome pays any less attention to the outside world now that he has moved under the earth. Despite his hermitic existence, he's proved to be very interested in what is going on around him. That's one of the reasons I hope to contact him this time."

"And assss you indicated, human, time issss a great factor." The drake lord considered matters. He seemed to come to a decision he found both daring and dismaying. The emerald leviathan studied the scholar for several breaths, then finally asked, "Are you and yours prepared to leave within the hour?"

The Dragon King very much wanted to finish this, but Wellen thought that Green might be pushing ahead too swiftly. Wellen would have preferred to leave after nightfall, thinking that quick enough, but as he had realized before, one did not argue with a drake.

Bedlam exchanged looks with Xabene. She nodded, seeing the inevitable.

"We can be ready," he said with confidence.

"Good! Lore."

The black man appeared from nowhere. How long had he been lurking nearby? "Your Majesty?"

"Have the animals been readied?"

"I ordered men to make them ready more than an hour ago . . . in anticipation."

"Ssssplendid."

"We are to ride?" questioned Asaalk. "Not teleport?"

"Not until late in the journey. Teleportation works best when one is familiar with the region." Commander Lore's bored look was a mask; Wellen knew he did not care to stay in the northerner's presence any longer than necessary. "There has been no reason to remember that area until now; it was like any other part of the region. With the exception of a few masters, such as Shade, most spellcasters are better off using line of sight for such unfamiliar places."

"We would need to see where we are going, yes?"

"Exactly." No longer needing to look at the blue man, Benton Lore awaited further commands.

The truth was that there would be no teleporting at all. Neither Wellen nor Xabene was capable of casting the spell, but that was not the reason why. After all, Lore, who was to follow behind in order to keep their backs covered from possible treachery, did have the capability. The Green Dragon, however, had pointed out that excessive spellcasting would only attract the attention of his fellow monarch. A small group of riders had a better chance, especially if Purple was intentionally looking for the telltale signs of teleportation.

Asaalk was the reason they hinted at utilizing teleportation at all. Whether he was not truly the blue man or was willingly serving the other drake lord, the figure beside them was not to be trusted as far as the Green Dragon was concerned. False information fed to him might make its way to Purple. That would give them two distractions. At the very least, it would certainly keep the blue man at a disadvantage.

Their efforts might be for nothing; the Purple Dragon by no means could see everything that went on in his domain. Wellen and the others could feasibly reach their destination, succeed or not at contacting the gnome, and return without any incidence of danger.

No one was willing to believe it would be so easy.

Wellen wanted to leave Prentiss Asaalk behind, but the master of Dagora Forest would not have that. Drakes were apparently fond of overdone subterfuge and the Green Dragon revelled in it. The scholar was certain only disaster would come of it in the end.

The drake lord shifted, bringing everyone's attention back to the situation at hand. "The time for talk is over, then. Lore, see what activity occurs in my brother's domain. Master Bedlam, you will ready yourself and see to it that your companions are ready." Hesitation, then, "Would that I could be there when he finally realizes he has been tricked and that *we* have gained access to what he, the Lords of the Dead, and all their predecessors failed to capture!''

Feeling uncomfortable with the Dragon King's overconfidence, Bedlam reminded him, ''The plan is hardly foolproof; the gnome may laugh at me from within his citadel! I am only relying on the thought that in certain cases, he and I are of like mind.''

''I have faith in you, human. Besides, as has been brought up more than once, nothing else has succeeded. Why not try *your* plan? At the most it can only fail!''

He was not certain whether the Dragon Lord was serious or not, but he could hardly ask. Wellen took one last look at the tapestry, exhaled sharply, and said, ''Let's hope that *is* all that happens.''

No one had to remind him of what failure by itself actually meant. Wellen and the others might still return to the forest, from there to continue on with their lives as best as possible. For Shade, however, it meant death sooner or later at the rotting hands of the Lords of the Dead.

That was, of course, assuming he was not dead already.

Prentiss Asaalk confronted him a short time later in the corridor by the former's chamber. Servants had taken what few things Wellen was going to carry and brought them ahead so they could be packed. The explorer had intended on trying to talk to the Green Dragon for the few minutes that still remained. There were details about the diversions he was uncertain about and wanted clarified.

''Wellen Bedlam, you and I must speak.''

The scholar's throat tightened. ''About what?''

''Please! Inside the room.'' Asaalk's voice was low and just a little uncertain.

After the necromancers' invasion, it was doubtful that anything could occur that Lore's soldiers would not respond to in a matter of seconds. Nonetheless, Wellen was somewhat leery about being alone with the blue man. ''Perhaps we could talk later, when—''

''No! It must be now!'' The massive northerner seemed to fill up the corridor. ''Please, Master Bedlam!''

The intensity with which Asaalk spoke, moved, even *breathed*, made Wellen acquiesce. Nodding, he allowed the blue man to lead the way into the chamber. Asaalk had never struck him as a man who did things for no reason and if he needed to speak so urgently with Wellen, then it might do the scholar some good to listen. Perhaps some questions the Green Dragon had brought up would be answered. Still, the scholar did not consider himself a complete fool. As he followed the northerner in, Wellen put one hand on the hilt of the sword that he had convinced the Dragon King to let him wear.

Asaalk studied the chamber, possibly seeking magical eyes that might report his words to the drake lord even as he spoke them. Satisfied, the blue man finally talked.

"Master Bedlam, I must warn you about myself."

"Warn me?"

The blue man's eyes darted back and forth. "I spoke of escaping the collar put on me by the Dragon Purple, yes?"

"Yes."

"I did not escape that collar, my friend."

"But the marks . . ." At one point when they had last spoken alone, Prentiss Asaalk had shown him the marks left by the metal collar. They were purplish, scaly scratches. Wellen had been certain at the time that removing the collar must have been painful if it had caused these.

"Aaah . . ." Asaalk gave him a grim smile and fingered one of the scars. "These do not show where the collar was, but where the collar *is*! Like the building whose master has buried it, the cursed thing lies *beneath* the surface, yes! Beneath the skin!"

Without thinking, Wellen started to reach forward to touch the other's neck. Asaalk jerked away. "No! Only I may touch it! Anyone else's touch is agony! One of my captors put a hand to the back of my neck, yes, and I almost doubled over!"

"How is it you are able to tell me? That hardly seems like a thing that the Purple Dragon would neglect to prevent. He does not mark me as a simple tyrant."

"And he is not, no. I have some small magic of my own and I have my own indomitable will." He swelled with pride. "I am never totally beaten! I always strike back!" Prentiss Asaalk twitched then, moving like someone just whipped. The blue man deflated a bit. "The collar always fights to regain even that bit of ground from me. I fear that sooner or later it will triumph, yes. Yet, no one can remove the collar, save the Purple Dragon and he will do that only if I obey his commands!"

"And what are those?"

"To bring you to him, of course."

"Me? In particular?" Wellen recalled standing before the pentagon and watching it vanish. Had the other Dragon King been observing and decided, like so many others had, that the would-be warlock was responsible? Wellen was beginning to wonder himself. Was he absolutely certain that the tingle he had felt had not originated from him? Absurd, yes, but still not entirely improbable. After all, he had not meant to bespell Shade, yet he had.

"You." The blue man seemed to bemoan this fact. "He has come to believe you must be here to steal the dragon tome from him . . . he is certain that it is his by right, yes."

"I only want to be left alone, to live in peace."

Asaalk shrugged. "But we cannot and now we must think of what to do."

"The Green Dragon might be able to do something."

"He cannot. I believe my accursed master, yes, when he says that he has planned for that, but"—suddenly, the crafty northerner's eyes narrowed—"could the gnome, do you think?"

Even from what little he knew about the short, squat figure, Bedlam thought it quite possible. "If he can do everything that's been hinted to me, then I think it's very possible that he can help you."

"That is good. If he cannot, I must face the wrath of the Dragon King. I assure you that he is not a forgiving creature, no."

Asaalk twitched again. Wordlessly, he stepped away from Wellen and turned his back to the scholar. The blue man's entire backside shook from effort. Bedlam purposely found other things to study, thinking that the struggling northerner deserved to preserve his pride. As much as he disliked many things about Prentiss Asaalk, he admired the blue man's spirit. Wellen was not so certain he could have been as strong under the circumstances.

At last, the blue man turned around. His countenance in no way betrayed his struggle with the pain Wellen had watched him go through. "You must let me come with you. I must speak to this little man."

The Green Dragon would forbid him doing that and Benton Lore would be with the trio to assure that the scholar obeyed.

Still, if there was anything he could do to aid the blue man, Wellen knew he had to try. "I'll see."

"I can ask no more."

They heard the sounds of armored men marching through the tunnel. As the two of them turned to face the entranceway, a guard stuck his head inside. He pulled it back almost immediately. There was some muttering, then Commander Lore stepped in.

"Everything is prepared. We do not know what Purple himself is doing, but our eyes watch his lackey's every move. He seems to be waiting, nothing more."

"Which means your lord wants us to leave now."

"Unless there is still urgent need to complete other matters, Master Bedlam. It is for your own sake, I must point out. His Majesty does not desire to endanger you any more than necessary. He cares."

"How noble," Asaalk sneered. Wellen gave him a severe frown, warning him not to provoke the major-domo.

Lore's eyes flared, but his visage remained polite and cool, as it always was around the blue man. "Yes, very much so. The same could certainly not be said for most of his kind, especially the tyrant whose land you reenter."

The blue man said nothing.

Wellen stepped between them, pretending interest only in the coming quest. "Have you provided Xabene with a map case for the tapestry? We need to keep it clean and out of sight."

"I have." The dark-skinned officer nodded, his eyes acknowledging his understanding of why the scholar had interrupted. "Even now, she waits by the mounts."

"Good. Then we had best be on our way."

"As you desire." Lore stepped aside and, with a sweep of his arm, indicated that the two outsiders should depart first. Asaalk stalked out of the chamber immediately, with Wellen following close behind. *A good thing we won't be here any longer than necessary!* he thought. *Each time these two meet, they come closer to blows!*

Whether or not they succeeded, he was determined to help the blue man free himself of the Dragon King's deadly ring. Then, Asaalk would be encouraged to go somewhere, *anywhere,* that he might like. Wellen intended to spend some time discussing the history of the realm with the Green Dragon, but he could hardly do that if Asaalk remained with him. Xabene also had a say in the matter, a very essential say, and her dislike of the blue man's ways was more than obvious.

It occurred to Wellen that he was assuming they would all be returning. That was still in doubt even with the information that Prentiss Asaalk had provided him.

Their footfalls echoed throughout the corridor, a feature of the caverns that he had grown so accustomed to that he barely noticed anymore. That was why when Benton Lore stepped up beside him that the shorter man was surprised when the officer commented, "The echoes have always fascinated me."

"Oh?"

"Actually, the acoustics of this entire system of caverns must be experienced over a long period of time to fully understand their complexity. One hears so much." The commander's expression was entirely innocent.

That settled the question of whether the Dragon King knew what the two foreigners had discussed. Wellen did not reply, but he took it as a mark of the monarch's trust that he had even been given a hint.

Prentiss Asaalk, several steps ahead, scratched his throat at the sore marks.

When they reached the animals, Xabene was there. Her eyes, first slits when she spied Asaalk, lit up when Wellen entered the chamber. He returned her smile, but his attention was momentarily fixed on his surroundings. They stood in what was an organized and very well-kept stable. Row upon row of stalls attested to the great capacity of the place. Most of the stalls were empty, but a few held tall, ready animals. The party's mounts were already saddled and waiting.

"Tell me, commander," Wellen said, noting the walls and ceiling of the chamber. "Was this entire system carved out or did any of it exist before the coming of the drakes?"

"Much of it was as you see it, sirrah. Even this place. But there have been many ruling races in this land, as my lord made mention, and some of those used this place before. We have had to make few additions."

"A ready-made kingdom," Xabene commented. "I hope the next rulers appreciate it as much as your masters do."

"Your mounts await you," Benton Lore reminded them, the enchantress's comment diplomatically ignored. It was impossible to believe he did not think about who those rulers would be. The Green Dragon had already hinted that the human race was becoming more and more an influential force in the realm. The major-domo himself was part of that force, having almost gained a kingdom of his own from the looks of things. The human habitations of this cavern system had to nearly equal in size those of the drake clans unless the entire cave system was even more extensive than it seemed. With men like Benton Lore to lead the way, humanity was indeed gaining a stronger foothold, especially in this region.

Not all the Dragon Kings were likely to appreciate that as much as the Green Dragon did.

Lore watched in silence as they mounted their horses. Because of Prentiss Asaalk, he did not mention that he would be following, but Wellen knew that they would barely be beyond the cave entrance before the commander himself mounted. He felt a little better knowing that Lore would be behind them; in some ways, the efficiency of the man reminded him of the late, lamented Yalso. Recollections of the captain, both before and *after* his death, renewed Wellen's decision to go ahead with this lunacy. Unlike Yalso, Shade might not yet be beyond his ability to save.

"You will be led to the entrance," the officer informed them solemnly. "From there, you will be on your own. You have the maps I gathered for you and you have the tapestry. That should be all you need. Follow the timetable we agreed on and there should be no trouble. Lord Purple will be too busy with other matters to watch out for you."

"Let us hope so." Asaalk's whisper was loud enough for all of them to hear.

"May the Dragon of the Depths watch over you," the black man concluded.

Two soldiers on horseback joined them. One of them, a dark-skinned man he recognized from the initial patrol, saluted and said, "Master Bedlam, if you and yours will follow me."

They did as he requested, Wellen and Xabene riding alongside one another and the blue man a length behind them. After the trio came the other soldier. Lore was taking no chances.

From the torch-lit stable they entered a darkened tunnel. The soldiers were undaunted by this change, but Wellen disliked it. There was no complaint from Asaalk, however, and Xabene, more used to the night than the day, likely was at peace. Wellen wished he could adjust his eyes to the way they had been during his sojourn into the realm of the dead.

A tiny light blossomed in the distance, the entrance to the outside. Bedlam wanted to ride hard toward it in order to escape the darkness, but he was aware how that might appear to the others. They would reach the light before long, anyway.

Then their troubles would truly begin.

XVI

The gnome smiled as he watched his adversaries play their games. The flurry of activity beyond his domain had given birth to a new, typically remarkable idea and he looked forward to implementing it when the time came.

The time was very near. Only a short *distance* from him, in fact.

When the time chosen for the diversion came, they acted as planned. They rode with speed and determination, their course rechecked just prior to the appointed hour. The citadel was still in the northwestern region, so close to where they had waited that it seemed almost a shame they had waited at all. Yet, wait they had, for no one, with the possible exception of Prentiss Asaalk, wanted to go charging in until their chances were best.

Somewhere behind them, Benton Lore was supposedly keeping pace. There had been no sign of the man, but the soldier was an expert at scouting . . . as he seemed to be expert at almost everything else.

Wellen's head, of course, pounded with dire warnings all the while. He needed no overly sensitive albeit consistent ability to tell him that he faced possible danger. He had known that from the first time the Dragon King had suggested this.

To the scholar's left, Prentiss Asaalk stared sullenly ahead. He had not forgiven them for their lack of trust, at least, that was what Wellen had decided. It was possible that would change if they were successful and the gnome showed them not only how to free Shade, but also how to rid the blue man of the magical collar just underneath his skin. The thought of the collar being there made Bedlam cringe every time he considered it; a fine but horrible piece of sorcery. He was amazed that anyone could live with such a thing attached, but the Dragonrealm probably held worse than that.

"It has to be just a short distance ahead!" shouted Xabene. "If we go too much farther, we'll be too much to the east!"

So far, there had been no sign of activity on the Purple Dragon's part. Wellen was both wary and relieved by that. True, the Green Dragon's deception was already at work, but from what he had heard of the master of this land, Bedlam could not help considering that this drake lord might not be so easily fooled.

Could it be he *wanted* them to locate the citadel for him? If so, how did the Dragon King think he was going to seize the prize? If the gnome deigned to speak to them, then they would surely be under some protection, as, of course, would be the tome everyone wanted so badly. If they failed, then Purple would be back where he started.

Benton Lore probably held the key. It would not have been surprising to learn that the lord of the Dagora Forest had held back a few plans even from Wellen. Not a betrayal, as Xabene or Asaalk might see it, but rather caution, for if the party did not know what else had been plotted, then it was doubtful anyone watching them would.

Raising a hand and slowing her mount, the enchantress cried out, "This is it! We're here!"

"Are you certain?" The blue man reined his horse to a stop. He peered around. "It all looks the same. I sense nothing, either."

"Let me look." She unrolled the tapestry. Wellen saw now another reason it was so small. Anything larger would have been cumbersome and nearly impossible to study while on horseback. Xabene glanced up several times, studied the landscape, then finally nodded. "If I'm correct, we're only about fifty feet from it."

"Which way?" Like Asaalk, Wellen could not see or sense anything that told him where the citadel might be buried. If they had not had the tapestry . . .

She rolled the magical item back up and placed it in the case Lore had given them. The enchantress then pointed to a spot to the southeast. "There. It lies somewhere just in front of us."

They dismounted. Bedlam experienced a sense of *déjà vu*,

save that this time he was hoping that the gnome's stronghold would reappear.

"You know," the sorceress said quietly, looking somewhat ashamed, "the first time you came here, when the place vanished, it wasn't entirely by your choice."

"I wondered."

"I was told to put the desire into your mind and enforce it. Given a choice, I would have preferred not to, but they were adamant. You can see how well it worked."

"Are you suggesting that I might have been influenced again?"

"By the drake who plays at being your friend?" Xabene shrugged. "I'd say I wouldn't be surprised, Wellen, although I do think he likes you. That might save your life in the end if it happens to be true."

"Or not. I've already considered the things you mentioned now, though, and I think I still would have come here. I owe Shade that, even if it's only to bring his body back."

She smiled sadly at him. "An idealist!"

"Worse. A dreamer." He did not try to explain the difference.

"Are we there yet?" asked the blue man, who had been trying all the while to find something, anything, that would lend credence to the tapestry's revelation.

Xabene took a few more steps, then stopped. "This should be good."

"Am I facing it?" Despite the danger of their situation, Wellen also feared the gnome's opinion of him if he happened to be facing the wrong direction. The wizened spellcaster's opinion was paramount, else he had not a chance of convincing the creature to hear him out.

"You should be. I'm sorry, but the tapestry was put together in quick fashion. As I said, if I'd had more time, I could have made it more elaborate."

"This will do."

"You are merely going to *talk*?" an incredulous Prentiss Asaalk spouted. "This is your massssstcr plan? This is to succeed where all other plans have failed?"

Wellen looked at him, trying not to think about how his own face must be turning red at the northerner's accusatory tone. "You knew that was what I planned."

"Yes, but I expected that . . ." The blue man trailed off. From his outburst, the scholar understood what Asaalk had left unsaid. Considering the distrust surrounding him, Asaalk had expected not to be told everything. That expectation had already been justified.

"Get on with it!" Xabene urged. "The longer we wait here the worse our chances."

Bedlam nodded. He reached down and removed the sword and scabbard he had been given in what he hoped was an obvious enough attempt to show the gnome he came in peace. Xabene stepped near, took the articles from him, and retreated again. Taking a deep breath, he organized his thoughts. "Master of the citadel, I know you by no name save 'gnome' but I hope you will hear me out this time. A plain and simple offer is what I bring. An exchange. I need your aid, your knowledge, to save a life and free another. I want nothing else from you. Your precious tome, what the Dragon King Purple and so many others have sought over the centuries, is none of my concern."

To one side, the enchantress wore a bitter mask. She had likely spent much of her service to the Lords of the Dead in pursuit of the very object he was telling the gnome he wanted no part of.

"In exchange, I can offer you only one thing. I come from a land beyond the seas east of here. My former home is one of only many, but I have spent my life, short as it is compared to your own, studying all those realms. You seem one forever searching for knowledge; I am the same. If you can aid me in my quest, a simple one for a spellcaster of your proven skill, then whatever I know I offer to share with you, scholar to scholar."

There was nothing more he could think of to say that would not make him sound like he was babbling. Wellen folded his arms and glanced Xabene's way again. She nodded her satisfaction. Prentiss Asaalk, a bit farther back, had eyes only for the patch of grassy ground before the shorter man. Wellen might have been invisible for all the interest the blue man had in him.

The scholar returned his own gaze to the still, innocuous-looking piece of field and waited.

Several minutes later, he was still waiting.

"We've failed," Xabene said at last, breaking the uneasy silence. "We'd better leave."

"Not yet."

"He won't respond, Wellen! We're all next to nothing to the

gnome, even the Dragon Kings!'' She stepped closer, intending to take his arm.

A powerful wind erupted in the grasslands Wellen watched. The startled sorceress stepped back.

The patch of grass shimmered, grew indistinct.

Asaalk muttered something that was lost in the roar of the unnatural wind.

The scant outline of a tall structure briefly formed before Wellen. He blinked, finally marking it down as wishful thinking when it did not rematerialize.

''Wellen, come away!''

''No! He musssst not!'' shouted the blue man. The ferocity in his voice so snared Bedlam that he started to turn toward the northerner.

A vaguely recalled tingle coursed through his body. He stumbled back, but not too far. His head barely throbbed and that meant that he was not in any true danger from what was happening . . . at least, not at the moment.

With a crackle of thunder, the five-sided citadel of the gnome once more stood before him.

There was a difference this time.

A hole just large enough to admit the scholar marred the otherwise smooth, featureless side of the sanctum.

''We can enter!'' Prentiss Asaalk raced toward the hole, which Wellen realized *was* an entrance, and tried to go through.

The wall sealed up just as he was about to put his hand into the opening.

The tall warrior pulled back his arm with a snarl. He pounded a fist against the blank wall and shouted, ''This is the last trick! Open! Open or I shall tear this place down around you!''

''I doubt *that* threat means much to him,'' a more practical Xabene interjected. She had quickly grasped the situation. ''Wellen, I think it's only meant for you.''

''What?'' Watching the fruitless pounding by Asaalk had made him think of something, but the notion faded like dew in the sunlight the moment the enchantress spoke. *Perhaps later,* he decided. ''What did you say?''

''I think . . .'' She put a hand against the wall. Her success was no better than that of the northerner. ''I think you might be the only one allowed to go inside.''

''It must be *all* of us!'' Asaalk argued.

"*We* do not have a say in the matter. Only the gnome, and he's chosen Wellen alone."

"Me . . . but I cannot leave you two out here!"

"I don't like it either, but you can't pass this up! It's you alone or no one."

She was probably right, but he did not like the thought of the two of them alone. Not merely because of the danger around them, but the certainty that the longer Xabene and Asaalk were alone together, the more likely they would come to blows about something.

Xabene confronted the taller man. "You. Move."

Seething, Prentiss Asaalk nonetheless obeyed. His eyes, more narrow than Wellen recalled them, darted back and forth between the scholar and the treacherous wall.

The hole sprouted into existence, this time more directly aligned with where an anxious Wellen stood.

"See what I mean?"

He nodded. "I do, but it's all of us or none of us. I cannot leave you behind." He faced the inviting hole. "All of us . . . that's not too much to ask for! I will vouch for them!"

There was no reason for the eternal to do anything but laugh at his daring. Nonetheless, he was determined that his companions join him. Even if Prentiss Asaalk was a spy for the Purple Dragon, certainly the gnome knew that already. With trepidation, Bedlam approached the gaping hole. It seemed to widen the nearer he came, as if seeking to accommodate him as well as possible. The way the stone, if that was what it was, shifted and flowed made him think of a gigantic maw opening to accept a meal. He wondered if the citadel was somehow alive, then tried quickly to drop the horrific thought as he ran out of distance between the structure and his body and discovered that his next step would take him inside.

One foot through. The hole remained still. It had not attempted to relieve him of his leg as part of him had secretly feared. Wellen leaned forward, planted his boot on the smooth, marble floor, and peered inside.

A blank corridor, impossibly long. He could not make out what was at the other end, although he assumed it was a doorway. The scholar recalled circling the pentagon and was certain that it had not been this lengthy. A trick of the eye? The citadel's master *was* a spellcaster of seemingly limitless ability. It could be real. Almost as an afterthought, he noticed a corridor on each side of him as well. For some reason, however, he did not give them the consideration that he gave the one in front.

He turned back to the others. "Inside. Quick."

The ancient mage might choose to crush his body in the very wall, but Wellen was willing to risk it. That the gnome had expressed interest in him at all meant that the mage might hesitate. The other two were of no consequence to the master of the citadel and he hoped they were hardly reason enough to send a certain presumptuous scholar to his gory death.

Asaalk removed his own weapons but held back, allowing Xabene to be the first. The enchantress, unarmed, walked up to the portal, but then hesitated at the threshold. Her fear was no mystery; she wondered if the hole would close as soon as she dared put a hand or foot through. This close to the goal her masters had set for her, the ivory-skinned sorceress was frozen.

Prentiss Asaalk solved the problem by *pushing* her through.

There was a collective gasp from Bedlam, the stumbling enchantress, and even an anxious Asaalk.

Nothing happened. Xabene continued across and then spun around, her eyes aflame and her hands twitching as if she sought to utilize what little strength remained to see that the blue man regretted his maneuver.

"Xabene!" the scholar hissed. "Remember where you are! For all our sakes!"

She did, and the knowledge drained her of the desire if not the anger. The seething woman relaxed as best she could and muttered, "I won't forget that, blue man!"

"I had faith," the northerner replied in cool tones. He dismissed her as if she had ceased to exist. Asaalk stepped calmly through the hole, gazed down the corridor, then turned to wait for Wellen.

The apprehensive explorer, moving with a speed enhanced by a well-honed sense of mistrust, finished crossing the unnerving portal, then stood transfixed in the corridor by the sheer thought of being inside what so many had fought fruitlessly to enter. Here was the domain of the enigmatic, immortal gnome.

"Wellen!"

Xabene's warning shout shook him from his stupor. He whirled about and watched in dismay as the circular portal shriveled. Smaller and smaller it grew, a gaping wound magically healing itself before their very eyes. Wellen reached toward it, then pulled his hand back when he realized that all he might succeed in doing was trapping his arm in the side of the citadel.

With a slight hiss, the hole ceased to be.

After some careful consideration, Wellen ran his fingertips across the region where the entrance had been. There was not even the slightest trace of its existence. For all practical purposes, it might never have been.

"What issss this?" Asaalk snarled. "Where is the gnome? Why is he not here?"

Turning, Wellen stared at the endless corridor. "I suspect that we're to go to him."

"Down the corridor?"

"Do you see anywhere else to go?" he asked. Sure enough, when Xabene and the blue man looked around, they too, saw that the corridor was the only path open to them. Wellen wondered if the same thought was going through their minds that had gone through his . . . had there not been other corridors running along each side? Now, there were only blank walls. The notion that they were being herded was not an attractive thought.

"Let us be done with this!" Prentiss Asaalk began stalking down the corridor, his lengthy strides taking him several yards from his comrades before either could even react. Wellen hurried after the northerner, not wanting Asaalk to run off too far on his own, for both his sake and theirs. Especially theirs. Xabene kept pace with him.

"Perhaps we should let him keep a distance ahead of us," she whispered. "Maybe there's a trap or two and he'll spring them."

"We stay together, *regardless* of you two."

"A pity."

The blue man, despite their best efforts, continued to lead the way. Wellen soon settled for merely keeping pace a few feet behind the warrior. He was not too concerned with Prentiss Asaalk's attempt to seize control of the situation. Let Asaalk lead the way; it was still Wellen who the mysterious gnome wished to see. The blue man could be no more than a minor irritant to someone as omnipotent as the lord of this magical place.

Several minutes passed without incident, but everyone sensed that something was awry. Still walking, Wellen glanced over his shoulder to observe the path they had already trodden, then faced forward again. While he was still mulling over his discovery, he heard a muttered curse from the figure before him.

"What ails our friend now?" Xabene asked quietly.

"He's likely discovered the same thing I did."

"What's that?"

"That we are no closer to the end of the hall than we were just after we *started*."

She blinked, scanned the entire corridor, and finally frowned. "I'd wondered . . . it didn't seem right, but . . ."

"I know. It's hard to sense it; part of the spell, I imagine." *Is he laughing at us?* Wellen asked himself. *Have we been admitted only to amuse him?*

Asaalk paused. When the others had caught up to him, he turned and snarled, "The faster I go, the less distance I seem to cover. What do you suggest we do, Master Bedlam?"

There was only one thing to do, but he dreaded telling it to the frustrated blue man. "We keep walking."

"*That* is all?"

"We could turn back."

"Never!"

The northerner's outburst was much too intense. Wellen regretted having him with them now, but it was too late. Perhaps Prentiss Asaalk merely fretted over the collar, which was reasonable enough, but his interest was more of a coveting nature. He wanted the dragon tome as much as the Lords of the Dead or the Purple Dragon did.

"Then we continue on." Wellen, taking Xabene's arm, stepped around the seething blue man and resumed his trek. As she passed, the enchantress could not help displaying to Asaalk a brief, mocking smile.

They walked for a time more and then it became obvious that while their progress was slow, it was definitely progress. Wellen squinted and thought he made out doors both at the end of the corridor and on the side walls farther ahead. He asked Xabene if she saw them.

"I do. What do you think lies behind them?"

"That's not the question that runs through my mind," he returned, eyeing the distant portals. Considering where the trio was, such doorways were tempting, indeed. "I was wondering whether we're allowed to open them or not."

The doors had also captured the blue man's curiosity. Prentiss Asaalk broke past his two companions and increased his pace further.

"Asaalk!"

The hulking figure ignored them. Now the distance melted away with a swiftness. In only a few minutes, the rows of doorways became apparent; Wellen estimated that there had to be over a hundred on each wall. They were simple in design and blended with the white walls. A handle was the only thing that decorated each, a plain, metal handle that like so much else, seemed austere in design for something conjured by one with the power to do almost anything he desired.

The more evident it became that they were nearing the doors, the faster Asaalk traveled. He moved as if the Dragon King himself was on his heels. The last few steps he fairly leaped. When at last he reached the doorways, the blue man did not hesitate. Asaalk seized the handle of the closest one and pulled.

It would not open.

He pulled harder. Despite his strength, the door did not even so much as shake. Cursing, the blue man released the handle and tried pulling the one next to it. That portal, too, rebuked his efforts.

"Asaalk! Wait!"

Ignoring them, the enraged northerner turned to the opposite wall and took hold of the handle of the nearest door there. It, like the others, refused him entrance. He put his foot against the wall beside the portal and tried to use his weight.

Still nothing.

"Asaalk, it's obvious these paths are not meant for us." Wellen tried to pull the ever more furious figure from his obsession, but the blue man pushed him away with a snarl. To his surprise, the smaller man barely saved himself from flying into one of the other doors. Instead, he rolled to a stop just inches away. Asaalk's strength was so incredible that Wellen was surprised his companion had not torn the entire door from its hinges.

"Stop that!" Xabene called, stepping toward Asaalk. She, like Wellen, was ignored.

"One of thesssse must open!" He turned toward the final portal at the end of the corridor. "Sssso be it!"

Before they could stop him, Prentiss Asaalk was running toward the far doors.

"He's gone mad!" the enchantress cried, helping Bedlam to his feet.

"Mad or ensorcelled! The collar, remember?"

"Then this was all—" She had no time to finish. Prentiss Asaalk had nearly reached his goal, and showed no sign of slowing down.

The hard, massive form of the blue man struck the twin doors where they met.

With a shriek of metal resounding through the hall, Asaalk's body continued through as the barrier before him gave way.

Wellen and Xabene rushed after the blue man. The scholar feared that all hope of peaceful contact with the gnome was lost. The citadel's master surely would not long tolerate this vandalism, this plundering.

"There!" roared Asaalk from within. The chamber was fairly well lit. With his large form blocking most of their view, however, they could not entirely make out what was in the room beyond, save that Wellen thought he saw some sort of pedestal upon which something lay.

There was an inhuman quality about the northerner now. His breathing grew heavy and fast and his stance was a bit awkward. He seemed even larger for a moment or two.

"At lasssst!" he hissed. "My *dragon tome!*"

"Did he say . . ." Xabene hesitated at the battered doorway. ". . . the dragon tome?"

Bedlam only partly heard her. He was still staring at Asaalk. A horrible, unthinkable notion was creeping into his mind, one he tried to reject but could not.

He started to move, realizing that whatever the truth, one thing was certain. "We have to keep him from taking that book!"

It was already too late. Heedless of whatever else might wait in the chamber, the blue man rushed toward his prize. As much as Wellen both hoped and dreaded it, nothing stayed the crazed figure. The scholar had some hope that he and the enchantress might still have a chance when Asaalk suddenly slowed just before the pedestal. The northerner, though, wasted only a few seconds as he seemed to study the area before him for traps. Evidently finding none, he reached for the massive book.

Wellen did not need any magical warning sense to tell him to stay back. He grabbed hold of Xabene's arm and pulled her to the floor.

Prentiss Asaalk lifted the dragon tome from its resting place. He laughed.

Then vanished.

With a heavy thud, the ancient tome fell to the marble floor. It bounced twice, then settled a few yards in front of the two gaping onlookers.

"Predictable in the end," commented a voice behind them. Wellen had a sense of great age and authority . . . and not a little pride. "Obsession will always do that, even to a creature like a Dragon King."

Very slowly, the two humans, still lying on the floor, turned around.

The figure towered over them, but only because they were not standing. *He cannot be any taller than my chest!* Bedlam decided. *And that if he can straighten up.* The latter seemed doubtful; the figure before them had been permanently bent by both centuries of study hunched over desks and by the centuries themselves, for though he might be immortal, this being was old.

The gnome, clad in a brown robe that nearly touched the floor, smiled at them. It was a smile reminiscent of a dragon, but without the warmth. "Rise, please."

The duo obeyed immediately. The master of the citadel glanced over Xabene, found nothing of interest, then studied Wellen. He stared longest at the scholar's eyes.

"A few flakes of crystal, I see. A throwback, no doubt. Most interesting."

His words raised questions, but nothing that Wellen would have dared ask now.

A staff was in the gnome's left hand. It had not been there the previous moment. With it, the aged figure prodded at the two humans. "Step aside."

Again, they obeyed without hesitation. The gnome moved with amazing grace to the fallen book. It lay flat with its pages fanning upward.

"*Wellen,*" Xabene whispered. "Do you sense anything?"

He thought about it. He had not sensed danger in the corridor and he had not sensed danger in the chamber, despite the trap offered by what had to be a false book.

His ability had vanished. From the moment Bedlam had entered this place, it had ceased to be. *How* had he missed its sudden absence?

The answer was the squat creature before him.

She understood his silence. "It's the same with my own power. I've lost it all now," the enchantress muttered. "I think it was the moment Asaalk touched the book."

Blocking out his ability to sense danger was one thing, but the citadel's lord must have known he would give his plot away if he stole the last of Xabene's power. Unlike Wellen, she was not one to fail to notice the absence of something so important to her.

"That it was him at all was the most fascinating part of all this," the smiling gnome explained to his baffled audience. He flipped through the pages of the tome and chuckled at something he saw within. "I have always wondered just how he planned to get in even if he succeeded in capturing me."

"What is it . . ." The scholar took a deep breath. "What is it you're saying?"

"You know very well," the gnome admonished him. "You know that he was not your companion of old."

Xabene's eyes rounded. "Not the blue man?"

"I would say that your blue friend . . . what was his name, my young friend?"

"Prentiss Asaalk," Wellen responded. "Is the true man dead, then?"

"Probably so. If this is the kind of spell I think it is, then he died the moment our scaly friend put on this form. That he mastered even a human one is astonishing, but that he wore the shape and form of one you knew, too, is impossible."

"Who is he talking about, Wellen? You and he both seem to understand what you're saying, but I—" The enchantress broke off. "He just said *scaly* . . ."

"Indeed I did, young woman." The staff turned to so much smoke as the gnome made use of both hands to hold the huge tome open. He held it much the way it had lain on the floor, both covers down and the pages all displayed like a peacock's feathers. "Allow me to show you what he looks like . . . without the spell of seeming that made him be your friend."

The spellcaster tore a page from the false tome and tossed it into the air before them. The single sheet fluttered about for several seconds, at last coming to earth roughly in the trio's midst. It did not settle, however, but rather continued to turn and turn, a top spun by an invisible hand.

The page stood on one end. Transfixed by this continuing

feat of sorcery, Wellen and Xabene watched as the paper expanded, swiftly rising to a height equal to the scholar's own and then rising even higher. Bedlam estimated it ceased growing when it was a little over eight feet tall.

It was still turning, but now that its growth had ended, it began spinning faster and faster, raising a breeze that forced the two humans to turn away until they could shield their eyes.

Beyond them, beyond the whirling page, the gnome chuckled.

As Wellen, his hand above his eyes, squinted, much of the sheet started to darken. The darker the paper grew, the slower the turning became. He made out a manlike form, but one taller and more massive than even Prentiss Asaalk.

The hairless spellcaster nodded. With a stop so jarring it made Wellen and Xabene jump, the page froze before them. There, in all its inhuman glory, stood what had truly traveled with the two humans to the citadel.

A demonic warrior clad in enshrouding scale armor. The monstrous countenance was all but hidden within a helm, but they could make out the fiery eyes and part of the flat, horrific face within nonetheless. Atop the helm was an elaborate dragon's head crest, a crest so lifelike that one expected the head to open wide its maw and snap up the onlooker. No weapon hung from the warrior's waist, but it was doubtful that any was needed. The gauntleted hands and the savage mouth looked readily able to tear apart a foe gobbet by bloody gobbet.

From head to toe, the fiendish knight was colored a very distinctive shade of purple.

"Allow me to introduce, albeit in a form much removed from his original, His Infernal Majesty, the lord of this land . . . the *Purple Dragon*."

The illustration on the page was so very lifelike that Wellen could see the evil, the power, and at the moment, the incessant frustration of the trapped drake lord.

It *was* the Dragon King.

Not an illustration. Not an image of the captured creature as he stood waiting in some hidden dungeon. The *true* dragon. Held prisoner on the very sheet of paper—a prison of only two dimensions—that stood before them.

The gnome shuffled toward them. It was all the humans could do to keep from stumbling back. There could be no doubting the short, squat mage's skills now, not that the scholar ever had.

"And since it seems time for introductions," the gnarled figure continued, closing the book with a finality that was all too noticeable, "you may call me *Serkadion Manee*."

XVII

Benton Lore had not believed that the outsider Bedlam would succeed with his insane, sophomoric plan, but his lord had thought differently. Now he saw that the Green Dragon must have made a careful study of both the outsider and the gnome, for who could have predicted Bedlam's success otherwise?

From his hiding place in a copse of trees not too distant from the featureless pentagon, he watched. There was little else to do until they exited the cursed place.

If they did leave, he wanted to speak with the scholar in private. Whatever secrets or even passing knowledge that Bedlam picked up would be useful to the major-domo's true cause. He could have cared less about the fate of the mad warlock Shade, whose chief concern, in Lore's eyes, was always his own existence. The gnome had the potential to give all humans their freedom from the Dragon Kings, make them master of their own fate. Wellen Bedlam represented a possible bridge for Lore to that knowledge and power.

His lord knew of his desire, of that the officer was aware. The Green Dragon, however, foresaw mankind's ascendancy as a certainty, whereas Lore saw it as something attainable only if he and those like him strained to reach it. Nothing was certain as far as the black man was concerned, especially freedom.

All of that would be a moot point if the trio never departed. Benton Lore and humanity would be back where they had left off. Nowhere.

He settled down to wait, knowing that his own sorcerous abilities would warn him of any approaching threat. The forces of the Dragon King Purple, however, were very absent tonight. That could only mean that they had fallen for the diversions. Asaalk was still a problem, but not one he could not handle. After all, it was not as if the blue man, human or not, were the Dragon King himself.

Another pair of eyes, white, soulless ones, also watched the pentagon. Another watcher, just as eager as the dark man, waited for the trio, especially the scholar, to leave the safety of the citadel.

The gnome spoke his own name with such authority that Wellen supposed that he should have recognized it. He did not. Neither, he saw, did Xabene. Name or not, though, Serkadion Manee was to be respected, if only because of his power.

Something about the name did strike him, however. Wellen could not say what it was, save that it reminded him of another name . . . two, in fact. Shade had used those names, Dru Zeree for the legendary lord Bedlam had known as Drazeree, and Sharissa Zeree, the wraith who had also been the lord's illustrious daughter. In fact, there had been another title with the same distinctive syllable at the end, a mysterious people called the Tezerenee.

Could Serkadion Manee, like Shade, be a representative of the same ancient race?

Xabene was not so concerned with history. Her priorities surrounded the menacing figure of the Dragon King, who literally seemed to be struggling to free himself of the page. "Can he escape?"

Manee glanced back at the prisoner. A brief frown crossed his unsightly visage. "He is stronger than I imagined; I had not thought it possible for him to fight it as much as he has." The rounded shoulders rose and fell in a shrug. "But struggle is all he shall do."

The bizarre, flat image did not seem to agree. The Dragon King only increased his visible efforts.

"How did he obtain such a near-human form?" the unnerved yet fascinated woman asked, ignoring the annoyed look on Serkadion Manee's visage. Wellen hoped he was not the type that used his sorcery to erase from his existence all those who irritated him, however slight the irritation might have been.

"There are ways, but it would have been a struggle. You see that while he has obtained size and the basic form, he would *hardly* have passed for human without the other spell. He has tried to compensate for his ineffectiveness by masking himself in a form that, at least from a distance, might pass.'' A chuckle. ''Although I can say without a doubt I have never seen such a beastly knight. Oh well, the helm hides his worst ugliness.''

Despite her anxiousness, Xabene was fascinated by the complex and physically draining spells that the Dragon King must have utilized to achieve as much as he had. Wellen could not blame her for the way she stared at the sight. He knew that she was wondering what she might have achieved with such ability available to her.

''Now, then,'' started the gnome. He paused when he saw that the two were still eyeing the ensnared drake. ''Whether in man form or beast, he *cannot* escape.'' Manee sighed and added, ''I can see that we will not be able to speak in peace so long as he is around. No matter, this was hardly a comfortable place for conversation.''

The three of them were suddenly in another chamber. Wellen's stomach rose and fell. He still detested traveling in such a manner, but it was becoming less and less disturbing to his system. Much of his pain was in his mind, anyway. The scholar knew that, but so far had not been able to convince his stomach of the fact.

Their new location was a place so very familiar to the scholar, not because he had seen it before but because he had seen its like. As with Xabene's secret domain, Wellen almost felt at home. Shelves of fascinating and mysterious objects lined the walls. The familiar desk with candles. Paper and quill pen. Notes and sketches laid here and there. It was evident that the room had been reorganized only recently, but things were already forming into random piles. It was a chamber typical of men like Wellen. Researchers and scholars.

''This should be much better.'' Once again, the gnome smiled and once again his guests were repulsed. ''Sit.''

He discovered then that Serkadion Manee's study was not so typical after all.

The floor beneath the two humans' feet swelled, throwing them off balance. Helpless, Bedlam fell backward. He envisioned the back of his skull striking the hard surface and cracking into a number of pieces. He saw Xabene's head do the same and the vision of her lying dead on the floor stirred him more than his own fate had.

Midway to his doom, something soft caught and nestled him.

A gasp from the enchantress informed him that she had met with a similar experience. He looked down at what his body rested in.

A chair had formed from the very substance of the floor. Wellen rubbed a finger over what should have been a harsh surface, only to find it smooth and pliable. He looked at his companion, who was likewise studying the astonishing sight. Even shaped as it was, the floor still retained an appearance of stone.

"I trust that is comfortable." Serkadion Manee, still standing, folded a partially obscured leg under him. Bedlam expected to see him teeter, perhaps even fall, but the ungainly sorcerer somehow maintained perfect balance.

Then, he folded the *other* leg under him and simply floated a few feet in the middle of the air.

Summoning up his courage, Wellen said, "Master Manee, I thank you for allowing us entrance to your domain. I know that you rarely have congress with others—"

"More often than you think." The smile broadened, no pleasant change. "You are hardly the first I've allowed entrance to, my young friends."

That contradicted everything that he had heard, but Wellen tried to take it as a good sign. Certainly, the gnome would not advertise that he dealt often with others, yet how could he keep it a secret?

"That is neither here nor there," Manee continued. His fingers absently stroked the book's cover.

"Please," Xabene asked, a bit more at ease now that she knew the chair was not going to swallow her whole. "Is that the dragon tome or not?"

Another chuckle. "In a sense."

"What does that mean?"

"It means what I said."

Wellen interrupted, already seeing that this was going to turn into a conversation of confusion, which the inhabitants of the Dragonrealm seemed to delight in creating. "You said we were hardly the first to be allowed inside. Why are there not tales of the others? I would think the Dragon Kings or the Lords of the Dead would have discovered them."

"I take measures." It was all the gnome would say on that subject. "I believe that you made me an offer, Master Wellen Bedlam."

The scholar burned within. He realized that he had set aside Shade's existence for a brief moment so that he might satisfy some of his curiosity. "Yes. Knowledge of the land from which I began this journey in exchange for aid for two of my companions . . . although it seems too late for one."

"Perhaps. We shall see. What of the other one then? What fate has befallen him? Explain carefully the details."

Wellen did. That the Lords of the Dead were involved did not shake Serkadion Manee for a moment. When Wellen hesitated after first introducing their threat to the tale, the gnome merely raised one hand from the book in his lap and indicated he should continue. The scholar told of the attack and Shade's determination to track down the necromancers and make them suffer.

When he spoke of Shade's claim of blood ties to the self-styled gods, Bedlam noticed Manee's eyes widen, then narrow. Curious as to what effect his encounter with the wraith would have on the aged sorcerer, he slowed down at that point and gave as descriptive an image of the scene as possible.

Serkadion Manee hung on every word. From his expression, he seemed to be thinking that what the mortal before him was relating was impossible yet true. It was very likely that the ancient mage could tell whether Wellen was lying or not, so everything that left the scholar's mouth was the truth. It was not the entire truth, but at least there were no falsehoods. Wellen did not want to give everything away if he could help it.

After the story ended, Serkadion Manee leaned back. Wellen expected him to fall, but the sorcerer shifted as if a chair also held him. He appeared to be speaking more to himself. "So Nimth still reaches forth from her far grave. She should be dead by now, and all her children little more than a few vague memories in the souls . . . or specks of crystal in the eyes . . . of their descendants."

"What is Nimth? I heard it mentioned."

"Nimth, my young mortal companion, was my home. It was the home once of those who call themselves the Lords of the Dead, although I consider them shadows now, not living examples of its former greatness like *myself*." It had already become obvious that Serkadion Manee held himself in great esteem. He scratched him chin in thought. "This Sharissa, who claims ancestry, fascinates me, but I will leave the visitation for another time. The one called Shade, the one you desire to free, he might also be *Vraad* after all. This is worthy of note.''

From the desk, a quill and a sheet of paper leaped into the air and darted to the waiting warlock. Manee did not take the items, but rather had them float to one side of him. The two newcomers watched as the paper stiffened and the pen readied its point just above the top of the sheet.

''Proceed,'' the gnome commanded the implement.

Writing at a furious pace, the quill filled the sheet with words. Manee's eyes were little more than slits. Although no words escaped his lips, he was evidently directing the pen's efforts.

When the first page was filled, a second flew from the desk and took its place. Xabene actually smiled at Wellen. The dancing quill and the soaring sheets seemed so fanciful, it might have been pulled from a child's dream.

After a third page, the pen froze. The final sheet joined the other two, which were floating serenely above the gnome's head, and then both paper and pen returned to the desk.

Manee was visibly amused by the attitudes of his two guests. Wellen was entirely baffled by the gnome. Was he as benevolent and understanding as he appeared now or was the master mage who had trapped the Purple Dragon more what the true Serkadion Manee was like? Could he trust the gnarled figure or was the gnome only biding his time for some reason?

''Tell me, Scholar Bedlam, did this Shade ever say the word 'Vraad'? I should have paid more attention to him, but he seemed only to watch, and the necromancers and the Dragon King were so much more interesting.''

One of Wellen's questions was partly answered. The true Serkadion Manee was more like the sorcerer who had tricked the drake lord and countless would-be conquerors through the ages. He enjoyed the challenges, even as certain as he was of the outcome of each. Over the centuries, or rather millennia, they had probably become one of his chief ways of battling boredom. Even the most avid scholar could not study *all* the time.

He wondered just how mad Serkadion Manee was.

Belatedly, Wellen recalled the gnome's question. He pretended to be considering the answer, then finally responded, ''He may or may not have. It sounds familiar, but I could be mistaken.''

The gnome uncrossed his legs and returned his feet to the ground. His eyes looked to the ceiling as he stared at something that existed only in his memory. "You have no idea what your ancestors were like, my young ones. We wielded power such as even the Lords of the Dead only dream of. Our world, Nimth, was our plaything... and play with it we did. We began to twist and turn its laws, make it a parody of both itself and us, its children."

Swinging one hand in an arc, Serkadion Manee summoned forth an image in the air. A landscape, but one that lived and breathed, not simply a flat picture. Clouds floated serenely overhead and a winged creature or two soared into and out of the tiny domain. Leaning closer, Bedlam saw that the landscape was sculpted, not natural, yet to such a masterful degree that one became so caught up in admiring it that one did not notice immediately the handiwork of the unknown artisan. In the distance, one or two high and elaborate buildings, possibly towers or castles, could be made out.

"This was the view from my domain." Manee seemed to age as he spoke. The spellcaster might deny it, but he missed his former world. He stared at the scene a breath or two longer, then wiped it away with a single slash of his hand. "But it exists no more and even as I chose to depart, knowing what was to come of our playing, it was *decaying* already."

He arced his hand again, summoning up the image. There was something different about it, however, something subtle that neither Wellen nor Xabene could define at first. The scholar only knew that he sensed a mood of uneasiness, almost like that of a person who suspects he is dying but does not wish to know the truth for fear he is correct. Clouds lingered too long in the sky. Nothing flew. Those were the only physical differences that Wellen could see, but that hardly proved a thing. If, as Serkadion Manee had said, this Nimth had already been decaying, much of that decay would begin with the unseen things, the breakdown of the natural laws that bound all.

Again, the gnome slashed his hand across the image, literally shattering it into a thousand ephemeral fragments that dissolved before they stuck the hard floor. "I can only imagine what the world this Shade and your kind left must have been like. A sick, twisted thing. The Lords of the Dead, they do not remember their own past very well, but I have often suspected that their domain is a mirror of those times.''

Wellen nodded. Shade had made a similar comment.

''I was right in abandoning that place.'' Manee drew himself together. ''But the Vraad still live on, if only in a distant manner, through you.''

Xabene leaned close to Wellen. ''He sounds more and more like Shade.''

The gnome put a gnarled hand to his bald head in obvious discomfort. ''None of that now!'' he reprimanded to the air. ''Struggling will achieve you nothing but more pain, you know!''

The scholar rose. Behind him, the chair instantly sank back into the rocklike floor that had birthed it. ''Are you all right?''

''The Dragon King is becoming a bit of a bother, nothing more. Some of them will not accept the inevitable. Some of them cannot accept that Serkadion Manee is ever their superior. I, a *Vraad* of the highest achievement! I was the one who *opened* the path of power to my kind, showed them what they could *do* . . . not that they listened properly! The drake lords are novices. I have in this place the accumulated knowledge of *two* worlds and it is all for my use whenever I need it!''

Despite his words, Manee winced. ''I can see that I will have to do something about him, but later.'' Serkadion Manee looked up at the two outsiders. ''My own words remind me of the task at hand; you have promised me knowledge in exchange for a service. I see no reason to delay any further. What little I have garnered from observing you makes me fascinated. I never thought to explore beyond the eastern seas or the Sea of Andramacus to the west.'' He indicated the citadel as a whole. ''How could I leave all that I had obtained over time? It would be better if I could take all of it with me, *then* . . .

Take it with him? Is that what he hopes to do? the explorer wondered, thinking of the sudden change in the citadel's location after all this time. Was the sorcerer trying to make his sanctum capable of transporting itself from one land to another? From one *continent* to another? What Wellen understood about teleportation indicated that Serkadion Manee needed to know much about a region before he could safely materialize there. He was probably capable of a blind teleport, but for something as distant as Bedlam's homeland, such a feat was too risky even for him.

Riskier still if he truly sought to teleport his entire citadel with him.

The idea did not defy Wellen's imagination, but it did defy his belief. He had never heard of a sorcerer with such power and ability.

"What about Shade?"

"His time will come after you have given me what is mine."

"He could be dead by then."

"If he is Vraad, then he is not. If he is not . . . then he perished long before you came to me, my young friend."

"What must I do?" Suddenly faced with the task, the scholar was uneasy. Manee might just as easily strip his mind clean, reduce him to less than a newborn child. That might even be what the gnome intended.

"Nothing much . . . just trust me." Serkadion Manee chuckled as he watched the two.

From his empty hand the robed spellcaster produced a flat, square object made of some gray material of the like Wellen had not seen. It was not the same substance as the citadel walls, but did have similarities in appearance. A piece of finely forged metal was wrapped around one end of the mysterious artifact and on the metal, inscribed in black, were runes of an unreadable language. Humans generally spoke one language, the *why* of that never having been settled, but there were records of other types utilized by some of the races that had preceded the Dragon Kings as rulers of this land.

Serkadion Manee held the metal-clad end toward the two waiting figures. He contemplated Xabene for a time.

She stepped back, shaking her head. "This was not *my* bargain, gnome! I made no offer to you to go stealing around in my head!"

"Perhaps you will change your mind before long," he retorted, the sinister smile playing on his lips again. His attention focused on Wellen. "And have you decided to back down from this deal?"

Shade's life aside, Bedlam pondered their fate if he chose to abandon his part of the bargain. Immediate ouster from the gnome's sanctum; that was the least they could expect, that and forever to be haunted by the hooded warlock's ghost. "Do what you have to."

"I always do. Please understand that."

While he was still attempting to mull over the last, something seized him. Xabene called out, but there was nothing that Wellen could do. Something had hold of his legs and his arms, something with tentacles as strong as iron. The enchantress, too, was tangled in tentacles. Wellen tried to make out their source, but he could only see a thick darkness behind her. Trying to glance over his own shoulder, the struggling man saw only shadows. The limbs just seemed to begin somewhere in the darkness.

The gnome was slowly moving toward him, the peculiar artifact held tight in his extended hand. Manee shook his head. "I'm sorry, but I find this necessary. Every time."

The cephalopodic limbs had him wrapped tight. Bedlam could barely move his head from side to side, which was what the wizened spellcaster desired. At an unspoken command, the scholar was pulled down to his knees. Serkadion Manee smiled one last time and touched the metal portion to his captive's forehead.

Wellen's head rocked back as what seemed like a lightning bolt shook him. A second shock, slightly less intense, rattled him just as he recovered from the first. The second was barely gone before a third, a bit less intense than the second, rocked him.

Only one variation jarred the otherwise rhythmic sequence. A brief flash of memory of the dismal domain of the Lords of the Dead interrupted things for only the blink of an eye. The vision of the tortured castle of the necromancers was enough to make him shiver.

The shock waves decreased with each successive one until finally he could sense them no longer. The scholar blinked, then realized that he had shut his eyes tight almost from the moment Serkadion Manee's toy had touched him. As the chamber came into focus, Wellen noticed slight alterations. Not understanding why and how Manee would change things during the few moments he had been out, he turned to where Xabene had been held.

She was not there, but the gnome was.

"That took longer than I expected," the squat figure commented in almost companionable tones. "Not many have dedicated themselves to knowledge as you have. Not in so short a life span, that is."

"What did you do to me?" Wellen's struggle was futile. The tentacles still held him tight. "Where's Xabene?"

"The typical questions. No originality? Here." Manee touched one of the limbs with a finger. The coils began to unwrap; the scholar was free in less than a minute.

"What did you do with her?"

"I sent her elsewhere. Would you have wanted her to wait in discomfort for so long?"

"So long?" He stared down at the stooped figure. "How long was I . . . it was only a few moments, wasn't it?"

Manee shook his head in sympathy. "Day has turned to night, my young scholar friend. There was much in your mind to gather, much more than even I had supposed. We are more alike than I thought. I must say it is refreshing to know that there is someone else."

Flattery was not what Wellen wanted to hear. "What did that thing do to me?"

"It merely read your mind, both the conscious part and the part where all you have learned or perceived is stored. Nothing is ever lost, you know. Even things you learned in passing are retained. My creation finds it all and reproduces it."

Bedlam eyed the magical artifact in the gnome's wrinkled hands. "What will you do with all that?"

"Go through it later. There's always time. It may be years, but there will always be time."

Wellen almost thought he sounded tired.

"Can you take me to Xabene?"

"Of course." Serkadion Manee touched his forehead and winced.

"What's wrong?"

"The Dragon King is becoming most offensive. Had I known he would be so much trouble, I would have left him outside pounding on the walls."

That brought something to mind that Bedlam had briefly contemplated earlier. "Why didn't you kill him? It certainly seems as if you had a chance."

"I've not studied him yet nor have I made a copy of his memories." Manee looked at Wellen as if all this should have been logical. "I waste nothing."

Then, they were standing in another room. Xabene, in the act of pacing, something she had evidently been doing for a long, long time, stiffened. The rage and frustration boiled over when she saw the gnome.

"You! How dare you keep me in here all this time!" She

rushed to Wellen and held him tight. "Are you all right? Say something!"

"I'm fine, Xabene. Other than a few jarring moments, I felt nothing. He didn't hurt me."

"Not that he would've cared!" Still holding the scholar, she glanced at Serkadion Manee. "Ask him about that, Wellen! Ask him if he would have cared if you were injured!"

"It would have been regrettable," Manee responded, not waiting for Bedlam to ask. "The loss of knowledge is always regrettable."

"More so than the loss of a life!"

"Life can be replaced; knowledge is often lost for too long, sometimes forever."

There was no doubt that he meant what he said. What similarities there were between the gnome and Wellen did not include this. Life was more important than anything. The death of those who had journeyed to this land, even the unseen, far-off death of Prentiss Asaalk, would remain with him to his own demise.

Serkadion Manee did not seem to see a problem with his way of thinking. "I do what I can to make certain that the process is safe. I will not waste what might again be useful."

Was this an example of their ancestors? Wellen hoped not. The ghost of Sharissa Zeree had not been at all like this. She had cared about life.

"We could discuss this until the end of all," Manee continued. "But I am assuming that you still desire your end of the bargain fulfilled."

Shade! "I do."

"Then we shall commence with it now."

"What should I do?" He expected the gnome to order him to lie down. The Lords of the Dead had put Xabene into some sort of trance. If the necromancers and the wizened spellcaster were of the same people, then it stood to reason that their methods would be similar.

Wellen was proved wrong. Manee looked up at him. "You should do nothing. All I require is your presence as a focus. You may sit, sleep, talk, or try to walk on the ceiling. As long as you stay nearby, I can search."

Opening his hands, Serkadion Manee suddenly held the dragon tome again. For the first time, Wellen had a good view of the stylized image on the cover. It was as had been described to him. A fierce and very elaborate design. The color of the book confused him, however, for he recalled that it had been some color other than gold. That he could not say for certain did not surprise him; events just prior to the mage's use of the memory device were still a bit cloudy. Bedlam hoped nothing had been lost permanently. He preferred his memories to fade away, not to be snatched.

"Here it is." Serkadion Manee ran his fingers down one of the pages. He winced at a momentary pain, then resumed his reading. "Yes. Short but complex. Simple thought would hardly do. No one could maintain all those patterns and still be able to search..." The gnome grew more and more interested.

Xabene had shifted to the scholar's side. "Is this wise? He might bring forth one of the lords themselves or, at the very least, a Necri!"

"It's too late now."

Manee was muttering under his breath, his eyes no longer on the page but staring up into another world. For the first time since he had entered the pentagon, Wellen felt the familiar throb of warning. With the Dragon King to control and the spell to complete, Serkadion Manee did not need to waste power on something as insignificant as the novice warlock's poor abilities.

He felt the enchantress shift beside him and knew that her powers, too, had returned. Wellen hoped she would not try anything at this juncture. If Xabene thought now an opportune time to strike back at the gnome, Manee might indeed summon forth something other than Shade. Something they might all live... for a short time... to regret.

A faint scent of decay and death turned their noses. Xabene, who should have been more adapted to the odor, shivered, possibly thinking that one of her former masters might be the next thing through Serkadion Manee's spell.

Then, the gnome frowned. He twitched once or twice, searching, Wellen decided, but why was there need? Manee had been confident that even the otherworldly realm of the necromancers could not hide from his prying senses.

With a sigh, the tiny figure finally opened his eyes. His gaze darted from one side of the chamber to the other, as if he expected to see the hooded warlock standing with his companions.

"What's happened?" the scholar asked. Was it too late? Was Shade beyond *everyone's* power to save?

"He should be here. In fact, it almost felt as if he had . . . impossible . . . not likely at all . . . could it?"

A moment ago, Wellen would not have been able to picture the gnome caught up in uncertainty. Serkadion Manee knew everything, orchestrated everything to satisfy his goals. Yet, here he was now, at a loss.

"It *has* to be!" the sorcerer finally muttered. "It has to be! Devious! Worthy of a Vraad!"

"What is he babbling about?" Xabene whispered.

"I don't—"

Serkadion Manee, his mind returning to the reality of the room, extended a twisted hand toward the duo. "Come! He *must* be there!"

This time, Wellen was prepared for the teleport.

They were in another corridor, but its contents did not immediately register with the scholar, for his attention was snared by the gnome, who was clutching his head in obvious agony. Bedlam started to reach for him, trying to give aid in some way, but Manee waved him back.

"It is nothing! Nothing!"

"You! You have tricked me!"

Wellen forgot all else at the sudden shout from far down the corridor. He turned, unable to believe that his ears had heard true.

"Wellen! He's here!"

Shade stood in the midst of the long, narrow hall, a demonic fury. Though distance and the hood shadowed his features as usual, there was no doubt as to the intensity of his anger, an anger directed not at Bedlam or the enchantress, but rather at the short, squat figure who had brought them here.

There was no sign of injury, no indication at all that the warlock had suffered in his battle against his cousins. Wellen knew that not all wounds were visible, but Shade seemed to suffer from none, not if his manic activity was a sign.

"Which one is it, Serkadion Manee?" the cloaked figure roared. "Which one is it? I've gone through shelves already and none of them have it!"

Shade picked up a massive, crimson book and threw it at one of the empty shelves. Wellen blinked; he had been so caught up in the discovery of the warlock that he had not even noticed what lined the walls of the corridor.

Books. Row upon row of books stretching far off into the

distance. If anything, this hall was longer than the first he had traveled. Perhaps it even went on forever.

All the books were identical in color and form. There were hundreds . . . no . . . *thousands* of volumes in this corridor alone and from the looks of things, there were side hallways in the distance. More shelves with more books? Small wonder that Shade was growing frustrated in his search for . . . for *what*?

Then the maddened spellcaster pulled another volume from one of the walls, allowing the scholar to at last see the cover.

A stylized dragon. Without seeing the other books, he knew that they, too, would have the same design.

"Which one is it?" Shade snarled. "Which one is the true *dragon tome*?"

Serkadion Manee chuckled. From his hands he produced the volume that Wellen and Xabene had watched him utilize only minutes before. The gnome tossed the book toward the enraged figure. It flew with unerring accuracy into the waiting fingers of the other spellcaster. Shade forgot the others and began paging through the tome. After several seconds, however, his anger began to resurface. What he sought was not in the book Manee had given to him.

"This is not it, either!" The book fell to the top of the pile that had accumulated at Shade's feet. "Another useless collection of dribble!"

The gnome's countenance darkened. "Dribble? Yes, you are Vraad! No concern with anything except what you desire! All else is to be swept aside as inconsequential!"

"I want only one thing! I want nothing else this accursed, parasitic world has offered! Where is the true dragon tome?"

He could not see it. Wellen pitied Shade, so caught up in his quest and his madness that he could not see what Serkadion Manee was trying to show him.

It was apparent to the gnome, too. He produced another book, identical in design but this time a forest green in color, and held it up before his shadowy counterpart.

"This is the *true* dragon tome."

"Give it to me!"

Manee ignored his demand. Releasing the book, he sent it floating a few feet before him. At the same time, a new volume materialized. This one was deep blue, but otherwise a twin of the others. "This is the true dragon tome."

Shade began to say something, but stopped. He simply stared at the gnome and the floating books.

A rainbow of literature formed before the eyes of all. Wellen had never seen so many variations of color at one time. He counted more than a dozen shades of green and was certain there were more. Book after book materialized and dematerialized, only to be replaced by another.

"These are *all* the true dragon tome." The gnome took amusement at the horrified expression stretching across the warlock's deathly visage. "As is every volume on every shelf in every hall."

"All . . . of them?"

There was something Serkadion Manee had not yet said that Bedlam suspected would finish whatever reserves of anger and hope that Shade had left.

"All of them, yes, my dark and annoying friend." Manee waved a hand and every book that had been torn off the shelves returned to its rightful resting place. The countless volumes that he himself had summoned also vanished, no doubt to their own shelves.

Serkadion Manee smiled widely and finally concluded, "And you have yet to see the *other* libraries."

XVIII

In Serkadion Manee's intricate trap, the Purple Dragon continued to struggle. Now and then, he found he made a little more progress. Soon, it would be enough to free him.

Soon.

The old sorcerer ran a hand over his hairless head. Wellen noticed him wince again. The jabs, or whatever they were, were becoming more frequent. He wondered if Manee understood that he was overtaxing himself.

Shade was still refusing to believe what he had heard. He took a few steps toward the master of the citadel. "You lie!

You have to be!'' With a sweep of his arm he indicated the other volumes. ''These are ploys, an elaborate plot to hide the one, true tome!''

Sounding much like a disappointed parent, Serkadion Manee returned, ''You know who I am, Vraad.''

''I do! Master Dru Zeree studied your works long and hard! It was because of your writings that he searched and found this accursed land!''

''I wish I had met him. From what else I have gathered, he was rather remarkable. A Vraad who did more than fulfill his childish fantasies was a rare one even in my time . . . and I have lived *much*, much longer than you, stripling!''

''Which is why I know you must have what I seek!'' Shade looked triumphant and not a little mad. ''You could not be alive otherwise! Not after all this time!''

Manee arched what had once been an eyebrow. ''Is that what you want? Is that all? A thousand thousand years of research and that is all you want?''

His almost matter-of-fact tone made all of them curious. If he was talking about immortality, a thing sought after by so many over the millennia, then his manner was puzzling. Wellen doubted that he could be so nonchalant about such an amazing discovery. No mage that he had ever met had discovered a way to tap into the world's life and extend his own for more than three, possibly four hundred years. Even the Dragon Kings were mortal.

Pulling back his hood and fully revealing his horrific state, the warlock almost pleaded. ''*Yes*, that *is* what I want! That is *all* that I want! I will give this world neither my body nor my soul!''

''Hmmph.'' Serkadion Manee saw what Shade could not. Wellen was certain that anyone other than the shadowy warlock would have noticed the truth. Shade had long ago given his body and soul to this world, or at least a good portion of each. The rest belonged to the place called Nimth. The warlock was a man caught between two worlds, neither of which he saw as promising him a simple and quiet fate.

Shade looked for help. ''Master Bedlam, I am sorry. The spell used on Xabene by my cousins urged me to a sudden and daring plan, a spell hidden in *your* mind. I desired no harm to come to you. This the Green Dragon and I agreed upon.''

They had both betrayed him. Only Xabene, who had proven

herself to him, still earned his trust. If not for her, Wellen would have wished that he had never thought of searching for the legendary Dragonrealm. It was a place of treachery and greed, nothing more. "How did you escape from the Lords of the Dead?"

"They are shadows of what we once were. Only I still have ties to Nimth, to the power that is both our right and our curse."

"He means he has broken through and linked himself to a world ravaged by my kind," Serkadion Manee argued. "Only a true Vraad would think of allying himself with a force I estimate had been perverted beyond repair."

"As have you."

"I have not."

"I don't believe you." There was, however, a touch of uncertainty in Shade's voice.

"It matters not what you believe." The gnome was disgusted. "I had forgotten what happens when two Vraad meet. Very well, before we come to blows, I shall give you what you desire and then you can leave." He winced. "Do not bother to come back. Our mutual heritage will not open this citadel to you again. Rather, it should have never let you inside."

"All I want is the secret of immorality. . . and the promise that Master Bedlam here will not become a part of your collection."

Serkadion Manee wore a pained expression. "He will remain here only so long as he chooses to. Now then," the gnarled spellcaster reached into the confines of his robe and removed yet another book. Pitch black, Wellen would have thought it more appropriate for death rather than immortality. Manee held it out. "This is what you were seeking. Read it, use it if you will, and depart. You may thank Master Wellen Bedlam for your safety and the fact that I am even giving you this one chance."

"He has my gratitude. I hope one day he will understand, if only for the sake of one we both know."

Bowing his head, Wellen would not meet the crystalline gaze. Whatever Shade or Gerrod had been to the scholar's ancestor, the warlock had to be a shadow of that man now. He truly lived up to his self-chosen appellation.

The warlock grabbed the proffered book and began thumbing through it. His eagerness made him bat the pages aside with such intensity that it was a wonder he was able to ready any of it. Serkadion Manee watched him for a breath or two, then *tsked* at the cloaked figure's impatience.

"That is not how you will find it. Do what you are doing and you will search through the tome forever. Simply think about what you desire. My book will do the rest."

Shade visibly debated believing the gnome, then decided it was worth a try. He held the dragon tome slightly away from him, unnecessarily, Wellen suspected, but Shade had always seemed to live the dramatic, and stared at it.

The pages flipped by. Nearly two-thirds of the way through the volume, they ceased. Shade slammed a gloved hand on the page, which made his counterpart frown, and pulled the book to him. He began to read avidly, not caring at all the sight his desperation made of him.

All was well at first, but then the warlock's brow furrowed. He reread part of the page, silently mouthing the words as if he could not believe what was written there.

"You cannot be *serious*!" he snarled. "You would not have done this! It would mean giving yourself up to this land and its accursed, covetous mind! It would mean forever being tied to this one place!"

"What you see is truth."

"You have been seen throughout the Dragonrealm!"

"There are ways. Temporary measures that allow me access and the ability to taste outside life."

Now it was Shade who was disgusted. "You are truly Vraad after all even though the rest of you belongs to this domain! I could only dream of such a travesty!"

Serkadion Manee held his head. "I have given you what you wanted. If you choose to decline it, then our business is ended. You may leave us any time you like."

"Leave you?" The warlock *threw* the dragon tome to the floor. One hand went up and pulled the hood back over. Shade was a different person when all but hidden by the voluminous cloak. "Only with them!"

"I knew he could not be trusted!" Xabene whispered. "He let you think he was a prisoner or nearly dead just so that you would help him gain entrance!"

"I don't know..."

Serkadion Manee had stepped in front of the duo. "They do not wish to depart with you. Leave now or not at all."

Holding out a hand, Shade tried to appeal to the confused scholar. "Master Bedlam, have him explain what has happened to the others he allowed inside! Ask him why neither the Dragon King nor any of the others who sought, foolishly, I see, the secrets of this monster ever questioned those folk! Ask him what became of them!"

"It is time you left." Serkadion Manee pointed at the other Vraad.

A brilliant emerald green aura bathed Shade. The warlock smiled and the aura winked out of existence as abruptly as it had formed.

"My cousins showed more imagination."

Helpless, Wellen and Xabene stepped back from Manee. The gnome ignored them. "You want imagination?"

Every book from the shelves before, next to, and behind the hooded figure shot forth.

Shade covered his face as the paper hailstorm battered and buried him. Though he must have sought to protect himself with his own skills, several volumes struck him soundly on the head. The warlock went down on one knee. The dragon tomes, what he had desired for so very long, continued to come to join their brethren in the assault.

Unable to stand it any longer, Wellen ceased his retreat and came up behind the gnome. Manee, still holding his head and now breathing with a little difficulty, paid him no mind as he concentrated on defeating his rival.

"A little knowledge is a dangerous thing!" snarled Serkadion Manee. Despite his seeming triumph, however, each passing second saw him more and more exhausted. He clutched his side.

Wellen's head screamed of the danger he was thrusting himself into, but the novice warlock patently ignored both the warning and the fear he felt rising. Perhaps it was still the memory of Shade and his silent talk with the phantasms of the scholar's ancestors or even Wellen's own brief conversation with Sharissa Zeree's specter, but he could not allow Serkadion Manee to continue.

Praying that something, *anything*, would happen, Bedlam touched the gnome's shoulder.

In the chamber where the Dragon King struggled, the magical page that held him prisoner burst into flames.

The Purple Dragon roared.

* * *

Wellen had hardly expected Serkadion Manee to scream, but the master of the citadel did so—and very loudly. Manee doubled over, falling to the floor. One hand still clutched his head. "Too much..." he muttered. "Too much...but it cannot be! Not me!" Then, "He will escape...he will..."

"What did you do?" the enchantress asked, joining Wellen. The gnome, curled up, seemed to be in shock, although it might have been the effect of sorcery. Slowly, his words became quieter. Serkadion Manee eventually froze in one position. Wellen stared at his hand, uncertain as to whether he was the cause or not. When Xabene moved even closer to him, he was almost afraid to touch her for fear the same fate that had befallen Serkadion Manee would befall her.

"I don't know...it *could* have been me..." He reached toward the fallen figure, but pulled his hand back at the last moment. Wellen had no desire to kill Manee. That might happen if he touched him again. He still had no control over his abilities.

Understanding his quandary, Xabene knelt and inspected Serkadion Manee for him. Her first touch was tentative, but when the still figure did not respond, she became less cautious. After a brief inspection, the enchantress pushed aside some hair that had fallen forward and said, "He's either in a trance or there's a spell on him."

"Is there anything you can do?"

"I could care less about doing anything for this parasite...but the answer is no; I can't. What has him is beyond my meager powers."

"I could try to touch him again," he suggested with some hesitation, his hands clenched, "but it might only harm him. I...I do not even dare touch *you*."

Xabene reached out and took hold of his left hand before he realized what she was about.

"No—" His protest faded when nothing happened. Bedlam glared at the woman.

She smiled. "You seem to work off your emotions. I counted on the fact that you wouldn't want to hurt me. I was right."

As a scholar, he would have argued her logic, especially as it did not take in so any other considerations. On a more personal level, he agreed with her . . . not that he planned on telling the enchantress that.

His eyes drifted beyond her, alighting on the massive pile of bulky tomes. "Shade!"

Nearly dragging Xabene along, he rushed to where the warlock had made his last stand. While Wellen could not forgive the mad spellcaster, as with Serkadion Manee, he wished Shade no injury. Wellen admitted to himself that there was still a trace of compassion for the warlock. In the same position, the scholar wondered how *he* would have held up. Would he have been as insane as Shade? Worse?

They dug their way into the pile. The scholar was amazed at both the sheer number of books and how none of them had been damaged in any way. Serkadion Manee's assault had initially surprised him, for he had not thought the gnome would risk his own work. Now he saw that the gnome had assured the condition of the dragon tomes before sending them at his adversary.

Deeper and deeper they burrowed, Wellen as swiftly as he could and Xabene with much reluctance. As far as she was probably concerned, two great problems had been removed from her life. Wellen was aware that the only reason she helped was because she knew he would not leave without trying.

The literary avalanche gave way in short order to his efforts, but still he could not find Shade. Bedlam began moving around the massive pile, thinking perhaps that he had chosen the wrong location to dig.

Shoving aside yet another dozen tomes, Xabene cursed in the name of her former masters and said, "Wellen, we have to forget him! I think it might be a good idea if we search instead for a way out of this place!"

"Not without Shade! He saved your life, remember!"

"And we've repaid him for that! Just because it turned out to be a ploy on his part . . ." She shivered, recalling something for the first time. "I wonder what he did to them. He *must* have defeated them." Her eyes grew round. "Gods, what power and skill!"

"Thank you . . ." came a hissing voice from where they had left the unconscious gnome. "It wasssss really nothing at all!"

A leviathan in scale armor, the Purple Dragon was a thing of nightmares. He filled the hall, so massive was he even in humanoid form. The dragon's head crest leering down on the twosome made him come nearly to the ceiling. Within the helm, they saw the reptilian eyes burning. Now and then, a forked tongue would dart out of a mouth filled with jagged teeth. The image of a monstrous knight was so real it was almost impossible to believe that the armor was actually just the Dragon King's scaly hide twisted by the spell that allowed him this shape.

With one hand he carried the unmoving form of Serkadion Manee. The other was raised toward the duo.

"You are mine at lasssst, manling! I have *everyting* now!" He indicated the two should come to him.

Wellen's body rose, although Wellen himself tried not to obey. Xabene was already moving toward the armored figure. He caught a glimpse of her horrified expression and wondered about his own.

The Purple Dragon made them pause just within arm's length. One swipe of his clawed hand could have torn both their throats out. This near, the scholar noticed that the drake was not as at ease as he had tried to make them believe. There were signs of strain. Wellen could see that Purple was feeling the weight of trying to maintain his control over the situation.

If nothing else, it was the sibilance in his voice that most betrayed the Dragon King. The more excited or weary he became, the more the hissing grew dominant. "At lassst! Now all I need issss the interfering warlock who wassss the final sssstraw!" The drake gave a raspy chuckle. "If not for him, I might sssstill be sssstruggling! Not that the outcome wassss not inevitable regardlesssss! I would have sssstill triumphed, jusssst a bit later!"

Wellen and Xabene once more moved without their own consent. Lugging the gnome with him, the Dragon King stepped between them and confronted the sea of knowledge under which Serkadion Manee had attempted to drown Shade.

"Let it be assss it wassss."

The dragon tomes flew back to their various shelves. There did not seem to be any order to what the Purple Dragon did. He did not seem to care about organizing the books, merely putting them where they would be out of the way. For the moment, Shade, the last loose end, was all that concerned him.

When all the books had flown away, however, there was no trace of the hooded warlock. The Dragon King stalked over to where the center of the mountain of tomes had stood and peered down at the floor.

"Bah!" He turned back to Wellen. "Your comrade issss either a victim of thissss damnable little sssssprite or hassss fled in mindlessss fear at my coming! Either way, he will trouble ussss no more!"

That Shade had turned coward was not a notion that Wellen Bedlam believed. That the warlock had fled, however, he found more likely. With Serkadion Manee's spell of rejuvenation not to his liking and the Dragon King now in control, there was no reason for Shade to stay.

Yet, he *had* fought with Manee over Wellen's freedom.

The Purple Dragon's breathing quickened. He put Serkadion Manee down and leaned against one of the corridor walls. For a brief moment, the horrific warrior shimmered.

Wellen found he could move his fingers. It was not a great victory in the scheme of things, but it was a victory nonetheless. It meant that the Dragon King was weaker.

Slowly, the drake regained control of himself. He glared at the two humans, daring either of them to comment on his weakness. Still under his spell, they could not have said anything even if they had been insane enough to want to. Satisfied, the drake contemplated his next move.

"There issss no need for the two of you for now," he informed them. The truth, Bedlam knew, was that like Serkadion Manee, it was becoming harder and harder for Purple to spread his power over so much. If he could find another way of keeping his two human prisoners secure, then it would allow him to redirect his efforts. "I shall sssend you to the royal caverns. Then, when the time permitssss, I will be better able to dissssect what information you know from your mindssss."

He waved a negligent hand at them, then hissed in anger when they simply stood there. The Dragon King stared at them long and hard. Wellen felt a faint tug, but it soon faded.

"Why do you not vanish? What holdssss you here?" The Purple Dragon picked up the wizened sorcerer at his feet and held him at eye level. "Thissss issss your doing! It will not ssssave you, though! Your precioussss tomessss are now mine and they shall stay mine!" A sinewy tongue darted out and in. "You would like me to assssk you for aid, would you not? You think I am foolish enough to risssssk your esssscape by freeing you from thissss ssssspell for *any* length of time? You will

neither move nor sssspeak until I can be certain your coopera-
tion issss assured!''

The fearsome knight lowered his motionless captive and then
scanned the library hall in both directions. There seemed no
end to the corridor no matter which way one looked. Cursing,
he turned back to the two helpless humans.

Wellen found himself able to move once more. He looked up
expectantly at the Dragon King.

"There issss no need for me to wasssste my strength on you,
manling. Neither you nor your mate have shown power of any
ssssignificant level. Therefore, you will hardly be able to
esssscape me should you both be mad enough to try.''

The scholar was well aware of their present chances. Later,
things might change, but for now they had little choice but to
obey. "I understand.''

"I am certain you do. Both of you.''

Xabene gasped as mastery of her body was once again hers.
She quickly nodded her agreement.

"We undersssstand one another. Good.'' The Dragon King
studied the corridor behind where he had originally materialized. He nodded to himself and added, "Ssssince I may not
teleport you out of thissss place, we musssst find a portal like
the one we entered by. You two will lead the way... jusssst in
casssse.''

Wellen reached for the enchantress, but the drake's free hand
came between then. Nothing was said but the message was
clear. The Dragon King did not trust their apparent weakness
that much. He would not allow his captives to conspire against
him.

Side-by-side but nearly an arm's length apart, the two began
walking. The horrific knight followed only a few paces back,
Serkadion Manee's small form not slowing his stride in the
least. The sorcerer was carried the way one might carry a light
sack, an ignoble position if ever there was one.

Their trek began in silence, the Dragon King possibly taking
inventory of his gains. Wellen doubted that his success was
going to be as complete as he imagined. Something about the
citadel, especially the libraries, seemed to hint at a reluctance
to accept this new master. If defeating Serkadion Manee was all
that the drake lord had needed to do to triumph, then why was
he unwilling to teleport *within* the pentagon even if teleportation

out of it was impossible? Surely if everything was now his, then there was no danger.

If that were the case, Purple would not be using them as shields. No, the Dragon King knew that the battle was not yet over. He had captured only the master, not the servant.

After a time, the scholar decided to chance talking to his captor. Anything to break the leaden silence that suppressed them all. "Is Prentiss Asaalk truly dead?"

Almost to his surprise, the reptilian sovereign responded. "The gnome had the right of it. Your azure companion quickly proved himsssself too devioussss to live. I tolerate ambition in thosssse who are usssseful, but only assss long assss they undersssstand their place. I knew he would never undersssstand and sssso I played on hissss very arrogance and ambition." A hissing laugh. "There are collarssss and there are collarssss. Assss if I would be so foolish assss to trusssst him with the tassssk of sssseeking you out and bringing you back to me!"

Asaalk had offered him to the Dragon King. *Would I have done the same in his position?* he asked himself.

"There will be one for you and your female eventually. Collarssss that will only teach you your place, however, unlike some of the otherssss I have usssssed in the passsst. I needed the blue one'ssss appearance and mind but not hissss untrussssstworthy wayssss. The collar he ignorantly donned drained him of all memoriesssss. It alwayssss workssss sssso much better when they are not aware of what issss to happen. Alasssss, it meant his eventual death, for in draining his memories, it destroyed what was left." A pause. "Pray that you do not annoy me assss he did. I might forget which collar to pressssent you."

The last brought a return to silence. Wellen exchanged glances with Xabene, but that was the extent of their communication. Escape was essential. The reptilian monarch's hint at their future had made that all too clear. Unlike the Green Dragon, this drake lord had no qualms about disposing of his guests on a whim.

Shelf after shelf after shelf of book after book after book. All of them forming the accumulation of the gnome's millennia-old search for knowledge. Did any of them hold a key to their rescue? He would have liked to thumb through a few of the volumes, if only to see what was contained within.

"Sssso much knowledge," the Dragon King commented in

what might have been an admiring tone. "Will there be time for all of it?"

For just that brief instant, the scholar and the Dragon King shared a desire.

"There are no titlessss on the sssspinessss. How does one know what issss contained in what?"

The question had bothered Wellen, too, but unless the drake chose to release Serkadion Manee now, he doubted he would ever find out.

"Manling."

As the Dragon King had not stopped, neither did Bedlam. He turned and waited for his captor to speak again.

"Doessss thissss place sssseem almost *alive* to you?"

He gave it some thought. "It wouldn't surprise me."

"Agreed." Burning eyes darted from one bookshelf to the next. "Sssso many marvelssss..." The look of admiration died as the drake lord turned his gaze forward. "But the one I could do without issss thissss cursed, endlesssss hall!"

The words no sooner escaped his lipless mouth then they saw a lone metal door in the distance. The discovery was so abrupt that Wellen eyed the ensorcelled gnome with some suspicion. Did Serkadion Manee still have mastery over his former domain?

The door, when they at last reached it, was a simple iron thing with only a handle. There was no lock, but then the ancient sorcerer had never needed one. Pausing, the party stared at the exit for several seconds. What lay on the other side only Serkadion Manee knew. After some silent debate, the Dragon King looked at the explorer. "You!" he hissed, thrusting a clawed finger at Wellen. "You will open it!"

Bedlam stepped forward, knowing he had no choice. All he could do was pray as his fingers wrapped around the handle and pulled the door open.

Xabene gasped.

"Nothing..." murmured the Dragon King. "Almosssst a dissssappointment."

His heart still pounding in his ears, Wellen surveyed what had been hidden behind the door. Only another hallway. No trap. No visible threat.

Save perhaps to one's eyes. Evidently, Serkadion Manee had his whimsical moments, for there seemed no other explanation for the design and pattern of the place.

They entered an immense hall that was a chess master's

board run amok. The floor, the walls, and the rounded ceiling were all covered in a black and white pattern resembling one massive game board. There were no doors, save at the far, far end. Neither were there fixtures or decorations. Because of the pattern, it was even hard to tell where the floor ended and the walls began. Wellen would not have been surprised if the party could have walked up one of the walls without even noticing the change.

"What issss thissss new madness? My head poundssss jusssst sssstaring at it!" Purple, squinting, turned to his two mobile prisoners. "The female will go first, I think. A few paces ahead. Then you and I, manling. Side-by-side. If you should stray even a foot beyond my reach, I will act. I do not need to touch you to kill you."

"I understand."

A taloned finger scraped the stubble that was growing on the scholar's neck. "I am sure that you do."

The trio started down the hall at a slow but steady pace. From his position, Wellen studied the profile of the horrific warrior. The Purple Dragon, marching along from square to square, looked like the soul survivor of some massive game in which he played both knight and king. The scholar pictured an entire board of such figures, with Serkadion Manee for some reason still coming to mind as the opposing lord. Xabene was a queen, but one whose side she was he had not figured out. As for his own position, Wellen could only see himself as a pawn in the middle.

But it is the pawn in the middle who starts the opening gambit sometimes . . .

It was a peculiar thought and he could not say what had caused him to summon it. Chess was a game he had once played avidly, but not during the past few years. In the end, the expedition had demanded his complete devotion. There had been no time for games.

"Issss there no hall in thissss accursed place that doessss not sssstretch on and on and on?" the Dragon King complained. The strain was beginning to show on the drake. Not only had he exhausted much power in escaping his prison and capturing Manee, but he was expending even more keeping the gnome secure while also, at least so Wellen assumed, probing for any sorcerous surprises left by the citadel's former master.

It rose through the floor, clad in black mail and plate armor, simply decorated but skillfully crafted. A helm obscured all trace of the fighter's countenance. In his gauntleted hands, the dark knight held a battle-ax nearly two-thirds the size of Wellen himself. As for the mysterious warrior, he topped the Dragon King in both height and build.

"A challenge?" mocked the drake. "No challenge at all!" He raised his free hand.

The newcomer glowed liquid-metal red.

Purple suddenly snarled and withdrew his hand as if something had bitten it. While he rubbed it, the silent guardian took two steps forward, then shifted a square to his right, bringing him parallel to the rounded form of Serkadion Manee.

Another figure, also black, rose behind the original position of the first. This one was smaller, but clad in nearly identical armor. He looked no less threatening for being shorter, although the ebony mace and shield he carried might have had something to do with that. The second guardian took two steps forward, then also waited.

The Dragon King hissed.

Scarlet tendrils of sorcery entwined the two attackers.

The larger one shook them off like so much mist. He took another step forward, then two to his left so that he ended up facing Xabene, who quickly backed away to where Wellen was standing.

After a brief struggle with the drake lord's attack, the second warrior took a single step toward the party.

Behind the black figures, two more, identical to the smaller one, joined the confrontation. Far to the scholar's left, a different gladiator rose. This one was almost as tall as the lead figure, but slimmer and carrying a crimson longbow. A sleek, glittering arrow of gold was already notched.

"We have to go back to the libraries," Xabene whispered. "I don't think the Dragon King will find these so simple to defeat!"

Nodding, Bedlam glanced back in order to locate the doorway. . . and found that it no longer *existed*. "It seems we have no choice in the matter." He faced forward again and squinted. "The other door is still there."

"But we have to go through them first."

Beside them, Purple heard everything. "They are nothing! I have disssscovered their weaknessss."

He held up his ensorcelled captive for the warriors to see. "I have your masssster here! Ssssurrender or I will kill him now!"

The archer took several steps forward until he was even with the original guardian. The Dragon King spun around and held Serkadion Manee between himself and the bowman, but the latter did nothing.

The shorter warriors all took one step forward.

It struck Wellen then what sort of predicament they faced. This hall was not simply decorated like a chessboard by chance. Rubbing his chin in thought, he happened to glance ceilingward.

"Xabene!" he whispered.

She followed his gaze.

More than half a dozen ebony warriors stood scattered on the upper walls and ceiling. They seemed not at all put out by the fact that in some cases, they stood completely upside down. Most were identical to the ones already confronting the trio, but there was one wearing black raiments and an obscuring hood who resembled some insidious cleric.

All of those clinging to the walls and ceiling were armed and eyeing the intruders below.

Hearing Wellen's voice, the Dragon King turned just enough to see the humans. When he caught them staring up, he glanced that way. "Dragon of the Depthsssss!"

The archer released his arrow.

It might have been an exceptional shot, but Bedlam was almost positive that only chance made the bolt miss Serkadion Manee, who still hung unknowing and unprotected from the massive Dragon King's hand. Hampered by his living baggage, Purple could not turn in time to avoid the arrow. He was, however, able to react fast enough with his sorcery to cause it to deflect. A normal arrow would not have concerned the Dragon King, but it was doubtful that Serkadion Manee would have been satisfied with such for this macabre, life-size game.

Yet another dark knight rose through one of the squares, this one out of the wall to their left. Though armored like the others, it had a definite feminine shape and in its hands it carried a jeweled scepter.

"Pawns, knight"—the scholar studied one of the archers, then continued—"rooks, I suppose, then bishops, and now a queen." Wellen glanced hurriedly around the mind-wrenching corridor. "But where's the king?"

"What are you talking about?" the enchantress muttered, her eyes still on the unsettling tableau above them.

"This is some bizarre and deadly chess game!"

If the drake lord heard them this time, he said nothing. His hands were full in more ways than one, for several of the stygian figures were moving toward him, each one following a peculiar movement pattern. Even the ones on the ceiling and walls were shifting closer. So far, only the archer, Serkadion Manee's idea of a rook, had posed any problem, but the attackers were slowly cutting off the party from any hope of escape . . . and there was no telling what powers the queen or the yet-to-be-seen king controlled. There might even be more than one. Who was to say that the gnome's version of chess was the same as the one the scholar was familiar with? With so large a board and so many dimensions, Wellen would have added pieces. He suspected that Manee had done just that.

The Purple Dragon unleashed another spell. Mist enshrouded the chessmen, for a moment bringing all movement to a halt. More was expected if the drake's irritation was anything to judge by. Hissing, the Dragon King muttered under his breath. The mist took on a greenish tinge.

The nearest pawn fell face first onto the floor and faded away.

"Ha!" Encouraged by his success, the Dragon King increased the intensity of the green mist. The knight in front remained still, but the other pieces moved closer, as if the death of one had strengthened the others.

Wellen saw the queen raise her specter. He was caught in a quandary. Warn the Dragon King? Let him be attacked? Either way he and Xabene lost. They needed the drake to save them from these silent sentinels, but they also needed the chessmen to rescue them from the clutches of the dragon.

He was saved that decision by the Dragon King himself, who noticed the queen at the last moment. The jewel in her scepter glowed a warm rose. Purple's eyes narrowed and darkness seemed to come from them. He reached out and swiftly blocked the queen's scepter. A crimson flash was all they could see, then the darkness vanished. The queen slowly lowered her royal weapon and stood there as if nothing had happened.

"Can't we do anything?" the enchantress asked. "I have some power! Perhaps I could pull one of those from the ceiling onto some of the ones coming toward us!"

"Do nothing!" the scholar uttered in sudden inspiration. Perhaps they were not in so great a danger after all!

She looked at Wellen as if he had lost all sense of reality. "If we do nothing, we die."

"If we do nothing," he responded in as low a voice as possible, "then they may ignore us completely. So far, they've only attacked the Purple Dragon!"

"I think I would prefer not to wait until they have killed him. By then we'll be surrounded!"

He nodded. "When I said do nothing, I meant only in terms of attacking them. I think that they may only be interested in the Dragon King"—Wellen pointed at the archer above—"or else we would have been dead already."

The original chess piece, the knight, finally attacked. With a rapid one-step, two-step run, he moved close to the Dragon King. He brought the axe up and around in a vicious arc, his speed so astonishing that the drake lord barely had time to react. Not trusting to his spells at so close a range, the reptilian monarch stumbled backward. It almost proved a fatal mistake, for Serkadion Manee's weight made just enough difference that the drake nearly fell.

Cursing, the Dragon King shot a glance at the frozen figure. With little ceremony, he dumped the still form of Manee on one of the squares a few feet back and to the side. In his now-free taloned hands materialized an incredibly long, curiously curved sword. No human that Wellen had ever met could have wielded so great a giant, but the Dragon King did so with ease.

He moves and acts with confidence, the scholar noted. *How long has he held this spell from the eyes of his brethren? One would almost think he had been born in such a body and not shaped himself through masterful sorcery!*

The ebony knight brought the axe around again, this time in a downward arc. The gleaming head missed its target by less than a foot, but it forced Purple back another square. If he was not careful, Wellen thought, he would be in danger of stepping on—

Serkadion Manee was no longer lying prone on the square where he had been so roughly deposited.

Xabene noticed it at the same time. "The gnome!" she hissed. "He's escaped!"

It hardly seemed possible, but there was no sign of the

libraries' creator. Wellen could not even say exactly when he had disappeared.

A golden streak flashed by them, narrowly missing him. Reflex action made him fall to the floor away from the path of the bolt.

"We may die whether they intend to kill us or not!" he managed to gasp.

There was no response from the sorceress. Fearful that she had somehow been struck down by the arrow, despite the fact that he was almost certain it had continued on, Wellen rolled over.

Xabene was gone.

Something heavy and metal crashed to the floor beside him. Not Xabene, as his mind first imagined, but the knight who had crossed weapons with the Dragon King. The helm was cracked and for the first time he caught a glimpse of the warrior within.

The sight almost made him sick. Within the armor, thankfully only barely visible, was the mummified visage of a man. By the explorer's calculation, he had been dead for years. There was hardly anything but dried skin and bone. By comparison, Shade almost looked robust.

Then, to his horror, the head began to *turn* slowly toward him. He scrambled back.

Something that would not be denied pulled him from every direction.

The chessboard corridor and his macabre companion faded. For the first time, Wellen welcomed a teleportation spell, regardless of where it might be sending him.

A darkened chamber formed around him. He breathed a sigh of relief . . . and looked up at the looming specter of a huge, ebony-armored warrior clad in scarlet cape and crown and bearing a long scepter upon which was fixed a rainbow gem whose power even an inept novice like Wellen Bedlam could sense.

He had found the king of Serkadion Manee's chess game at last . . . or perhaps the king had found *him*.

XIX

The black king continued to stare in silence. Wellen remained where he had materialized, uncertain if even the slightest movement was allowed.

After a long, breath-holding wait in which the ebony figure did not stir, the scholar began to wonder if he had misjudged the situation. He looked at the visored head and dared talk to it. "Are you the one who saved me?"

Nothing. Yet, knowing the abominable thing that must lie within, he could not take a lack of response as meaning that he was safe. "I'd like to stand, if you have no objections to that."

He decided to take the silence for agreement. Wellen slowly rose from the floor, his eyes ever locked on the monarch of night. The armor spoke of a being gargantuan in proportions, larger than even the humanoid form of the Dragon King. While such giants were not unknown among humanity, it was possible that the armor enhanced its wearer, made the thing within appear larger than it was.

Either way, if it chose to strike him down, he doubted he would be able to defend himself.

When he stood before it, and it did not react, the shorter scholar took a step toward it. Still nothing. He continued until he was well within arm's reach. The scepter did not rise and crush his skull. The gauntleted hand did not seize him by the throat and squeeze.

He reached up and touched the black king lightly on the chest. The chessman might as well have been a marble column for all he moved.

"Praise be!" Bedlam exhaled. Thinking of the need for a weapon, Wellen tried to take the scepter. It was held so tight, in fact, that it was more likely he would end up crushed under the fallen figure of the king if he continued. Exasperated,

Wellen stepped back from the monstrous toy and finally studied his new surroundings.

Choking down a gasp of disgust, Wellen for the first time saw the *other* playing pieces of the gnome's macabre game. A full score at least, all surrounding him, a legion of the dead. There were a few more black pieces and an entire range of white. There were duplicates, too, evidently in case one of the others became too damaged to use again. They were the only things he could see in the chamber, but that was not surprising, since the only illumination was a pale blue ball just above him.

He was alone. No Xabene. No Serkadion Manee. Where they had vanished to he had no idea. Worse, where *he* had vanished to was a complete mystery. Just how vast was the gnome's citadel? The libraries alone were a phenomenon in size, but now he was discovering corridor after corridor and room after room.

There was little choice but to seek a way out of this place and hope he could find Xabene. Then, the two of them would have to find a means of escaping Manee's paradoxical pentagon. What happened between the Dragon King and the gnome was of no interest to him. Wellen merely wanted his freedom.

Choosing a direction unpopulated by the grisly warriors, the explorer started out. The throbbing in his head had begun again, although he could not say exactly when, but here it was fairly useless. There was too much within a near distance that was genuinely a threat to the would-be warlock. His ability informed him of nothing he did not already know about. Had one of the chessmen raised a weapon against him, Bedlam would have been no better warned.

If this was the extent of his powers, then he doubted he would ever be a competent sorcerer. At this point, he doubted he was much more competent at *anything*.

He found, to his relief, that the blue light followed him as he progressed. It would at least be possible to wander about without having to worry about walking into something in the dark. The illumination was still not the best, but it always kept a yard or two of the path around him visible, which had been more than he could have hoped.

Now if only I can find a doorway or a gate out of this chamber! The fear that this was a place accessible only by a teleportation spell had already occurred to him, but Bedlam tried not to think about the possibility. If such was the case, then he was doomed to capture, or even worse, to die here and become one more rotting corpse.

Wellen increased his pace.

After what he estimated to be at least three or four minutes, Wellen began puzzling over the lack of walls. Not once had he noticed one, not even when he had stood in the midst of the chessmen. Looking up, he realized that there was no visible *ceiling* either. Only the floor beneath his feet, the blue globe floating over his head, and the horrific army he had left behind seemed to exist. There was no sound, save his breathing and his footfalls. He might have been in limbo.

Limbo . . .

He came to a dead halt, trying to hear again the voice whispering in his head. Had it been his imagination? A single word, one sounding more like a gust of wind than speech, that was all it had been. Just a trick of his anxious mind?

Mind . . .

Again, a single word! "Is someone there?"

The proverbial silence of the tomb was all that greeted him, but Wellen was certain it had been another who had spoken.

"Where are you?" His voice did not echo. Even sound died here.

Died . . .

This time, Wellen thought he noted a direction. It was difficult to say if he was imagining *that*, too, for the voice still appeared to exist in his head alone. Yet, he felt that turning to his right and walking in that direction for a time was the correct choice. Perhaps the only choice.

"Please," the scholar whispered, running a hand through his hair as he tried to think. Despite a quick and lengthy stride, Wellen still saw nothing. "Who are you? I don't mean any harm."

It could all be another game, either Serkadion Manee's or the Dragon King's, but he doubted it. With each other to have to concentrate upon, neither could waste time on such a game with him.

Having little other choice, he continued walking. Wellen guessed that he might be underneath the rest of the citadel. Perhaps this was a storage area for Serkadion Manee's abandoned experiments or his monstrous toys, if the chess pieces were any indication. Either way, the scholar only cared about escape.

No escape . . .

"No escape? But . . ." He closed his mouth. The voice

within was not speaking of his fate, but rather its *own*. For the first time, he sensed the mournful, beseeching tone, the sense of agony and loss.

The cry for release.

More than mere words were being conveyed into his head. Emotions. Vague memories. A warning.

Its fate *could* be his, if he was not careful.

"But where are you?" He had to find out what the source of the voice was. He needed to know if he could free it from whatever torment held it. Wellen had to find out if he could avert his own fate.

Then, the dim blue illumination touched an array of small, glittering objects before him.

They stood upon a pedestal, each in its own little slot. Vials no bigger than his index finger. There were ten vials in all, each sealed tight with wax. What was within he could not say, only that it shifted as he tried to see it, almost as if it did not want to be seen. His scholarly side seized control. Wellen crouched near the pedestal and surveyed the scene from eye level. The slots had been designed to securely hold the containers. No simple jostle of the pedestal would shake them loose. For that matter, the stand itself had been created from the same stonelike substance that formed the pentagon itself. The pedestal literally grew from the floor, which made it doubtful that anything short of a dragon would actually be able to disturb it in the first place.

"But what is it?" he muttered.

There came an almost undeniable urge to reach forward and touch the nearest vial. The urge was desperate, needy, and not of his own doing. It was the same sensation as the voice. Whoever or whatever had chosen to speak through his mind desired him to touch one of the vials. It pleaded through sheer emotion for him to do so. He started to comply, but as he eyed the odd array, the arrangement of the containers registered.

He was staring at a pentagram. The pattern was almost identical to that utilized by the Lords of the Dead. This was not just a display, but part of a complex spell of which the sealed vials were likely of the utmost importance. There was one at each point of the pentagram. The only difference was that instead of an eleventh container, a clear gemstone filled the center. It was not an overly brilliant stone, which was why he had not paid that much attention to it, but he saw now that someone had cut the stone to certain specifications. If things followed as they had with the necromancers, then the center-piece was a focus of sorts.

What was in the vials, that they were used in this spell? What sort of power had the gnome captured in each?

What was he doing with it?

The urge to reach for the nearest vessel struck him again, but he shook it off. Touching the magical construct of a creature like Serkadion Manee could easily prove very, very fatal. He had his life to consider. His and Xabene's. She was still trapped here somewhere, perhaps the captive of the immortal.

Trapped . . . A chill wind enshrouded him. Indignation amidst despair rocked his senses. Pleading struck him again while he fought off the other emotions.

There's more than one! the scholar thought. More than one . . . soul? . . . trapped . . . *trapped?* Wellen dared lean close enough to minutely study the foremost flask.

A soul? No, not a soul. A mind.

Ten of them.

"Lord Drazeree protect me!" he uttered, falling back on the inaccurate version he had grow up with. This was what Shade had hinted at! This was what the twisted gnome did with those he invited in! *He doesn't like to waste anything. He said so himself!*

How did he progress? Did he take their memories, as he had taken Wellen's, and then used their bodies for whatever purpose the gnome needed them for? No, the bodies had to be the last thing, else the minds would have been damaged, possibly destroyed.

The possibilities became too grotesque. Bedlam forced the thoughts to the back of his mind, but they continued to make their presence felt. He concentrated on the vials. Within was something not quite white, not quite liquid, that tried to hide from his sight. Each vial held similar contents.

With a deep breath, Wellen took hold of the closest.

Pleadingsobbingshatterchildrenfatherhelphusband . . .

Wellen gasped and tore his hand away from the vessel.

"Too much!" he shouted at the mind he had touched. "I can't take that all in!" The memories and the message had kept mixing. It was probably as confusing and difficult for the trapped thing within as it was for the scholar.

Shatter, he recalled. *It said 'shatter.'* A plea to destroy the vial? That would *kill* it—

He shook his head. Not kill it. In truth, the ten were already dead; they had just not been allowed to rest. How long since they had been forced into this tortured nonexistence? The minds must burn out eventually, but they went through agony in the meantime. Bedlam had felt that. Not just from the one he had touched, but from all of them.

There were many questions the dark-haired explorer desired answers to, but to delay in what had to be done would only be adding to the cruelty that Serkadion Manee had instigated.

The vials would not come free of the pedestal; Wellen had learned that during his brief physical contact with the vessel. He would need something to smash them with, but his choices were sorely limited. Anything that could have been used as a weapon had been removed. While he did not want the immortal's victims to suffer further, Wellen did not relish using his bare hands.

He looked down, trying to think, and noticed his boots. They were of the sturdy kind, designed for the tremendous trek originally intended. Comfortable, but with sturdy enough soles and a bit of heel that, admittedly, had been added in vanity to give him a little more height than nature had provided.

Stepping back, Wellen measured the pedestal. If he raised his leg high enough . . .

Balancing himself, Wellen kicked with as much force as he could muster.

The vial shattered, pieces flying everywhere.

Something like a whisp of smoke shot forth from the remains of the vessel. A trilling sound assailed the explorer's ears as the smoky form whirled about his head once. Wellen caught a glimpse of a face, or at least thought he had, belonging to a woman. That was all he could see. The smoke curled around itself then and, without further fanfare, *dissipated*.

He became awash in a sea of emotion. Pleading and hope from those still trapped. The ease with which he had liberated the first still somewhat surprised Bedlam, but it was possible that Serkadion Manee had never considered an intruder down here. Wellen suspected that the reason he was here in the first place was due to the very beings he was now aiding. The Dragon King's presence likely had something to do with their sudden freedom to act in their own behalf.

Shifting his stance, Wellen brought his boot up again. This time, he aimed so that more than one vial would be in the path of his heel. The sooner this was finished the better.

Three more containers shattered under the impact of his second strike. A harmony arose as three tiny forms intertwined with one another and then, like the first, circled his head once. He saw no ghostly visages this time, but he felt their overwhelming gratitude, their relief at being freed from their torment.

As the three faded, the scholar studied the remaining ones. The anticipation they exuded permeated him, making Wellen all that more desirous to put an end to the travesty. He considered his arm. The vials were actually fairly fragile, perhaps a necessity for the spell. While his hands were unprotected, his arm was covered in cloth. One good sweep of his arm could do what would have required his heel two or three attempts to complete.

He stepped around to the other side of the pedestal, measured, and pulled his arm back.

His head shrieked a dire warning.

Wellen fell to the floor and rolled away from the pedestal, the blue light, as was its manner, shifting to compensate. The scholar came to a crouching position. The pedestal was only a dim outline at the edge of the ball's illumination. He could see no threat to warrant the alarm.

"What . . . have . . . you . . . *done*?" came a voice from somewhere behind the vials.

The despair he felt was not just that emitted by the minds in the vials. His own more than matched theirs.

"Do you know what you've done?" What was most frightening about the voice was its detached quality, almost as if the questioner had gone beyond anger to something far colder and far deadlier.

An inferno lit up the region, momentarily blinding Wellen. When he was able to see again, a tiny part of the scholar's mind noted that beyond himself, the pedestal, and the newcomer, there seemed to be nothing but emptiness.

Emptiness and Serkadion Manee.

"Six left," the wizened gnome commented, looking down at the broken pentagram. "But not at all in a viable configuration. That means that control is gone."

Perhaps it was Wellen's imagination, but he thought he felt an aura of satisfaction emanating from the remaining victims.

"He shall treat you no better than I, my little friends," the gnome snarled. His attention turned to the human. "And you

have finally made a place for yourself in the Dragonrealm."
Manee indicated the now empty slots.

Wellen knew his only hope was to stall. It was the only thing
left to him, a momentary halt to the inevitable. Unless a
miracle occurred, nothing would prevent Manee from adding
him to his vile collection.

He wondered if Xabene had already been added. Was one of
the minds hers?

"I'd like to ask a question if I may?"

Something much like the strange square memory device
materialized in the gnome's wrinkled hand. "I have no time for
questions or rebellious creations! Each moment allows that
infernal lizard to further set back my precious work! The
chessmen do not respond now and the corridors are beginning
to buckle . . . and you have made the situation intolerable!
Without a properly coordinated system to maintain the balance,
this entire structure cannot exist! The libraries will fold in on
themselves as they try to take up limited space . . . and they will
not be concerned with the presence of any of us!"

"Stealing my mind will hardly give you the added control
you need."

Serkadion Manee glanced at the vials. "I can create another
viable configuration, one that will work until I've gathered
enough replacements. The female, for one. Perhaps the drake,
too. I've never tried one of his kind." Despite his talk of time
limits, the sorcerer became caught up in his own suggestions.
"I had to rely on elves and dwarfs and the like. They lasted
longer, but were too scarce. When humans appeared, they
looked to be perfect, but they only last two or three centuries."
He scratched his chin. "What would be perfect is an immortal,
but the drakes live centuries. They will do perhaps as a good
substitute."

"How do you propose to get the Dragon King to accept such
a task?" Wellen asked. If his choices consisted of three
hundred years of agony or a quicker death in the collapse of the
citadel, he would take the latter. He only hoped the destruction
was imminent.

"Once I have this realigned, I will have time to consider
that." Manee smiled. "A pity we do not have more time to
discuss things. You have potential. Unfortunately for you, it is
time for me to make use of some of that."

Wellen's legs abruptly gave way, sending him to a kneeling

position on the floor. He felt the other minds mourn their lost hope and his lost life.

"Just one thing," Wellen asked, no longer trying to stall but wanting to know. "Where's Xabene? What have you done with her?"

The gnome's smile soured. "I do not have your companion, but do not worry, my young friend; she will be joining you soon. There is no way out of here without *my* assistance."

"You weren't responsible for the chessmen?"

"Talkative until the end?" Manee stepped around the pedestal. "Yes, I was . . . in the beginning. The drake's presence has muddled things. I lost control and these"—he indicated the vials—"*these* dared to exert some independence."

Their hatred for their captor could be felt even now. Serkadion Manee shrugged it off. "Their agony cannot be helped, nor will yours. It is essential that my work continue and that the results are available for possible later study. I need this spell to maintain that system. I could use the memory disks, of course, but they do not last. The memories fade." The gnome's smile broadened again. He appeared to be trying to be kind about the situation, as if Wellen had a choice. "Otherwise I certainly would not do this, believe me."

He help up the gray, square device with the metal side toward the straining human. "You will find this a bit more shocking than the other one."

Whether it was his own latent ability come to the forefront in this desperate moment or some carelessness upon the immortal's part, the novice spellcaster felt a weight lift from his entire body. Movement was his again.

Wellen did the only thing that he could think of under the circumstances. He *threw* himself against the shorter Manee.

The gnome just had time to open his mouth before the two of them met. As they fell, his disk slipped from his hand. Wellen cared not; if Serkadion Manee recovered, the gnome could easily retrieve his dark device. The scholar had to keep his adversary off balance. Only if he succeeded could he even consider the menacing artifact.

Manee struck something solid, jarring both men hard.

The pedestal! Wellen, taking advantage of the fact that the sorcerer had taken the brunt of the collision, lifted the much lighter gnome and threw him over the top of the stand.

There was a crackling noise as the immortal sprawled over the pedestal.

Stumbling back, the explorer watched in relief and awe as the six remaining victims were released. For a breath or two, the smoky creatures cavorted over the stunned figure of their murderer and enslaver. Then, they drifted over to Wellen, enveloped him in a wave of gratitude, and drifted off, fading as they went.

A tremendous groan marked their passage. Wellen felt the floor beneath him shift.

Without the imprisoned minds to coordinate his spell, could Serkadion Manee's libraries be beginning to collapse?

"No!" Rolling off the pedestal, the gnome turned and gazed upward. After a quick study of something that Wellen could not see, Manee glared at the scholar. Wellen found himself again frozen in place. "I hope you enjoyed your moment of magical glory, my young, impetuous friend, because even if you can manage another spell, it will not be as easy to escape from my domain as it was to break free of the holding spell!"

"What are you going to do?" He fully expected the worst. He had possibly caused the destruction of the work of ages. The scholarly side mourned its imminent passing but the practical side reminded him that it had to have been done. Whatever fate awaited him would be better than what the immoral had planned.

In point of fact, however, Serkadion Manee was smiling, albeit this time without any pretense of enjoyment. With grim satisfaction, he replied, "No, things are not quite ready to crumble yet. You have caused, though, an imbalance. Things will begin to shift in an attempt to keep the citadel from collapsing . . . and that will cause yet more chaos. Worse, there is no control over anything." The gnome shook his head in mock pity. "But I am hardly in dire straits. I planned for this eventuality. There is a method, albeit a rather drastic one, by which I can restore control of this place. If I could only remember what it entailed I could . . ."

"You speak of a lack of control? Does that mean you've lost control of the citadel?"

Manee did not answer his question. Staring off into the emptiness, he said, "It has been too long. I can't remember what it was." He reached out to his motionless prisoner. "Come. We have a book to read."

Once more, they suddenly stood in the libraries.

It was not the same corridor, not unless the tomes had changed the color of their bindings. These books were sky blue. Again, Wellen was amazed at the sheer volume of Serkadion Manee's studies.

"This way." Under the gnome's guidance, the scholar followed his captor down the corridor. Manee seemed at ease despite the fact that somewhere the Dragon King was searching for them.

The gnarled sorcerer began running his fingers over the spines of one particular row of books. He muttered something under his breath. Wellen could do nothing but walk and watch.

"Here!" Manee pulled out one of the volumes. He opened it. Like a living creature, the pages began to turn of their own accord. Manee perused them, telling the book to continue when he did not find what he was looking for.

"Ah! Stop!"

The pages flattened out.

A bent finger ran down the length of the left page. Serkadion Manee nodded to himself. "Of course! How silly of me! That's why I created it like that in the first place." He *tsked* and looked up at his captive. "Time takes its toll even on the most brilliant of minds. It has been so long that I forgot and yet what I forgot was so simple in the first place!"

Closing the dragon tome, the gnome sent it floating to its rightful place. He started to speak, then squinted at something behind Wellen. The scholar, of course, expected the worst.

"Odd. The corridor did not end so close. The pentagon must be readjusting itself. I'd hoped the control had not slipped that badly."

Wellen said nothing but his eyes widened as the part of the corridor he was forced to gaze at abruptly ended no more than a few yards behind the gnome. When they had first appeared, it had been as endless as any. Now, a shelf full of books, *silver* copies, adorned the area.

Noting the look, Serkadion Manee turned. "Nimth's blood! This is more fouled than I imagined!" he snarled at his reluctant companion. "It is only appropriate that since you are responsible for this disarray that you be the sole means by which it is tidied up."

Wellen expected to find himself teleported again, but the gnome did nothing but fold his arms. For several seconds, the human pondered what it was that Manee intended. Then, a prickling sensation coursed through his feet. He wanted to look down, but Manee's spell prevented him from looking anywhere but in the direction the squat mage stood.

"What's happening to me?"

"I regret this, I really do, my overcurious friend. It will be a waste. You probably will not last more than, oh, three or four years, being mortal, but I have no better choice at the moment. A pity you are not immortal, like myself. Then, you'd last forever. The spell for that takes too long to prepare, however. You would need the life span of a Vraad for that and I am afraid the blood has been watered down by too long exposure to this world." The gnome became thoughtful again. "Perhaps I can entice the hooded one into returning. He might be useful once you fade. Yes, I'll have to consider that."

The unnerving sensation had spread upward to Wellen's knees now. He gritted his teeth and asked again, "What are you *doing* to me? At least *tell* me!"

"Now that it has progressed so much, I suppose I can. It appears your own power will not save you this time. You are more of a carrier than a mage. I suspect that your children . . . which you will not have, of course . . . would have been exceptional sorcerers." Serkadion Manee reached up and tapped Bedlam on the chest. "As for satisfying your curiosity, it is the least I can do for a fellow scholar. Put quite simply, you are going to become part of my domain. At present, the floor is slowly encroaching upon you. It lives in a sense, have I mentioned that? It has no higher thought, only base instinct, but that might change now. I have never really tested its potential; so much else to do, you know. It is a radical solution and I fear you will not be as efficient as the matrix was, but this will have to do."

Wellen tried to struggle, but the part of him that had not succumbed to the encroaching floor was still frozen. Manee had only allowed him speech. "For god's sake, don't do this!"

"I am the closest thing to a god around here, I imagine, and this *is* for my sake. Bear with it, won't you please? I have other things to look up. There is still your companion to find and a rather annoying pest to clean out." The insidious gnome bowed. "I am afraid that I will not be back before it is too late. Please believe me, Master Wellen Bedlam, when I say that it was both a pleasure and a pain to meet you. Who knows? Perhaps enough of you will remain coherent so that we might have a discourse or two in the future."

With that, Serkadion Manee vanished.

Blinking, the scholar realized he could move again. Unfortunately, that meant being able to move only the top half of his body, for the living stone that was the citadel had already crept up to his waist and was continuing its climb at far too fast a pace.

Xabene! was his first thought, but she was probably almost as powerless as he seemed to be. Shade was the only one who might be able to help him but he had vanished, either a victim of Manee or simply a wiser soul who had departed the moment he could. Still, Wellen wished that one or both of his companions were here. Perhaps there was some spell they knew that would free him or—

Before him stood both the hooded warlock and the pale enchantress.

To say they were as surprised as he was would have been understating matters. Xabene looked as if she expected either the Dragon King or the gnome to snatch her. When she realized who it was she stood next to, the sorceress stepped away. Her gaze drifted to Wellen, but her sudden joy died when she saw the fate that had befallen him.

"Wellen! By the Lords of the Dead!" She took hold of him and tried to pull him free, not understanding the true nature of his predicament.

"Stop! Unless you desire to become a part of him permanently!" Shade separated the two. Xabene raised her hand, but instead of the spell that the warlock likely expected, she *slapped* him instead.

Shade looked at her, mouth a grim, straight line, and then laughed. "I think I like you after all, female, despite the fact that you remind me too much of my dear, unlamented family."

"Like me or hate me; I could care less! Do something about Wellen!"

"I was going to." The warlock turned glittering eyes on the scholar. "You need not have shouted in my head, Master Bedlam; a simple summons would have been sufficient."

"Shout?" The shadowy figure extended a gloved hand, which Wellen immediately took hold óf. All at once, he felt able to move his legs again.

"You brought us here, you know. That infernally unpredictable power of yours."

Looking down, the novice spellcaster saw that the stone was receding. It had taken on an almost liquid quality and was so soft he was able to pull one of his legs entirely free. With a hand from both of his companions, he was soon away from the treacherous spot. The trio watched as the floor reformed its flat self, then solidified.

"A Vraad through and through," muttered the ancient warlock.

Now free, Wellen took hold of Xabene. "Where were you? What happened to you in that madcap corridor?"

She gave Shade a chilly glare. "*He* did. It was he who rescued me."

"I would have rescued you also," the hooded warlock added, "but you vanished before I could. It was Manee, then, who took you."

"No, Manee didn't." Wellen relayed what had happened to him, not excluding even the tortured minds he had discovered.

When Wellen was done, Shade shook his head. "Worthy of Lady Melenea." When the other two stared at him blankly, the warlock added, "An old acquaintance. Your ancestor, Master Bedlam, was the last to see her before she herself vanished forever. No loss." He grimaced. "All this activity stimulates the memory too much. I was better left dreaming in my cavern, going ever more mad."

"You are welcome to return to your madness," Xabene snapped, "but not until we've escaped this place!"

"Xabene—"

Shade raised a hand to forestall arguing. "Have no fear that I take her words the way she meant them. I am a child of the clan of the Tezcrenee, the dragon men." He paused dramatically for reasons Wellen would never understand. At last, twisting his dry features into something resembling pleasure, he finished, "I have been threatened and bullied by far more intimidating forces than her."

"Listen you—"

"This can wait," Wellen said, taking charge, much to his surprise. "What concerns us now is escaping."

"Do you have an idea?" Shade asked. His parchmentlike countenance had slipped back into the shadows of his hood.

"No."

"Then," responded the master warlock, reaching into his flowing cloak, "perhaps you might be interested in my idea, after all."

His gloved hand emerged with a dragon tome of a pale white that reminded the scholar of the color of the undead Yalso's decaying flesh.

"What's so special about that particular volume?" the raven-haired enchantress asked. She no longer seemed to have any interest in the gnome's treasures. In fact, the very presence of all the other books had made her even more anxious. Wellen had seen her gazing at them every now and then out of the corner of his eye and her expression had not been one of desire but the opposite.

He found he was glad.

"This," Shade said, "tells us the citadel's weaknesses in detail."

"You're joking! Why would he put together something like that?"

"Because," the dark warlock replied, opening to a particular page and turning it toward them, "he *is*, after all, Serkadion Manee."

In another corridor of the vast libraries, the gnome rematerialized. By now, the unfortunate mortal scholar was a well-integrated part of his citadel, but it would take a little time for the shock to recede. It was much the same as the first few minutes after a mind had been introduced to the pentagram. Not until the spell completely took control was it worth trying to get what had once been a living being to obey even the simplest of instructions.

That meant that the citadel was open to further infestation by the Dragon King and there was only one thing that Serkadion Manee knew of that was quick and cunning enough to foil the intruder.

A creak made him glance around, but he saw nothing out of the ordinary. With no guidance, the citadel's vast interior was shifting randomly. This was not the first such noise he had heard and he doubted it would be the last. Things would need time to return to normal.

A gray book leaped into his hand from one of the shelves. The pages turned until he found what he wanted. Manee read and, by reading, cast the spell.

The squat gnome allowed himself a chuckle as he sent the dragon tome back to its resting place. That would teach the would-be conqueror a thing or two. It would almost be worth the risk just to watch the drake open one of the books now.

See how much you learn now! The stooped Vraad chuckled again. The spell had almost been a joke when he had devised it, a change of pace from his more serious work. Now, it would be the final strike in his counterattack.

Jagged streaks of pain shook his body. He felt moisture on his back and neck. The world around him began to blur.

What is happening to me? It almost feels—was his last coherent thought.

He fell to the floor, the blood from the gaping tear in his neck and shoulders spilling over onto the floor.

Looming over the quivering figure of the dying gnome, the Purple Dragon dropped his spell of hiding and wiped his bloodied talons on Serkadion Manee's robe, only briefly pondering what it was that might have amused the former immortal so much.

XX

Torches lit by themselves as the trio teleported into the chamber.

"Where are we now?" Wellen asked. He looked forward to a time when he could once more travel purely by conventional means. *Still, I suppose to a spellcaster teleportation is a conventional method.*

"In the lair of the beast," Shade replied, unfurling himself. There was something foul about the way he teleported, something so different that Wellen had so far been unable to pinpoint it. The grotesque manner in which the warlock twisted himself... and the two of them, this time... before each teleport was not what the scholar wondered about. It was the way Shade's magic always made him want to shy away.

To a lesser extent, the same applied to Serkadion Manee's power, albeit with the gnome it had always seemed more of a residue, as if he no longer drew from the same source that his counterpart did.

What was the land called? Nimth, that was it.

"I could think of many other places to be than Serkadion Manee's private study," Xabene muttered, her eyes darting around the room as if she expected the gnome at any moment.

Quite possibly that just might happen, but they had no choice. Shade had indicated that a key to their release lay in the very heart of the immortal's domain.

Wellen was not entirely trustful of the shadowy spellcaster, but Shade had rescued him more than once.

"What are we looking for?" he asked.

The quiet laugh startled him. "A key, of course."

"A key?"

"Serkadion Manee is either often literal-minded or has a touch of dry humor. The key to opening the portal in the wall without his aid is to use a *key*. He apparently created a few precautions in case something happened to his powers. Very kind of him, don't you think?"

Neither Wellen nor the enchantress bothered responding. The trio commenced a rapid search of the crowded chamber, discovering almost immediately that like so much else in the citadel, appearances were deceiving. The more they searched, the more to search there seemed to be. It was as if random things simply materialized from some pocket world, like the one in Xabene's tree. In only moments, they were already wading in stack after stack of abandoned experiments and notes. Wellen could not help returning to his early days as a student, when all of his assignments had seemed so mountainous.

"What do we have here?" Shade finally asked.

The others quickly joined him. It was not a key he had found, however, but a tapestry.

Looking it over, the master warlock could not keep the admiration out of his tone. "Exceptional work! Still so new! It might have been weaved yesterday!"

"It reminds me of the tapestry *I* weaved," whispered Xabene to Wellen.

"I would not be surprised," Shade interjected. "Since in that respect it serves a similar purpose to the one Serkadion Manee influenced you to create."

"*He* did?" A flush of red filled the cheeks of the pale sorceress. She did not like being used, but especially by the crafty gnome.

"It appears so, but this is not a Vraad thing. I think, despite its condition, that it was weaved even before our cursed host came to this world." Shade touched the side of the cloth artifact gingerly. "Yes, no doubt about that. He may have learned the method of its creation and passed it on to you, but this was created by another hand . . . or claw, depending on who ruled here then.''

"That's it! I will not be used again!" Xabene raised a hand toward the artifact. Shade, seeking to protect the tapestry, caught hold of her wrist. Wellen saw the look on her face and tried to warn the aged warlock, but it was too late. Not caring what happened, the enraged sorceress unleashed raw power at the struggling Shade.

He shrugged it off as a dog might shrug off rain.

With the release of her anger, Xabene grew sullen. Letting go of her wrist, the hooded figure blinked his crystalline eyes and said, "That tickled. Was that your intention?"

Wellen took hold of her before her anger, now directed at Shade, renewed itself sufficiently. "Forget it! We need him. He needs us."

"He doesn't need us. He could find this thing and leave without dragging us along with him."

The cloth-enshrouded mage shook his head. "I abandoned her. I will not abandon her children."

She looked at him in angry puzzlement. "And what does that mean?"

"Master Bedlam knows." Leaving it at that, Shade returned to admiring the tapestry. "If he did not weave this, then at the very least the gnome has made many changes in its usage. Some of them quite new. I can sense as well as see them. I wonder what purpose this marvel now serves."

Wellen, caught up by Shade's interest, was forced to admit to himself that the tapestry was certainly worthy of the attention being given to it. As with Xabene's creation, it was a representation of a region, but with such stark detail that it was like gazing at a true image. A tiny book marked the location of the libraries. Scanning further, he easily noted the hills to the east, but then did not recognize something that lay to the southwest. He pointed at it and asked Shade, "What is that? A town? Every building looks to be there."

"Penacles. One of the human habitations that the Purple Dragon allows in his domain. Only a small human town now, but once, long before refugees from Nimth foolishly invaded the Dragonrealm and even before the reigns of the Dragon Kings, the Quel, or a dozen races who preceded them, Penacles was known as a city of knowledge. Its original builders, who may have also created this tapestry, were not human, I think...at least not in the end."

"It seems a strange coincidence that Serkadion Manee would pick this location," Wellen commented. His eyes narrowed and he looked at the hooded warlock. "Could he have been here that long?"

"Perhaps, but I suspect it predated even him. Despite his talk of a thousand thousand years, Manee is not that old. Not hardly. Perhaps it just seems so long to him, I do not know." Shade put a hand to his face, as if growing exhausted. "I think he must have stripped the city's ancient bones of whatever he could find, though. I once searched its ruins, even spied upon the human town in the course of my own desires, but I learned all too soon that ancient Penacles was bare of anything that might have aided me. I wondered then where it had gone. That was before I knew of him." He leaned forward. "Interesting. The entire plain, I see, was part of the original city."

"Is this thing of any use to us or are we wasting precious time?"

"It may very well be useful to us, enchantress." Shade reached up and removed it from where it hung. "This is the method by which our host may reenter the citadel directly from no matter where he is. Normal teleportation does not work, as you know. Not even for Serkadion Manee. This would have been good for times when it was vital to materialize within and not outside. I wonder..."

Wellen noticed a tiny slot in the wall where the tapestry had been hung. He reached into it and felt something metallic. "I think I've found our key."

"Be careful, Wellen!"

Despite Xabene's warning, he was not worried. So comfortable had Serkadion Manee become in his private quarters that he had evidently felt little reason to overprotect them. Those few who he had allowed in had never had free access to this chamber.

The key, if that was what it was, had a rounded end for holding and a stem, but that was all that resembled a key that Wellen would have recognized. The other end, the part that must touch the wall, was a wicked five-pronged affair that looked as it if were more designed for torture than opening a lock. The scholar wondered how it was supposed to work. Turning it so that the prongs faced him, he noted that with so

much else here, the five points made up the corners of a tiny
pentagram. He mentioned this to his companions.

"A Vraadish taste, that. Pentagrams and fives." Shade folded
the tapestry and thrust in into his deep cloak. He reached for
the key, but Wellen chose to hold onto it. The master warlock
already had the book and the tapestry. Shade took it in stride.
"We have no more need to be here, then. It is time to leave this
infernal place. Let the gnome and the lizard decide who its
master is."

He was just beginning the spell that would teleport them out
when his entire frame coursed with light. Shade, a burning sun,
gasped once and fell.

"The decisssssion hasssss been made, thank you."

The Purple Dragon stretched forth a taloned hand and flames
from the torches encircled the two mortals. Xabene tried a
counterspell, but the flames would not be denied. Wellen tried
to shift out of the way. He failed. Like a snake, the magical fire
followed him, then darted around him again and again, tightening
its circle until he could no longer move without burning
himself.

"Thissss has been a mosssst informative conversation. I
appreciate your effortssss on my behalf." The key flew from
Bedlam's fingers and into the waiting hand of their captor. The
Dragon King gazed at it in fondness. "At last! The cursssssed
gnome hassss made it impossssible to open the portals without
thissss!"

A scratching sound made them look down. Shade was still
alive. His gloved hand scraped against the floor, as if even
while unconscious he sought to escape.

"Ressssilient. I ssssuppose I shall have to take you with
me," the drake lord said to the still figure. "You might have
some knowledge of worth."

Shade's body rose into the air, making him look like a limp
marionette with invisible strings. The Dragon King turned to
his other two captives. "This time, I will not trust to chance.
My will is your will. Your bodies will move as I command."

Wellen, with Xabene beside him, staggered toward the
drake. This time, Purple had assured that his control was
complete. The only movements left to the scholar were blinking and breathing. He could not even ask the question that
burned on his tongue.

The Dragon King must have noted his expression, however,

for he held one of his taloned hands before the human. "For an immortal, the gnome died asssss eassssily assss any mere mortal!" Straightening, the drake looked at the key, then back at his prisoners. "Now I truly have everything. All I need issss to ssssecure you ssssafely and then I can return and begin the processss of going through thissss treasure trove." Purple's eyes blazed with anticipation. "Sssso much to do!"

Even if he had been able to speak, Wellen Bedlam would have not contradicted the Dragon King. Let the drake believe that it would now be a simple task to escape. If there was one thing the young scholar had learned, it was that nothing was simple in this place. Serkadion Manee might be dead, if what the Dragon King had said was true, but this *was* his creation.

The Purple Dragon could continue to believe his own words, as far as Bedlam was concerned. Let him think that he could simply walk out of this place. Let him believe that with the gnome no more, he was now unchallenged master of the libraries and their contents.

Wellen knew better. Even without their creator, the libraries were *lethal*.

Had the Dragon King waited for a few more moments after delivering the mortal blow to Serkadion Manee, he would have perhaps seen a strange thing happen to the Vraad sorcerer. With a few vestiges of life still remaining, the body began to *sink* into the false marble floor and, as it sank, it changed, becoming less and less the gnome and more a part of the very floor itself.

Serkadion Manee had designed his libraries so that nothing would be ever be wasted.

Not even him.

In the corridor where they had first entered, the party appeared. Shade was still a silent corpse. He might truly have been dying for all Wellen knew, but there was nothing that could be done about it at the moment. All of their lives were in the scaly claws of the Dragon King and his concern at present had little to do with their well-being.

Holding out the pronged key, Purple returned control of the scholar's body to him. Wellen savored the ability to move, then looked up at his captor.

"How doessss thissss work? There issss no hole."

"Shade knew," Bedlam replied with some satisfaction. "But you made certain he wouldn't be able to help."

For his remark, he received a backhanded blow to the face. It was only a tap, but from the Dragon King it was enough to send the human falling back. When Wellen rose, he felt blood trickling down the left side of his mouth. Now, not only did his head throb, but so did his jaw.

"Again, how doesssss thissss work? Another flippant remark and I shall tear your head off! Then, we shall sssee if your female will be more obliging!"

The threat to Xabene was sufficient. Looking at the blank wall and then back at the key, Wellen shrugged. "I would guess that the first step would be to place it against the wall. From what little the—*Shade* said, it sounds like the only thing you *can* do." He had almost mentioned the single volume that the hooded warlock still had secreted on his person. That single dragon tome might yet save their lives. "After that, I can only assume that it will either open or you'll have to turn it first."

"Ssssimple. Sssssensible. I agree." The Dragon King stepped past his captives and placed the key against the stonelike wall.

Nothing happened. He tried turning the key, causing it to scrape against the substance. Wellen almost expected the living stone to rebel against the sharp prongs of the key, but that was not so.

This time, there was a reaction.

With great hesitation, the wall began to separate around the region where the prongs of the key had touched it. The drake quickly pulled the device away and hissed in triumph as the crack became a circular opening which in turn grew larger and larger. Once again, the scholar was reminded of a giant maw, only this time he was inside looking out. Not a comfortable thought.

"Much better!" Purple roared. "Much better!"

The opening of the wall was much slower this time than when they had first arrived here. Now, with success at hand, the Dragon King grew impatient. He stood before the expanding portal and tried to use physical means to make it widen faster. That failed. In an attempt to keep his impatience at a minimum, the drake turned away from the exit and faced Wellen.

"Conssssider yoursssself fortunate, manling. You have been witnessss to the end of one era and the beginning of the next. Thissss will be the dawning of a new kingdom. The Dragon

Emperor will sssssoon on longer ssssit in the Tyber Mountains. He shall rule from here! From... from a new *Penaclessss*, yesss! I shall ressssurrect the ancient city!'' It was obvious that the Purple Dragon did not intend to turn over the gnome's vast knowledge to his golden counterpart but rather intended that *he* become new lord of the realm. Even with the knowledge of Serkadion Manee, Wellen wondered whether Purple was taking on more than he was capable of controlling. Certainly, the other monarchs would have something to say.

The portal was now large enough to admit the Dragon King through. Wellen was surprised to see that the sun was setting. Was it the same day? Another? Time here, he was certain, did not pass as it did outside.

Purple started to step through, then recalled something. He turned and went back to the silent form of Shade. With little care, the drake rolled the warlock onto his backside and reached into the volumnous cloak.

Move, Shade! Bedlam expected a trick, expected the spellcaster to leap up and take on the Dragon King, but Shade remained motionless. This was no ploy, which meant that now there truly was no hope.

''Dragon of the Depthsssss! How far mussssst I reach to find it?'' A moment later, the horrific knight smiled. He pulled his hand from the confines of the cloak. In his claws he held the tapestry. ''Yesss. Lessst I forget it and it remain losssst in your infernal clothes. Thissss piece issss definitely worth insssspecting.''

Outside, a wind whipped up the nearby grass. Wellen contemplated running for the portal, but he could not leave Xabene nor even Shade.

Rising, the Dragon King looked over the intricate work of the artifact. ''I wonder. A few changessss and I may be able to usssse thissss. No more keyssss. *I* will have the only way in. and out.''

A flutter of wings caught Wellen's attention.

A huge, white form that seemed all claws and wings darted through the portal and made for the backside of the drake.

The reptilian knight dropped both the key and the tapestry as he went down under the onslaught of a monstrous Necri.

Acting on sheer instinct, Wellen rushed to Xabene's side. She, of the three of them, was the only one still under a spell of paralysis. Shade, after all, was hardly in a condition to crawl, if he was even still alive. Taking hold of the enchantress by the waist, he started to drag her toward the opening.

Despite his lack of height and his scholarly background, he was far from weak. Xabene was also light, which helped. Even before Purple had recovered from his initial surprise and started to fight back, Wellen had her in the mouth of the portal.

What he hoped to gain, he could not say. Wellen was aware that he could not carry her all the way to safety. There was nowhere to hide for miles. No matter who won the battle, the victor would easily be able to chase down the runaways.

Still, he did not give up. Wellen would not have been able to forgive himself. Too many had died. If he could even buy Xabene a little time...

The wind cooled him a little bit, which helped, but the soil was too soft. He could not get much traction. The oncoming darkness, which he would have once thought a plus, also worked against him. Both the Necri and Purple would be able to find him, day or night. Wellen, on the other hand, could already tell that he was no longer gifted with night vision. Bumbling around in the dark, with Xabene an unwieldly load, he would not be far from the pentagon when the winner came to reclaim the two of them.

"You look as if you could use my aid, sirrah."

Bedlam swore.

"Such language," Benton Lore said, adding a chuckle.

"Does no one walk or simply ride anymore? Did you have to materialize right behind me?"

"I did nothing of the sort. I crept here."

Feeling somewhat abashed, the scholar apologized.

The black man waved his apology aside. "Never mind that. Let me help you with her."

A single touch of his hand to her forehead and Xabene was released from the Dragon King's spell.

"Lords of the Dead!" she muttered.

"Good," Lore commented almost clinically. "I did not think he would waste anything fancy upon you."

"How are you feeling?" Wellen asked her.

"Good enough to run if we have to."

"There is no need, my lady. I can teleport us all back." The major-domo raised his hand.

Wellen wanted to go. He wanted to travel as far as he could, and then find ways of allowing him to journey farther. By no means did he desire a return to Serkadion Manee's former domain. yet . . .

"I can't leave him, Xabene."

She seized his arm. "There's a Dragon King and a Necri in there! *My* Necri! If that thing should win or be fought off, it'll come for me! I failed the Lords of the Dead! Shade may have repelled them, but that monstrosity won't care! It only knows that I have betrayed its creators!"

"Go with Commander Lore, then. I have more than one reason for going back! Just trust me!" He tore free of her and hurried back to the gaping hole.

She did not cry out for him, but Bedlam knew she was still behind him, refusing to leave if he did not. Wellen hoped that neither Xabene nor Benton Lore would suffer because of his decision.

The drake and the Necri had taken their battle farther down the corridor. Wellen had expected the batlike creature to fall quickly under the massive power of Purple, but the dragon appeared to be holding back. Either he was weaker than Wellen had thought or he was afraid to unleash his full strength so near his precious books. The drake had, after all, resorted to physical violence when he had finally taken down Serkadion Manee. Neither the gnome nor the dragon had likely been able to utilize their full strength.

Shade was where he had been left. The fear that he had accidentally been included in the deadly duel had proved false. Wellen slipped through the circular entranceway and rushed over to the warlock, ever careful to keep an eye on the combatants. With two such as they, the battle could turn at any moment.

"Shade!" There was no response to his whisper. He was forced to begin dragging the injured figure as he had Xabene. Unfortunately, Shade's much larger and more limp body proved at least twice as laborious to carry as the slighter enchantress. The false marble floor added to the difficulties, for Wellen found that he was in danger of slipping now and then.

Something fell from the cloak. Wellen leaned down and saw that it was the dragon tome that the aged spellcaster had appropriated much earlier. He picked it up and stuffed it into his shirt. There would be time to deal with it later.

Benton Lore called to him from the other side. "Do you need help?"

"Take Xabene and leave!"

"She does not desire to be reasonable, sirrah, and I find that neither do I!"

He sighed. A part of him could not help but he relieved at their reappearance. "Help me, then."

The black man came around and took Shade's feet. "I tried to teleport you out, but it did not work for some reason."

"One of the gnome's tricks..." Thinking of tricks, he started to look around. A metal object a few feet to his left caught his eye. "Wait!" Lowering Shade, he reached over and retrieved the pronged key that the drake lord had dropped during the initial assault. Wellen pocketed the key and re-spositioned himself.

"What is that?"

"Something which could buy us time." Continuing his search as he began to back through the gateway, the scholar finally located the tapestry. It had evidently been carried partway down the hall with the two combatants. Wellen calculated his chances. Once Shade was outside, he might still have time to—

He heard the Necri shriek.

Both Wellen and Benton Lore turned to the agonized cry. Far down the corridor, the Dragon King had finally gained the upper hand. His adversary was pinned under him. The talons of the drake had torn both the demonic creature's wings to shreds and now an odd foam was spreading over the batlike horror. Purple released his hold on his opponent and stepped back to watch as his spell enveloped the dying beast. The Dragon King himself did not look well. He was bleeding from severe wounds. His stance was none too steady.

"We have to hurry, Master Bedlam!"

They had the warlock nearly through when he began to mutter and struggle. Wellen heard Shade speak to someone he referred to as his father, warning him about some scheme. Then, Lore lost his grip and Wellen stumbled. The warlock's words grew garbled, but he did not cease struggling.

The anxious scholar looked up in the direction of the Dragon King.

The reptilian knight had noticed them. With some effort, he started toward the open portal.

"Step through!" Wellen roared. "Pull him out from my side!"

As the soldier hastened to obey, the scholar reached into his pocket and pulled out the key. His idea was desperate, but not completely mad.

"What are you doing?"

"Just pull him through!"

Xabene joined them, much to his annoyance. *We can all die together!* "Go back!"

She ignored him. Leaning, the enchantress helped Lore with the mad warlock. Shade's words were complete nonsense now, but his hampering of their efforts was not.

Wellen could wait no longer. He reached forward with the key, choosing a part of the wall just to the left of the portal.

A crash nearly made him drop the key.

"It's all right!" Xabene called. "I reached in with one hand and blocked his spell with one of my own! It was a weak attack!"

"He will summon up something much more troublesome in a moment, I'm certain!" the officer added. He gave a final tug. "Your friend is free, Master Bedlam!"

All too aware that he might be totally mistaken, Wellen turned the key as the drake had done, only in the *opposite* direction.

The mouth of the portal began closing.

The party fell back as sorcerer's tendrils reached forth from within. They were not the target, however. Instead, the tendrils sought to keep the entrance open. The spell on the citadel was far more potent, however, and the portal continued to shrink unabated.

Even as the tendrils failed, Purple stood at the threshold.

"If he gets outside, we're lost!" the enchantress shouted. "He could shift form!" Both she and Lore unleashed their sorcery.

Their spells died at the wall. They could not hope to repel the drake unless he was outside, and if he was, then it would be too late.

Wellen looked at Shade. The injured spellcaster's eyes had opened, but it was apparent he was not seeing the world around him. *If only we had his strength! We might be able to do it!*

Perhaps there was yet time for one more miracle.

Hurrying over to Shade's side, he knelt and took the warlock's head in his arm. Wellen faced his mad companion toward the portal and leaned down to whisper. He was working on an assumption, one based solely upon the master warlock's triumphant return from the dank domain of the Lords of the Dead. "Shade, they've broken their word! Your cousins have broken their word! They're coming!"

Purple had a claw through what remained of the gateway and was crawling through. Despite his wounds, he shrugged off the desperate attacks of Benton Lore and Xabene.

Shade stirred, but still did not act.

Wellen tried the last thing he could think of. "They want her, Shade. They want her descendents. They want Lady Sharissa!"

Crystalline eyes blazed. Shade gritted his teeth. For a moment, a much younger, more arrogant figure lay in the scholar's lap.

"It's coming through the hole, Shade! It's coming for her!"

The Vraad glared in the direction of the Dragon King.

A rain of needlelike thorns shot forth at the drake. Concerned only with his escape, he did not see them. Only when they first pierced his armored hide did the drake realize his danger.

A full score more struck home. Several entered wounds left by the Necri. Roaring his agony, the drake lord tried to pull them free, but for every one he pulled out, more than a dozen found root. In mere seconds, he looked like some sort of grotesque parody of a pincushion.

Still the needles flew.

His breathing a ragged hiss, Purple finally realized that to remain outside was to invite certain death. He began to slide back even as more of Shade's missiles hit. His pace was too slow, however. It was clear that he would not escape the closing portal on his own.

Then, just before the blood-covered knight would have been crushed, Wellen saw a small hand drag him back.

The gateway closed.

He breathed a sigh of relief. "Thank you, Shade. Thank you."

Then the weary Bedlam looked down and realized he was holding nothing but air.

XXI

"We think he has returned to his caverns beneath the realm of the Dragon Emperor," Benton Lore informed them. "With Shade it is almost impossible to tell, but our spies reported sightings of a cloaked and shadowy wraith." He smiled. "I can think of no one else to whom that description would be appropriate."

"Why did he leave?" Xabene asked.

Wellen, the enchantress, and the Green Dragon's major-domo sat astride horses in the middle of a glen just west of the main portion of the Dagora Forest. In the four weeks since escaping Purple and the citadel of Serkadion Manee, the scholar and his bride had made the small settlement of Zuu their temporary home. The two of them had both agreed that they needed to find a quieter, safer place than even that, but not until Wellen was satisfied as to Shade's fate. Even Xabene agreed they owed the ancient mage that much.

"I think the madness has returned," Lore replied, his smile fading a bit. "He is said to seem a bit at a loss, as if his memory is incomplete or, at the very least, muddled. He may not even recall that he was ever inside the citadel. His failure to secure a method of achieving immortality may have also sent him back to the real of fantasy. From what I have discerned, it would not be the first time."

"I'm not so certain I would ever want to be an immortal. The Lords of the Dead dangled that above my head, but the price seems too high now."

"Two or three hundred years is enough for the two of you, then?"

"Enough," Wellen agreed. One of the benefits of sorcery, even for an inept carrier like himself, was an extended life span. Both he and Xabene might live another two centuries, maybe more, and most of it looking little older than they did now.

"No one has yet seen Purple depart the libraries," Lore said, changing the subject. "Perhaps he will be trapped forever."

"Perhaps." The scholar still had the key. Just in case. He was not so certain that the Dragon King would not escape someday, though. Given time, if he survived his wounds, Purple would eventually reason out the tapestry and how it could be used.

He had not spoken to anyone about the hand he had seen, a hand belonging to an obviously short being.

"My lord fears what his brother will unleash if he does escape. All that knowledge in his vile claws."

Here, Wellen relaxed. He smiled at Xabene, who nodded. It was time to show Benton Lore what they had discovered. Reaching into a pouch, he removed the book.

The black man's eyes widened. "A dragon tome! You have one!"

"Here."

Lore caught the book and quickly opened it. After a few pages, he looked mystified. "It is *blank*!"

"Not quite. Think of a subject involving the construction of a magical fortress . . . like Serkadion Manee's pentagon."

The major-domo did. Before his eyes, the pages began to turn. At last, they stopped. The smile reappeared, then almost instantly disappeared again. "What *is* this gibberish? It looks almost like a . . . like a riddle or a poem! I do no understand!"

"Shade stole that particular volume, then lost it. I picked it up, intending on giving it to him if we escaped, but then he vanished first." He looked a bit abashed. "I know I didn't mention its existence, but my curiosity got the better of me. I promise you I would have told the Green Dragon everything."

"I believe you and so will he." Lore inspected the riddle. "What does it mean?"

"The secret is within, one merely has to be willing to spend the time . . . years, even."

"Then . . ." The officer laughed. "If Purple lives it may take him years just to decipher one?"

Wellen joined him in laughing. "It gets worse. Unless you really work at it, what you read in the book will not be retained in your memory. You can't even write it down. Somehow, it always disappears."

"The gnome must have done this!"

"I think so. Just before he died, I imagine." *Was* he dead, though? What had Wellen seen?

"So the price of Purple's victory is endless searching for even the minutest bit of information. He may spend his lifetime simply deciphering a simple experiment for telling time!"

Knowing how complete the knowledge contained in the libraries was, Wellen had no doubt that there was such information listed. The Dragon King might have won, but his victory would keep his ambitions curtailed. If anything, the rest of the Dragonrealm had gained much more than it had lost with the change in masters.

Xabene glanced at the sinking sun. "It's time we returned to Zuu. Tomorrow, we head north. I know a settlement up there that the Dragon King Bronze never bothers with. A pleasant place."

"You would both be welcome here. It would be safer. What about the Lords of the Dead?"

"Shade did something to them, that's all we know," Bedlam replied. "We can only tell you that we have this feeling that they will not bother us, neither in this life nor the next."

No one desired to contemplate what could have made the necromancers abandon their plans and their vengeance.

"I think this would be better off in your hands," Lore finally decided. "I only ask that you share whatever you find." The dragon tome was returned to Wellen. "I shall depart, then. Farewell to both of you. Good luck with everything."

"Farewell to you, Commander Lore," the enchantress said, taking a tighter hold of the reins.

Wellen simply nodded. He was savoring being his own master at last, not to mention riding a horse rather than teleporting. His children, on the other hand, would likely be materializing and dematerializing before they were adults. Still, much of the fact that he was now able to live his own life was due to one person. As Benton Lore rode off, he muttered, "May you find your future, Gerrod."

"Shall we go?" Xabene asked him.

They urged their horses to a trot. The sorceress, her lengthy dark hair fluttering, moved her mount alongside Wellen's and asked, "What do you really think is going on in the gnome's place? Couldn't Purple be dead?"

"He might be, but I doubt it. He probably won't recover completely for some time, but I think he survived."

She did not care to think about that. "At least we no longer have to worry about Serkadion Manee. His death is the one good thing we can thank the Dragon King for."

"Mmm . . ." Wellen turned the dragon tome over and stared at the cover. He was tempted to throw the book away and try to forget Serkadion Manee, but curiosity made him put it back where he had originally packed it. It might not hurt to try and decipher the contents. Besides, unlike the Purple Dragon, Wellen only had *one* book to muddle through.

With two hundred years ahead of him and some peace at last, he was certain to make *some* progress.

Hissing, the Dragon King threw the yellow-backed book across the corridor. His rage unspent, he cleared shelf after shelf until finally, exhausted, he slumped against one of the library walls.

"You seem ill-tempered. How may I serve you?"

"You again?" Purple whirled on the tiny, calm figure. "You are *dead*! Dead! Leave me!"

The gnome bowed. "I am here only to serve you, the present master of the libraries. It is all I exist for now, thanks in great part to you."

"Sssstop ssssaying that, cursssse you!" The Dragon King reached forward and took hold of the gnome by the collar. The bald figure simply stared back blandly. This further antagonized the drake. "I killed you once and I shall do sssso again!"

He brought a taloned hand down on the gnome's head.

The squat figure vanished.

"Perhaps if you tell me what it is you search for," came the voice again, this time from behind him. When the Dragon King turned, he once more found himself facing the libraries' former master.

"I want out of thissss place! I want the secret of why it hassss turned mad!" He picked up one of the tomes and held it open for the other to see. "Mosssst of all, I want to know what you have done to thesssse precious volumessss! What is thissss foolishnessss written here?"

The gnome calmly held forth another book. "I am only an extension of the libraries' purpose; I cannot aid you in that. The one you have there is the wrong volume, however. The one with the information you seek is this one here."

A hand batted the book away. "I *cannot* decipher it!"

"Perhaps if there was someone to help you . . ."

"There issss no one but me!" Purple stepped back and glared at the shelves. "When I am free of thissss place, I will rebuild Penaclessss! I will take humanssss, who are insssssuffer-ably adaptive, and educate them! The besssst will work to aid me in ssssolving these quandaries!''

"That seems a reasonable course.''

"But I have to find the way *out* of here first!''

"It is in the book . . .'' responded the gnome, bending over to retrieve the volume. "All you have to do is read it.''

Hissing in frustration, the Dragon King fell to his knees. "Very well, then. Give it to me.''

"This is a simple one, truly,'' the shadow that resembled Serkadion Manee commented. "At the most, it would take one as clever as you no more than forty, perhaps fifty years to solve it. Possibly as little as a year or two.''

In sullen silence, the Purple Dragon took the proffered tome and began reading. His eyes narrowed and his breathing slowed. He knew he would need all his concentration to decipher the cursed poem/riddle. He also knew that he would have to struggle to retain whatever he read.

"The key . . .'' the drake lord muttered. "It would have been sssso much easssssier with the key.''

"Yes, my lord.'' There *was* still the tapestry, which the gnome recalled presently lay in an obscure part of one of the hallways, but it was not his place to offer such information. His purpose now consisted entirely of maintaining and protecting the libraries, as he himself had commanded before his demise. That was all he was to do and he would perform that task until the libraries themselves were no more, for he, unlike the minds trapped in the vials that had once monitored his creation, had tied his own immortality to this place.

As he watched the new master of the libraries at work, the gnome could not help but smile.